WORLD'S END I.

Upton Sinclair's theme is the world of the first half of the twen ti eth century. Readers of the other ten nov els in this se ries will be glad to dis cover what has been happening to the far-flung Budd family and their friends. As with each book of this series, this one can be enjoyed for its own sep a rate story, or as a part of the sweep ing ac count of the era.

Each vol ume is pub lished in two parts: I and II.

WORLD'S

END I.

Upton Sinclair

When I say "his to rian," I have a mean ing of my own. I por tray world events in story form, because that form is the one I have been trained in. I have sup ported my self by writ ing fic tion since the age of six teen, which means for forty-nine years.

... Now I re al ize that this one was the one job for which I had been born: to put the pe riod of world wars and rev o lu tions into a great long novel. ...

I cannot say when it will end, because I don't know exactly what the characters will do. They lead a semi-independent life, be ing more real to me than any of the peo ple I know, with the sin gle ex cep tion of my wife. ... Some of my char ac ters are peo ple who lived, and whom I had op por tu nity to know and watch. Oth ers are imaginary—or rather, they are com plexes of many people whom I have known and watched. Lanny Budd and his mother and fa ther and their var i ous rel a tives and friends have come in the course of the past four years to be my daily and nightly com pan ions. I have come to know them so in ti mately that I need only to ask them what they would do in a given set of cir cum stances and they start to en act their roles. ... I chose what seems to me the most re veal ing of them and of their world.

How long will this go on? I can not tell. It de pends in great part upon two pub lic fig ures, Hit ler and Mussolini. What are they go ing to do to man kind and what is man kind will do to them? It seems to me hardly likely that ei - ther will die a peace ful death. I am hop ing to out live them; and what ever happens Lanny Budd will be some where in the neigh bor hood, he will be "in at the death," ac cord ing to the fox-hunting phrase.

These two foxes are my quarry, and I hope to hang their brushes over my mantel.

In the course of this novel a num ber of well-known per sons make their ap - pearance, some of them living, some dead; they appear under their own names, and what is said about them is fac tu ally cor rect.

There are other char ac ters which are fic ti tious, and in these cases the au thor has gone out of his way to avoid seem ing to point at real per sons. He has given them un likely names, and hopes that no per son bear ing such names ex ist. But it is im pos si ble to make sure; there fore the writer states that, if any such coincidence occurs, it is accidental. This is not the customary "hedge clause" which the au thor of a *ro man à clef* pub lishes for le gal pro - tec tion; it means what it says and it is in tended to be so taken.

Var i ous Eu ro pean con cerns en gaged in the man u fac ture of mu ni tions have been named in the story, and what has been said about them is also ac cord - ing to the re cords. There is one Amer i can firm, and that, with all its af fairs, is imag i nary. The writer has done his best to avoid seem ing to in di cate any ac tual Amer i can firm or fam ily.

...Of course there will be slips, as I know from ex pe ri ence; but *World's End* is meant to be a his tory as well as fic tion, and I am sure there are no mis takes of im por tance. I have my own point of view, but I have tried to play fair in this book. There is a var ied cast of char ac ters and they say as they think. ...

The Peace Con fer ence of Paris [*for example*], which is the scene of the last third of *World's End*, is of course one of the great est events of all time. A friend on mine asked an au thor ity on mod ern fic tion a ques tion: "Has any - body ever used the Peace Conference in a novel?" And the reply was: "Could any body?" Well, I thought some body could, and now I think some - body has. The reader will ask, and I state ex plic itly that so far as con cerns his toric char ac ters and events my pic ture is cor rect in all de tails. This part of the manu script, 374 pages, was read and checked by eight or ten gen tle men who were on the Amer i can staff at the Con fer ence. Sev eral of these hold im por tant po si tions in the world of trou bled in ter na tional af fairs; oth ers are col lege pres i dents and pro fes sors, and I prom ised them all that their let ters will be con fi den tial. Suf fice it to say that the er rors they pointed out were cor rected, and where they dis agreed, both sides have a word in the book.

Contents:

BOOK ONE

God's in His Heaven

1

Music Made Visible

I

THE American boy's name was Lanning Budd; people called him Lanny, an agreeable name, easy to say. He had been born in Switzerland, and spent most of his life on the French Riviera; he had never crossed the ocean, but considered himself American because his mother and father were that. He had traveled a lot, and just now was in a little village in the suburbs of Dresden, his mother having left him while she went off on a yachting trip to the fiords of Norway. Lanny didn't mind, for he was used to being left in places, and knew how to get along with people from other parts of the world. He would eat their foods, pick up a smattering of their languages, and hear stories about strange ways of life.

Lanny was thirteen, and growing fast, but much dancing had kept his figure slender and graceful. His wavy brown hair was worn long, that being the fashion for boys; when it dropped into his eyes, he gave a toss of the head. His eyes also were brown, and looked out with eagerness on whatever part of Europe he was in. Just now he was sure that Hellerau was the most delightful of places, and surely this day of the Festspiel was the most delightful of days.

Upon a high plateau stood a tall white temple with smooth round pillars in front, and to it were drifting throngs of people who had journeyed from places all over the earth where art was loved and cherished; fashionable ones among them, but mostly art people, writers and critics, musicians, actors, producers—celebrities in such numbers that it was impossible to keep track of them. All Lanny's life he had heard their names, and here they were in the flesh. With

1

two friends, a German boy slightly older than himself and an English boy older still, he wandered among the crowd in a state of eager delight.

"There he is!" one would whisper.

"Which?"

"The one with the pink flower."

"Who is he?"

One of the older boys would explain. Perhaps it was a great blond Russian named Stanislavsky; perhaps a carelessly dressed Englishman, Granville Barker. The boys would stare, but not too openly or too long. It was a place of courtesy, and celebrities were worshiped but not disturbed. To ask for an autograph was a crudity undreamed of in the Dalcroze school.

The three were on the alert for the king of celebrities, who had promised to be present. They spied him at some distance, talking with two ladies. Others also had spied him, and were doing as the boys did, walking slowly past, inclining their ears in the hope of catching a stray pearl of wit or wisdom; then stopping a little way off, watching with half-averted gaze.

"His whiskers look like gold," murmured Lanny.

"Whiskers?" queried Kurt, the German boy, who spoke English carefully and precisely. "I thought you say beard."

"Whiskers are beard and mustaches both," ventured Lanny, and then inquired: "Aren't they, Rick?"

"Whiskers stick out," opined the English boy, and added: "His are the color of the soil of Hellerau." It was true, for the ground was reddish yellow, and had glints of sunlight in it. "Hellerau means bright meadow," Kurt explained.

II

The king of celebrities was then in his middle fifties, and the breeze that blew on that elevated spot tossed his whiskers, which stuck out. Tall and erect, he had eyes as gay as the bluebells on the meadow and teeth like the petals of the daisies. He wore an English tweed suit of brown with reddish threads in it, and when he threw his head back and laughed—which he did every time he made a joke —all the flowers on the bright meadow danced.

The trio stared until they thought maybe it wasn't polite any more, and then turned their eyes away. "Do you suppose he'd answer if we spoke to him?" ventured Lanny.

"Oh, no!" exclaimed Kurt, the most strictly brought up of the three.

"What would we say?" demanded Rick.

"We might think up something. You try; you're English."

"English people don't ever speak without being introduced."

"Think of something anyhow," persisted Lanny. "It can't hurt to pretend."

Rick was fifteen, and his father was a baronet who preferred to be known as a designer of stage sets. "Mr. Shaw," he suggested, with Oxford accent and polished manner, "may I take the liberty of telling you how much I have enjoyed the reading of your prefaces?"

"That's what everybody says," declared Lanny. "He's sick of it. You try, Kurt."

Kurt clicked his heels and bowed; he was the son of an official in Silesia, and couldn't even imagine addressing anyone without doing that. "Mr. Shaw, we Germans count ourselves your discoverers, and it does us honor to welcome you to our soil."

"That's better," judged the American. "But maybe the Bürgermeister has already said it."

"You try it then," said Rick.

Lanny knew from his father and others that Americans said what they wanted to, and without too much ceremony. "Mr. Shaw," he announced, "we three boys are going to dance for you in a few minutes, and we're tickled to death about it."

"He'll know that's American, all right," admitted Rick. "Would you dare to do it?"

"I don't know," said Lanny. "He looks quite kind."

The king of celebrities had started to move toward the tall white temple, and Kurt glanced quickly at his watch. "*Herrgott!* Three minutes to curtain!"

He bolted, with the other two at his heels. Breathless, they dashed into the robing room, where the chorus master gazed at them sternly. "It is disgraceful to be late for the Festspiel," he declared.

But it didn't take three boys long to slip out of shirts and trousers, B.V.D.'s and sandals, and into their light dancing tunics. That they were out of breath was no matter, for there was the overture. They stole to their assigned positions on the darkened stage and squatted on the floor to wait until it was time for the rising of the curtain.

III

Orpheus, the singer, had descended into hell. He stood, his lyre in hand, confronting a host of furies with a baleful glare in their eyes. Infernal music pounded forth their protest. "Who is this mortal one now drawing near, bold to intrude on these awful abodes?"

Furies, it is well known, are dangerous; these trembled with their peculiar excitement, and could hardly be restrained. Their feet trod with eagerness to leap at the intruder, their hands reached out with longing to seize and rend him. The music crashed and rushed upward in a frenzied presto, it crashed and rushed down again, and bodies shook and swayed with the drive of it.

The spirits stood upon a slope within the entrance gates of Hell; tier upon tier of them, and in the dim blue light of infernal fires their naked arms and legs made, as it were, a mountain of motion. Their anger wove itself into patterns of menace, so that the gentle musician could hardly keep from shrinking. He touched his lyre, and soft strains floated forth; tinkling triplets like the shimmering of little waves in the moonlight. But the fiends would not hear. "No!" they thundered, with the hammer-strokes of arms and the trampling of feet. In vain the melodious pleading of the lyre! "Furies, specters, phantoms terrific, let your hearts have pity on my soul-tormenting pain."

The musician sang his story. He had lost his beloved Eurydice, who was somewhere in these realms of grief, and he must win her release. His strains poured forth until the hardest hearts were melted.

It was a triumph of love over anger, of beauty and grace over the evil forces which beset the lives of men.

The mountain of motion burst forth into silent song. The denizens of Hell were transformed into shades of the Elysian fields, and showers of blessings fell upon them out of the music. "On these meadows all are happy-hearted; only peace and rest are known." In the midst of the rejoicing came the shy Eurydice to meet her spouse. Rapture seized the limbs now shining in bright light; they wove patterns as intricate as the music, portraying not merely melody but complicated harmonies. Beautiful designs were brought before the eye, counterpoint was heightened through another sense. It was music made visible; and when the curtain had fallen upon the bliss of Orpheus and his bride, a storm of applause shook the auditorium. Men and women stood shouting their delight at the revelation of a new form of art.

Outside, upon the steps of the temple, they crowded about the creator of "Eurythmics." Emile Jaques-Dalcroze was his name, a stocky, solidly built man with the sharply pointed black beard and mustache of a Frenchman and the black Windsor tie which marked the artist of those days. He had taken the musical patterns of Gluck's *Orpheus* and reproduced them with the bodies and bare arms and legs of children; the art lovers would go forth to tell the world that here was something not only beautiful but healing, a way to train the young in grace and happiness, in efficiency and co-ordination of body and mind.

Critics, producers, teachers, all of them were devotees of an old religion, the worship of the Muses. They believed that humanity could be saved by beauty and grace; and what better symbol than the fable of the Greek singer who descended into Hell and with voice and golden lyre tamed the furies and the fiends? Sooner or later among the children at Hellerau would appear another Orpheus to charm the senses, inspire the soul, and tame the furies of greed and hate. Wars would be banished—and not merely those among nations, but that bitter struggle of the classes which was threatening to rend Europe. In the Dalcroze school children of the well-to-do classes danced side by side with those of workers from the factory suburbs. In the temple of the Muses were no classes, nations, or races; only humanity with its dream of beauty and joy.

Such was the faith of all art lovers of the year 1913; such was the creed being taught in the tall white temple upon the bright meadow. In these fortunate modern days the spread of civilization had become automatic and irresistible. Forty-two years had passed since Europe had had a major war, and it was evident to all that love and brotherhood were stealing into the hearts of the furies, and that Orpheus was conquering with his heaven-sent voice and golden lyre.

IV

All Lanny Budd's young life he had played around with music. Wherever he was taken, there was always a piano, and he had begun picking at the keys as soon as he was old enough to climb upon a stool. He remembered snatches of everything he heard, and as soon as he got home would lose himself in the task of reproducing them. Now he had discovered a place where he could play music with arms and legs and all the rest of him; where he could stand in front of a mirror and see music with his eyes! He was so excited about it that he could hardly wait to jump into his clothes in the morning before dancing downstairs.

At Hellerau they taught you an alphabet and a grammar of movement. With your arms you kept the time; a set of movements for three-part time, another for four, and so on. With your feet and body you indicated the duration of notes. It was a kind of rhythmic gymnastics, planned to train the body in quick and exact response to mental impressions. When you had mastered the movements for the different tempi, you went on to more complex problems; you would mark three-part time with your feet and four-part time with your arms. You would learn to analyze and reproduce complicated musical structures; expressing the rhythms of a three-part canon by singing one part, acting another with the arms, and a third with the feet.

To Lanny the lovely part about this school was that nobody

thought you were queer because you wanted to dance; everybody understood that music and motion went together. At home people danced, of course, but it was a formal procedure, for which you dressed especially and hired musicians who played a special kind of music, the least interesting, and everybody danced as nearly the same way as possible. If a little boy danced all over the lawn, or through the pine woods, or down on the beach—well, people might think it was "cute," but they wouldn't join him.

Lanny was getting to an age where people would be expecting him to acquire dignity. He couldn't go on capering around, at least not unless he was going to take it up as a career and make money out of it. But here was this school, to provide him with a label and a warrant, so to speak. His mother would say: "There's Lanny, doing his Dalcroze." Lady Eversham-Watson would put up her ivory and gold lorgnette and drawl: "Oh, chawming!" The Baroness de la Tourette would lift her hands with a dozen diamonds and emeralds on them and exclaim: *"Ravissant!"* "Dalcroze" was the rage.

So Lanny worked hard and learned all he could during these precious weeks while his mother was away on the yacht of the gentleman who had invented Bluebird Soap and introduced it into several million American kitchens. Lanny would steal into a room where a group of boys and girls were practicing; nobody objected if a graceful and slender lad fell in and tried the steps. If he had ideas of his own he would go off into a corner and work them out, and nobody would pay any attention, unless he was doing it unusually well. There was dancing all over the place, in bedrooms and through corridors and out on the grounds; everybody was so wrapped up in his work that there would have been no special excitement if Queen Titania and her court had appeared, marking with their fairy feet the swift measures of the *Midsummer-Night's Dream* overture.

V

Lanny Budd had made two special friendships that summer. Kurt Meissner came from Silesia, where his father was comptroller-general of a great estate, a responsible and honorable post. Kurt was the youngest of four sons, so he did not have to become a government official or an officer in the army; his wish to conduct and possibly to compose music was respected, and he was learning in the thorough German way all the instruments which he would have to use. He was a year older than Lanny and half a head taller; he had straw-colored hair clipped close, wore pince-nez, and was serious in disposition and formal in manners. If a lady so much as walked by he rose from his chair, and if she smiled he would click his heels and bow from the waist. What he liked about the Dalcroze system was that it *was* a system; something you could analyze and understand thoroughly. Kurt would always obey the rules, and be troubled by Lanny's free and easy American way of changing anything if he thought he could make it better.

The English boy had a complicated name, Eric Vivian Pomeroy-Nielson; but people had made it easy by changing it to Rick. He was going to be a baronet some day, and said it was deuced uncomfortable, being a sort of halfway stage between a gentleman and a member of the nobility. It was Rick's idea of manners never to take anything seriously, or rather never to admit that he did; he dressed casually, made jokes, spoke of "ridin' " and "shootin'," forgot to finish many of his sentences, and had chosen "putrid" as his favorite adjective. He had dark hair with a tendency to curl, which he explained by the remark: "I suppose a Jew left his visiting card on my family." But with all his pose, you would make a mistake about Eric Pomeroy-Nielson if you did not realize that he was learning everything he could about his chosen profession of theater: music, dancing, poetry, acting, elocution, stage decoration, painting—even that art, which he said was his father's claim to greatness, of getting introduced to rich persons and wangling their cash for the support of "little theaters."

Each of these boys had a contribution to make to the others. Kurt knew German music, from Bach to Mahler. Lanny knew a little of everything, from old sarabands to "Alexander's Ragtime Band," a recent "hit" from overseas. As for Rick, he had been to some new-fangled arts-and-crafts school and learned a repertoire of old English folk songs and dances. When he sang and the others danced the songs of Purcell, with so many trills and turns, and sometimes a score of notes to a syllable, it became just what the song proclaimed—"sweet Flora's holiday."

All three of these lads had been brought up in contact with older persons and were mature beyond their years. To Americans they would have seemed like little old men. All three were the product of ripe cultures, which took art seriously, using it to replace other forms of adventure. All were planning art careers; their parents were rich enough—not so rich as to be "putrid," but so that they could choose their own activities. All three looked forward to a future in which art would go on expanding like some miraculous flower. New "sensations" would be rumored, and crowds of eager and curious folk would rush from Paris to Munich to Vienna, from Prague to Berlin to London—just as now they had come flocking to the tall white temple on the bright meadow, to learn how children could be taught efficiency of mind and body and prepared for that society of cultivated and gracious aesthetes in which they were expecting to pass their days.

On a wide plain just below Hellerau was an exercise ground of the German army. Here almost every day large bodies of men marched and wheeled, ran and fell down and got up again. Horses galloped, guns and caissons rumbled and were swung about, unlimbered, and pointed at an imaginary foe. The sounds of all this floated up to the tall white temple, and when the wind was right, the dust came also. But the dancers and musicians paid little attention to it. Men had marched and drilled upon the soil of Europe ever since history began; but now there had been forty-two years of peace, and only the old people remembered war. So much progress had been made in science and in international relations that few men could contemplate the possibility of wholesale bloodshed in Europe. The art lovers were not among those few.

VI

When the summer season at the school was over, Lanny went to join his mother. He had tears in his eyes when he left Hellerau; such a lovely place, the only church in which he had ever worshiped. He told himself that he would never forget it; he promised his teachers to come back, and in the end to become a teacher himself. He promised Rick to see him in England, because his mother went there every "season," and if he tried hard he could persuade her to take him along.

As for Kurt, he was traveling with Lanny to the French Riviera; for the German lad had an aunt who lived there, and he had suggested paying her a visit of a couple of weeks before his school began. He had said nothing to her about an American boy who lived near by, for it was possible that his stiff and formal relative would not approve of such a friend. There were many stratifications among the upper classes of Europe, and these furies had never yielded to the lure of Orpheus and his lute.

Kurt was like an older brother to Lanny, taking charge of the travel arrangements and the tickets, and showing off his country to the visitor. They had to change trains at Leipzig, and had supper in a sidewalk café, ordering cabbage soup and finding that the vegetable had been inhabited before it was cooked. "Better a worm in the cabbage than no meat," said Kurt, quoting the peasants of his country.

Lanny forgot his dismay when they heard a humming sound overhead and saw people looking up. There in the reddish light of the sinking sun was a giant silver fish, gliding slowly and majestically across the sky. A Zeppelin! It was an achievement dreamed of by man for thousands of years, and now at last brought to reality in an age of miracles. German ingenuity had done it, and Kurt talked about it proudly. That very year German airliners had begun speeding from one city to another, and soon they promised air traffic across all the seas. No end to the triumphs of invention, the spread of science and culture in the great capitals of Europe!

The boys settled themselves in the night express, and Lanny told his friend about "Beauty," whom they were to meet in Paris. "Her friends all call her that," said the boy, "and so do I. She was only nineteen when I was born." Kurt could add nineteen and thirteen and realize that Lanny's mother was still young.

"My father lives in America," the other continued; "but he comes to Europe several times every year. The name Budd doesn't mean much to a German, I suppose, but it's well known over there; it's somewhat like saying Krupp in Germany. Of course the munitions plants are much smaller in the States; but people say Colt, and Remington, and Winchester—and Budd."

Lanny made haste to add: "Don't think that my parents are so very rich. Robbie—that's my father—has half a dozen brothers and sisters, and he has uncles and aunts who have their own children. My mother divorced my father years ago, and Robbie now has a wife and three children in Connecticut, where the Budd plants are. So you see there are plenty to divide up with. My father has charge of the sales of Budd's on the Continent, and I've always thought I'd be his assistant. But now I think I've changed my mind—I like 'Dalcroze' so much."

VII

Beauty Budd did not come to the station; she seldom did things which involved boredom and strain. Lanny was such a bright boy, he knew quite well how to have his bags carried to a taxi, and what to tip, and the name of their regular hotel. His mother would be waiting in their suite, and it would be better that way, because she would be fresh and cool and lovely. It was her business to be that, for him as for all the world.

Kind nature had assigned that role to her. She had everything: hair which flowed in waves of twenty-two-carat gold; soft, delicate skin, regular white teeth, lovely features—not what is called a dollbaby face, but one full of gaiety and kindness. She was small and delicate, in short, a delight to look at, and people turned to take their share of that delight wherever she went. It had been that way ever since she was a child, and of course she couldn't help knowing about it. But it wasn't vanity, rather a warm glow that suffused her, a happiness in being able to make others happy—and a pity for women who didn't have the blessed gift which made life so easy.

Beauty took all possible care of her natural endowment; she made a philosophy of this, and would explain it if you were interested. "I've had my share of griefs. I wept, and discovered that I wept alone—and I don't happen to be of a solitary nature. I laugh, and have plenty of company." That was the argument. Wasn't a beautiful woman as much worth taking care of as a flower or a jewel? Why not dress her elegantly, put her in a charming setting, and make her an art-work in a world of art lovers?

Her name was an art-work also. She had been born Blackless, and christened Mabel, and neither name had pleased her. Lanny's father had given her two new ones, and all her friends had agreed that they suited her. Now she even signed her checks "Beauty Budd," and if she signed too many she did not worry, because making people happy must be worth what it cost.

Now Lanny's mother was blooming after a long sea trip among the fiords, having kept her complexion carefully veiled from the sun which refused to set. Her only worry was that she had gained several pounds and had to take them off by painful self-denial. She adored her lovely boy, and here he came hurrying into the room; they ran to each other like children, and hugged and kissed. Beauty held him off and gazed at him. "Oh, Lanny, how big you've grown!" she exclaimed; and then hugged him again.

The German boy stood waiting. Lanny introduced him, and she greeted him warmly, reading in his eyes astonishment and adoration —the thing she was used to from men, whether they were fourteen or five times that. They would stand awe-stricken, forget their manners, become her slaves forever—and that was the best thing that could happen to them. It gave them something to look up to and worship; it kept them from turning into beasts and barbarians, as they were so strongly inclined to do. Beauty had put on for this occasion a blue Chinese silk morning robe with large golden pheasants on it, very gorgeous; she had guessed what it might do to Lanny's new friend, and saw that it was doing it. She was charming to him, and if he adored her he would be nice to her son, and everybody would be that much happier.

"Tell me about Hellerau," she said; and of course they did, or Lanny did, because the German boy was still tongue-tied. Beauty had had a piano put in the drawing room, and she ran to it. "What do you want?" she asked, and Lanny said: "Anything," making it easy for her, because really she didn't know so very many pieces. She began to play a Chopin polonaise, and the two boys danced, and she was enraptured, and made them proud of themselves. Kurt, who had never before heard of a mother who was also a child, revised his ideas of Americans in one short morning. Such free, such easygoing, such delightful people!

The boys bathed and dressed and went downstairs for lunch. Beauty ordered fruit juice and a cucumber salad. "I begin to grow plump on nothing," she said. "It's the tragedy of my life. I didn't dare to drink a glass of milk at a *saeter*."

"What is a *saeter*?" asked Lanny.

"It's a pasture high up on the mountainside. We would go ashore in the launch and drive up to them; the very old farmhouses are made of logs, and have holes in the roof instead of chimneys. They have many little storehouses, the roofs covered with turf, and you see flower gardens growing on top of them. One even had a small tree."

"I saw that once in Silesia," said Kurt. "The roots bind the roof tighter. But the branches have to be cut away every year."

"We had the grandest time on the yacht," continued Beauty. "Did Lanny ever tell you about old Mr. Hackabury? He comes from the town of Reubens, Indiana, and he makes Bluebird Soap, millions of cakes every day, or every week, or whatever it is—I'm no good at figures. He carries little sample cakes in his pocket and gives them to everybody. The peasants were grateful; they are a clean people."

The boys told her about the *Orpheus* festival, and Bernard Shaw and Granville Barker and Stanislavsky. "It's quite the loveliest place I've ever been to," declared Lanny. "I think I want to become a teacher of 'Dalcroze.'"

Beauty didn't laugh, as other mothers might have done. "Of course, dear," she answered. "Whatever you want; but Robbie may be disappointed." Kurt had never heard of parents being addressed by such names as Beauty and Robbie; he assumed it was an American custom, and it seemed to work well, though of course it would never do for Silesia.

They were having their pastry; and Beauty said: "You might like to stay over for an extra day. I'd like to have a chance to see more of Kurt, but I've accepted an invitation to spend a fortnight in England, and then go to Scotland for the shooting." Lanny was disappointed, but it didn't occur to him to show it, because he was used to seeing his mother in snatches like this; he understood that she had obligations to her many friends and couldn't be expected to stay and entertain one boy, or even two.

Kurt, also, was disappointed, having thought he was going to feast his eyes on this work of art, created in far-off America and perfected in France. He made up for lost time, and was so adoring, and at the same time respectful and punctilious, that Beauty decided he was an exceptionally fine lad and was glad that dear Lanny had such good judgment in the choice of friends. Lanny had written who Kurt's parents were, and also of the aunt in Cannes, the Frau Doktor Hofrat von und zu Nebenaltenberg. Beauty didn't know her, but felt sure that anybody with such a name must be socially acceptable.

VIII

In the afternoon they went to an exhibition of modern art. "Everybody" was talking about the Salon des Indépendants, and therefore Beauty had to be able to say that she had seen it. She had a quick step and a quick eye, and so was able to inspect the year's work of a thousand or more artists in fifteen or twenty minutes. After that she had a dress fitting; the business of being an art-work oneself didn't leave very much time for the art-works of others. Lanny's mother, flitting through life like a butterfly over a flower bed, was so charming and so gay that few would ever note how little honey she gathered.

She left the two boys to share the display between them. The painters and sculptors of a continent had turned their imaginations loose, and the boys wandered past wall after wall covered with their efforts. Each seemed to shriek: "Look at me! I am the ne plus ultra!" Few seemed willing to paint in the old accepted way, so as actually to reproduce something. Here faces were made into planes and conic sections; eyes and noses changed positions, trees became blue, skies green, and human complexions both. It was the epoch of the "Nude Descending the Staircase"; this nude consisted of spirals, zigzags which might have been lightning flashes, a tangle of lines resembling telephone wires after a cyclone. You couldn't form the least idea why it was a "nude," and wished you might know the artist and ask if it was a colossal spoof, or what.

There were plenty of recognizable nudes; they were shown in the morgue, on the battlefield or the operating table. There were women with great pendent paunches and breasts, men with limbs diseased or missing. You got the definite impression that the "independent" artists of the continent of Europe were a disturbed and tormented lot. Perhaps they lived in garrets and didn't get enough to eat; Lanny and Kurt, neither of whom had ever seen a garret or missed a meal, did not think of that explanation. They could only wonder why, in a world with creatures like Lanny's mother, painters should prefer ugly and repulsive subjects. There was something wrong; but the riddle couldn't be solved by the son of Beauty Budd nor yet by the son of the comptroller-general of Castle Stubendorf in Upper Silesia.

Beauty had an engagement for dinner, so the two boys went to a cinema, an art which was still in its rough-and-tumble days. The French equivalent of a custard pie was, it appeared, a bucket of paperhanger's paste; the paperhanger was mistaken for a lover by a jealous husband, and the pursuit and fighting ended with the pot of paste falling from a ladder onto the husband's head, to the hilarious delight of the husband-haters of Paris. In the orchestra pit a solitary man sat in front of a piano and a book of scores marked for different kinds of scenes—love, grief, or battle, whatever it might be. He would turn hastily to the proper page, and when the ladder was about to topple he was ready with the thunderstorm passage from the *William Tell* overture. Quite different from the Salon des Indépendants, and also from Hellerau; but the tastes of boys are catholic, and they laughed as loudly as the least cultured bourgeois in the place.

Next morning Beauty did not get up until nearly noon, so the boys drove about; Kurt had never been to Paris before, and Lanny, quite at home, showed him the landmarks and gave him history lessons. Later came a polo-playing American by the name of Harry Murchison, a scion of the plate-glass industry; he had a fancy car, and drove them out to Versailles, where they had lunch in a sidewalk café, and wandered through the gardens and forests, and saw the Little Trianon, and were told by a guide about Marie Antoinette and the Princesse de Lamballe and other fair ones of the vanished past—but none of them so fair as Beauty! Both Lanny and Kurt were a bit jealous of the handsome young American who sought to monopolize the mother; but she was kind and saw to the equal distribution of her favors.

When they were back in the hotel she had them show some "Dalcroze" to her friend while she dressed. Harry was taking her to the opera, it appeared; but first they had dinner, and then drove the boys to the station and saw them on the *rapide* for the Côte d'Azur. Beauty always had tears in her eyes at partings, and so did Lanny, and—unexpectedly—so did Kurt. Beauty kissed him good-by; and when the two boys were settled in their compartment and the train was under way, Kurt exclaimed: "Oh, Lanny, I just *love* your mother!"

Lanny was pleased, of course. "So does everybody," was his reply.

2

Côte d'Azur

I

ON THE eastern side of a little peninsula which juts out into the Mediterranean stood the tiny village of Juan-les-Pins, looking across a bay, the Golfe Juan, with the Estérel mountains in the background. On this lovely sheltered coast was a villa, with a tract of two or three acres, which Robbie Budd had given to Lanny's mother years ago. He had put it in trust so that she could not sell or even mortgage it, thus placing her in an odd position, with financial ups and downs that made no real difference. Just now "Juan," as it was called, was enjoying a mild prosperity; land was being divided up into *lotissements*, considerable sums were being offered, and Beauty had the thrill of being worth a hundred thousand francs. In due course would come a depression, and she would be "ruined," and sorrowful about it; then would come a terrific "boom," then another "slump"—and Beauty believing in each one. But always she and Lanny would have a home, which was the way Robbie intended it to be.

This had been Lanny's nest ever since he could recall. In its deeply shaded pine woods he had picked the spring flowers and learned the calls of birds. On its slowly shelving sand-beach he had paddled and learned to swim. Down the shore were boats of fishermen drawn up, and nets spread out to dry, and here was the most exciting kind of life for a child; all the strange creatures of the deep flapping and struggling, displaying the hues of the rainbow to the dazzling sun, with fisherboys to tell him which would bite and sting, and which could be carried home to Leese, the jolly peasant woman who was

17

their cook. Lanny had learned to prattle in three languages, and it was a long time before he was able to sort them out; English to his mother and father, French to many guests and occasional teachers, and Provençal to servants, peasants, and fisher-folk.

The house was built on the top of a rise, some way back from the sea. It was of pink stucco with pale blue shutters and a low roof of red tiles. It was in Spanish style, built round a lovely court with a fountain and flowers; there Lanny played when the mistral was blowing, as it sometimes did for a week on end. Along the road outside ran a high wall with a hedge of pink and white oleanders peering over it, and a wooden gate with a bell which tinkled inside the court, and on each side of the gate an aloe, having thick basal leaves and a tall spike with many flowers—"God's candelabra," they were called.

Here was a happy place for a boy, with no enemies and few dangers. His father taught him to swim in all sorts of water, and to float as peacefully and securely as a sea turtle. He learned to row and to sail, and to come in quickly when storms gave their first warnings. He learned so much about fishing, and about the nuts which the peasants gathered in the forests and the herbs which they found in the fields, that Beauty used to say, if they ever got really poor, Lanny would feed them. He learned also to make friends, and to share in so many occupations that he would never need to be bored.

His mother, being a lady of fashion, naturally worried now and then about the plebeian tastes of her only child, and when she was there would invite the children of her rich friends as playmates. And that was all right with Lanny, the rich children were interesting too; he would take them down the shore and introduce them to the fisherboys, and presently they would be ruining their expensive clothes learning to cast a hand net for shrimp. They would plan a walking trip into the hills, and rest at the door of some peasant cottage, and when they came back would tell how they had learned to weave baskets. Beauty would say with a laugh that Robbie's forefathers had been farmers, though of course in Connecticut they weren't the same as peasants.

II

Lanny Budd had never been to school, in the ordinary sense of the word. For one thing, his mother so often took him on journeys; and for another, he taught himself as many things as it seemed safe to put into one small head. He remembered phrases of every language he heard, and that was saying a lot on the Riviera. He was forever picking at the piano, and if he saw people dance a new dance, he had learned it before they got through. All his mother had to do was to show him his letters, and presently he was reading every book in the house that had pictures. You might be surprised to hear that Beauty Budd considered herself a lady of literary tastes; it meant that she noted the names of the books she heard people talking about, bought them, read the first few pages, and then was too busy to look at them again. Sooner or later Lanny would get hold of them, and if he didn't understand them, he would start pestering somebody with questions.

A good part of his education had come from listening. All sorts of people came to the house, and a well-bred little boy would sit quietly in a chair and not say a word. As a rule, people would forget that he was there, and have no idea that he was stowing things away in his mind: society and fashion, what people wore and what they ate, where they went and whom they met; the aristocracy of Europe and its titles; the rich people and their stocks and bonds, dividends and profits; the new cars, the new restaurants; the theaters and what they were showing, the operas and the names of the singers; the books that people were talking about; the journalists, the politicians, the heads of states—everything that was successful and therefore important.

When they were alone, the child would start in on his mother. "Beauty, what is taffeta, and what do you mean by cutting it on the bias? What are penguins and why are they like French politicians? What were the Dreyfusards, and why did the abbé get so excited when he talked about them?" It was hard on a mother who had developed to a high degree the art of taking part in conversation without bothering too much about details. With Lanny she had to get things right, because he would remember and bring them up again.

He had developed at a very early age the habit of cherishing some profound remark that he had heard one of his elders make, and getting it off in other company. Of course it would cause a sensation; and of course an active-minded child did not fail to enjoy this, and to repeat the performance. He had the advantage that he was operating behind a screen; for the elders seldom realize how shrewd children are, how attentively they listen, and how quickly they seize upon whatever is of advantage to them. The elders would say anything in a little boy's presence—and then later they would be astonished to find that he knew about such matters!

The city of Cannes lay only a few miles from his home, and the mother would betake herself there for shopping, and to have her charms attended to. Lanny, having promised never to go away with anybody, would find himself a seat on a street bench, or in a sidewalk café; and sooner or later there would be someone taking an interest in a bright lad with wavy brown hair, lively brown eyes, rosy cheeks, and a shirt of gray oxford cloth open at the throat.

In this way he had met, during the winter before he went to Hellerau, Colonel Sandys Ashleigh-Sandys—do not pronounce the y's—late of His Majesty's Royal Highlanders in the Indian Northwest. The colonel had white mustaches and a complexion like yellow parchment; it was trouble with his liver. He wore a linen suit, comfortably cut. A member of the exclusive "British colony," he would have turned away from any grown person who ventured to address him without a proper introduction; but when the tables were crowded and a small boy invited him to a seat, he did not think it necessary to decline. When the boy began to chat with all the grace of a man of the world, the colonel was inwardly amused and outwardly the soul of courtesy.

Lanny chose to talk about the latest popular novel he was halfway through. The old martinet with parasites in his liver questioned him about his reading, and found that this benighted lad had never read a novel of Scott, had never even heard of Dickens, and all he knew about the plays of Shakespeare was the incidental music of *A Midsummer Night's Dream*, written by a Jewish fellow. Lanny asked so many questions, and was so serious in his comments, that before they parted the colonel offered to send him a one-volume edition of the poet which he happened to be able to spare. One condition would be imposed—the lad must promise to read every word in the book.

Lanny had no idea of the size of that promise. He gave it, and also his name and address, and a couple of days later there arrived by the post an elegant tome weighing several pounds. It was the sort of work which is meant to be set upon a drawing-room table and dusted every day but never opened. Lanny kept his pledge literally, he began at the title page and spent a month reading straight through, in a state of tense excitement. He wore his mother out at mealtimes, telling her about the lovely ladies who were accused of dreadful crimes which they had not committed. Just what the crimes were supposed to be was vague in Lanny's mind, and how was his mother to answer his questions? What did a man mean when he said he knew a hawk from a handsaw, and what were maidenheads and how did you break them?

Presently there was Lanny making himself swords out of laths and helmets out of newspapers, and teaching fishermen's children to fence and nearly poke one another's eyes out! Shouting: "Zounds!" and "Avaunt, traitor!" and "Lay on, Macduff!" down on the beach! Spouting poetry all over the place, like an actor—maybe he might turn out to be that—how was any woman to know what she had brought into the world? It was evident to her that this child's imagination was going to carry him to strange places and make him do uncomfortable things.

III

Lanny and Kurt, arriving at Cannes, parted company before they left the train. The German boy was to be met by his aunt; and this widow of the Court-Counselor von und zu Nebenaltenberg was a person with old-fashioned notions who would probably disapprove of Americans on general principles. The situation turned out to be even more difficult, for the aunt knew or professed to know all about "that Budd woman," as she called Beauty, and was shocked that her nephew had met such a person. She wouldn't say what it was—just one word: "*Unschicklich!*"

Kurt asked no questions. "Mrs. Budd has gone to Scotland for the shooting season," he remarked, casually. He sat erect in the stiff chair, facing the meager, severe old lady, telling her the news about the many members of their family. He ate a sound German luncheon of rye bread with slices of *Leberwurst* and *Schweizerkäse*, followed by a small *Apfelkuchen* and a cup of weak tea with milk. When the two had finished this meal, the aunt laid out the proper portions of food for her solitary maid, and then opened a cedar chest which stood between the windows of the dining room, and stowed all the remaining food therein, and carefully locked the chest with one of a bunch of keys which she carried at her waist. "You can't trust these native servants with anything," said the Frau Doktor Hofrat. Her husband had been dead for ten years, but she still wore black for him and of course carried his titles.

However, she was a woman of culture, and in due course asked about Hellerau, and Kurt told her. She was prejudiced against Jaques-Dalcroze because he had a French name and beard; but Gluck's music was *echt deutsch*, so the Frau Doktor Hofrat asked questions and wished that she might have seen the Festspiel. Only after Kurt had awakened her curiosity to the utmost did the budding diplomat mention that his American boy friend had a real gift, and might assist him to give a Dalcroze demonstration. He was a very well-bred and polite boy, Kurt assured his aunt; he was only thirteen, and probably knew nothing about the "*Unschicklichkeit*" of his mother. Furthermore, he was an artist, or going to be, and one should not judge persons of that sort by ordinary standards. Consider Wagner, for example. Concerning even Beethoven there had been rumors . . .

By such insidious devices Kurt won his aunt's permission to invite Lanny Budd for tea. A telegram was dispatched, and the Budd chauffeur drove Lanny over at the proper hour. He entered a plain, immaculate apartment, clicked his heels, bowed from the waist, and apologized for his German—which really wasn't so bad, because he had had two German tutors, each for several months. He ate only one tiny sandwich and one cooky, and declined a second cup of tea. Then while Kurt played the piano he gave demonstrations of what the Dalcroze people called "plastic counterpoint"; the elderly widow played folk songs which Lanny did not know, and he listened, and invented movements for them, and made intelligent comments while he did so. The Frau Doktor Hofrat did not tell him that she had once lost a little boy who had brown hair and eyes like his; but she invited him to come again, and gave her consent for Kurt to visit his home.

So all was well, and the youngsters were turned loose to enjoy life in their own fashion. The luncheon that Kurt had with Lanny wasn't any frugal German meal. Leese prepared a *mostele*, an especially good fish which the boys caught; also an omelet with fresh truffles, and then fresh figs with cream and cake; that was the way they lived at the Budds', and any peasant woman was happy to serve two handsome lads who had such good appetites and paid so many compliments to the food.

The two boys lived in bathing trunks, which sufficed for clothing in this free and easy playground of Europe. They walked out along the peninsula to the Cap d'Antibes, where you could dive off the rocks into thirty feet of water so clear that you expected to reach the bottom. They hauled a seine on the shallow beach and brought in shrimp and squid and crabs and other odd forms of life which had swarmed in these waters for ages and had been hauled out by Roman boys, Greek boys, Phoenicians, Saracens, Barbary corsairs—children of unnumbered races which had invaded this "Azure Coast" since the land had sunk and let the water in.

From his earliest days Lanny had lived in the presence of this long past. He had learned geography in the course of motor trips, and his history lessons had come from asking about old ruins. People didn't always know the answers, but there would be a guidebook in one of the pockets of the car, and you could look up Arles or Avignon or whatever it might be. Antibes, which lay on the other side of the promontory, had once been a Roman city, with baths and an arena and an aqueduct; it was fascinating to look at the remains and think about the lives of people long gone from the earth which once they had held with pride and confidence. Not long ago, there had been dug up a memorial tablet to the little "Septentrion child" who had "danced and pleased in the theater"; Lanny Budd might have been that child come back to life, and he wondered how his predecessor had lived and what had brought him to his untimely end.

The two boys of the year 1913, having no idea what their ends were to be, wandered happily over the hills and valleys which run back from this coast. There was an endless variety of scenes: swift rivers, deep gorges, broad valleys; olive groves and vineyards, forests of cork oak and eucalyptus, meadows full of flowers; crowded villages, with terraced land cultivated to the last precious inch; palaces of Carrara marble with elaborate gardens and flowering trees—so many things to look at and ask questions about! Kurt couldn't talk to the peasants, but Lanny would translate for him, and the women noted the bright blue eyes and yellow hair of the strange lad from the North, and had the same thought as Pope Gregory, who had inspected the war prisoners and remarked: "Not Angles, but angels."

IV

High above Antibes is an ancient monastery, with a church, Notre-Dame-de-Bon-Port, from which the sailors of Antibes, barefooted and wearing white shirts, carry an image of the Virgin in a procession, so as to enjoy her protection from storms. From here there is a view of all the seas, the white cities of the Riviera, and distant Italian mountains capped with snow. To this place the boys brought their lunch, and Lanny pointed out the landmarks: to the west the Estérels, mountains of blood-red porphyry, and to the east the large city of Nice, and beyond it Monaco on its rock. Directly below them, in the bay, French warships were anchored; it was their favorite resting place, and sailors swarmed in the little town.

The boys spent the afternoon on this height, talking not merely of the scenery, but of themselves and what they planned to make of their lives. So serious they were, and so conscientious! Kurt was an ethical person, and when he revealed the moral compulsions of his soul, Lanny was quite awe-stricken.

"Did you ever think how few really cultured persons there are in the world?" inquired the German boy. "There are whole races and nations with practically none, and in the rest just a handful, holding aloft the banner of good taste, among so many millions of Hottentots."

"What are Hottentots?" asked Lanny, naïvely.

Kurt explained that this was a way of referring to persons without culture or ideals. The great mass of men were like that, and civilization was kept going by the labors of a devoted few. "Suppose they were to fail—what then?"

"I never thought about it," admitted the other, worried.

"We should sink into barbarism again, into another dark age. That is why the mission of art is such a high one, to save humanity by teaching a true love of beauty and respect for culture."

Lanny thought that was a very wonderful way to look at it, and said so. Kurt went on:

"We who understand that have to discipline ourselves as if for a priesthood. We have to make the most of our powers, living an ordered life and not wasting ourselves as so many musicians have done. I have made up my mind to be one who lives a life of reason, like Bach or Brahms. Do you know about them?"

"Not very much," Lanny had to admit.

"Of course I don't know how much talent I may have——"

"Oh, I'm sure you have a wonderful talent, Kurt!"

"Whatever it is, I want to cherish it and put it to service. Have you thought about doing that with your life?"

"I'm afraid I never had any great thoughts like yours, Kurt. You see, my parents don't take things so seriously."

"Surely they have taught you some ethical standards!"

"Well, they told me to enjoy the beautiful things I came upon;

and of course to be polite to people, and kind, and learn what I can from them."

"That's all right, only it's not enough. One must have a wider vision, nobler aims."

"I see it, Kurt, and I appreciate your telling me about it."

"Of course, one doesn't talk about such things except to a few chosen persons, who are capable of understanding one's soul."

"I realize that," said Lanny, humbly; "I'll try to be worthy of the trust. I'll be a sort of disciple, if I may."

The older lad agreed to accept him on that basis. They would correspond and tell each other their deeper longings, not keeping them locked up, as one had to do in a world of shallow and thoughtless people. When the sun began to drop behind the Estérels and the pair started down the road, they felt that they had had a sort of religious experience, such as might have come to the monks who through many centuries had paced the corridors of that monastery.

V

It was Kurt's idea that his new disciple should be invited to visit the great Castle Stubendorf during the Christmas holidays; and to this end it was desirable that he should cultivate the esteem of the Frau Doktor Hofrat, whose recommendation would decide the matter. So Lanny came several times to the apartment in Cannes, and danced "Dalcroze" for some of the friends of the severe and straitlaced German lady. Never once did anyone mention his mother or his father, or any of his American associates; but the Frau Doktor Hofrat probed his mind, and made certain that he had a genuine respect for the contributions of the Fatherland to the world's culture. At Kurt's suggestion, Lanny borrowed a volume of Schiller's poetry, and struggled diligently with it and asked the old lady's help now and then.

She also interested herself in his musical education, which had been of a deplorably irregular character. Kurt, like his aunt before him, had had a sound German training in piano technique; a veritable military drill; arms and wrists stiff, knuckles depressed, second joint elevated, fingers pulled up and sharply pushed down. But poor Lanny had got a hodge-podge of everything that friends of his mother had been moved to recommend. First had come Professor Zimmalini, protégé of the mother-in-law of Baroness de la Tourette. Having been a pupil of a pupil of Leschetizsky, the professor laid great stress upon equality of the fingers; the wrists depressed, the knuckles arched, the fingers rounded, the elbows curved even in ordinary legato. Lanny had been taught that for a whole winter; but then had come the London season, and after that Biarritz, and by the time they returned to their home, the professor had moved to Paris.

So then Lanny had a spell of the Breithaupt method, at a still higher price. He was told about forearm rotary motion, the importance of relaxation, and the avoidance of devitalization. But the excitable French professor who taught him all this suddenly fell under the spell of a stout concert singer and went off to the Argentine as her accompanist. Now Beauty had heard about a Professor Baumeister, who had recently come to Cannes, and she had told Lanny in her offhand way to take lessons from him if he wanted to. But Lanny hadn't got around to thinking about it yet.

When the Frau Doktor Hofrat heard all this her orderly German soul was shocked. This poor child was playing the piano half a dozen ways at the same time; and the fact that he was perfectly happy while doing so made it even worse. She assured him that the Herr Professor Baumeister was no better than a musical anarchist, and recommended a friend who had once taught at Castle Stubendorf and would impart the official German technique. Lanny promised to put this recommendation before his mother, and thereby completed his conquest of Kurt's aunt. She took the two boys to a concert—the one extravagance she permitted herself.

When the time came for Kurt to leave, he told his disciple that the aunt had consented to write to her brother, endorsing Lanny as worthy of guesthood. The American boy was extraordinarily delighted about it, for by this time he had heard so much about the

castle and the wonders of life there that it had come to seem to him
a place out of Grimm's fairy tales. He would meet Kurt's family,
see how Kurt lived, and become acquainted with the environment
in which his friend's lofty ideals had been nurtured.

VI

Kurt went away, and Lanny settled down to reading German,
practicing finger drill, and teaching fisherboys to dance Dalcroze.
He was never lonely, for Leese and the housemaid Rosine loved him
as if he were their own. He knew that Beauty would come in the
end, and a month later she came, full of news and gaiety. Then, out
of the blue, came a telegram from Robbie, saying that he was leaving Milan and would arrive the next day.

That was the way with Lanny's father, who thought no more of
sailing for Europe than Beauty did of going in to Cannes to have a
fitting. He didn't bother to cable, for he might be taking a train
for Constantinople or St. Petersburg, and he couldn't know how
long he would be there. Post cards would come, sometimes from
Newcastle, Connecticut, sometimes from London or Budapest. "See
you soon," or something like that. The next thing would be a telegram, saying that he would arrive on such and such a train.

Robbie Budd was still under forty and was the sort of father
any boy would choose if he were consulted. He had played football, and still played at polo now and then, and was solid and firm
to the touch. He had abundant brown hair, like his son, and when
you saw him in bathing trunks you discovered that it was all over
his chest and thighs, like a Teddy bear's. From him Lanny had got
his merry brown eyes and rosy cheeks, also his happy disposition
and willingness to take things as they came.

Robbie liked to do everything that Lanny liked, or maybe it was
the other way around. He would sit at the piano and romp for
hours, with even worse technique than his son's. He was no good at
"classical" music, but he knew college songs, Negro songs, musical
comedy songs—everything American, some of it jolly and some sen-

timental. In the water he did not know what it was to tire; he would stay in half the day or night, and if he thought you were tiring, he would say: "Lie on your back," and would come under you and put his hands under your armpits, and begin to work with his feet, and it was as if a tugboat had taken hold of you. He had ordered two pairs of goggles, to be strapped around the head and fitted tight with rubber, so that he and Lanny could drop down and live among the fishes. Robbie would take one of the three-pointed spears used by the fishermen; he would stalk a big *mérou*, and when he struck there would be a battle that Lanny would talk about for days.

Robbie Budd made quantities of money—he never said how much, and perhaps never knew exactly—but he left a trail of it behind him. He liked the smiling faces of those who have suddenly been made prosperous. He needed a lot of people to help him, and that was the way he persuaded them—a little bit at a time, and collecting the service quickly, before the debt was forgotten!

He expected some day to have the help of his son at this money-making; and because, for all his gaiety and his cynicism, he was a far-seeing and careful man, he had devised a system of training for this, his first and most dearly loved child. It appeared quite casual and incidental, but it had been thought out and was frequently checked for results. Robbie Budd caused his son to think of the selling of small arms and ammunition as the most romantic and thrilling of all occupations; he surrounded it with mysteries and intrigues, and impressed upon the boy the basic lesson that everything concerned with it was a matter of most solemn secrecy. Never, never, was the son of a munitions salesman to let slip one word about his father's affairs to any person, anywhere, under any circumstances! "On the whole continent of Europe there is nobody I really trust but you, Lanny"—so the father would declare.

"Don't you trust Beauty?" the boy asked, and the answer was:

"She trusts other people. The more she tries to keep a secret, the quicker it gets out. But you will never dream of saying a word to anybody about your father's business; you will understand that any one of Beauty's rich and fashionable friends may be trying to find out where your father has gone, what contracts he's interested in, what cabinet minister or army officer he has taken for a motor ride."

"Never a hint, Robbie, believe me! I'll talk about the fishing, or the new tenor at the opera." Lanny had learned this lesson so thoroughly that he was able to recognize at once when the Conte di Pistola or the wife of the attaché of the Austrian embassy was trying to pump him. He would tell his father about it, and Robbie would laugh and say: "Oh, yes, they are working for Zaharoff."

Lanny wouldn't have to hear any more; Zaharoff—accent on the first syllable—was the gray wolf who was gobbling up the munitions plants of Europe one by one and who considered the placing of a contract with an American as an act of high treason. Ever since he was old enough to remember, Lanny had been hearing stories of his father's duels with this most dangerous of men. The things Lanny knew about him might have upset every chancellery in Europe, if there had been any way to get them published.

When Robbie stepped off the train—he had come all the way from Bulgaria—both Beauty and Lanny were there to welcome him. He gave the latter a bear hug and the former a friendly handshake. Having a wife, in Connecticut, Robbie didn't stay at the house, but at the hotel near by. He and Lanny ran a race down to the boathouse to get into their swimming trunks, and when they were out in a boat, far enough from all prying ears, Robbie grinned and said: "Well, I landed that Bulgarian contract."

"How did you do it?"

"I made a mistake as to the day of the week."

"How did that help?" There were so many strange ways of landing contracts that the brightest boy in the world couldn't guess them.

"Well, I thought it was Thursday, and I bet a thousand dollars on it."

"And you lost?"

"It was last Friday. We went to a kiosk on the corner and bought a Friday newspaper; and of course they couldn't have had that on Thursday." The two exchanged grins.

Lanny could guess the story now; but he liked to hear it told in Robbie's way, so he asked: "You really paid the debt?"

"It was a debt of honor," said the father gravely. "Captain Borisoff is a fine fellow, and I'm under obligations to him. He turned in a report that Budd carbines are superior to any on the market. They really are, of course."

"Sure, I know," said the boy. They were both of them serious about that; it was one of the fixed laws of the universe that Americans could beat Europeans at anything, once they put their minds to it. Lanny was glad; for he was an American, even though he had never set foot upon the land of the pilgrims' pride. He was glad that his father was able to outwit Zaharoff and all the other wolves and tigers of the munitions industry. Americans were the most honest people in the world, but of course if they had to, they could think up just as many smart tricks as any Levantine trader with Greek blood and a Russian moniker!

VII

It might occur to you that all this was hardly the best kind of moral training for a child; but the fact was that Lanny managed to preserve a sort of gay innocence toward it. Other boys got their thrills out of the "pulps" and the movies, but Lanny Budd got his from this wonderful father, his diplomatic and conspiratorial aides, and the generals, cabinet ministers, financial tycoons, and social high lights whom the boy met and would continue to meet so long as he was Robbie Budd's son.

The father's attitude toward these people was suave, even cordial, but behind their backs he laughed at them. They were the *crème de la crème* of Europe; they lived a life of many formalities and solemnities, gave themselves fancy titles, covered themselves with orders and decorations, and looked upon an American munitions salesman as a crude commercial fellow. Robbie didn't pay them enough of a tribute to resent these pretensions; he would chuckle as he told his son about the absurdities and weaknesses of this great one and that.

He would refer to the stout Countess Wyecroft as a "puller-in," and to the elegant and monocled Marquis de Trompejeu as a pimp. "They'll all do anything if you pay them enough—and guarantee them against being caught!"

Robbie had constructed a complete suit of intellectual armor to protect himself and his business against criticism, and he made a smaller-sized suit for Lanny and taught him to wear it. "Men hate each other," he would say. "They insist upon fighting, and there's nothing you can do about it, except learn to defend yourself. No nation would survive for a year unless it kept itself in readiness to repel attacks from greedy and jealous rivals; and you have to keep your weapons up to date, because the other fellow's always improving his. From the beginning of time there was a duel between those who made shields and those who made swords and spears; nowadays it's war between the makers of armorplate and the makers of shells and torpedoes. This will go on as long as there's any sort of progress."

The munitions industry was the most important part of every nation, insisted the head salesman of Budd Gunmakers Corporation; the one upon which all others depended. Most people would admit that, but they had the notion that the makers of guns and shells ought to work only for their own country, and that there was something unpatriotic in supplying other nations with such products. "But that's just people's ignorance," said Robbie; "they don't realize that propellants"—it was the industry's way of speaking of the various kinds of powder—"deteriorate fast, and after a few years they're worthless. So you can't store up the product and feel safe; you have to keep your producing machinery in order, and how can you do it unless you give it something to do? Are you going to stay at war just to keep your munitions workers in practice?"

Back there in the state of Connecticut was an establishment which Budd's had been building for three generations. Lanny had never seen it, but many pictures had been shown him and many stories told. In the beginning was a Connecticut Yankee who first thought of the idea of making guns with interchangeable parts, exactly alike, so they could be replaced and manufactured wholesale. Lanny's great-grandfather had been one of those who took up the idea and helped the country to put down the Indians, conquer Mexico, preserve the Union, and free Cuba and the Philippines. "That's the kind of service the armament people render," said Robbie. "They do it when it's needed, and at the time everybody's mighty glad to have it done!"

America hadn't had a really big war for half a century, and so American armaments plants were small by European standards. American wages were so much higher that the only way to compete was to turn out a better product—and to persuade the customers that you were doing so. This last was Robbie's job, and he worked hard at it, but was never satisfied; he grumbled at Europe's inability to appreciate Yankee brains. Americans labored under another handicap, in that their plants used English inches as their standard of measurement, whereas Europe employed the metric system. Robbie had persuaded his father to install machinery of the latter sort, and he now had the duty of keeping that costly machinery running. The business he did never satisfied him; the contracts were "mere chicken-feed," he would say—but he was a well-fed and handsome chicken, all the same!

Some day Lanny would visit the Budd plant across the seas and learn its secrets. Meantime, he must get to know Europe, its different races and tribes and classes, what arms they needed, and how to get there with the right samples and grease the right palms. Said Robbie: "It's a serious matter to realize that thousands of workmen and their wives and children are dependent upon your business foresight. If Zaharoff had got the contract for the carbines from Bulgaria, it would have been British or French or Austrian workingmen who would have had the work and the wages, and not merely would workers' children in Connecticut have gone hungry, but storekeepers would have been bankrupted and farmers would have had no market for the food they grew." So it was not for himself and his family, but for a whole townful of people that Robbie Budd practiced the tricks of salesmanship, and lost large sums of money at poker or betting that it was Thursday when he knew it was Friday!

Of course it was terrible that men went to war and killed one another; but for that you had to blame nature, not the Budd family. Robbie and his son would put on their goggles and drop down among the fishes for a while, and when they came up and sat on the rocks to rest, the man would talk about the life that went on in that strange dim world. Uncounted billions of microscopic creatures called plankton were produced in the sunshine at the surface, and tiny fish and shrimp and other creatures fed upon them. Larger fish devoured the small ones, and monsters like the sharks preyed upon these. All reproduced themselves incessantly, and this had gone on for tens of millions of years, with changes so slight that they were hardly to be noticed. Such was life, and you could no more change it than you could stop the rising and setting of the sun; you just had to understand the sun's behavior and adjust yourself to it.

This was a lesson which Robbie preached incessantly, so that to Lanny it became like the landscape and the climate, the music he heard and the food he ate. Robbie would enforce it with picturesque illustrations; he would bring up a lame fish that had had one of its fins bitten off, and he would say: "You see, he didn't keep up his armaments industry!"

Now Lanny heard more of this, and decided that he had better put off telling his father about becoming a Dalcroze dancer. And what about all those noble ideals which Kurt Meissner had revealed to him, and which had impressed him so greatly a month or so ago? What was the use of thinking about religion and self-dedication and all that, if men were shrimps and crabs, and nations were sharks and octopi? Here was a problem which men had been debating before Lanny Budd was born and which it would take him some time to settle!

3

Playground of Europe

I

BEAUTY stayed a couple of weeks, and so did Robbie, with the result that Lanny's life became what the newspapers call one continuous round of social gaieties. Beauty gave a tennis party, with afternoon tea, and a row of fashionable ladies decorating the sidelines. She gave a dinner party, with dancing on the loggia, and Venetian lanterns hanging, and an orchestra from Cannes. When they were not having or preparing things like these, they were motoring to the homes of friends up and down the coast, for motorboat races, or bridge, or fireworks, or whatever it might be.

Lanny had his part in these events. People who had heard about "Dalcroze" would ask for a demonstration, and he would oblige them without having to be begged. Lady Eversham-Watson put up her ivory and gold lorgnette and drawled: "Chawming!" and the Baroness de la Tourette lifted her hands with a dozen diamonds and emeralds on them and exclaimed: *"Ravissant!"*—all exactly as Lanny had foreseen. This attention and applause did not spoil him, because it was his plan to take up the role of teacher, and here was a beginning. He liked to please people, and everybody loved him for it; or at any rate they said they did, and Lanny took the world for the gay and delightful thing it strove so hard to appear.

It was a world of people who had money. Lanny had always taken it for granted that everybody had it. He had never known any poor people; or, to be more exact, he had never known about their poverty. The servants worked hard, but they were well paid and had plenty to eat and enjoyed working in the rich homes, knowing the rich people and gossiping about their ways. The Provençal peasants partook of nature's bounty, and were independent and free-spoken. The fishermen went to sea and caught fish; they had done that all their lives, and liked to do it, and were healthy, and drank wine and sang and danced. If now and then one was hurt, or lost his boat, a collection would be taken, and Lanny would tell Beauty about it and she would contribute.

The rich people had the function of exhibiting elegance and grace to the world, and the Côte d'Azur was a place set apart for that performance. It was the winter playground of Europe; the wealthy and fashionable came from all over the world and either built themselves homes or stayed in luxurious hotels, dressing in the latest fashions and displaying themselves on waterfront parade grounds such as the Boulevard de la Croisette in Cannes and the Promenade des Anglais in Nice. They danced and played baccarat and roulette, golf and tennis; they motored and sailed, and ate and drank in public, and lay about on the beaches under gaily striped umbrellas. Photographers took pictures of them, and newspapers and magazines all over the world paid high prices for them, and so the exhibition of elegance had become a large-scale business.

The ladies who lent their charms to this parade were spoken of as professional beauties, and they took their profession with the same seriousness as a physician takes the healing of bodies or a priest the saving of souls. It was an exacting occupation and left its devotees little time to think about anything else; during the exhibition periods, known as "seasons," they made it a rule to change their costumes four times a day, thus keeping the cameramen on the jump; during the "off seasons" they hardly got a chance to recuperate, because they had to spend their time planning with *couturiers* and *marchands de modes* and others to keep them at the head of the next procession.

It would seem as if a woman by the name of Beauty Budd had been especially cut out for such a career. And she might have had it, but for the fact that she was so poor. All she had was this home, and a thousand dollars a month which Robbie allowed her. He was strict with her; had made her promise not to incur debts, and never to gamble unless it was a business matter, with Robbie himself taking part. Of course you couldn't take that too literally; she had to play bridge, and couldn't very well insist upon paying cash for the clothes she ordered—the makers would have thought there was something wrong with her.

Thus in the view of Lanny Budd the meaning of "being poor" was that his lovely mother was outclassed in the race for attention. She would never be listed as one of the "ten best-dressed women of Paris." Fortunately she was of a happy disposition and did not let these hardships mar her life; she learned to make a joke of them, and also a virtue. She would talk about her unwillingness to "pay the price," a remark which some of her friends might have resented as a reflection upon themselves.

But these were matters beyond Lanny's understanding as yet. He would try to console his mother. "I'm glad you're poor. If you weren't, I wouldn't see even a little of you!"

She would hug him, and tears would come into the lovely blue eyes. "You're the best thing in the whole world, and I'm a foolish woman ever to think about anything else!"

"That's the way I'd like it!" Lanny would grin.

II

The reason why Robbie stayed so long on this trip was that he had another deal on, and Beauty was helping him. That was an aspect of their relationship which Lanny had learned about, and in which he also took part according to his abilities. Customers had to be met "socially," something far more effective than mere business acquaintanceship. In the latter case they would be thinking only about money, but in the former they would like you; at any rate they would pretend they did, and you would try to make it real. You had to "entertain" them, and for this purpose what could be more helpful than a woman with the charms of Beauty Budd? For this well-recognized part of the selling of munitions Robbie paid generously.

The Russian Minister of War would be planning to visit Paris with his wife. Robbie had scouts who kept him posted, and he would telegraph Beauty, who would at once inquire among her friends and find someone who knew either the minister or his wife, and would invite them down for a few days to warm their old bones. Beauty would meet them and make an engagement for tea, and wire Robbie, who would come in a shiny new car and take the tired old couple motoring, and show them the Corniche road, and maybe let them have a fling in the Casino at Monte Carlo.

Robbie's agents would have provided him with a regular dossier about such guests, including their tastes and their weaknesses. Beauty would have several duchesses and countesses at the tea party, and when the minister took his seat at the gaming table, Robbie would slip him a bundle of thousand-franc notes and tell him laughingly to take a "flier" for him. The old gentleman would do so, and if he lost Robbie would tell him to forget it, and if he won he would forget it without being told. Later, when Robbie would tell him news about the marvelous new sub-machine gun which Budd's were putting on the market, the minister would be deeply interested and would make a date for Robbie to demonstrate it in St. Petersburg.

When Robbie was leaving to keep that date, he would say to Beauty: "I can't motor to St. Petersburg. I'd get stuck like Napoleon in the snow." Yes, there was snow in Russia, impossible as it might seem in Juan-les-Pins, where everybody lay around on the beach absorbing sunshine. "That old car of yours is beginning to look shabby," he would add. "You better take mine. But don't let anybody swindle you on the old one; you ought to get five or six thousand francs for it at least." If Beauty protested that he was too generous, Robbie had a formula: "It goes on the expense account."

A marvelous phenomenon, the expense account of a munitions salesman, which could be stretched to include both his business and his pleasures. It included the newspaper man who brought the tip, and the detective who prepared the dossier. It included the car, and the chauffeur, and the gambling losses. It included the tea party and, strange to say, it might even include some of the duchesses and countesses—those who were so important that it was an honor for a Russian cabinet minister to meet them, instead of for them to meet a Russian cabinet minister.

Such subtle distinctions you had to know thoroughly if you wanted to land contracts. The great ladies knew their own value and the value of the service expected. If it was to get the wife and daughter of an American millionaire presented at the Court of St. James's, that might be worth a thousand pounds; but if it was just a matter of introducing you to a politician or a financier, that might be done for a thousand francs.

Of course there were members of the nobility who were not for sale. Some English milords were so rich they could afford to be dignified. Some of the old French families were poor as church mice, but chose to live in retirement, dress dowdily, and pray for the return of the Bourbon pretender. But the people Robbie Budd made use of belonged to the *grand monde;* their pleasure was to shine in public, and the ladies especially were frequently in debt and ravenous for money. Beauty made it her business to know them, and with her woman's tact she would find out what service they could render, and what they would expect. Some were frank, and would name their price and be prepared to haggle over it; others took a high tone, and said they would do it to oblige dear, darling Beauty. These were the persons who got more.

Thus Lanny, opening his eyes to the world in which he was to live, came to realize that among the swarms of elegant and showy people who passed through his home there were all sorts and sizes, and each had to be treated differently. A few were friends whom his mother loved and trusted; others were there for business reasons, and might turn out to be "horrid people," who would go off and say mean things about her behind her back. When that happened she would cry, and Lanny would want to kick those false

friends the next time he met them. But that was another lesson of
the *grand monde* which you had to learn; you never kicked anybody, but on the contrary were as effusive as ever, and the most
you allowed yourself was a sly little thrust with a sharp stiletto of
wit.

III

The new deal was to be with Rumania, which was about to supply part of its army with automatic pistols; this had become necessary because Bulgaria had just done the same. Several countries in
southeastern Europe had fought two wars among themselves in the
past three years, and no one could guess when the next one would
start, or who would be fighting whom. Budd's was putting out for
the European trade a new eight-cartridge 7.65 mm. automatic
which it claimed was the best in the world. Of course Robbie always had to claim that, but in this case he told Lanny that he really
believed it.

He had in Paris a fellow by the name of "Bub" Smith, who had
been a cowboy and could shoot the head off a hatpin, and would
have done it while the hat was on a lady's head if there had been
any female willing to face a William Tell from Texas. Robbie had
arranged for this man to come whenever needed, because army
officers were generally so impressed by good marksmanship that
they would attribute it to the gun. Now he was going to bring Bub
to the Riviera to meet a certain Captain Bragescu, a member of the
commission which was making preliminary investigations prior to
the final tests in Bucharest. Robbie laughed about that phrase "preliminary investigations," which meant that the captain wanted to
look into Robbie's pocketbook before he looked into his pistol.

The captain arrived unannounced, just after Robbie and Beauty
had gone off to a dinner dance. A taxi drew up in front of "Bienvenu," the bell at the gate tinkled, and Rosine ushered into Lanny's
presence a mincing and elegant figure with mustaches dyed black
and twisted to sharp points, in a sky-blue military uniform fitting

tightly and drawn in at the waist so that you knew he was wearing corsets. You might have found it hard to believe that an army officer would have his cheeks painted and powdered and would smell strongly of perfume, but so it was.

Lanny was embarrassed, because he had on some old fishing togs and a fisherboy named Ruggiero was waiting for him down on the beach. But he welcomed the guest courteously, and explained where his father and mother had gone, and offered to telephone them at once. "Oh, no!" said Captain Bragescu. "I would not think of interfering with their engagement."

An idea occurred to Lanny. "I wonder if you'd be interested in seeing torch-fishing."

"What do you get?" asked the officer. It turned out that he had done a lot of fishing at home.

So Lanny ran down to the boathouse, where there were some of Robbie's old clothes and a warm sweater—for it turns cold on the Riviera the moment the sun disappears behind the Estérels. The captain took off his corsets, and proved to be not in the least effeminate. Down the beach they met an Italian fisherboy, a year or two older than Lanny, and strong as his work required. The Rumanian spoke good French, but had trouble with a mixture of Provençal and Ligurian, so Lanny had to help out.

While Ruggiero rowed the heavy boat out toward the Cap, the army officer told about the fishing he had seen in his boyhood, at the mouth of the Danube, for the huge sturgeon. It was a rather ghastly procedure, for they cut out the roe, containing seven million eggs, and then threw the fish back alive. This was the black caviar, the epicure's delight—but Lanny wouldn't enjoy it quite so much for a while.

The sea was smooth except for long swells, and when the torch was blazing you could see much farther into the depths than you could reach with the trident. Peering down among the rocks, you would see a *langouste* poking out his greenish-gray head. You would get the three-pronged spear poised above him and strike, and up he would come, snapping his heavy tail back and forth. He was pleasanter to have in the boat than an American lobster, because he had no big claws that might take off one of your fingers.

Also, there were fishes of many hues and sizes; they seemed to be dazzled by the light, and even an amateur like the captain could hit one now and then. Presently he saw a head underneath some waving branches of a sea plant; he struck, and was all but jerked into the water. "Look out!" shouted the fisherboy, and leaped to help him. It was fortunate the officer didn't have those corsets on, for now he needed every particle of muscle and wind he had.

They brought up a huge green moray, the largest of all the eels, and the most dangerous. Ruggiero gaffed him, but cried: "Don't haul him into the boat!" He clubbed and stabbed the creature until the life was all gone out of him, for he had teeth as sharp as razor blades. He was more than six feet long, and when you saw him down in the water you thought he was clad in elegant green velvet.

He had been esteemed as a food fish ever since the days of the ancient Romans; so the pair had a fine story to tell Beauty and Robbie in the morning. Lanny's reputation as an entertainer of customers was much enhanced; for Captain Bragescu might have thought that dinner dances were got up for business reasons, but he couldn't doubt that this eager lad really admired his prowess as a fisherman.

IV

Bub Smith showed up on the morning train; a stocky fellow with a funny flat face—his nose had been broken in a fall from a horse and there had been nobody to set it, so he just let it stay as it was. But there was nothing the matter with either his eyes or his hands. "I'm feeling fine this morning," he said; "I could shoot holes through the side of a barn." He looked at Lanny with a twinkle in his pale blue eyes; they were old pals, and Bub had taught Lanny cowboy songs. He was introduced to the army captain, and was just about speechless at the spectacle of a man with paint and powder on his face and corsets under his sky-blue uniform.

Well, they motored back into the hills, where there was a little valley with a heavy forest of eucalyptus, and a peasant who for a few francs would let them shoot holes in his trees. The chauffeur lugged a couple of heavy boxes out of the car, one with the 7.65 mm. automatics and the other with the cartridges; Bub took a card-board target and tacked it onto a big tree about thirty paces away. Meantime Robbie was loading the pistols. "I want to show you how quickly it can be done," he said. Pretty soon Bub took his stand, and quick as a flash threw up his arm and fired. The shots came so fast it was just a whir, and there was the target with the central bull's eye shot clean out.

Captain Bragescu, of course, was enraptured by such a perform-ance. Pierre, the chauffeur, ran and got the target for them. You could see parts of the circle made by each bullet, but there wasn't any hole that wasn't part of one big hole. "I'll take that back to Bucharest with me!" said the captain.

"Wait," replied Bub; "I'll make you a few more." So they tacked up another target, and Bub took a different gun and did it again; he was ready to do it as long as the ammunition held out.

But the officer was convinced. "*C'est bon*," he said. He wouldn't be too enthusiastic, for it was a matter of business, but he repeated several times: "*Oui, c'est bon.*"

He tried it himself, and spattered the target all over with his shots. Bub showed him how to swing up the gun, and how to keep it from jerking, and then he did better. Robbie took his turn. He knew all about shooting, of course, and apologized to the captain for being too good; it was just a matter of understanding this remarkable weapon, he said.

Then Lanny took his turn. The army weapon was too heavy for him, but he had brought along his own thirty-two. Lanny was pretty good, but nobody seemed really good after Bub Smith. When the captain learned that Bub had been a cowboy, he exclaimed:

"*Ça s'explique!* I have seen them in the cinema. We need men who can ride and shoot like that in Rumania. We are troubled with moun-taineers who don't like to pay taxes."

V

They went home to lunch, and Beauty had some friends in; but you could see that Beauty herself was company enough for Bragescu. He could hardly take his eyes off this delicate creation in pink and cream and gold. She, being used to that sort of thing, was kind, but sedate and never the least bit flirtatious. Lanny always got plenty of motherly attention at such times. He was too young to understand these subtleties, but he played up to her all the same, and they made a sweet and sentimental pair.

It was the Baroness de la Tourette who was supposed to do the entertaining of the officer. Sophie Timmons had been her maiden name, and her father owned a chain of hardware factories in several towns of the Middle West. He sent his only daughter lots of money, but never enough for her husband the baron, who lived in Paris and had very expensive tastes. The baroness had one of those henna heads, and had what you might call a henna laugh; she talked fast and loud, half in French and half in English, and was considered to be the life of every party. Lanny was too young to observe that while she chattered her eyes would roam restlessly, as if her mind were not entirely on her work. She was his mother's best friend, and had a kind heart in spite of all her smartness.

The captain was taken off by Robbie to have the drawings of the Budd automatic pistol explained to him. Afterward they all went for a sail, and watched the sun sink into the Mediterranean; then they dressed and went to Cannes to dine at a fashionable resort, and later came home to play poker. Lanny was just getting into bed when he heard them come in and settle themselves at the table, and he peeked in at the door for a bit.

They made a pretty sight in front of the big open fire of crackling pine; the men in evening dress, except the Rumanian in a blue and gold dress uniform; the ladies in lovely soft dresses cut halfway down their smooth white backs. They had picked up friends at the restaurant, including Lord and Lady Eversham-Watson. She was another rich American who had married a title, but she had used better judgment; his lordship was a large, solid, and rather dull gentleman past middle age, but he admired his gay wife and liked to see her shine in company. She was a talkative little woman who managed him and made it acceptable by joking; her money came out of a Kentucky whisky known as "Petries' Peerless."

Lanny had never been taught to play poker, but had watched it sometimes. They might still be playing when he woke up in the morning, and would go on playing most of the day; he was used to the sight of Petries' Peerless and soda bottles on the side table, and half-empty glasses, and the not very pleasant odor of stale tobacco smoke, and little ashtrays filled with stubs. He was used to hearing how "rotten" his father was as a poker player, and would smile to himself, for this was one of the secrets which he shared with Robbie, who used as much skill in losing as other people did in trying to win.

Always to the right man, of course! This time Captain Bragescu would be the lucky one. Robbie, bland and smiling, would draw cards every time, and wait until the captain gave signs of having a strong hand, then raise him, and finally quit and drop his cards without showing them. After this had happened a few times the captain would realize that it was safe for him to bet heavily, and when Robbie would propose to raise the limit, he would agree. This would go on for hours, until the lucky officer had most of the chips piled in front of him, and would think that he owned the world. At the end Robbie would say: "It's amazing how you've mastered our American game." It was such a decent way to arrange a contract for guns that the captain could not fail to appreciate it. The guns were all right, of course, and the Rumanian army would be safe from the Bulgarians and able to capture the rebel mountaineers and collect the taxes.

VI

Robbie motored to Marseille to meet some member of his family who was coming from Egypt, and Beauty went to dance at a ball which a friend was giving in one of the white marble palaces on the heights above Nice. It would last until morning, and she would sleep there and return later. Lanny settled himself to the reading of a well-worn novel which somebody had picked up on a bookstall and left in the house.

It was a story about slum life on the outskirts of an American industrial town. The district was known as the "Cabbage Patch," and in it lived an Irish washerwoman with a brood of children, all dreadfully poor, but so honest and good that it touched your heart. Lanny, whose heart was always being touched by one thing or another, found this the dearest and sweetest of stories. By next morning he was nearly through with it and, sitting in the warm sunshine of the court, with narcissus beds around him and a huge bougainvillaea throwing a purple mantle over the kitchen porch, he yearned to have been born in a slum, so that he might be so generous and kindhearted and hard-working and helpful to everybody around him.

There came a tinkling of the bell, and Lanny went to the front gate and was confronted by his Uncle Jesse, his mother's brother. Jesse Blackless was a painter of a sort—that is to say, he had a small income and didn't have to work. He lived in a fishing village some distance to the west, a place where "nobody ever went," as Beauty phrased it. But it was just as well, because Jesse didn't seem to care about visitors, nor they about him; he lived alone in a cottage which he had fixed up in his own fashion. Lanny had been there once, when Uncle Jesse was sick and his sister felt it necessary to pay a duty call, taking along a basket of delicacies. That had been two or three years ago, and the boy had a vague memory of soiled dishes, a frying pan on the center table, and half a room filled with unframed paintings.

The artist was a man of forty or so, wearing a sport shirt open at the neck, a pair of linen trousers, not very well pressed, and tennis shoes dusty from his walk. He wore no hat, and his hair was gone entirely from the top, so that the brown dome was like a bronze Buddha's. He looked old for his years, and had many wrinkles around his eyes; when he smiled his mouth went a little crooked.

His manner was quizzical, which made you think he was laughing at you, which wasn't quite polite. Lanny didn't know what it was, but he had got the impression that there was something wrong about his Uncle Jesse; Beauty saw him rarely, and if Robbie spoke of him, it was in a way implying disapproval. All the boy knew definitely was that Uncle Jesse had had a studio in Paris, and that Beauty had been visiting him at the time she met Robbie and fell in love.

Lanny invited him into the court and got him a chair and, as Uncle Jesse looked hot after his walk, called Rosine to bring some wine. "Mother's gone to the ball at Mrs. Dagenham Price's," said the boy.

"She would," was Jesse's comment.

"Robbie's gone to Marseille," Lanny added.

"I suppose he's making lots of money."

"I suppose so." That was a subject Lanny did not discuss, so the conversation lagged.

But then Lanny recalled the Salon des Indépendants, and said he had been there. "Are they spoofing, or aren't they?" he asked.

"No doubt many of them are," said Uncle Jesse. "Poor devils, they have to get something to eat, and what do critics or buyers know about original work?"

Lanny had picked up ideas concerning the graphic arts, as well as all the others. Many painters lived along the Côte d'Azur and reproduced its charms; a few were famous, and now and then someone would persuade Beauty that it was a cultural action to invite one to a tea party, or perhaps be taken to his studio to inspect his work. Now and then she would "fall for" something that was especially praised, and these hung as showpieces in the home. The most regarded was a blazing sunrise painted by a certain van Gogh, who had lived at Arles, which you passed when you motored to Paris; in fact he had gone crazy there and had cut off one of his ears. Also there was a pond covered with shining water lilies by Monet. These canvases were becoming so valuable that Beauty was talking about having them insured, but it cost so much that she kept putting it off.

VII

There was, of course, a limit to the amount of time that a specialist in the art of painting cared to devote to exchanging ideas with a youngster; so presently the conversation lagged again. Uncle Jesse watched the bees and the hummingbirds in the flowers, and then his eyes happened to fall upon Lanny's book, which had been laid back up on the grass. "What are you reading?" he inquired.

Lanny handed him the volume, and he smiled one of those twisted smiles. "It was a best-seller many years ago."

"Have you read it?" inquired the boy.

"It's tripe," replied Uncle Jesse.

Lanny had to be polite at all hazards, so after a moment he said: "It interests me because it tells about the slums, which I don't know about."

"But wouldn't it be better," asked the uncle, "if you went and looked at them, instead of reading sentimental nonsense about them?"

"I'd be interested," replied the lad; "but of course there aren't any slums on the Riviera."

Uncle Jesse wanted to laugh again, but there was such an earnest look in his nephew's eyes that he checked himself. "It happens that I'm going to pay a visit in a slum this afternoon. Would you like to come?"

The boy was much excited. It was exactly what he had been longing for, though without having formulated it. A "cabbage patch" in Cannes—imagine such a thing! And a woman who lived there for the same noble and idealistic reasons that Lanny had been dreaming about! "This woman is poor," his uncle explained, "but she doesn't need to be. She is highly educated and could make money, but she prefers to live among the working people."

Leese gave them some lunch, and then they walked to the tram and rode cheaply into the city. When they got off, they walked into the "old town," picturesque and fascinating to tourists. They turned into a lane where the tall buildings came closer together at the top, and very little light got down. There are thousands of such tenements in towns all along the Mediterranean shore; built of stone, several stories high, and having been there for a hundred years or more. There will be steps in the street, and many turns, and archways, and courts with balconies above, and at the end perhaps a dead wall, or a glimpse of an old church, prompting the tourist to unsling his camera.

Of course Lanny knew that people lived in such tenements. Babies swarmed on the steps, with flies crawling over their sore eyes; chickens dodged beneath your feet, donkeys jostled you with their loads, and peddlers shouted their wares into your ears. But somehow when you were thinking about antiquities you forgot about human beings; things that are ancient and artistic are lifted into a different realm. The son of Beauty Budd might have walked through such "old towns" for years and never once had the idea of going inside for a visit. But now Uncle Jesse turned into one of the small doorways. It was dark inside, no electric light, not even gas; the steps felt as if they were made of rotten boards, and the odors seemed as old as the house. Doors were left ajar and fresh smells came out; food cooking, and clothes—"Let's hope they're in separate kettles," said the sardonic visitor. Babies squalled, and one very nearly got caught between their legs. Yes, it was a "cabbage patch"!

VIII

The man knocked on a door, a voice called, and they went in. There appeared to be only one room; it had one window, and a woman was sitting near it. She seemed to be old, and was wrapped in a shawl; the light made a silhouette of her face, which was emaciated, and yellow in hue, as happens when the blood goes out of the skins of these swarthy Mediterranean people. Her face lighted when she saw who it was, and she greeted Jesse Blackless in French and held out to his nephew a hand in which he could feel all the bones.

The woman's name was Barbara Pugliese; pronounced Italian fashion, Pool-yay-say. They were evidently old friends, but had not met for some time. Uncle Jesse was anxious about her cough, and she said it was about the same; she was well taken care of, since many here loved her, and brought her food. She asked about Jesse's health, and then about his painting; he said that nobody paid any attention to it, but it kept him out of mischief—but perhaps that was just his way of making a joke.

They talked part of the time in Italian, of which Lanny understood only a little; perhaps they thought he didn't understand any. He gathered that they knew the same persons, and talked about what these were doing. They discussed international affairs, and the diplomats and statesmen, of whom they thought badly—but so did most people in France, the boy had observed. He knew the names of many politicians, but was hazy about parties and doctrines.

His eyes roamed over the room. It was small, the furniture scanty and plain. There was a single bed, or perhaps it was just a cot, with a couple of worn blankets on it; a chest of drawers; a table with odds and ends piled on it, mostly papers and pamphlets; a lot of books on a trunk—apparently no other place for them; a curtain covering one corner, presumably with clothes behind it. This was how you lived in a slum!

Lanny found himself watching the woman again. He had never seen so much grief in a face. To him suffering was a theme for art, so he found himself remembering Christian martyrs as painted by the Italian primitives; he kept trying to recall one of the saints of Cimabue. The woman's voice was soft and her manner gentle, and he decided that she was truly a saint; yes, she lived in this terrible place out of pity for the poor, and must be an even more wonderful person than Mrs. Wiggs of the Cabbage Patch.

When they went out Lanny hoped that Uncle Jesse would tell him about her; but the painter was an unsatisfying sort of companion. All he said was: "Well, you've seen a slum."

"Yes, Uncle Jesse," replied the boy humbly. Presently he added: "Don't you think we ought to take her some food, or something?"

"It wouldn't do any good. She'd just give it away."

The man appeared to be wrapped up in his own thoughts, and Lanny hesitated to disturb him. But finally he asked: "Uncle Jesse, why do there have to be poor people like those?"

The other replied at once: "Because there are rich people like us." That was confusing to the boy, who had always been led to believe that it was the rich people who gave the poor people work; he knew of cases in which they had done it out of kindness, because they were sorry for the poor.

Lanny tried again. "Why doesn't somebody clean up places like that?"

"Because somebody is making money out of them."

"I don't mean the landlords," Lanny explained. "I mean the city officials."

"Maybe they're the landlords; or else they're collecting graft."

"In France, Uncle Jesse?" Lanny had been given to understand that that happened only in America.

The painter laughed one of his disagreeable laughs. "They don't publish it here," he said. They were in front of the Mairie, and he waved his hand toward it. "Go dig in there, and you'll find all you want." As they walked on, he added: "As much as in the munitions industry."

Of course Lanny couldn't discuss that, and perhaps his uncle knew it. Perhaps Uncle Jesse had argued too much in his life, and had grown tired of it. Anyhow, they had come to the tram, where their ways parted. The boy would ride home alone, because his uncle's home lay to the west, and a long way off. Lanny thanked him and said he had enjoyed the visit, and would think over what he had seen and heard. Uncle Jesse smiled another of his twisted smiles, and said: "Don't let it worry you."

IX

Walking from the tram in Juan, Lanny had got to the gate of his home when a car tooted behind him, and there was Robbie just arriving. They greeted each other, and Robbie said: "Where have you been?" When Lanny replied: "I went to Cannes with Uncle Jesse," the father's manner changed in an unexpected way.

"Does that fellow come here?" he demanded. The boy answered that it was the first time in a long while. Robbie took him into the house, and called Beauty into her room, and Lanny also, and shut the door.

It was the first time the boy had ever seen his father really angry. Lanny was put through a regular cross-examination, and when he told about Barbara Pugliese, his father exploded in bad language, and the boy learned some of the things that Uncle Jesse had not chosen to explain to him.

The woman was a prominent leader of the "syndicalist" movement. That was a long word, and Lanny didn't know what it meant, until Robbie said that for practical purposes it was the same as anarchism. The boy had heard enough about that, for every once in a while a bomb would go off and kill some ruler or prime minister or general, and perhaps some innocent bystanders. It had happened in Russia, in Austria, Spain, Italy, even in France; it was the work of embittered and deadly conspirators, nihilists, terrorists, men and women seeking to destroy all organized government. Only last year a band of them had been robbing banks in Paris and had fought a regular battle with the police. "There are no more depraved people living!" exclaimed the father.

Lanny broke in: "Oh, surely, Robbie, she isn't like that. She's so gentle and kind, she's like a saint."

Robbie turned upon the mother. "You see! That snake in the grass, imposing upon the credulity of a child!"

He couldn't blame Lanny, of course. He controlled his anger, and explained that these people were subtle and posed as being idealists, when in their hearts were hatred and jealousy; they poisoned the minds of the young and impressionable.

Beauty began to cry, so the father talked more quietly. "I have always left Lanny's upbringing to you, and I have no fault to find with what you've done, but this is one thing on which I have to put down my foot. The black sheep of your family—or perhaps I had better say the red sheep of your family—is certainly not going to corrupt our son."

"But, Robbie," sobbed the mother, "I hadn't the least idea that Jesse was going to call."

"All right," said Robbie. "Write him a note and tell him it's not to happen again and Lanny is to be let alone."

But that caused more weeping. "After all, he's my brother, Robbie. And he was kind to us; he was the only one who didn't raise a row."

"I've no quarrel with him, Beauty. All I want is for him to keep away from our son."

Beauty wiped her eyes and her nose; she knew that she looked ugly when she wept and she hated ugliness above all things. "Listen, Robbie, try to be reasonable. Jesse hasn't been here for half a year, and the last time he came Lanny didn't even know it. It will probably be as long before he'll be moved to come again. Can't we just tell Lanny not to have anything to do with him? I'm sure this child isn't interested in him."

"No, really, Robbie!" The boy hastened to support his mother. "If I'd had any idea that you objected, I'd have made some excuse and gone away."

So the father was persuaded to leave it that way; the lad gave his promise that never again would he let his Uncle Jesse take him anywhere, and there would be no more slumming tours with anybody. The concern of his father, who was usually so easygoing, made an indelible impression on the boy. Robbie behaved as if his son had been exposed to leprosy or bubonic plague; he probed Lanny's mental symptoms, looking for some infected spot which might be cut out before it had time to spread. Just what had Jesse Blackless said, and what had that Pugliese woman said?

Some inner voice told Lanny not to mention the remark about graft in the munitions industry; but he quoted his uncle's explanation of why there had to be poor people—because there were rich people.

"There's a sample of their poison!" exclaimed the father, and set out to provide Lanny with the proper antidote. "The reason there

are poor is because most people are shiftless and lazy and don't save
their money; they spend it on drink, or they gamble it away, and
so of course they suffer. Envy of the good fortune of others is one
of the commonest of human failings, and agitators play upon it, they
make a business of preaching discontent and inciting the poor to
revolt. That is a very great social danger, which many people fail to
realize."

Robbie became a bit apologetic now for having lost his temper
and scolded Lanny's mother in Lanny's presence. The reason was
that it was his duty to protect a child's immature mind. Lanny,
who adored his handsome and vigorous father, was grateful for this
protection. It was a relief to him to be told what was true and thus
be saved from confusion of mind. So in the end everything became
all right again; storm clouds blew over, and tears were dried, and
Beauty was beautiful as she was meant to be.

4

Christmas-Card Castle

I

THERE had come to the Frau Robert Budd a formal and stately
letter, almost a legal document, from the comptroller-general of
Castle Stubendorf in Silesia, saying in the German language that it
would give him pleasure if *der junge Herr* Lanning Budd might be
permitted to visit his home during the Christmas holidays. *Der junge
Herr* danced with delight and carried the letter around in his pocket
for days; the Frau Budd replied on fashionable notepaper that she
was pleased to accept the kind invitation on behalf of her son. The

hour arrived, and Lanny's *smoking* and his warm clothes were packed into two suitcases, and Leese prepared fried chicken and bread and butter sandwiches, just in case the dining car might run out of food. In a nice new traveling suit, and with a heavy overcoat and a French copy of Sienkiewicz's *With Fire and Sword*, Lanny was ready for an expedition to the North Pole.

Since Robbie had gone back to Connecticut, the mother bore the responsibility for this journey. All the way into Cannes she renewed her adjurations and Lanny his promises: he would never step from the train except at the proper stations; he would never allow anyone to persuade him to go anywhere; he would keep his money fastened with a safety pin in the inside pocket of his jacket; he would send a telegram from Vienna, and another from the station of the castle; and so on and so on. Lanny considered all this excessive, because he had just celebrated his fourteenth birthday and felt himself a man of the world.

He brushed away his tears, and saw Beauty and the chauffeur and the familiar Cannes station disappear. The sights of the Riviera sped by: Antibes, Nice, Monaco, Monte Carlo, Menton, and then suddenly it was Italy, and the customs men coming through the train, asking politely if you had anything to declare. Then the Italian shore, and the train plunging through short smoky tunnels, and out into sight of little blue bays and fisherboats with red sails. Presently came Genoa, a mass of tall buildings piled up on a steep shore. The train went inland and wound through a long valley, and ahead were the southern Alps shining white. In the morning they were in Austria, and everywhere was snow; the houses having steeply pitched roofs weighted with heavy stones and the inns having carved and gilded signs.

A wonderful invention, these international sleeping cars; among the many forces which were binding Europe together, mingling the nations, the cultures, the languages. There were no restrictions upon travel, except the price of the ticket; you paid and received a magical document which entitled you to go to whatever places you had chosen. On the way you met all sorts of people, and chatted with them freely, and told them about your affairs, and heard about theirs. To travel far enough was to acquire an education in the business, politics, manners, morals, and tongues of Europe.

II

As his first traveling companions the fates assigned to Lanny two elderly ladies whose accent told him they were Americans. From them he learned that in the land which he considered his own there was a state as well as a city of the name of Washington; this state lay far in the northwest and provided the world with quantities of lumber and canned salmon. In the city of Seattle these two ladies had taught classes of school children for a period of thirty years, and all that time had been saving for the great adventure of their lives, which was to spend a year in Europe, seeing everything they had been reading about all their lives. They were as naïve about it and as eager as if they had been pupils instead of teachers; when they learned that this polite boy had lived in Europe all his life, they put him in the teacher's seat.

At Genoa the ladies departed, and their places were taken by a Jewish gentleman with handsome dark eyes and wavy dark hair, carrying two large suitcases full of household gadgets. He spoke French and English of a sort, and he too was romantic, but in an oddly different way. The ladies from the land of lumber had been brought up where everything was crude and new, so their interest was in the old things of Europe, the strange types of architecture, the picturesque costumes of peasants. But this Jewish gentleman— his name was Robin, shortened from Rabinowich—had been brought up among old things, and found them dirty and stupid. His job was to travel all over this old Europe selling modern electrical contraptions.

"Look at me," said Mr. Robin; and Lanny did so. "I was raised in a village near Lodz, in a hut with a dirt floor. I went to school in another such hut, and sat and scratched my legs and tried to catch the fleas, and chanted long Hebrew texts of which I did not understand one word. I saw my old grandmother's head split open in a pogrom. But now I am a civilized man; I have a bath in the morning and put on clean clothes. I understand science, and do not have any more nonsense in my head, such as that I commit a sin if I eat meat and butter from the same dish. What I earn belongs to me, and I no longer fear that some official will rob me, or that hoodlums will beat me because my ancestors were what they call Christ-killers. So you see I am glad that things shall be new, and I do not have the least longing for any of the antiquities of this continent."

It was a novel point of view to Lanny; he looked out of the car window and saw Europe through the eyes of a Jewish "bagman." The nations were becoming standardized, their differences were disappearing. An office building was the same in whatever city it was erected; and so were the trams, the automobiles, the goods you bought in the shops. Said the salesman of electrical curling irons: "If you look at the people on this train, you will see that they are dressed much alike. The train itself is a standard product, and by means of it we travel from town to town selling products which are messengers of internationalism."

Lanny told where he was going, and how Kurt Meissner said that art was the greatest of international agents. Mr. Robin agreed with that. Lanny mentioned that he had a van Gogh in the dining room of his home, and it developed that Mr. Robin lived in Holland, and knew about that strange genius who had been able to sell only one painting in his whole lifetime, though now a single work brought hundreds of dollars. Said Mr. Robin: "How I wish that I knew such a genius now alive!"

This salesman of gadgets was a curious combination of shrewdness and naïveté. He would have got the better of you in a business deal, and then, if you had been his guest, he would have spent twice as much money on you. He was proud of how he had risen in the world, and happy to tell a little American boy all about it. He gave him his business card and said: "Come and see me if you ever come to Rotterdam." When he took up his heavy cases and departed,

Lanny thought well of the Jews and wondered why he didn't know more of them.

III

From Vienna the traveler enjoyed the society of a demure and sober little Fräulein a year or two younger than himself; she was returning from her music studies in Vienna, and had eyes exactly the color of bluebells and a golden pigtail at least two inches in diameter hanging down her back. Such a treasure was not entrusted to the chances of travel alone, and Fräulein Elsa had with her a governess who wore spectacles and sat so stiff and straight and stared so resolutely before her that Lanny decided to accompany Sienkiewicz to Poland of the seventeenth century, and share the military exploits of the roistering Pan Zagloba and the long-suffering Pan Longin Podbipienta.

But it is not easy to avoid speaking to people who are shut up in a little box with you all day long. With true German frugality the pair had their lunch, and it was difficult to eat it and not offer their traveling companion so much as one or two *Leibnitzkeks.* Lanny said politely: "No, thank you," but the ice was broken. The governess asked where the young gentleman was traveling to, and when he said he was to spend the holidays at Schloss Stubendorf, a transformation took place in her demeanor. *"Ach, so?"* cried she, and was all politeness, and a comical eagerness to find out whose guest he was to be. Lanny, too proud of himself to be a snob, hastened to say that he did not know the Graf or the Gräfin, but had met the youngest son of the comptroller-general and was to be the guest of his family.

That sufficed to make pliable the backbone of Fräulein Grobich. *Ja, wirklich,* the Herr Heinrich Karl Meissner had a post of great responsibility, and was a man of excellent family; the Fräulein knew all about him, because the husband of the Fräulein's sister had begun his career in the office of Schloss Stubendorf. She began to tell about the place, and her conversation was peppered with *Durchlauchts* and *Erlauchts, Hoheits* and *Hochwohlgeborens.* It was a great property, that of the Graf, and the young gentleman was fortunate in going there *zu Weihnachten*, because then the castle would be open and the great family would be visible. Fräulein Grobich was thrilled to be in the presence of one who was soon to be in the presence of the assembled *Adel* of Stubendorf.

She wanted to know how Lanny had met the son of the Herr Comptroller-General; when he said at Hellerau, the governess exclaimed: *"Ach, Elsa, der junge Herr hat den Dalcroze-Rhythmus studiert!"* This was permission to enter into conversation with the shy little girl; the bright blue eyes were turned upon him, and the soft well-modulated voice asked questions. Of course nothing pleased him more than to talk about Hellerau; he couldn't offer a demonstration in the crowded compartment, and his German was but a feeble stammering compared with the eloquence which filled his soul.

As for the soul of Fräulein Grobich, what filled it was a sound and proper German respect for rank and position, the phenomenon which was most to impress Lanny during his visit. What you heard about in Silesia was *Ordnung*. Everyone had his place, and knew what it was; each looked up to those above him with a correctly proportioned amount of reverence, unmingled with any trace of envy. As the guest of an important official, Lanny would share the dignity of his host. The shy little maid and her vigilant governess gave him the first taste of this agreeable treatment, and he was sorry when he had to say his *Lebewohls*.

IV

There was a local train waiting on a siding. It had only two cars, and Lanny had to crowd himself into a seat with a farmer who had been to town to sell some of his cattle. He had a large red face and much beer on his breath, and was extremely sociable, telling the little foreign boy about the crops of the district and its important landmarks. When he learned that the boy had come all the way from France to visit the son of Herr Comptroller-General Meissner, he was even more impressed than the governess, and tried to crowd himself up and leave more room for "*die Herrschaft*," as he began to call the young stranger. From then on he waited for *die Herrschaft* to ask questions, so as to be sure he was not presuming.

The little train was winding up a valley; it had turned dark, and presently the farmer pointed out the lights of the castle on a distant height. There was a whole town built around it, said the farmer, and everything belonged to the Graf, who was referred to as *Seine Hochgeboren*. There were vast forests filled with stags and buffalo and wild boar which *Seine Hochgeboren* and his guests hunted. Six weeks ago *Seine Majestät der Kaiser* himself had visited the place, and there had been the greatest hunt that anyone in the district could remember. Now everything was covered with heavy snow and no more hunting was done; the creatures came to the feed racks, where hay was put out for them so that they would not starve.

Ja, gewiss, said the farmer, he knew the Herr Comptroller-General; he was the business manager of all these properties, and had several assistants, or heads of departments. He had four sons, of whom three were in the army. The farmer knew the *jungen Herrn* Kurt Meissner, a fine lad, he studied music, and would probably play at some of the festivals. Then Lanny was told about the noble family, the wife and the sons and daughters and brothers and sisters of *Seine Hochgeboren*. The farmer was a tenant of the estate, but it was so big that he did not get off until the second station beyond that of the castle. When they came to the latter, he insisted upon taking Lanny's bags and carrying them out to the platform for him; he bowed and touched his hat, and was still doing it when Kurt came running up and grabbed Lanny.

My, how happy those two lads were to see each other again; and how many handshakes and pats on the back they exchanged! Snow was falling, making a blur of the station lights. Kurt had a sleigh with a fine team of horses; he tucked Lanny in under a big fur robe and gave him a pair of mitts to put on, and away they went. They couldn't see much, but the horses knew the way, winding to the height on which the castle stood. Lanny talked about his trip, and Kurt about the festivities which were coming; so much news they had to pour out, and so many plans for their ten days together! Friendship and youth make a delightful combination.

Lanny saw dark masses of buildings with many lights; he got out and was taken indoors and presented to a large family of large people: the father stout, but erect and military, with close-cut gray hair and mustaches trimmed in imitation of his Kaiser's; the kind and comfortable mother, having a great bosom ornamented with a rope of pearls; two sons, tall blond fellows straight as ramrods, with hair cut close like Kurt's, clicking their heels and bowing formally; a sister a year older than Kurt, slender, fair-haired, still in the pigtail stage, but ready to become a temporary mother to a visiting stranger. There were other relatives, a large company, all full of the sentimentality of Christmas and eager to share it with their guest.

Kurt had grown an inch or two since Lanny saw him. He was going to be a fine, tall fellow like his brothers; would he wear a monocle and turn himself into a walking ramrod? Probably so, because he admired them, and would serve his term in the army. His rather severe face was pale, because he had been working hard. But his love of *Ordnung* would always be tempered with the sweetness of music, and he would be Lanny's friend and appreciate the gay, easygoing disposition which Lanny had got from both mother and father. So, at any rate, Kurt assured him when they were up in Kurt's den which they were to share. He was kind and affectionate, but very serious, and talked grandly about his work and purposes, his devotion to art, and to friendship, something which one did not undertake lightly, but with deliberation and moral purpose.

V

Next morning Lanny looked out of the window and saw the great Schloss, five or six stories high, its roofs and turrets covered with fresh snow, gleaming like a Christmas card in the light of the newly risen sun. The picture made him think of all the fairy tales and romances of knights and princesses that he had ever read. To a boy

who had spent most of his life on the Riviera, the mere presence of
snow was an adventure; to put on his big overcoat and the mitts
that Kurt lent him and go out and run, and see his breath in the
air, and throw snowballs and get tumbled in a snowbank—that was
fairyland. To go back into the house and be served *Pfannkuchen*
and broiled venison for breakfast, and be told that it had been shot
by *Seine Majestät* himself—could you beat that for thrills?

The Graf Stubendorf and family were expected on the morning
train from Berlin, and it would be better for the guest to see the
castle before they arrived. So after breakfast the boys ran up the
long drive through the park, and climbed the score of steps to the
gray stone building; they were admitted by bowing servants in blue
uniforms, white gaiters, and white gloves. There was an entrance
hall three stories high, and a reception room as big as a theater.
All the front of the castle had been built in the last century, but
there was an old part in the rear which was six hundred years old
and had been captured and recaptured in some of those cruel wars
which Lanny had been reading about on the train.

The modern part was splendid with white and gold woodwork,
and walls upholstered in hand-embroidered silk, and furniture with
scarlet brocade. There was a great deal of heavy carved furniture,
and the general atmosphere of a museum. The old part was the most
interesting to Lanny, because there were a tower and a donjon keep,
an armor room, and a refectory having a huge fireplace with a black
pot hanging on a hook. Lanny wondered if Pan Zagloba had ever
drunk wassail in that hall. He hefted huge halberds and battle-axes,
and tried to imagine what the world must have been like when men
went about armored like crabs and lobsters.

They walked about the environs of the castle. It was as the
farmer had said, a town, the old part medieval and crowded, the
new parts well laid out. Stubendorf was a *Gutsbezirk*, and the Graf
was a state functionary, which meant, in effect, that he had his own
court of justice, police force, and jail; the feudal system combined
with modern plumbing and street paving. But this didn't occur to
Lanny, who was living in a lovely fairy tale.

They came back in time to witness the arrival of *Seine Hochgeboren* and family. The great ones drove from the station in limousines; all the servants of the castle, a hundred or two, were lined up on the steps in costumes of long ago, the men on one side, the women on the other. The uniforms of the men bore indications of their rank, while the women had white aprons and lace fichus and white cotton stockings, and wore their hair in plaits down their backs. All were drilled once a week in a system of etiquette complete to the opening of doors.

The Graf Stubendorf was known in Germany as a poet and aesthete, and also as one of the Kaiser's intimates. He was a large man, stoutish and pasty, with a soft brown beard and gracious smile. His three sons were the orthodox military men with shaven heads and mustaches twisted to sharp points; they marched up the stairs in order of seniority, making grave acknowledgment of the bows of the servants. The mother, an elegant lady dressed in the latest Paris fashion, walked behind her sons, and the daughters walked behind her. Of course that may have been an accident; or it may have been because their Kaiser had prescribed the proper concerns of women—kitchen, children, and church—listed presumably in order of importance.

VI

In the afternoon the boys put on high boots and took repeating shotguns for hunting. Kurt's father had arranged it with the Oberforstmeister, an important personage in a green uniform with silver braid; he furnished them a Jäger, who would carry a rifle for their protection. It was not permitted to shoot roebuck or large game, but there were plenty of hare and pheasants in the forest.

They drove in the sleigh, following a wood road, slowly because of the fresh drifts of snow. They passed racks where the deer came to feed; the great stags lifted their heads and kept watch, but made no move to escape. They behaved like cattle, and it didn't seem much like hunting to go out and take post on a wooden platform, with a high-powered rifle and telescopic sight, and have beaters drive such creatures in front of you. When Lanny's father went after game it was in the Canadian wilderness, where the moose were not stall-fed; or out in the Rockies, where mountain sheep ran like the devil, leaping over boulders high up among the clouds.

Kurt said that would be fun, of course, but in Germany shooting was a privilege of the land owners, and the upper classes made a ceremony of it. The Jäger told them about the recent visit of the Kaiser. *Seine Majestät* had a special uniform, buff in color, and a splendid bird in his hat; he took his post on a high stand, and his entourage watched him shoot buffalo as they ran by, and boars, and stags, picking out the largest with the best heads. Afterward a pile of the game was made and the Kaiser had his picture taken, standing in front of it. A rather expensive sport, because it was estimated that to raise a single stag cost several thousand marks. But Kurt explained that none of it was wasted; the carcasses were distributed among those who had a right to them, and Lanny would eat his fill three times a day.

Lanny had never seen either buffalo or wild boars, and was greatly excited by the idea. The former was not the shaggy American bison, but smooth-skinned creatures that had been domesticated in Egypt and brought to Europe by the ancient Romans; now they ran wild in the forests and were very dangerous if wounded. As for the boars, they did not molest human beings—but still, it was well to have a rifle along.

After hunting through a great stretch of forest, they came upon a clearing with a tiny farm and a cottage that might have been the home of the witch in Grimm's fairy tales. They stopped to rest, and found no witch, but a peasant mother with half a dozen little ones, the boys with bullet heads and the girls with braided hair, all staring with wide blue eyes at *die Herrschaften*. There was only one room and a shed in back; the beds were shelves against the walls, and a good part of the room was taken up by a large stove, polished like a patent-leather shoe. Everything in the place had been manicured by this lean and toilworn woman, with tendons in her arms showing like whipcords. She was excited by the visit, and ran to get milk for *die Herrschaften*, as she called them over and over; she stood while they drank it, and apologized because she had nothing better, and because her husband was not at home, and because she had only a hard bench for them to sit on, and so forth. When they left, Lanny looked back and saw a pile of children's faces in the window of the hut, and it stayed with him as one of the sights of Germany.

They returned with a large bag of game, and a still larger appetite. They had a meal to match it, with half a dozen courses of meats and fowl. When they rose from the table they all took hands and danced gaily around it, crying "*Mahlzeit!*" Afterward they gathered round the piano and sang sentimental songs in melting voices, also Kurt and his guest were asked to show what they had learned at Hellerau. Lanny was *echt deutsch* that night, and stowed in his memory two lines of poetry which his friend quoted, to the effect that when you hear singing you may lie down in peace, because evil people have no songs.

VII

"*Fröhliche Weihnachten*," said everybody next morning, for it was the day before Christmas. The young people took a long sleigh ride and saw the country, and in the afternoon they played music, and Lanny danced with Kurt's sister. In the evening the Christmas celebration took place, and there were presents for all the family and the servants; not under the Christmas tree, but on separate little tables, covered with linen cloths. After the tree was lighted, the presents were given out. The Herr Comptroller said a few words, and shook hands with each of his servants, and they all kissed the hand of his wife. Everything was warmhearted, everybody wished happiness to everybody else, and they sang "*Stille Nacht*" with tears in their eyes.

Next morning they had a preliminary breakfast, eating a long kind of bun called *Dresdner Christstollen*, with raisins in it and sugar on top; also eggs, and many kinds of homemade jam, and coffee with hot milk. That was supposed to carry you until half-past ten, when you had the so-called "fork-breakfast." It appeared that ideas of diet reform which were spreading among Lanny's American friends had never been heard of in this Prussian province, and such things as *Hasenpfeffer*, fresh pork sausage, and several other kinds of meat could be eaten in great quantities in the morning.

Later on there was to be a celebration at the Schloss, and everybody dressed, the men in uniforms and decorations, and the ladies with their jewels, silks, and laces. They came in a happy solemn mood as to a church festival. For the tenants and employees it was the one time in the year when they might pass the portals of the great building which dominated their lives. They waited respectfully outside until the last of the dignitaries had entered and taken their places; then the crowd streamed into the great hall, the men taking off their hats before they ascended the steps, the peasant women with kerchiefs or shawls over their heads, curtsying to everybody. Those for whom there were no seats packed themselves around the walls.

Seine Hochgeboren and family came in by a private entrance, and everybody stood and said *"Fröhliche Weihnachten."* The pastor said a prayer, quite a long one, and they all stood again and sang a hymn, in such volume as to drown out the organ. The Graf gave them all Christmas greetings in a fatherly talk, full of assurances of concern for their welfare, and declaring the divine origin of *"deutsche Treu und Werde."* In their happy land, so favored by God, peace and order prevailed, and every man and woman cherished the sacred flame of loyalty in his heart. In this happy Christmas season they renewed their pledges to the Kaiser and Fatherland. The applause which followed seemed to indicate that *Seine Hochgeboren* was completely justified in his faith.

A great fir tree out of the forest stood in a corner of the hall, and there were presents for everyone, even to the toilworn peasant woman and the half dozen little ones who had stared at Lanny out of the window of the hut. Four men in uniform called the names on the packages and handed them out; but even with this procedure it took long to distribute them all. Not a person left the hall, and *Seine Hochgeboren* shook hands with each man and woman. Lanny was not bored, because these were Kurt's people, and he was interested to watch their faces and their costumes.

Next day the Comptroller-General went to report to his employer upon the state of affairs. He was invited to a smoker that evening, together with his eldest son. Other neighboring land owners came, and several of the higher officials of the estate, the chief of police, the head forester, and so on. Over pipes and beer they discussed the state of the country, both local and national, and the Graf honored them by reporting upon matters of importance on which he had special sources of information. The following evening Herr Meissner told his family what had gone on at this smoker, and gave his own views of the matters discussed. Everybody in the household listened respectfully to what the stout and imposing father said, and no one ventured to question anything. The guest from a foreign land could not understand all the long words, but listened attentively, and afterward had matters explained to him by Kurt.

Seine Hochgeboren had reported that other nations, jealous of German diligence and skill, had surrounded the Fatherland with a wall—*die Einkreisung,* was the phrase. Either that wall would be taken down by agreement, or it would have to be broken, because the Germans were a growing people, and would not be denied their place in the sun. The Graf had spoken of a dark cloud of barbarism in the eastern sky, and by that, of course, he meant Russia. The nobility and land owners of Upper Silesia got along well with their neighbors, the nobility and land owners of the Tsar's realm, and had no quarrel with them; but they were exasperated by the alliance with France, which was putting up huge sums of money for the arming of Russia. For what purpose? the Graf wished to know. There could be but one answer—a contemplated attack upon Germany.

Also, *Seine Hochgeboren* had talked about enemies within the Fatherland; he described them as rats, gnawing and nibbling. Of course he meant the Social-Democrats, said Herr Meissner. They had no strength in Stubendorf, where the good old ways prevailed; but in all the industrial districts they never ceased their hateful agitation, and at the next elections to the Reichstag they might win an actual majority. If that happened, steps would undoubtedly have to be taken to put them down by force.

Lanny was moved to tell his friend Kurt about his visit to the "cabbage patch" of Cannes. He didn't mention that he had an uncle who was a "red sheep"—that was too terrible a family secret; he said merely that somebody had taken him to meet a woman "Red," and he had been deceived into thinking that she was a good person. Kurt replied: "No doubt many of these agitators are sincere fanatics. Indeed, it's rather the fashion nowadays to say smart and cynical things against the government." He added: "There's more Socialist sentiment in Silesia than perhaps *Seine Hochgeboren* realizes; there are many coal mines in the province, and in the open portions are large industries and a lot of discontent among the workers."

Kurt talked in his usual lofty way about social problems. He said that art and culture would filter down from the cultivated classes and ultimately would civilize and regenerate the common people. He was especially certain that the artist must hold himself above the squabbles of politics. Solemnly he declared: "Just as knowledge is power, so is beauty; those who create it are masters of the Idea, which precedes everything in human affairs. As the idea of the chair comes before the making of the chair, so the idea of beauty, good-ness, justice, has to be nourished in creative minds. In the beginning was the Word"—and so on for a great many words.

Lanny did not know that all this was German philosophy with a capital P; that a learned professor in Königsberg had sat in his study with his eyes fixed upon a church steeple for twenty years, spinning mental cobwebs made of such high-sounding polysyllables. Lanny did not know that twenty-three centuries previously a wealthy gentleman of Athens of the name of Plato had walked up and down under a portico doing the same thing, and that his doctrines had spread to Alexandria, and from there had reached a Jewish enthusiast by the name of John. What Lanny thought was that his friend, Kurt Meissner, had worked up all this for himself, and he was quite overcome with awe.

VIII

The ten days passed rapidly, and one morning the two boys packed their belongings, said their farewells, and were driven to the station. They rode together to the junction, renewing their pledges of everlasting loyalty. At the junction their roads parted, and Kurt, whose train came first, made sure that his guest had his ticket in a safe place, and that the station master would see him aboard his train. Lanny watched Kurt depart; and then, because a cold wind was blowing, he went into the café of the station and ordered a cup of hot cocoa.

While he was sipping it and thinking over adventures the memory of which would always delight him, a man came into the room, looked around, and then came to Lanny's table. There were other tables, but the man appeared to be sociable, and Lanny was glad to chat with anyone in this agreeable country. The stranger said: "*Guten Morgen*," and Lanny returned the greeting, and at the same time took the man in with a swift appraisal.

The stranger was small, rather dark, and sallow; his hat, tie, and overcoat were lacking in those touches of elegance which meant a "gentleman." He wore glasses, and his thin face had a worried look; his fingers were stained with tobacco. He ordered a glass of beer, and then remarked: "*Ein Fremder, nicht wahr?*" When Lanny replied that he was an American, the man began to speak somewhat hesitating English. He had seen Lanny with Kurt Meissner, and said that he knew Kurt; had Lanny been staying at the Schloss?

Lanny explained where he had been staying, and they talked about the visit. Lanny enjoyed nothing more than telling about what a good time he had had, and how kind everybody had been. The man seemed to know all about affairs at the castle. *Ja, ja*, he knew the Herr Comptroller-General, also his sons; they had gone back to the army. No time to be lost in the army; that very morning a company of light artillery had gone into the mountains for practice, the guns mounted on sleds, the troops on skis. Lanny said he had seen them getting off the train; wonderful how fast they had

slid those guns off the flatcars. The stranger said that was part of the
drill and was timed to the second. The Fatherland had many enemies
and must ever be on the alert.

Lanny was interested to hear this from another German.
Apparently it was the first thought in the mind of everyone in the
country. He told the stranger about the political discussions which
had taken place, and how Graf Stubendorf had warned his officials
of the dark cloud hanging over the east and of the rats within which
were gnawing and nibbling. "He must mean the Social-Democrats,"
said the stranger; and Lanny replied, yes, that was what Herr
Meissner had explained to his family.

Lanny's father had carefully posted him as to the dangers of
talking about the munitions industry; but it never occurred to the
lad that there could be any reason for not discussing the patriotic
sentiments of the defenders of the Fatherland. The stranger wanted
to know exactly what *Seine Hochgeboren* had said, and where and
how he had said it; so Lanny told about the smoker, and who had
been present at it. *Seine Hochgeboren* had said that if the "rats"
were to carry the Reichstag at the next elections, it might be necessary to put them down by force; the comptroller-general had agreed
with this idea.

Lanny mentioned also the hunting, and what he had learned about
the Kaiser's extraordinary prowess as a slaughterer of game. The
stranger said that photographs of it had been published in the
papers; there was one in a magazine which Lanny could buy on the
newsstands. He would observe that the Kaiser kept his left arm
behind him; one would always find that in any picture of him, for
he had a withered arm and was very sensitive about it. Had they
mentioned how he had a special knife and fork, made in one piece,
so that he could eat with one hand? Lanny said, no, they hadn't
told him things like that. A flicker of a smile crossed the little man's
sallow face.

The stranger went on to set forth how in the castle they had
prepared every day a special newspaper for the Kaiser, printed in
gold. Lanny said that didn't sound as if it would be easy reading.

The other agreed; but it would never do for the All-Highest to read a common newspaper, such as any of his subjects could buy for ten pfennigs. Had they told him whether everybody in the room had to rise and click his heels when the Kaiser addressed that person?

There had come what seemed a note of sneering in the man's voice, and the boy became vaguely uneasy and changed the subject. He told how they had shot hare and pheasants in those wonderful forests; and about the farm with the cottage and the pretty children. Lanny said how much he had been impressed by the cleanness and order he had seen in that cottage, and in fact throughout the domain of the Graf, and by the evidences of loyalty and discipline. "Ach, yes!" replied the man. "You see, Napoleon never got here."

The youngster didn't know enough history to understand that remark, so the other explained that wherever the French armies had penetrated, they had distributed the lands among the peasants, and so had broken the feudal system. If Lanny had been in France, he must know how independent and free-spoken the peasants were; none of this bowing and kowtowing to the masters, the everlasting *Hoheits* and *Hochgeborens*. Lanny said that he had noted that difference.

"Perhaps I ought to tell you," continued the stranger, "that I am a journalist. I am indebted to you for some very useful information."

Lanny felt something fall inside and hit the pit of his stomach. "Oh!" he cried. "Surely you're not going to quote what I've been saying!"

"Don't worry," said the other, smiling. "I am a man of tact. I promise not to mention or indicate you in any way."

"But I was a guest there!" exclaimed Lanny. "I haven't the right to repeat what they told me. That would be shameful!"

"By your own account many persons heard what Stubendorf said. Any one of them might have told it to me. And as to Meissner——"

"It was in his own house!" cried the boy. "Nothing could be more private."

"He'll be saying it to many persons, and he won't have any idea how it came to my ears."

Lanny was so bewildered and embarrassed he didn't know what to answer. Such an ending for his holiday! The other, reading his face, continued apologetically: "You must understand that we journalists have to take our information where we find it. I am one of the editors of the *Arbeiterzeitung,* a Social-Democratic newspaper, and I have to consider the interests of the oppressed workers whom I serve."

Again something hit Lanny's stomach, even more heavily than before. "What interest can the workers . . . ?" he began; but then speech failed him.

Said the editor: "Our people take seriously their rights as citizens; but their opponents, it appears, do not share that view. The Comptroller-General of Schloss Stubendorf announces that if the workers win at the polls, the masters will not submit to the decision, but will resort to force and counter-revolution. Don't you see how very important that news will be to our readers?"

Lanny could not find words to answer.

"You came here as a guest," continued the other, "and you found everything lovely. There was nobody to take you behind the scenes and show you how this charming Christmas puppet show is worked. You are too young to form any idea of what it means to live in the Middle Ages; but I will give you facts which you can think about on your journey. You admire the fairy-story cottage in the forest and the pretty children—but nobody mentioned that the first of them might be the child of your host, the Herr Comptroller-General."

"Oh, surely not!" cried Lanny, outraged.

"He scattered his seed freely when he was younger. And I'll tell you more for your own welfare. You are a charming boy, and if ever you come for another visit, do not attract the attention of the Graf Stubendorf, or under any circumstances be left alone in the room with him."

Lanny, staring at his interlocutor, didn't know just what the man meant, but he knew it was something very bad, and the blood was climbing to his cheeks and forehead.

"I will not offend your young mind with the details. Suffice it to say that some men in the Kaiser's intimate circle have extremely evil ways of life. A few years ago there was a public scandal which forced one of the Kaiser's best friends to retire from public life. Stubendorf is an exquisite fellow, highly sentimental, and thinks he is a poet; but I tell you that neither boys nor girls are safe in this feudal principality which has seemed to you like a set of Christmas cards."

There came a roaring outside the station, and the uniformed official came to the door. *"Der Zug, junger Herr,"* said he, with feudal politeness. The Social-Democratic editor rose quickly and went out by another door, while the station master took Lanny's bags and put him safely into the right car.

Lanny never learned the name of that editor, and never knew what he published. For a while his happiness was poisoned by the fear of a scandal; but nothing happened, so apparently the man had kept his promise. Lanny was ashamed of his lack of discretion and resolved never to tell anyone about the incident. A bitter and hateful fellow, that editor; repeating slanders, or perhaps making them up. Lanny decided that Social-Democrats had minds warped with envy, and must be fully as dangerous as anarchists. But all the same he couldn't help wondering if the stories were true—and whether perhaps it mightn't have been better if Napoleon had got to Stubendorf!

5

The Facts of Life

I

LANNY came home with the idea fixed in his head that he ought to go to school; he wanted to settle down to hard study and be disciplined and conscientious like those Germans. The idea somewhat alarmed his mother, and she asked, just what did he want to learn. Lanny presented a list: he wanted to understand what Kurt called philosophy, that is, what life was, and why it was, and how the Idea always preceded the Thing; second, he wanted to understand the long German words that he had heard, such as *Erscheinungsphänomenologie* and *Minderwertigkeitscomplexe;* third, he wanted to know how to calculate trajectories and the expansive forces of propellants, so as to understand Robbie when he was talking to the artillery experts; and, finally, he wanted to learn to multiply and divide numbers.

Beauty was puzzled; she didn't know any of these things herself, and wasn't sure if there was any school in the neighborhood where they were taught. She pointed out that if Lanny went away to boarding school, he wouldn't be on hand for the visits of his father; also he would miss a great deal of travel, which was another kind of education, wasn't it? So finally it was decided that the way to solve the problem was, first, to buy a large dictionary and a twenty-volume encyclopedia; and, second, to get a tutor who understood arithmetic.

So it came about that Mr. Ridgley Elphinstone entered into Lanny Budd's young life. Mr. Elphinstone was an Oxford student whose health had weakened, and he was living *en pension* in the village. Beauty was introduced to him at a bridge party, and when the hostess mentioned that the young man was poor, Beauty had the bright idea to inquire if he could teach arithmetic. He answered sadly that he had forgotten all he had ever known, but doubtless he could brush up; that was the way of all tutors, he explained, they got advance information as to what was expected, and they brushed up. Mr. Elphinstone came and made an inventory of Lanny's disordered stock of knowledge, and told Beauty that it might be difficult to make an educated man of him, but since he was going to have money, why did it matter?

After that Mr. Elphinstone came every morning, unless Lanny was otherwise engaged. He was a thin person of melancholy aspect, with dark Byronic hair and eyes, and spent his spare time composing poetry which he never showed to anyone. Apart from his code as an English gentleman, he appeared to have only one conviction, which was that nothing was certain, and anyhow it made no difference. His method of instruction was most agreeable; he would tell Lanny anything he wanted to know, and if neither of them knew it, they would look it up in the encyclopedia. Incidentally, Mr. Elphinstone fell in love with Beauty, which was as she expected; being poor but proud he never said anything, which made the most pleasant arrangement possible.

So far, Lanny's pronunciation of his own tongue had been modeled upon that of his father, who was a Connecticut Yankee. But the Oxford accent is most impressive, and the boy now lived in daily contact with it, so presently he was being heard to declare that he "had bean," and that he knew "we-ah" he was going, he saw "cle-ahly" what was his "gaoal." He would say that he "re-ahlized" that his education was "diff'rent," but that it was "mod'n," and he wanted it to be "thurrah." He developed aristocratic sentiments, and when he discussed politics would say: "We must not shut ahr eyes to the fact that it is necess'ry for someone to commahnd." If one of the boys invited him to play tennis he would reply: "Ah-i will luke and see the tah-eem." When Robbie returned he "tuke" some amused "lukes" at his son, and informed him that the sound of "oo" as in the word "loot" came from the quite unfashionable North of England.

II

Among the guests at one of the tea parties was a Russian baron of the name of Livens-Mazursky. The friend who brought him said that he was rich and important, owned a newspaper in St. Petersburg, had diplomatic contacts, and would be a valuable person to Robbie—all that sort of thing. He was of striking appearance, large, with flourishing black whiskers, pale cheeks, and lips so red that you wondered if he did not stain them. His eyes were prominent and bright, and he talked with animation in whatever language the company preferred. He spent his money freely, so everybody liked him.

Baron Livens came to the house several times and seemed to take an interest in the handsome boy. Lanny was used to that, many people did it; also he was used to the ardent temperament of the Russians and thought he would be helping the American munitions industry by making friends with a brilliant man who had once been a cavalry officer, and who seemed like a character stepping out of *With Fire and Sword*.

One afternoon Lanny went with his mother to Cannes, and while she did some shopping he went to a kiosk and got a magazine, and sat down to read and wait for his mother in the lobby of one of the fashionable hotels. Baron Livens happened in, and sat beside him, and asked him what he was reading, chatted about magazines, and finally told Lanny that he had some wonderful reproductions of Russian paintings in his suite upstairs. So they went up in the lift, and the baron ushered Lanny into a showy drawing room, and got the prints, and they sat down at a table together to look at pictures.

Presently one of the man's arms was about Lanny, and that was all right; but then he bent down and kissed the boy on the cheek. All boys in those days had the experience of being kissed with whiskers, and didn't like it. When the action was repeated, Lanny shrank and said: "Please don't." But the baron held on to him, and Lanny became alarmed; he looked, and discovered a half-crazy stare in the man's eyes. A panic seized the boy and he cried: "Let me go!"

Lanny had not forgotten what the Social-Democratic editor had told him about Graf Stubendorf; he had tried to imagine what he was being warned against, and now it flashed into his mind that this must be it! He struggled and started to scream, which frightened the man, so that he let go his hold, and Lanny sprang up and rushed to the door.

It was locked; and this discovery gave Lanny the wildest fright he had ever known. He shrieked at the top of his voice: "Help! Help! Let me out!" The baron tried to quiet him, but Lanny got a big upholstered chair between them, and yelled louder; until the man said: "Be quiet, you little fool, and then I'll open the door." "All right, open it," panted Lanny. When it was open he made the man step away from it, and then dashed out and down the stairs without waiting for the lift.

In the lobby he took a seat, pale and shivering; for a while he thought he was going to be nauseated. Then he saw the bewhiskered baron bringing the magazine which had been left behind. Lanny jumped up and kept backing away; he wouldn't let the Russian get near him. The man was agitated too, and tried to plead; it was all a misunderstanding, he had meant no harm, he had little boys of his own whom he loved, and Lanny reminded him of them.

Such was the situation when Beauty appeared. She saw that something had happened, and the baron tried to explain; the dear little boy had misunderstood him, it was a cruel accident, most embarrassing. Lanny wouldn't speak of it, he just wanted to get out of there. "Please, Beauty, please!" he said, so they went out to the street.

"Have you been hurt?" asked the frightened mother.

But Lanny said: "No, I got away from him." He wouldn't talk about it on the street, and then he wouldn't talk in the car, because Pierre, the chauffeur, could hear them. "Let's go home," he said, and sat holding his mother's hand as tightly as he could.

III

By the time they reached Bienvenu, Lanny had got over some of his agitation, and was wondering whether he could have been making a mistake. But when he told his mother about it she said, no, he had been in real danger; she would like to go and shoot that Russian beast. But she wouldn't tell the youngster what it was about; a kind of fog of embarrassment settled over them, and all Lanny got out of it was anxious monitions never to let any man touch him again, never to go anywhere with any man again—it appeared that he couldn't safely have anything to do with anybody except a few of his mother's intimates.

Beauty had to talk to somebody, and called in her friend Sophie, Baroness de la Tourette. Oh, yes, said that experienced woman of the world, everybody knew about Livens; but what could you do? Have him arrested? It would make a journalist's holiday, he would fight back and blacken you with scandals. Shoot him? Yes, but the French laws were rather strict; the jury would have to be made to weep, and lawyers who can do that charge a fortune. The thing to do was to make the child understand, so that it couldn't happen again.

"But what on earth can I say to him?" exclaimed Beauty.

"Do you mean you haven't given him a straight talk?" demanded her friend.

"I just can't bring myself to it, Sophie. He is so innocent——"

"Innocent, hell!" retorted Sophie Timmons, that henna blonde with the henna laugh; the daughter of a hardware manufacturer who was a piece of hardware herself. "He plays around with these peasant children—don't you suppose they watch the animals and talk about it? If you heard them you would pass out."

"Oh, my God!" lamented Beauty. "I wish there was no such thing as sex in the world!"

"Well, there's plenty of it on this 'Coast of Pleasure,' and your little one will soon be ready for his share. You'd better wake up."

"His father is the one who ought to tell him, Sophie."

"All right then, send a cablegram, 'Robbie come at once and tell Lanny the facts of life.'" They both laughed, but it didn't solve the problem. "Couldn't the tutor do it?" suggested the baroness finally.

"I haven't the faintest notion what his ideas are."

"Well, at the worst I should think they'd be better than Livens'," responded the other, dryly.

The Baroness de la Tourette of course told the story all over the place, and Baron Livens-Mazursky found himself cut off from a number of calling lists; he suddenly decided to spend the rest of the winter at Capri, a place which was not so puritanical as Cannes. Lanny's mother repeated her warnings to the boy, with such solemnity that he began to acquire the psychology of a wild deer in the forest; he looked before he ventured into any dark places, and if he saw anyone, male or female, getting close to him he moved.

IV

But even the wild deer in the forest enjoys life, and Lanny couldn't be kept from wanting to talk to people and find out about them. Soon afterward came the Adventure of the Gigolo, which was the last straw, so Beauty declared. The story of Lanny's gigolo spread among the smart crowd up and down the Riviera, and every now and then someone would ask: "Well, Lanny, how's your gigolo getting along?" He knew they were making fun, but it didn't worry him, for his mind was firmly made up that his gigolo was really a very kind man, much more so than some of the persons who tried to win money from his mother at bridge.

It was another of those occasions when Beauty was having herself made more so. This time it was a ravishing evening gown of pale blue chiffon over cloth of silver, which was being "created" by M. Claire, the couturier in Nice, at a specially moderate price because of the advertising he would get. It meant long sessions of fitting in which Beauty got a bit dizzy, and Lanny preferred to sit out under the plane trees and watch the traffic go by, the fashionable people strolling, and the *bonnes* with the pretty children.

He sat on a bench, and along came a gentleman of thirty or so, wearing correct afternoon attire in the morning, and a neatly trimmed little black mustache and a cane with a ball of polished agate for a handle. He had an amiable expression, and perhaps recognized a similar one on the face of the boy. Certainly he could see that the boy was fashionably attired. It was now the height of the season, and the town was full of tall slender youths from England and America, wearing sports shirts, linen trousers, and tennis shoes. or sandals.

The gentleman took a seat on the bench, and after a while stole a glance at the book in Lanny's lap. "*J'ai lou cela,*" he remarked.

Which told Lanny right away that he was a countryman, a native of Provence. These people do not pronounce the *u* as do the French; the name of Lanny's town was not spoken in French fashion, or in Spanish, but "Jou-an." Lanny answered in Provençal, and the stranger's face lighted up. "Oh, you are not a foreigner?" Lanny explained that he was born in Switzerland and had lived most of his life in "Jou-an." The stranger said that he came from the mountain village of Charaze, where his parents were peasants.

That called for explanation; for the sons of peasants do not as a rule spend their mornings strolling under the plane trees of the Avenue de la Victoire, dressed in frock coat and striped trousers trimmed with black braid. M. Pinjon—that was his name—explained that he had risen in the world by becoming a professional dancer. Lanny said that he too was a dancer of a sort, and wished to learn all he could about that agreeable art. M. Pinjon said that what counted was that one had the spirit, the inner fire. Yes, assented Lanny; so few had that fire, which was the soul of every art. Kurt had said that, and Lanny remembered it and used it to excellent effect.

So you see the acquaintance started upon the very highest plane. Lanny was moved to tell about Hellerau, and the tall white temple loomed as a place of magic to which M. Pinjon might some day make a pilgrimage. Lanny described the technique of Eurythmics;

a little bit more and he would have been giving a demonstration on the sidewalk of the avenue.

V

Out of the fervor of his nature as an artist and a son of the warm South, M. Pinjon told the story of his life. He was a child of a large family, and the little plot of earth in Charaze was too small to sustain them all. So he, the youngest, had fared forth to make his fortune in the world, and for a while had not found it easy. He had lived in a wretched lodging—there was a "cabbage patch" also in Nice, and much refuse was dumped into the streets, and the smells were painful to a countryman who was used to thyme and lavender on the hillsides.

M. Pinjon had become a waiter, a menial position in a small café; but he had saved every sou, and bought himself this costume, patterned carefully after those he had observed in the *grand monde*. At home he had been a skillful dancer of the farandole, and had soon begun a study of modern dancing, no simple task, since twenty-eight forms of the tango were now being danced on the Riviera, besides such American innovations as the "turkey trot" and the "bunny hug."

Having cultivated his ten talents, M. Pinjon had obtained an opening in one of the casinos. He was what was called, somewhat unkindly, a "gigolo." True, there were evil men in the business, ready to take advantage of opportunities; but M. Pinjon was a serious person, a French peasant at heart, and his purpose in life was to save up a sufficiency of *livres* to purchase a bit of land which he had picked out near his ancestral home and there to live as his forefathers had done, cultivating the olive and the vine and saying prayers against the return of the Saracens.

Ladies came in great numbers to the casino; ladies who were lonely, mostly because they were middle-aged, and the men, whether old or young, preferred to dance with young partners. However, middle-aged ladies were reluctant to bid farewell to their youth, and to the enjoyment which we all crave. M. Pinjon spoke quite feelingly and at the same time instructively about the problem of the middle-aged lady. Why should she not dance—having nothing else to do? Since the men did not invite her, she was compelled to pay for partners, and it was in this way that M. Pinjon gained a modest living. He danced with strange ladies in a dignified and respectful way, and if they wished to be taught he helped them to improve their style.

He seemed anxious that this polite and intelligent boy should agree with him that this was a proper thing to do; and Lanny did agree with him. M. Pinjon came back to the subject of Dalcroze, and asked if there was a book about it. Lanny gave him the name of a book and he wrote it down. The boy was moved to add: "If you ever come to Juan, and will call at our home, I'll be glad to show you as much of it as I can." The dancer wrote down Lanny's address, and said he would surely not fail; he played the piccolo flute, and would bring it and render old Provençal tunes and Lanny would dance them.

At this point came Beauty, tired and a little cross after the ordeal of "fitting." Lanny introduced her to his new friend, and of course Beauty had to be polite, but at the same time most reserved, because she could perceive social subtleties which a boy couldn't, and this wasn't the first time that Lanny's habit of picking up strange persons had caused embarrassment. When they got into the car and were driving home, Lanny told her about his new friend, and—well, of course Beauty couldn't be angry with the child, but, oh, dear, oh, dear—she had to sink back into the cushions of the car and laugh. She thought how Sophie would laugh, and how Margy would laugh—that was Lady Eversham-Watson. And they did, of course; everybody did, except Lanny.

The worst of it was there was no way to keep the man from calling. The mother had to explain carefully to Lanny that there are certain social differences that just can't be overlooked. "You'll of course have to be polite to this poor fellow, but you mustn't ask him to call again, nor promise to go and see him dance at the casino. Above all, I won't meet him again."

M. Pinjon rode all the way from Nice in an autobus, his first free day. He brought his piccolo, and they sat out on the terrace, and he played shrill little tunes, "Magali," and the "Marche des Rois," and Lanny danced them, and the son of the warm South became inspired, and played faster and more gaily, and danced while he played. Beauty, who happened to be at home, peered through the blinds of a window now and then, and watched the dapper little man with the neat black mustache capering with such agility; she had to admit that it was a touching scene—out of the childhood of the world, as it were, before social classes came into being.

Afterward Rosine brought wine and cake. M. Pinjon was treated with every courtesy—except that he did not again see the face of the loveliest of grass widows. The Provençal chansons which tell of troubadours singing in castles and carrying away princesses somehow did not fit the circumstances of the year 1914 on the Côte d'Azur.

VI

After that episode Beauty Budd decided that she could no longer leave her child in ignorance of the facts of life. She sought out her friend Sophie, who had a new suggestion. There was in Nice an Austrian-Jewish physician of the name of Bauer-Siemans, practitioner of a method known as psychoanalysis, just now sweeping Europe and America. Ladies in the highest social circles discovered that they had inferiority complexes—that was the German jawbreaker *Minderwertigkeitscomplexe,* called "the Minkos" for short. Ladies and gentlemen talked quite blandly about their Oedipus fixations and their anal-erotic impulses; it was horrible, but at the same time fascinating. The thing that carried ladies off their feet was the fact that for ten dollars an hour you could employ a cultured and intelligent gentleman to hear you talk about yourself. It cost many times that to give a dinner party—and then you discovered that the gentlemen wanted to talk about *them*selves!

"I don't know how much I believe of that stuff," said the Baroness de la Tourette; "but at least the man knows the facts and won't mind talking about them."

"But will he want to bother with a child, Sophie?"

"Hand him an envelope with a hundred-franc note in it, and let nature do the rest," said the practical-minded baroness.

So Mrs. Budd telephoned and asked for an hour or two of the valuable time of Dr. Bauer-Siemans, and took Lanny with her and left him in the outer office while she told about the baron, and then the gigolo.

The psychoanalyst was a learned-looking gentleman having a high forehead topped with black wavy hair, and gold pince-nez which he took off now and then and used in making gestures. He spoke English with a not too heavy accent. "But why don't you talk to the boy yourself, Mrs. Budd?" he demanded.

More blood mounted to Beauty's already well-suffused cheeks. "I just can't, Doctor. I've tried, but I can't speak the words."

"You are an American?" he inquired.

"I am the daughter of a Baptist minister in New England."

"Ah, I see. Puritanism!" Dr. Bauer-Siemans said it as if it were "poliomyelitis" or "Addison's disease."

"It seems to be ingrained," said Beauty, lowering her lovely blue eyes.

"The purpose of psychoanalysis is to bring such repressions to the surface of consciousness, Mrs. Budd. So we get rid of them and acquire normal attitudes."

"What I want is for you to talk to Lanny," said the mother, hastily. "I would like you to consider it a professional matter, please." She handed over a scented envelope, not sealed but with the flap tucked in.

The doctor smiled. "We don't usually receive payment in advance," he said, and laid the envelope on the desk. "Leave the little fellow with me for an hour or so, and I'll tell him what he needs to know." So Beauty got up and went out; meantime the doctor glanced into the envelope, and saw that Lanny was entitled to a full dose of the facts of life.

VII

The boy found himself seated in a chair facing the desk of this strange professional gentleman. When he heard what he was there for, the blood began to climb into *his* cheeks; for Lanny, too, was a little Puritan, far from the home of his forefathers.

However, it wasn't really so bad; for the Baroness de la Tourette had been right. Lanny had not failed to see the animals, and the peasant boys had talked in the crudest language. His mind was a queer jumble of truth and nonsense, most of the latter supplied by his own speculations. The peasant boys had told him that men and women behaved like that also, but Lanny hadn't been able to believe it; when the doctor asked why not, he said: "It didn't seem dignified." The other smiled and replied: "We do many things which do not seem dignified, but we have to take nature as we find it."

The doctor's explanations were not by means of the bees and the flowers, but with the help of a medical book full of pictures. After Lanny had got over the first shock he found this absorbingly interesting; here were the things he had been wondering about, and someone who would give him straight answers. It was impossible for Lanny to imagine such desires or behavior on his own part, but the doctor said that he would very soon be coming to that period of life. He would find the time of love one of happiness, but also of danger and strain; there arose problems of two different natures, man's and woman's, learning to adjust themselves each to the other, and they needed all the knowledge that was to be had.

All this was sensible, and something which every boy ought to have; Lanny said so, and pleased the learned-looking doctor, who gave him the full course for which the mother had paid, and even a little extra. He took up a subject which had a great effect upon the future of both mother and son. "I understand that your mother is divorced," he remarked. "There are many problems for children of such a family."

"I suppose so," said Lanny innocently—for he was not aware of any problems in his own family.

"Understand, I'm not going to pry into your affairs; but if you choose to tell me things that will help me to guide you, it will be under the seal of confidence."

"Yes, sir," said Lanny. "Thank you very much."

"When families break up, sooner or later one party or the other remarries, or perhaps both do; so the child becomes a stepchild, which means adjustments that are far from easy."

"My father has remarried and has a family in Connecticut; but I have never been there."

"Possibly your father foresees difficulties. How long have your mother and father been divorced?"

"It was before I can remember. Ten years, I guess."

"Well, let me tell you things out of my experience. Your mother is a beautiful woman, and doubtless many men have wished to marry her. Perhaps she has refused because she doesn't want to make you unhappy. Has she ever talked to you about such matters?"

"No, sir."

"You have seen men in the company of your mother, of course."

"Yes, sir."

"You haven't liked it, perhaps?"

Lanny began to be disturbed. "I—I suppose I haven't liked it if they were with her too much," he admitted.

Dr. Bauer-Siemans smiled, and told him that a psychoanalyst talked to hundreds of men and women, and they all had patterns of behavior which one learned to recognize. "Often they are ashamed of these," he said, "and try to deny them, and we have to drag the truth out of them—for their own good, of course, since the first step toward rational behavior is to know our own selves. You understand what I am saying?"

"I think so, Doctor."

"Then face this question in your own heart." The doctor had his gold pince-nez in his hand, and used them as if to pin Lanny down. "Would you be jealous if your mother were to love some man?"

"Yes, sir—I'm afraid maybe I would."

"But ask yourself this: when the time comes that you fall in love with some woman—as you will before many years are past—will you expect your mother to be jealous of that woman?"

"Would she?" asked the boy, surprised.

"She may have a strong impulse to do it, and it will mean a moral struggle to put her son's welfare ahead of her own. My point is that you may have to face such a struggle—to put your mother's welfare ahead of yours. Do you think you could do it?"

"I suppose I could, if it was the right sort of man."

"Of course, if your mother fell in love with a worthless man, for example a drunkard, you would urge her against it, as any of her friends would. But you must face the fact that your mother is more apt to know what sort of man can make her happy than her son is."

"Yes, sir, I suppose so," admitted the son.

"Understand again, I know nothing about your mother's affairs. I am just discussing ordinary human behavior. The most likely situation is that your mother has a lover and is keeping it a secret from you because she thinks it would shock you."

The blood began a violent surge into Lanny's throat and cheeks. "Oh, no, sir! I don't think that can be!"

Aiming his gold pince-nez at Lanny's face, the other went on relentlessly. "It would be a wholly unnatural thing for a young woman like your mother to go for ten years without a love life. It wouldn't be good for her health, and still less for her happiness. It is far more likely that she has tried to find some man who can make her happy. So long as you were a little boy, it would be possible for her to keep this hidden from you. But from now on it will not be so easy. Sooner or later you may discover signs that your mother is in love with some man. When that happens, you have to know your duty, which is not to stand in her way, or to humiliate or embarrass her, but to say frankly and sensibly: 'Of course, I want you to be happy; I accept the situation, and will make myself agreeable to the man of your choice.' Will you remember that?"

"Yes, sir," said Lanny. But his voice was rather shaky.

VIII

Beauty had been wandering around in the shops, in a state of mind as if Lanny were having his tonsils out. A great relief to find him whole and sound, not blushing or crying or doing anything to embarrass her. "Dr. Bauer-Siemans is a well-informed man," he said with dignity. He was going to take it like that, an affair between men; his mother need not concern herself with it any further.

"Home, Pierre," said Beauty; and on the way they were silent.

Something was going on in Lanny's mind, a quite extraordinary process. There used to be a popular kind of puzzle, a picture in which a cat was hidden, a large cat filling a good part of the picture in such a way that you had a hard time to find it. But when once you had found it, it stood out so you could hardly see anything else; you couldn't imagine how you had ever looked at that picture without seeing the cat.

So now with Lanny Budd; he was looking at a picture, tracing one line and then another; until suddenly—there was a large cat grinning at him!

Farther out on the peninsula of Antibes, a mile or so from the Budd home, lived a young French painter, Marcel Detaze. He was several years younger than Beauty, a well-built, active man with a fair mustache and hair soft and fine, so that the wind blew it every way; he had grave features and dark melancholy eyes, in striking contrast with his hair. He lived in a cottage, having a peasant woman in now and then to cook him a meal and clean up. He painted the seascapes of that varied coast, loving the waves that lifted themselves in great green masses and crashed into white foam on the rocks; he painted them well, but his work wasn't known, and like so many young painters he had a problem to find room for all his canvases. Now and then he sold one, but most were stored in a shed, against the day when collectors would come bidding.

Beauty thought a great deal of Marcel's work, and had bought several specimens and hung them where her friends would see them. She watched his progress closely, and often when she came home from a walk would say: "I stopped at Marcel's; he's improving all the time." Or she would say: "I am going over to Marcel's; some of the others are coming to tea." There were half a dozen painters who had their studios within walking distance, and they would stop in and make comments on one another's work. It had never struck Lanny as strange that Beauty would go to meet a painter, instead of inviting him to her home to tea, as she did other men.

Many circumstances like that Lanny had never noticed, because he was a little boy, and the relationships of men and women were not prominent in his thoughts. But Dr. Bauer-Siemans had put the picture in front of him and told him to look for the cat; and there it was!

Marcel Detaze was Beauty's lover! She went over there to be with him, and she made up little tales because she wanted to keep the secret from Lanny. That was why the painter came so rarely to the house, and then only when there was other company; that was why he didn't come when Robbie was there, and why he had so little to do with Lanny—fearing perhaps to be drawn into intimacy and so betray something. Or perhaps he didn't like Lanny, because he thought that Lanny stood between Beauty and himself!

If the boy had found out this secret without warning it would have given him a painful shock. But now the learned doctor had told him how to take it—and he would have to obey. But not without a struggle! Lanny wanted his mother to himself; he had to bite his lip and resolve heroically that he would not hate that young French-man with the worn corduroy trousers and little blue cap. He painted the sea, but he didn't know how to swim, and like most French peo-ple on the Riviera he seemed to have the idea it would kill him to get caught out in the rain!

Well, the doctor had said that Beauty was to select her own lover, with no help from her son. So Lanny forced himself to admit that the painter was good-looking. Perhaps he had attracted Beauty be-cause he was so different from her; he appeared as if nursing a secret sorrow. Lanny, having read a few romances, imagined the young painter in love with some lady of high degree in Paris—he had come from there—and Beauty taking pity on him and healing his broken heart. It would be like Lanny's mother to wish to heal some broken heart!

Another part of the "cat" was Beauty's relations with other men. There had been a stream of them through her life, ever since Lanny could remember. Many were rich, and some were prominent; some had come as customers of Robbie—officials, army officers, and so on —and had remained as friends. They would appear in elaborate uniforms or evening dress, and take Beauty to balls and parties; they would bring her expensive gifts which she would gently refuse to accept. They would gaze at her with adoration—this was something which Lanny had been aware of, because Beauty and her women friends made so many jokes about it.

For the first time Lanny understood a remark which he had heard his mother make; she would not "pay the price." She might have been rich, she might have had a title and lived in a palace and sailed about in a yacht like her friends, Mr. and Mrs. Hackabury; but she preferred to be true to her painter. Lanny decided that this was a truly romantic situation. Marcel was too poor to marry her; or perhaps they thought Robbie wouldn't like it. The boy suddenly realized that it was exciting to have such a beautiful mother and to share the secrets of her heart.

IX

The two, returning from the visit to the doctor, came to their home, and Lanny followed Beauty into her room. She sat down, and he went and knelt by her, and put his head against her and his arms around her waist. That way he couldn't see her face, nor she his, and it would be less embarrassing. "Beauty," he whispered, "I want to tell you something."

"Yes, dear?"

"I know about Marcel."

· He felt her give a gasp. "Lanny—how"—and then: "That doctor?"

"He doesn't know—but I guessed it. I want to tell you, it's all right with me."

There was a pause; then to his astonishment, Beauty put her face in her hands and burst into tears. She sobbed and sobbed, and only after some time managed to blurt out: "Oh, Lanny, I was so afraid! I thought you'd hate me!"

"But why should I?" asked the boy. "We are going to understand each other, always—and be happy."

6

Arms and the Man

I

IT WAS February; springtime on the Riviera. The garden was carpeted with irises and anemones, and overhead the acacia trees were masses of gold. It was the height of the "season"; the boulevards blooming with gay parasols trimmed with lace and with large, floppy hats with flowers and fruits on them. On the beaches the ladies wore costumes so fragile that it seemed too bad to take them into the water, and many didn't. There was opera every night, and gambling in scores of casinos, and dancing to the music of "nigger bands"— thumping and pounding on the Côte d'Azur as if it were the Gold Coast of Africa.

There had come a postcard from Robbie in London, then another from Constantinople, and now a "wireless" from a steamship expected to dock in Marseille next day. Beauty having engagements, Pierre took Lanny in the car to meet him. It was the Route Nationale, the main highway along the shore, becoming ever more crowded with traffic, so that the authorities were talking about widening and improving it; but to get things done took a long time in a land of bureaucracy. The traveler passed scenes of great natural beauty, embellished with advertisements of brandies, cigars, and mineral waters. You wound upward into the Estérels, where the landscape was red and the road dangerous. Then came the Maures, still rougher mountains; in the old days they had been full of bandits, but now disorder had been banished from the world, and bandits appeared only in grand opera.

Pierre Bazoche was a swarthy, good-looking fellow of peasant origin, who had entered the service of Mrs. Budd many years ago and seemed unaffected by contact with wealth; he put on his uniform and drove the car whenever that was desired, and the rest of the time he wore his smock and cut the dead wood which the mistral blew down. He spoke French with a strong accent of Provence, and pretended that he didn't know English; but Lanny saw the flicker of a smile now and then, which led him to believe that Pierre was wiser than he let on. Like all French servants—those in the country, at any rate—he had adopted the family, and expressed his opinions with a freedom which gave surprise to visitors.

Pierre Bazoche and Lanny were fast friends, and chatted all the way. The boy was curious about everything he saw, and the chauffeur was proud of his responsibility, having been cautioned many times and made many promises. He could tell the legends of the district, while Lanny dispensed historical information from the guidebook. Toulon, the great French naval base: Lanny read statistics as to the number of ships and their armament, and wondered if any of it had come from Budd's.

The journey wasn't much more than a hundred miles, but cars were not so fast in those days, nor was the highway built for speed. When they got to the Quai du Port, the ship *Pharaoh* wasn't in sight yet, so they went to a waterfront café and ate fried cuttlefish and endives, and then strolled and watched the sights of one of the great ports of the world, with ships and sailors from the seven seas. If the pair had ventured into side streets, they would have found a "cabbage patch" of vast dimensions; but such places were dangerous, and they had promised to stay on the main avenues and never under any circumstances become separated.

II

The steamer was warped up to the quay, and there was Robbie waving, looking brown and handsome in a white linen suit. Presently they were settled in the back seat of the car, both of them beaming with happiness and the boy talking fast. Robbie wouldn't discuss business until they were alone, but Lanny told about his visit to Germany, including even the Social-Democratic editor, now six weeks in the past. Robbie took that seriously, and confirmed his son's idea that Social-Democrats were fully as reprehensible as anarchists; maybe they didn't use bombs, but they provided the soil in which bombs grew, the envy and hatred which caused unbalanced natures to resort to violence.

"I'm on another deal," the father said. "There's a big man staying on the Riviera and I have to convince him that the Budd ground-type air-cooled machine gun is the best." That was all he would say until next day, when he and his son went sailing. Out in the wide Golfe Juan, with little waves slapping the side of the boat, "That's my idea of privacy!" laughed the representative of Budd Gunmakers Corporation. Anchored here and there in the bay were the gray French warships, also keeping their own secrets. Lanny would keep his father's, as he had been so carefully trained to do.

There was another crisis in the affairs of Europe, Robbie reported; one of those underground wars in which diplomats wrestled with one another, making dire threats, always, of course, in polished French. It didn't mean much, in the father's opinion; the story of Europe was just one crisis after another. Three years back there had been a severe one over the Agadir question, and that had broken into the press; but now the wise and powerful ones were keeping matters to themselves, a far safer and more sensible way.

It was a game of bluffing, and one form it took was ordering the means to make good your threats; so came harvest-time for the munitions people. When Russia heard that Austria was equipping its army with field-guns that could shoot faster and farther, the Russians would understand that Austria was getting in position to demand that Russia should stop her arming of Serbia. So then, of course, the munitions people, who had sold field-guns to Russia and Serbia two years ago, would come hurrying to St. Petersburg and Belgrade to show what improvements they had been able to devise since that time.

It was most amusing, as Robbie told it. He knew personally most of the diplomats and statesmen and made it into a melodrama of greeds and jealousies, fears and hates. They were Robbie's oysters, which he opened and ate. Sometimes he had to buy them, and sometimes fool them, and sometimes frighten them by the perfectly real dangers of having their enemies grow too strong for them.

Robbie's talks to his son were history lessons, repeated until the lad understood them thoroughly. He told how in the last great war Germany had conquered France, and imposed a huge indemnity, and taken Alsace and Lorraine with their treasures of coal and iron ore. Now whenever French politicians wanted to gather votes, they made eloquent speeches about *la revanche,* and the French government had formed an alliance with Russia and loaned huge sums of money for the purchase of armaments. The secret undeclared wars now being waged were for support of the near-by smaller states. "The politicians of Rumania sell out to France and get a supply of French money and arms; so then the Germans hire a new set of Rumanian politicians, and when these get into power you hear reports that Rumania is buying Krupp guns." So Robbie, explaining the politics of Europe in the spring of 1914.

Britain sat on her safe little island and watched the strife, throwing her influence in support of the side which seemed weaker; it being the fixed policy of the British never to let any one nation get mastery of the Continent, but to help strengthen the most promising rival of the strongest. Just now Germany had made the mistake of building a fleet, so Britain was on the side of France and had made a secret deal to render aid if France was attacked by Germany. "That has been denied in the British Parliament," Robbie declared, "but the British diplomat's definition of a lie is an untrue statement made to a person who has a right to know the truth. Needless to say, there aren't many such persons!"

So the armaments industry was booming, and anybody who could produce guns that would shoot or shells that would explode could feel sure of a market. But an American firm was at a disadvantage, because it got practically no support from its own government. "When I go into a Balkan nation to bid against British or French, German or Austrian manufacturers, I have to beat not merely their salesmen and their bankers, but also their diplomats, who make threats and promises, demanding that the business shall come to their nationals. The American embassy will be good-natured but incompetent; and this injures not merely American businessmen and investors, but workingmen who suffer from unemployment and low wages because our government doesn't fight for its share of world trade."

This situation was now worse than ever, the father explained, because a college professor had got himself elected President of the United States, an impractical schoolmaster with a swarm of pacifist bees in his bonnet. As a result of his preachments American business was discouraged, and the country was on the way to a panic and hard times. Somehow or other the businessmen would have to take control of their country, said the representative of Budd Gunmakers.

III

Robbie mentioned to his son that the deal he had made with Rumania was in danger of falling through, and that he might have to go back to Bucharest to see about it. "Is it Bragescu?" asked Lanny —for he considered the captain as his man, in a way.

"No," replied the father. "Bragescu has played straight, at least so far as I can judge. But politicians have been pulling wires in the war department, and I've just learned that Zaharoff is behind it."

Once more this sinister figure was brought before Lanny's imagination. Zaharoff was "Vickers," the great munitions industry of Sheffield; and "Vickers" had the Maxim machine gun as their ace card. It wasn't as good as the Budd gun, but how could you prove it to officials who knew that their careers depended upon their remaining unconvinced? Robbie compared Zaharoff to a spider, sitting in the center of a web that reached into the capital of every country in the world; into legislatures, state and war departments, armies and navies, banks—to say nothing of all the interests that were bound up with munitions, such as chemicals, steel, coal, oil, and shipping.

Basil Zaharoff believed in the "rough stuff"; he had learned it in his youth and never seen reason to change. He had been born of Greek parents in Asia Minor, and as a youth had found his way to Constantinople, where he had been a fireman and a guide, both harmless-sounding occupations—until you learned that the former had meant starting fires for blackmail or burglary, while the latter had meant touting for every kind of vice. Zaharoff had become agent for a merchant of Athens, and in a London police court had pleaded guilty to misappropriating boxes of gum and sacks of gallnuts belonging to his employer.

Returning to Athens, he had represented a Swedish engineer named Nordenfeldt, who had invented a machine gun and a submarine. War was threatened between Greece and Turkey, and Zaharoff persuaded the Greek government that it could win the war by purchasing a submarine; then he went to Constantinople and pointed out to the Turkish government the grave peril in which they stood, with the result that they purchased two submarines. Said Robbie Budd: "Forty years' adherence to that simple technique has made him the armaments king of Europe."

New instruments of death were invented, one after another, and the Greek would seek out the inventor and take him into partnership. Robbie laughed and pointed out that a thing had to be invented only once, but it had to be sold many times, and that was why the ex-fireman always had the advantage over his partners. The toughest nut he had to crack was a Maine Yankee of the name of Hiram Maxim, who invented a machine gun better than the Nordenfeldt; the latter gun took four men to handle it, while the Maxim gun took only one and could shoot out the bull's eye of a target just as Bub Smith did with the Budd automatic.

Many were the stories concerning that duel between New England and the Levant; Robbie had got them directly from the mouth of his fellow-Yankee, and so had learned to fight the old Greek devil with his own Greek fire. More than once the devil had got Maxim's mechanics drunk on the eve of an important demonstration; it appeared that in those days it was impossible to find a mechanic who could have any money in his pocket without getting drunk. Later on, Maxim demonstrated his gun to high officers of the Austrian army, including the Emperor Francis Joseph, and wrote the Emperor's initials on the target with bullet holes. Basil Zaharoff stood outside the fence and watched this performance, and assured the assembled newspaper men that the gun which had performed this marvel was the Nordenfeldt—and the story thus went out to the world! Zaharoff explained to the army officers that the reason for Maxim's astonishing success was that Maxim was a master mechanic, and had made this gun by hand; it could not be produced in a factory because every part had to be exact to the hundredth part of a millimeter. This news held up the sale for a long time.

The result of the duel was that Zaharoff learned respect for the Maxim gun, while Maxim learned respect for Zaharoff. They combined their resources, and the Nordenfeldt gun was shelved. Later on Maxim and Zaharoff sold out for six and a half million dollars to the British Vickers; Zaharoff was taken into the concern, and soon became its master. The combination of British mechanical skill with Levantine salesmanship proved unbeatable; but that was all going to be changed, now that the president of Budd Gunmakers Corporation had been persuaded to let his youngest son come over to Europe and show what a Connecticut Yankee could do in the court of King Basil!

IV

When the head salesman of a large business enterprise took time to explain such details to a boy, he pretended that he wanted to unbosom himself; but of course he was following out his plan of preparing the boy for his future career. Robbie Budd had for his son a dream which was no modest one; and now and then he would drop a hint of it—enough to take away the boy's breath.

Basil Zaharoff was sixty-five now, and couldn't last forever. Who was going to take his place as master of the most important of all trades? And where was the industry of the future to be situated? In Sheffield, England? In the French village of Creusot? In the German Ruhr, or at Skoda in Austria, or on the Volga, as the Russian Tsar was daring to dream? Robbie Budd had picked out a far safer location, up the Newcastle River in Connecticut. "It'll not be an extension of Budd's," he explained; "but a new and completely modern plant. No enemy can ever get to it, and when it's in operation it will mean three things: American workingmen will supply the world, an American family will collect the money, and America will stand behind its ramparts, able to defy all the other nations put together. That's what we'll some day have to do, so why not get ready?"

Robbie went on to explain what Zaharoff was doing in France. The country's armament trust was known as Schneider-Creusot, and for years the old Greek devil had been intriguing to get control of it and share the profits of the rearming of Russia. He had bought a popular weekly paper so that he could tell the French people what he wished to have believed. He had endowed a home for retired French sailors and been awarded the rosette of the Legion of Honor. He had bought a Belgian bank, so as to become a director in Schneider's; and when his rivals had kicked him out, he had proceeded to tie up Europe in a net of intrigue in order to bring them to their knees.

First, he had gone to Turkey, and as "Vickers, Limited" had signed a contract to provide that country with warships and arsenals. This had frightened Russia, whose dream was to get Constantinople; so the old rascal had proceeded to that country, and pointed out to its officials the grave danger to them of remaining dependent upon foreign armaments. Zaharoff offered, through his British Vickers, to build a complete modern plant at Tsaritsyn on the Volga, and to lease all the Vickers patents and trade secrets to Russia. This, in turn, had frightened the French; for they could never be sure of the position of Britain in any future war, and if Russia got help from Britain, it would no longer need help from France. To make matters worse, Zaharoff had spread the story that the German Krupps were buying the Putilov arms plant in Russia. All this had broken the French nerve, and Schneider had had to give way and let Zaharoff have his share of the money which France had just loaned to Russia.

"That's why you have to watch the papers," said the father, and showed an item he had clipped that very day. Vickers had received orders from the Russian government for thirty-two million dollars' worth of armaments. "More than one-fourth the whole French loan!" sighed Robbie—deeply grieved because his country had no part in it. America's arms plants were pitifully small, and the business they could pick up in Europe was the crumbs that fell from a rich man's table. "But you and I are going to change all that!" said the salesman to his son.

V

They let down their anchor for a while and caught some fish, and Lanny told about Mr. Elphinstone, and got teased about his new English accent. Then Robbie mentioned that he had to go to Monte Carlo the following day, having an appointment with a Turkish pasha who was interested in buying ground-type, air-cooled machine guns. Robbie had found out that France was lending money to Turkey, with which to pay Zaharoff for his warships and arsenals; so the Turkish officials had plenty of cash. "It's a queer mix-up," Robbie said; "I'm not sure if I'll ever understand it. Even though the French are lending money to Turkey, they appear to distrust it, and don't want it armed too fast; but the Germans seem to want Turkey

armed—at French expense, of course. I am dealing with Turkish officials who are secretly in German pay, or so I have reason to believe."

Lanny said he was getting dizzy at that point.

"Yes, it's funny," the father agreed. "The minister I talked with
in Constantinople said that our guns were too cheap; they couldn't
possibly be good at that price. Of course he wanted me to put the
price higher, and give him a Rolls-Royce, or sell it to him second-
hand for a hundred dollars. Finally I was advised to take up the matter with another minister who is disporting himself at Monte Carlo."

"Oh, yes," said Lanny, "I saw him at the motorboat races; he wore
a large striped necktie and yellow suede shoes." The father smiled
and remarked that Oriental peoples all loved color.

Robbie told a sensational story about what had happened on board
the ship. A few hours before reaching Marseille, the door of his
cabin had been jimmied, and a portfolio of his papers, relating to this
Turkish deal, had been stolen. Fortunately the most secret letters,
which might have cost the life of that minister in Constantinople,
had been sewed up in the lining of Robbie's coat—he patted the spot.
But it was highly inconvenient to lose the drawings of the gun. "Of
course it was Zaharoff," the father added.

"You mean that he was on that ship?" asked Lanny.

The other laughed. "No; the old wolf did that sort of thing when
he was young, and belonged to the *tulumbadschi*, those firemen of
Constantinople who were really gangsters. But now he's an officer in
the Legion of Honor, and when he wants a burglary done he hires
somebody else."

Lanny was excited, of course. "You need a bodyguard!" he exclaimed; and then, a marvelous idea: "Oh, Robbie, why don't you
take me with you to Monte?"

The father laughed. "As a bodyguard?"

"If you have something you want taken care of, they wouldn't
suspect me; and I'd hang onto it, believe me!"

Lanny's fervor mounted, and he began a campaign. "Listen, Robbie, I stayed home and didn't go to school for fear I'd miss seeing
you; and then you come and only stay one day, and maybe you'll be

called to Bucharest as soon as you get through at Monte. But if you'll let me go with you I can see you a lot—you're not going to be with that Turk all day and night. When you are, I'll keep out of the way —I'll get things to read, or go to a movie, and I'll stay in the hotel room at night, honest I will. Please, Robbie, please, you really ought to have somebody with you, and if I'm ever to learn about the industry—you just can't imagine what it'll mean to me. . . ."

And so on, until the father said: "All right." Lanny was so happy he stood on his head in the stern of the boat and kicked his bare legs in the air.

VI

Beauty insisted upon lending them her car, so that Pierre would go along to help take care of Lanny. They would have a Budd automatic in the car, and Pierre knew how to use it—he couldn't fail to learn in a household where boxes of cartridges lay around like chocolates in other homes. Robbie laughed and said he didn't think Zaharoff had had any murder done for some years; but anyhow, it gave a fourteen-year-old boy more thrills than all the movies produced up to February 1914.

The road from Antibes to Nice is straight and flat, and there were advertising signs and a big racetrack, many motorcars, and in those days still a few carriages. When you pass Nice you travel on one of three roads, called *corniches*, which means "shelves"; if you wanted scenery you chose the highest shelf, and if you wanted to get there you chose the lowest, but in either case you kept tooting your horn, for no matter how carefully you made the turns, you could never tell what lunatic might come whirling around the next one.

Monaco is a tiny province with a ruler of its own. The "Prince" of those days was interested in oceanography, and had constructed a great aquarium; but this wasn't such a novelty to Lanny, who had learned to expel the air from his lungs and sink down to where the fishes live. "Monte," as the smart people call it, is a small town on a flat rocky height which juts out into the sea. There are terraces below it, carved out of the rock, and you can look over the water from your hotel windows; down below you hear incessant shooting, for next to playing roulette and baccarat, the favorite amusement of the visitors is killing pigeons. The tender-minded comfort themselves with the thought that somebody eats those that fall, and presumably the hawks end the troubles of those that fly away wounded.

Lanny had been here before, and there was nothing new to him in a street of fashionable shops and hotels. They went to the most expensive of the latter, and Robbie engaged a suite, and sent up his card to the Turkish dignitary, whose secretary came and requested in polished French that "M. Bood" would be so kind as to return in an hour, as the pasha was "in conference." Robbie said, certainly, and they went out to stroll in the beautiful gardens of the Casino, which have walks lined with palm trees and flowering shrubs. There was a little circle of flower beds, and as they came to it, Robbie said, in a low voice: "Here he comes."

"Who?" whispered Lanny; and the answer was: "The man we talked about in the boat."

The boy's heart gave a jump. He looked and saw a tall, gray-haired gentleman turning onto the other side of the circle. He paid no attention to them, so Lanny could take a good look.

Basil Zaharoff had been a vigorous man in his youth, but had grown heavy. He wore the garment of an Englishman on formal occasions, which is called a frock coat, cut large as if to hide his central bulk, and hanging down in back all the way to his knees; a smooth, black, and very ugly garment supposed to confer dignity upon its wearer. Added to it were striped trousers, shoes with spats, and on his head a tall cylinder of smooth black silk. The munitions king had a gray mustache and what was called an "imperial," a tuft of hair starting from the front of his chin, and hanging down three or four inches below it. He walked with a cane, stooping slightly, which made his hooked nose the most prominent thing about him and gave the odd impression that he was smelling his way.

"Having his constitutional," said Robbie, after Zaharoff had passed. Lanny took a rear view of the man who was worth so many

millions, and had got them by having other men's papers stolen.
"He comes here often," explained the father. "He stays at the hotel
with his duquesa."

"He is married?" asked the boy, and Robbie told the strange
story of this master of Europe who could not buy the one thing he
most wanted.

Some twenty-five years ago, when the ex-fireman had got well
under way as a salesman of munitions, he went to Spain on a deal,
and met a seventeen-year-old duchess of that realm, owning almost
as many names as Zaharoff now owned companies. Robbie, who
liked to make fun of the pretensions of Europe, said that the only
case he had ever heard of a person having more names was a run-
away slave whom his great-uncle had rescued by way of the "underground railroad." The Spanish lady was María del Pilar Antonia
Angela Patrocino Simón de Muguiro y Berute, Duquesa de Marqueni y Villafranca de los Caballeros. Legend had it that Zaharoff
had met her on a sleeping car, by rescuing her from the cruelties of
her husband on her wedding night. However that may be, it was
certain that the husband had become violently insane, and was confined in a cell, and for twenty-five years Zaharoff and the lady had
been living together, but couldn't marry because the Catholic
Church, of which she was a devout member, does not permit
divorce. It was usually possible to persuade the Church authorities
to annul a marriage on some pretext, but it would have been embarrassing in this case, for the reason that the mad duke happened
to be a cousin of King Alfonso.

The couple were devoted to each other, and Robbie said that
might be one of the reasons for the business success of the ex-
fireman; he was proof against traps which men bait for one another with women. The former peasant boy naturally felt honored
to have the love of a duquesa, and she helped him to meet the
right people. "Like you and Beauty!" remarked Lanny.

VII

Father and son went back to the hotel, and Robbie was invited upstairs to his pasha. Lanny had one of those little Tauchnitz novels in his pocket, and was going to sit quietly in a big armchair and read. But first, being young and full of curiosity, he stood looking about the entrance hall of this imitation palace where the millionaires of Europe came to seek their pleasures both greedy and cruel. Zaharoff came with his duquesa; Turkish pashas came with their boys; English milords, Indian maharajas, Russian grand dukes— Lanny knew, because his mother had met them. Battles were fought here, part of the underground war that Robbie talked about, for the ownership of armaments, of coal and steel and oil. . . .

Lanny's eyes, sweeping the lobby, saw a man in chauffeur's uniform come in at the front door, walk the length of the red plush carpet to the desk, and hand an envelope to the clerk. "M. Zaharoff," he said, and turned and retraced his steps to the door.

Zaharoff! Lanny's eyes followed the clerk and saw him turn and put the letter into one of the many pigeonholes which covered the wall behind him. Lanny marked the spot; for even a pigeonhole is of interest when it belongs to a munitions king.

Lanny hadn't known that his mind could work so fast. Perhaps it was something that had already reasoned itself out in his subconsciousness. Zaharoff had stolen Robbie's papers, including the drawings of the Budd ground-type air-cooled machine gun, essential to the making of deals. Somebody ought to punish the thief and teach him a lesson; as Robbie had put it in his playful way: "Fight the old Greek devil with his own Greek fire."

The clerk, who looked as if he had just been lifted out of a bandbox, was bored. He tapped his pencil on the polished mahogany top of the counter which separated him from the public; the midafternoon train had come in, and no automobiles were arriving. Two bellhops, in blue uniforms with rows of gold buttons, sat on a bench around a corner of the lobby, and poked each other in the ribs and tried to shove each other off their seats; the clerk moved over to where he could see them, and at his stern taps the bellhops straightened up and stared solemnly in front of them.

Around this corner sat a young lady who attended to the telephone switchboard; she too was mentally unoccupied—there being no gossip over the wires. The clerk moved toward her and spoke, and she smiled at him. Lanny moved to where he could see them; it was what the French call *le flirt,* and promised to last for a few moments. Lanny noted that the clerk had passed the point where he could see the pigeonholes.

The boy did not dart or do anything to reveal the excitement that had gripped him. He moved with due casualness to the far end of the counter, raised the part which was on hinges and served as a gate, and stepped behind it, just as if he belonged there. He went to the pigeonholes, took out the Zaharoff letter, and slipped it into his pocket. A bright idea occurring to him, he took a letter from another pigeonhole and slipped it into the Zaharoff hole. The clerk would think it was his own mistake. Still quietly, Lanny retraced his steps; he strolled over to one of the large overstuffed chairs of the lobby and took a seat. *Le flirt* continued.

VIII

It was Lanny Budd's first venture into crime, and he learned at once a number of its penalties. First of all, the nervous strain involved; his heart was pounding like that of a young bird, and his head was in a whirl. No longer did he have the least interest in a Tauchnitz novel or any other. He was looking about him furtively, to see if anybody hiding behind a pillar of the lobby had been watching him.

Second, he discovered that stealing involves lying, and that one lie requires others. What would he say if anyone had seen him? He had thought that the letter was in the pigeonhole of his own room. A mere mistake in numbers, that was all. But why had he not asked the clerk for the letter? Well, he had seen the clerk busy talking with the young lady. What were the chances that the clerk would

know the name of Budd, and realize that Budd and Zaharoff were
rivals for the armaments trade of the world?

Third, the moral confusion. Lanny had always been a good little
boy, and had done what his parents asked him, and so had never had
any serious pangs of conscience. But now—should he have done it
or not? Did one bad turn deserve another? Should you really fight
the devil with fire? After all, who was going to punish Zaharoff if
Lanny didn't? The police? Robbie had said that Zaharoff could do
anything with the police that he chose—was he not the richest man
in France and an officer of the Legion of Honor?

Lanny wished that his father would come and decide the matter
for him. But the father didn't come; he had a deal to discuss, and
might be gone for a long time. If Lanny got hungry, he was to go
to the restaurant of the hotel and have his supper. But Lanny didn't
think he'd ever be hungry again. He sat and tried to figure out, was
he ashamed of himself or was he proud? It was the famed New
England conscience at work, a long way from home.

He tried to imagine what might be in that letter. His fancy went
off on excursions wild as the *Arabian Nights*. The agent who had
stolen Robbie's portfolio from the ship was waiting to tell what he
had found, and where it was now hidden; Robbie and Lanny would
go at once to the place, and with the help of the Budd automatic
would retrieve the property. The shape of the envelope suggested
that the letter might be from a lady. Perhaps a woman spy—Lanny
knew about them from a recent American movie.

What might the handwriting reveal? After many cautious glances
Lanny took out the letter and, keeping it covered by his book,
studied the inscription. Yes, undoubtedly a woman's. Lanny held
the book and letter up to his nose; still less doubt now. The old
rascal, living in this fashionable hotel with his duquesa, was receiv-
ing assignation notes from another woman! Lanny knew about such
doings, not merely from movies, but from gossip of his mother's
friends. He had heard how politicians and others were trapped and
plundered by blackmailers. Robbie would let Zaharoff know that he
had this incriminating document in his hands, and Robbie's property

would be returned to him by a messenger who would neither ask nor answer questions.

Persons came into the hotel, and others departed; Lanny watched them all. Some took seats and chatted, and Lanny tried to hear what they were saying; from now on he was surrounded by intrigues, and any chance phrase might reveal something. Two ladies sat near him, and talked about the races, and about a skirt cut in the new fashion, with slits on the side. They were shallow creatures, heedless of the undeclared war now going on in Europe. Lanny got up and moved to another chair.

Presently came a sight which he had been expecting. Through the revolving glass doors of the entrance strode a large figure in a voluminous black frock coat, with a black silk tower on his head. The doorman in gorgeous uniform was revolving the doors for him, lest he have to make even that much effort with his hands. The bellhops leaped to attention, the clerk stood like a statue of gentility, the conversation in the lobby fell to whispers, the whole world was in suspense as the munitions king strode down the pathway of red velvet, smelling his way with his prominent hooked nose.

He stopped at the desk. Lanny was too far away to hear a word that was spoken, but he could understand the pantomime just as well. The clerk turned and took a letter from a pigeonhole and handed it to the great man with a respectful bow and murmur. The great man looked at it, then handed it back to the clerk. The clerk looked at it and registered surprise. He turned hastily and began taking other letters from pigeonholes and looking at them. Finally he turned to the great man with more bows and murmurings. The great man stalked to the lift and disappeared.

IX

Robbie came at last; and Lanny said quickly: "Something has happened. I want to tell you about it." They went up to the room, and Lanny looked around, to be sure they were alone. "Here's a letter for Zaharoff," he said, and held it out to his father.

The other was puzzled. "How did you get it?"

"I took it out of his box downstairs. Nobody saw me."

Even before the father said a word, almost before he had time to comprehend the idea, Lanny knew that he shouldn't have done it; he wished he hadn't done it.

"You mean," said Robbie, "you stole this from the hotel desk?"

"Well, Robbie, he stole your papers, and I thought this might refer to them."

Robbie was looking at his son as if he couldn't quite grasp what he was hearing. It was most uncomfortable for Lanny, and the blood began burning in his cheeks. "Whatever put that into your head, son?"

"You did, Robbie. You said you would fight the old devil with his own Greek fire."

"Yes, Lanny—but to steal!"

"You have had papers stolen for you—at least I got that idea, Robbie. You told me you had got some papers belonging to that Prince Vanya, or whoever it was, in Russia."

"Yes, son; but that was different."

A subtle point, hard for a boy to get. There were things you hired servants to do, detectives and that sort of persons, whose business it was. But you wouldn't do these things yourself; your dignity was offended by the very thought of doing them. Lanny had stepped out of his class as a gentleman.

Robbie stood staring at the piece of fashionable stationery, addressed in a lady's handwriting; and the boy's unhappiness grew. "I honestly thought I'd be helping you," he pleaded.

The father said: "Yes, I know, of course. But you made a mistake."

Another pause, and Robbie inquired: "Do you know if Zaharoff has come back to the hotel?" When Lanny answered that he had, the father said: "I think you must take this letter to him."

"*Take* it, Robbie?"

"Tell him how you got it, and apologize."

"But, Robbie, how awful! What excuse can I give?"

"Don't give any excuse. Tell him the facts."

"Shall I tell him who I am?"

"That's a fact, isn't it?"

"Shall I tell him that you think he stole your papers?"

"That's a fact, too."

Lanny saw that his father was in an implacable mood; and, rattled as the boy was, he had sense enough to know what it meant. Robbie wished to teach him a lesson, so that he wouldn't turn into a thief. "All right," he said. "Whatever you say."

He took the letter and started toward the door. Then, an idea occurring to him, he turned. "Suppose he beats me?"

"I don't think he'll do that," replied the other. "You see, he's a coward."

X

Lanny went by the stairway, not wanting anybody to see him. He knew the room number. He knocked, and to a young man who came to the door he said: "I have a letter for M. Zaharoff."

"May I have it, please?" asked the man.

"I have to hand it to him personally."

The secretary took him in with practiced professional eye. "Will you give me your name?"

"I would rather give it to M. Zaharoff. Just tell him, please, that I have a letter which I must put into his hands. It'll only take a moment."

Perhaps the secretary saw about Lanny Budd those signs which are not easy to counterfeit, and which establish even a youngster as entitled to consideration. "Will you come in, please?" he said, and the lad entered a drawing room full of gilt and plush and silk embroidery and marble and ormolu—all things which fortify the self-esteem of possessors of wealth. Lanny waited, standing. He didn't feel at home and didn't expect to.

In a minute or two a door was opened, and the master of Europe came in. He had changed his ugly broadcloth coat for a smoking jacket of green flowered silk. He came about halfway and then said: "You have a message for me?" The boy was surprised by his voice, which was low and well modulated; his French was perfect.

"M. Zaharoff," said Lanny, with all the firmness he could summon, "this is a letter of yours which I stole. I have brought it to you with my apologies."

The old man was so surprised that he did not put out his hand for the letter. "You *stole* it?"

"My father told me that you caused his portfolio to be stolen, so I thought I would pay you back. But my father does not approve of that, so I am bringing the letter."

The old spider sensed a trembling in his web. Such a trembling may be caused by something that spiders eat, or again it may be caused by something that eats spiders. The cold blue eyes narrowed. "So your father thinks that I employ thieves?"

"He says that is your practice; but he doesn't want it to be mine."

"Did he tell you to tell me that?"

"He told me that whatever questions you asked me I was to answer with the facts."

This, obviously, was something which might be of importance. Wariness and concentration were in every feature of Basil Zaharoff. He knew how to watch and think, and let the other person betray himself. But Lanny had said his say, and continued to hold the letter.

So finally the munitions king took it; but he did not look at it. "May I ask your name, young man?"

"My name is Lanning Prescott Budd."

"Of Budd Gunmakers Corporation?"

"That is my family, sir."

"Your father is Robert Budd, then?"

"Yes, sir."

Another silence; Lanny had the feeling that everything that had ever been in his soul was being read and judged. He felt sure that the prominent hooked nose was smelling him. "Have a seat, please," said the old man, at last.

Lanny seated himself on the front half of a chair, and the Greek sat near. He examined the letter, then opened it slowly. A smile relieved the concentration on his face, and he handed the document to the boy, saying: "Oblige me, please."

Lanny thought it was his duty to read it. It said, in French:

"The Marquise des Pompailles requests the pleasure of the company of M. Zaharoff and the Duquesa de Villafranca to tea at five this afternoon to meet the Prince and Princess von Glitzenstein."

"A little late," said the munitions king dryly.

"I am sorry, sir," murmured Lanny, his face burning.

"We should not have gone," said the other. In all Lanny's imaginings, it had never occurred to him that an old Greek devil might have a sense of humor; but it was now plain that he did. His lips smiled; but oddly enough, Lanny felt that the blue eyes were not smiling. They still watched.

"Thank you, sir," said Lanny, returning the letter.

Another silence. Finally the old gentleman remarked: "So Robert Budd thinks I have had his portfolio stolen! May I inquire where this happened?"

"On board the steamer *Pharaoh*, sir."

"The thief has not yet reported to me; but as soon as he does, I promise that I will return the property unopened—just as you have done with mine. You will tell your father that?"

"Certainly, sir. Thank you." Lanny was quite solemn about it, and only afterward did he realize that Zaharoff had been "spoofing" him.

"And you won't feel that you have to intercept any more of my invitations?"

"No, sir."

"You are going to be an honorable and truthtelling young gentleman from now on?"

"I will try, sir," said Lanny.

"I, too, used to have the same thought upon occasions," said the munitions king. Was it wistfulness or was it humor in his soft voice? "However, I found that it would be necessary for me to retire from my present business—and unfortunately it is the only one I have."

Lanny didn't know how to reply, so there was another silence.

When Zaharoff spoke again, it was in a business-like tone. "Young man, you say that your father told you to state the facts."

"Yes, sir."

"Then tell me: does your father wish to see me?"

"Not that I know of, sir."

"You don't think that he sent you here for that purpose?"

Lanny was taken aback. "Oh, no, sir!" he exclaimed. Then realizing the full implication of the question, he decided to fight back. "My father once told me about Bismarck—who said that the way he fooled people was by telling them the truth."

The old man smiled again. "You are a clever lad," said he; "but don't let Bismarck fool you with nonsense like that. Do you think your father would object to seeing me?"

"I don't know why he should, sir."

Zaharoff had in his hand the letter from the Marquise des Pompailles. He went to the escritoire and sat down and did some writing on it. Then he handed this to the boy, saying: "Read it again." Lanny saw that Zaharoff had marked out some of the words and written others over them. He read:

"M. Basil Zaharoff requests the pleasure of the company of M. Robert Budd and his son to tea this afternoon to discuss the problems of the armaments industry."

XI

The duquesa did not appear for the occasion. The waiter who brought the tray poured whisky and soda for the two gentlemen, and tea for Lanny; then he retired with quick bows.

The peasant boy from Asia Minor had become a citizen of whatever country he was in; so now he was an American businessman, using American business language. He sat erect and spoke with decision. He said that while he had never met Mr. Budd, he had watched him from a distance and admired him. Zaharoff himself had been a "hustler" in his time, although the Americans had not yet taught him that word. He said that the leaders of the armaments industry ought to understand one another, because theirs was the only trade in which competitors helped instead of harming. The more armaments one nation got, the more the other nations were compelled to get. "We are all boosters for one another, Mr. Budd."

It was flattering to be called one of the leaders of the armaments industry, but Robbie tried not to feel too exalted. He said that the future of the industry had never looked so bright to him as it did just then; they could all afford to be "bullish." The other replied that he could say even more than that; they were going to have to learn to go into a new element, the air. Robbie agreed with this also. Basil Zaharoff forgot now and then that he was an American, and set down his glass and rubbed his hands together, slowly and thoughtfully.

He soon made it clear why he had asked for a conference. He looked at Robbie and then at Lanny, and said: "I suppose this bright little man never talks about his father's affairs?" Robbie answered that whatever mistakes the little man might make, he would never make that one.

Tactfully, and with many flatteries, the Greek trader declared that he had conceived a great admiration for the methods of New England Yankees. He wanted to do for Mr. Budd what he had done nearly forty years ago for the Maine Yankee named Maxim. He gave Mr. Budd to understand that he was prepared to make him an excellent proposition; he added that he meant those words in the most generous sense; he made a gesture of baring his heart.

Robbie answered with equal courtesy that he appreciated this honor, but was unfortunately compelled to decline it. No, it was not merely that he was under contract; it was a question of home ties and loyalties. Zaharoff interrupted him, urging him to think carefully; his offer would not merely satisfy Mr. Budd, but even surprise him. The business he was doing at present would be small indeed compared to what he could do if he would join forces with Vickers, Limited. The whole world was open to them——

"Mr. Zaharoff," said the younger man, "you must understand that Budds have been making small arms for some eighty years, and it's a matter of prestige with us. I am not just a munitions salesman, but a member of a family."

"Ah, yes," said the old gentleman. "Ah, yes!" Had this young fellow meant to give him a sword prick? "Family dignity is an important thing. But I wonder"—he paused and closed his eyes, doing his wondering intensely—"if there might be the possibility of a combination—some stock that might be purchased . . . ?"

"There is stock on the market," replied Robbie; "but not very much, I imagine."

"What I meant is if your family might see the advantage . . . ? We have Vickers in most of the countries of Europe, and why not in the States? Do you think that members of your family might care to sell?"

Their eyes met; it was the climax of a duel. "My guess is, Mr. Zaharoff, they would rather buy Vickers than sell Budd's."

"Ah, indeed!" replied the munitions king. Not by the flicker of an eyelash would he show surprise. "That would be a large transaction, Mr. Budd."

It was David defying Goliath; for of course Budd's was a pygmy compared to Vickers. "We can leave it open for the moment," said Robbie, blandly. "As it happens, my son and I have one advantage which we have not earned. I am under forty, and he is fourteen."

Never was war more politely declared, nor a declaration of war more gracefully accepted. "Ah, yes," said the munitions king—whose duquesa had no sons, only two daughters. "Perhaps I have made a mistake and devoted myself to the wrong industry, Mr. Budd. I should have been finding out how to prolong life, instead of how to destroy it. Perhaps thirty years from now, you may decide that you have made the same mistake." The speaker paused for a moment, and then added: "If there is any life left then."

A man who wishes to succeed in the world of action has to keep his mind fixed upon what he is doing; he has to like what he is doing, and not be plagued with doubts and scruples. But somewhere in the depths of the soul of every man lurk weaknesses, watching for a chance to slip past the censor who guards our conduct. Was it because this naïve little boy had broken into the munitions king's life with his odd problem of conscience? Or had the father touched some chord by his reference to age? Anyhow, the master of Europe was moved to lift a corner of the mask he wore. Said he:

"Have you noticed, Mr. Budd, the strange situation in which we find ourselves? We spend our lives manufacturing articles of commerce, and every now and then we are seized by the painful thought that these articles may be used."

Robbie smiled. If a civilized man has to face the secrets of his soul, let him by all means do it with humor. "It appears," he suggested, "the ideal society would be one in which men devoted their energies to producing things which they never intended to use."

"But unfortunately, Mr. Budd, when one has perfected some thing, the impulse to try it out is strong. I have here a torpedo"— the munitions salesman held it up before the mind's eye—"to the devising of which my great establishment has devoted twenty years. Some say that it will put the battleship out of business. Others say no. Am I to go to my grave not knowing the answer?"

Robbie felt called upon to smile again, but not to answer.

"And this new project upon which we are all working, Mr. Budd—that of dropping bombs from the air! Will that be tried? Shall we have to take our armies and navies into the skies? And ask yourself this: Suppose some nation should decide that its real enemies are the makers of munitions? Suppose that instead of dropping bombs upon battleships and fortresses, they should take to dropping them upon de luxe hotels?"

The mask was up, and Lanny knew what his father meant when he said that Zaharoff was a coward. The magnate who was supposed to hold the fate of Europe in his hands had shrunk, and had become a tormented old man whose hands trembled and who wanted to break down and beg people not to go to war—or perhaps beg God to forgive him if they did.

But when Lanny made this remark to his father afterward, the father laughed. He said: "Don't fool yourself, kid! The old hellion will fight us twice as hard for the next contract."

BOOK TWO

A Little Cloud

7

The Isles of Greece

I

ROBBIE went to Bucharest, and then back to Connecticut, and the vacant place in Lanny's life was taken by Mr. and Mrs. Ezra Hackabury and their yacht *Bluebird*.

They arrived several days late, because they had a bad passage across the Atlantic. But their friends didn't have to worry, for they had sent frequent messages. The message from Madeira said: "Ezra sick." The message from Gibraltar said: "Ezra sicker." The one from Marseille said: "Ezra no better." When finally the *Bluebird* showed up in the Golfe Juan and the soap manufacturer and his wife were brought ashore, he had to be helped out of the launch by two of his sailors in white ducks. He was a large, florid-faced man, and when the color went out of his skin it made you think of that celebrated painting—futurist, cubist, or whatever it was—"The Woman Who Swallowed the Mustard-Pot."

They got him into the car, and then to Bienvenu. He asked them to put him in a lawn swing, so as to "taper him off"; he insisted that the columns of the veranda were trying to hit him. He was one of those fellows who make jokes even when they have to moan and groan them. He was afraid to take even a drink of water, because the drops turned to rubber and bounced out of his stomach. All he wanted was to lie down and repeat, over and over: "Jesus, how I hate the sea!"

Nobody could have afforded a better contrast to Mr. Hackabury than the lady he had chosen for his partner. The sea and the wind hadn't disturbed so much as one glossy black hair of her head. Her

119

skin was white and soft, her coloring was of pastel shades which she never changed; in fact, she didn't have to do a thing for herself, so the other women enviously declared. She didn't have to be witty, hardly even to speak; she just had to be still, cool, and statuesque, and now and then smile a faint mysterious smile. At once the men all started to compare her to Mona Lisa and throw themselves at her feet. She was somewhat under thirty, at the height of her charms; she knew it, and was kind in a pitying way to this large, crude Middle Westerner who had had his sixty-third birthday and who made soap for several million kitchens in order to provide her with the background and setting she required.

Edna Hackabury, née Slazens, was the daughter of a clerk in the office of an American newspaper in Paris. Being poor and the possessor of a striking figure, she had served as a model for several painters, one of them Jesse Blackless, Beauty's brother. She had married a painter, and when he became a drunkard, had divorced him. It was Beauty Budd who had helped to make a match for her with a retired widower, traveling in Europe with a man secretary and looking for diversion after a lifetime of immersion in soap.

Edna's beauty had swept the manufacturer off his feet; he had married her as quickly as the French laws permitted, and had taken her on a honeymoon to Egypt, and then back to the town called Reubens, Indiana. Reubens had been awe-stricken by this elegant creature from Paris, but Edna had not reciprocated its sentiments; she hadn't the remotest intention of living there. She stayed just long enough to be polite, and to make sure that her three stepsons, all married men with families, understood the soap business and would work hard to provide her with the money she required. Then she began pointing out to her husband the folly of wasting their lives in this "hole" when there were so many wonderful things to be enjoyed in other parts of the world.

So they set forth, and when they got to New York, Edna tactfully broached the idea that, instead of traveling in vulgar promiscuity on steamships and trains, they should get a yacht, and be able to invite their chosen friends to whatever place might take their fancy. Ezra was staggered; he was a bad sailor, and hadn't the least notion why it was "vulgar" to meet a lot of other people. But his wife assured him that he would soon get his sea legs, and that when he met the right people, he would lose interest in the wrong ones. The money was his, wasn't it? Why not get some fun out of it, instead of leaving it to children and grandchildren who wouldn't have the least idea what to do with it?

So the Hackaburys went shopping for yachts. You could buy one all ready-made, it appeared, with officers and crew and even a supply of fuel oil and canned goods. They found a Wall Street "plunger" who had plunged too deep, and they had bought him out, and sailed to Europe in lovely spring weather, and attended the Cowes regatta of 1913 in near-royal style. This was the summer that Lanny had spent at Hellerau; the Hackaburys had explored the fiords of Norway, taking Lord and Lady Eversham-Watson, and the Baroness de la Tourette and her friend Eddie Patterson, a rich young American who lived all over Europe; also Beauty Budd and her painter friend, Marcel Detaze, and a couple of unattached Englishmen of the best families to dance, play cards, and make conversation.

At first it had seemed shocking to Ezra Hackabury to have as guests two couples who weren't married, but who visited each other's cabin and stayed. But his wife told him this was a provincial prejudice on his part; it was quite "the thing" among the best people. The baroness was the victim of an unhappy marriage, while Beauty was poor, and of course couldn't marry her painter; however, she was dear and sweet and very good company, and had helped Edna to meet her Ezra, for which they both owed a debt of gratitude which they must do their best to repay. The considerate thing would be for Ezra to buy a couple of Marcel's seascapes and hang them in the saloon of the *Bluebird*. Ezra did so.

II

The cruise proved such a success that another had been arranged, and the guests were arriving with their mountains of luggage, ready

to set out for the eastern Mediterranean. Edna and Beauty had one
of their heart-to-heart talks, and Beauty told about Baron Livens
and Dr. Bauer-Siemans, and how cleverly Lanny had guessed about
Marcel. Edna said: "How perfectly dear of him!" She was a long-
time friend of that polite little boy, and at once suggested that he
should go along on the cruise. "He never gets in anybody's way,
and it'll be educational for him." Beauty said she was sure he would
love it; and the mistress of the yacht added: "We can put him in
the cabin with Ezra."

It was going to be a delightful adventure for all of them. Marcel
Detaze was looking forward to painting the Isles of Greece, where
burning Sappho loved and sung. The poetry of Byron being famous,
as well as that of Sappho, everybody looked upon the region as one
of glamour, and the guidebooks all agreed that it was a paradise in
early spring. Everybody was pleased except poor Ezra, who knew
only one fact: that every isle was surrounded by water. "The sea
is insane," he kept saying. At first he refused to go; but when he
saw tears in his wife's beautiful dark eyes, he said: "Well, not till
I've had some food."

The soapman's appetite came back with a rush, and next day he
was able to move about the garden, and the day after that he
wanted to explore the Cap d'Antibes; no, not a drive, but a walk,
actually a walk of several miles. The only person who was capable
of such a feat was Lanny, who took charge of the one-time farm-
boy and answered his questions about how the country people lived
here, and what they ate, and what things cost.

The pair sat on the rocks of the Cap and looked at the water, and
Mr. Hackabury admitted that it was fine from that vantage point;
the coloring varied from pale green in the shallows to deep purple
in the distance, and on the bottom were many-colored veils and
palm fronds waving like slow-motion pictures. "Could you catch
those fish?" asked Mr. Hackabury; and then: "Are they good to
eat?" and: "What do the fishermen get for them in the market?"
He looked at the anchored vessels of the French navy, and said: "I

hate war and everything about it. How can your father stand to be thinking about guns all the time?"

He told Lanny about the soap business; where the fats came from and how they were treated, and the new "straight-line" machinery which turned out cakes of soap faster than you could count them. He told about the selling, a highly competitive business; making the public want your kind was a game which would take you a lifetime to learn and was full of amusing quirks. In fact, Ezra Hackabury selling kitchen soap sounded remarkably like Robbie Budd selling machine guns.

Also Mr. Hackabury talked about America; he thought it was terrible that a boy had never seen his own country. "They are a different people," he said, "and don't let anybody fool you, they are better." Lanny said his father thought so too, and had told him a lot about Yankee mechanics and farmers, how capable and hardheaded they were, and yet how kind. The soapman told about life in a small village, which Reubens had been when he was a boy. Everybody was independent, and a man got what he worked for and no more; people were not worldly, the stranger was welcomed and not suspected and snubbed. Pretty soon the lilacs and honeysuckle would be in bloom.

"Yes," said Lanny, "I've seen them. Mrs. Chattersworth, who lives up on the heights above Cannes, has some in her gardens, and they do very well."

To this the other replied: "I suppose they'll live here if they have to, but they won't like it."

In short, the old gentleman was homesick. He said that back in Reubens were fellows who had grown up with him, and would now be pitching horseshoes on the south side of a big red barn where the snow melted early. Lanny had never heard about pitching horseshoes and asked what it was. "I know where the peasants have their horses shod," said he. "I'll take you there and maybe we can buy some shoes."

So that's what they did next morning. Since Pierre was driving the ladies for shopping, Mr. Hackabury rented a car, and they were taken to the blacksmith's place, and to the man's bewilderment Mr. Hackabury paid him three times too much for some clean new shoes, and gave him several little cakes of soap besides. When the ladies came home after lunch to dress for a tea party, they found that this oddly assorted couple had picked out a shady corner of the lawn, and Mr. Hackabury with his coat off was showing Lanny the subtle art of projecting horseshoes through the air so that they fell close to a stake.

III

In short, there sprang up one of those friendships which Lanny was always forming with persons older than himself. Such persons liked to talk, and Lanny liked to listen; they liked to teach, and he liked to learn. So when the stores were all on board the yacht, and the passengers packed and ready to follow, Mr. Hackabury took his new friend aside. "See here, Lanny; do you like motoring?" When Lanny replied that he did, the soapman said: "I've been studying the guidebooks, and I have a scheme. We'll motor to Naples and pick up the yacht there, and so I'll escape two or three days and nights of seasickness."

Lanny said: "Fine," and the owner of the yacht made the announcement to his surprised guests. He proposed to hire a car; but Beauty said there would be no one to use her car while she was away, and she would feel a lot safer if they had Pierre to drive them.

So for three days and nights the boy stayed with this homesick manufacturer, and absorbed a lifetime's lore about the civilization of Indiana. Ezra told the story of his life, from the time he had raised his first calf, an orphan which he had fed with his fingers by dipping them in the milk. A drunken hobo who worked on the farm at harvest-time had shown Ezra's father how to make a good quality of soap, and presently Ezra was making it for the neighbors, earning pocket money. He began saving pocket money to buy machinery to make more soap, and that was the way a great business had started.

For fifty years now Ezra Hackabury had lived with his nose in soap. Before he was twenty-one the people of the village of Reubens, seeing his diligence, had helped to finance the erection of a brick factory, and all these persons were now well-to-do and able to play golf at the country club. The soapman quoted from Scripture: "Seest thou a man diligent in his business? He shall stand before kings." Ezra hadn't done that, but he said: "I reckon I might if I put my mind to it."

There was a box of soap in the car, having a bright bluebird on the box, and one on the wrapper of each cake. The soapman had chosen this symbol because the bluebird was the prettiest and cleanest thing he had seen in his boyhood, and the people of the Middle West all understood his idea. Later on a fellow had written a play of the same name, which Ezra regarded as an infringement and an indignity. People assumed that he had named the soap for the play, but of course the fact was the other way around, said the manufacturer.

The box in the car contained little sample cakes. Mr. Hackabury was never without some in his pocket, his contribution to the spread of civilization in backward lands. Every time a motorcar stopped in Italy, a swarm of ragged urchins would gather and clamor for pennies; the American millionaire would pull out a fistful of his Bluebird packages, and the children would grab them eagerly, and either smell or taste them, and then register disillusionment. Lanny said: "Most of them probably don't know what soap is for." Mr. Hackabury answered: "It's terrible, the poverty of these old nations."

That was his attitude to all the sights of Italy, which he was seeing for the first time. He thought only of the modern conveniences which were not at hand; of the machinery he would like to install, and the business he could do. He wasn't the least bit interested in getting out and looking at the windows of an old church; all that was superstition, of a variety which he called "Cath'lic." When they came to Pisa and saw the leaning tower, he said: "What's the use? With modern steel they could make it lean even more, but it don't do anybody any good."

So it went, the whole trip. Carrara with its famous marble quarries reminded Mr. Hackabury of the new postoffice they were building in Reubens; he had a picture postcard of it. When he saw a dog lying in the road, he was reminded of the hound with which he had hunted coons when he was a boy. When the soapman saw a peasant digging in hard soil, he told about Asa Cantle, who was making a good living raising angleworms to be planted in soil to keep it aerated. There were a million things we could learn about nature that would make life easier for everybody on earth. Ezra told as many of them as there was time for.

They could watch the sea part of the time, and it stayed smooth as the millpond from which the Bluebird soap factory derived its power. But Mr. Hackabury was not to be fooled—he was sure that when they got on it they would find it was heaving and sinking. "The food ain't so good in these Eye-talian inns," he said, "but what I eat I keep. And anyhow, we can say we've seen the country."

IV

They bade farewell to Pierre and the motorcar, and went on board the yacht, which put to sea. The smells improved—but the treacherous element behaved just as Mr. Hackabury had said, and he took to his cabin and did not appear again until they were under the shelter of the rocky Peloponnesus.

Meanwhile a new friendship opened up for Lanny Budd. On the deck sat Marcel Detaze before his easel, wearing his picturesque little blue cap and his old corduroy trousers; he had sketched out a view of the Bay of Naples with Capri for a background, and a fisherboat with a black sail crossing the dying sun. Marcel worked on this for days, trying to get the thing which he called "atmosphere," which made the difference between a work of art and a daub. "Do you know Turner's atmosphere?" he asked of Lanny. "Do you know Corot's?"

Marcel was one of those painters who don't mind talking while they work. So Lanny drew up a camp chair and watched every stroke of the brush, and received lectures on technique. Every painter has his own style, and if you took a microscope to the brushwork, you could tell one from another. The despair of Marcel was the infinity of nature; a sunset like this shifted its tints every moment, and which would you choose? You had to get the effects of distance, and you had to make a flat surface appear endless; you had to turn a dead mineral substance into a thousand other things —not to mention the soul of the painter who was looking at them all. "No landscape exists until the painter makes it," said Marcel.

When his work wasn't going right, he was restless, and wanted to pace the deck. Lanny liked to walk too, so they kept each other company. The boy was so used to being with grown people, it didn't occur to him as surprising that a serious-minded artist should give so much time to him. Only gradually he realized that Marcel was availing himself of this opportunity to make friends. Hitherto he had had to hide from Lanny, but now he was taking him into the family—Marcel's family.

The boy was pleased to find the painter a person who worked so hard at his job. Marcel deliberately refused to learn to play cards, and while the others stayed up half the night, he went to bed, like Lanny, and, like Lanny, was fresh in the morning. He would get up early to watch the pearly tints in the sky, and when he told Lanny about this, the lad got up early too, and heard a discourse on color, and learned the names of many shades, and something about how paints are mixed. Lanny began to think that maybe he was missing his true vocation; he wondered what his father and mother would say if he were to get himself an easel and a palette and join one of the art classes which painters conducted on the Côte d'Azur.

This relationship between Lanny and Marcel seemed strange to a Middle Western American, but not in the least to a Frenchman.

The painter was prepared to become an extra father to Lanny, if this was permitted, and it was. The boy observed what was going on between Marcel and his mother, and realized that the man was trying to persuade her to give less of her time and energy to these fashionable people, and more of it to him. Marcel thought that Beauty was wearing herself out running about to social functions, depriving herself of sleep, and being so excited that she hardly took time to eat. Every now and then these "smart" ladies would find themselves threatened with a breakdown, and would have to go away and take baths or cures or what not to restore themselves. "It's a silly way of life," declared the hard-working man of art.

V

A cold wind was blowing from the snow-covered Mount Olympus, and the yacht sought shelter behind the long island called Euboea. Here was a wide channel, blue and still and warm; Mr. Hackabury said: "This is all I ever want to see of the Isles of Greece, and let's stay right here."

The channel ran for a hundred and fifty miles, and they would steam to a new place and anchor, and the party would be rowed ashore to some bedraggled village, and would climb a hill, and there would be the ruins of an ancient building, the stones once white now mottled and grayish, a great column lying in the dust, the segments which composed it having come apart, so that it looked like a row of enormous cheese boxes laid end to end. Sheep grazed among the ruins, and the bronzed old shepherd had built himself a hut of brush, pointed at the top like an Indian tepee.

Marcel had a guidebook, and would read about the temple which had stood there, and who had built it. Most of the company would be bored, and wander off in pairs and chat about their own affairs. One ruin was just like another to them. But the painter knew the differences of styles and periods, and would point these out to Lanny; so came a new stage in the boy's education. He had never known much about Greece, but now he became excited. Something wonderful had been here, more than two thousand years ago. A great people had lived, and had dreamed lovely things, such as Lanny caught gleams of in music and tried to catch and express in a dance. Now those splendid people were gone, and it was sad; when you stood among their old marbles and watched the sun going down across the blue-shadowed bay, feelings of infinite melancholy stole over you; you felt that you too were dying and being forgotten.

Marcel had a book with verses and inscriptions of these ancient ones. Invariably the verses were sad, as if the people had foreseen the fate which was to befall them. "Perhaps they had seen ruins of earlier people," suggested Lanny; and the painter said: "Civilizations rise and fall, and nobody has been able to find out what kills them."

"Do you suppose that can happen to us?" asked Lanny, a bit awe-stricken; and when the painter said that he believed it would happen, the boy watched the sun go down, with shivers that were not entirely from the north winds.

Marcel Detaze developed a great interest in this newly adopted son. The rest of the company were well-bred people, whom it was pleasant to travel with, but they were conventional and had little understanding of what went on in the soul of an artist. But this boy knew instinctively; something in him leaped in response to an art emotion. So Marcel would supplement the guidebook with everything he knew about Greek art, and he found that Lanny remembered what he heard. Later on, when they visited Athens, the boy found an English bookstore with books about ancient Greece, and so was able to read the history which had provided English statesmen with their examples, and the mythology which had provided English poets with their similes, for three or four hundred years.

Marcel and Lanny and Mr. Hackabury did the walking for the party. The latter had no interest in ruins, but he toiled up the slopes because he didn't want to put on more weight. While the younger pair examined columns Ionic or Corinthian, Mr. Hackabury would wander off and talk in sign language to the shepherds. Once he bought a lamb; not because he wanted it, but because of his curiosity as to prices current in this country. He put out a handful of coins, and pointed, and the shepherd took one small piece of silver. Ezra gave him some soap for good measure, and tucked the lamb under his arm and carried it to the ship. When the ladies heard that they were to have it for dinner, they said it was a horrid idea; they were used to eating roast meat, but not to seeing the creature first!

V I

Warm sunshine and peace settled over the Aegean Sea, and the *Bluebird* ventured forth to explore the islands famed in song and story. They are the tops of sunken chains of mountains, and to the unpoetic they look much alike; the fact that Phoebus Apollo was born on one and Sappho on another didn't mean much to modern society ladies. What counted was the fact that they had no harbors, and you had to be rowed ashore, and there was nothing to see but houses of plastered stone, and men with white starched skirts like ballet dancers. Swarms of children followed you, staring as if at a circus parade, and it was not very interesting to buy laces and sponges which you didn't need, or to eat pistachio nuts when you weren't hungry. Having once drunk coffee out of copper pots with long handles, and discovered that it was sticky and sweet, you decided that it was pleasanter on deck dancing to the music of a phonograph or trying to win back the money you lost at bridge the night before. Ezra, in his capacity as host, would propose a party to visit one of the "hanging monasteries," but his wife would say that she was tired and would prefer to rest and read a novel; one of the gentlemen would say that he would stay and keep her company; others would follow suit, and so it would come to the usual trio of sightseers, Ezra, Marcel, and Lanny.

There were several little dramas going on among these guests, which Lanny Budd was too young to understand or even suspect.

Of the two young Englishmen who had been brought along, one was named Fashynge; he had no special occupation, but was welcomed because he was a good dancer and cardplayer, and had the right sort of conversation, difficult for anybody to understand unless he knew a certain small set of people, their personal peculiarities, what had happened to them, and what they thought was funny. Society ladies like to have such men about, and Cedric Fashynge devoted himself to Beauty Budd, uninvited and without asking any return. Marcel said he was an ass, but probably a harmless one. Lady Eversham-Watson was attracted by him, and Beauty would playfully tell "Ceddy" to dance with Margy and do this and that with her; but "Ceddy" didn't obey—and anyhow, his lordship was always about, seeing to it that his wife received every attention that she required.

The other Englishman was older and more serious; Captain Andrew Fontenoy Fitz-Laing was his name, abridged to "Fitzy." He had got a bullet through his hip in some obscure skirmish with the Afghans, and would wince now and then when he got up out of his chair suddenly, but would say casually that it was "nothing." He was tall and erect, and had a fine golden mustache and fair pink skin about which the ladies teased him. He had the devil in his blue eyes, so Beauty declared; and anybody who watched them closely would see them turn in the direction of Edna Hackabury. If Edna's black eyes happened to encounter them, there would take place a slow deepening of color in the alabaster cheeks and throat of the soap manufacturer's wife. Of the eleven passengers on the yacht, there were only two who had not observed this phenomenon—Lanny and the soap manufacturer.

It had been going on for quite a while, for Fitzy had been on the cruise to Norway. Having a much worse hip at that time, he had not been able to go ashore and visit the *saeters*, so Edna had often stayed to keep him company. He had been among the guests who had accompanied the Hackaburys on their return to the States the previous fall, and had been with them at Key West and the Bahamas, and also crossing the Atlantic. This had been fortunate,

for otherwise Edna would have had no company at all while they
were at sea.

VII

They went to Athens—partly because everybody would ask if
they had been there, and partly in order to refuel. The port is called
the Piraeus, and there isn't much of a harbor—the tugs just turned
the *Bluebird* around and set her against a stone pier, and there were
the venders of laces and sponges, and swarms of hackmen clamoring
in various tongues to drive them to town. The weather was pleasant,
and they let themselves be driven about the avenues of a small city,
and saw that there was a museum, and on a height some distance
away ruins which the hackman said were the Parthenon. Did anybody want to look at any more ruins?

Marcel and Lanny did; and Mr. Hackabury went along for company. They rode up on the backs of donkeys, in the company of
thin American schoolteachers and stout German tourists. Ezra sat
down to rest while the younger pair wandered among these noble
remnants, which had been blasted by a powder explosion during a
siege, and from which Lord Elgin had taken all the beautiful statu-
ary. Marcel told what gods had been worshiped here and what arts
practiced, more than twenty centuries before. Now it was a shrine
to lovers of beauty; not long ago Isadora Duncan had danced here,
and when the police had wished to stop her she had told them it was
her way of praying.

They had planned to stay all day, and study diligently; but the old
gentleman called to them and said he guessed he'd have to go down;
he didn't feel quite right; maybe it was a touch of the sun, or something he had eaten. He told them to stay, but they insisted on going
with him—they could just as well come back next day.

So they drove to the boat, and went on board. Ezra went to his
cabin, and Marcel and Lanny stayed on the afterdeck, telling Beauty
and some of the others about the sights they had seen. They were interrupted by shouts from inside the yacht, and loud, crashing noises.

Lanny, the most agile among them, was the first to dash into the saloon and down the corridor from which the sounds came.

He saw an extraordinary spectacle—the owner of the yacht, having apparently recovered his health, had taken from the wall a red-painted fire ax, and with it was vigorously chopping at the lock of one of the cabin doors. "Open up!" he would shout; then, without waiting for anyone to obey, he would give another mighty whack. A steward in white duck jacket, and a deckhand, also in white, stood staring with wide eyes; the first mate came running, and then Lanny, Marcel, Lanny's mother, Lord Eversham-Watson, the baroness—all crowding into the corridor and standing speechless.

Two or three more whacks and the door gave way, and the owner of the *Bluebird* stood gazing inside. The others couldn't see—they kept away from the ax, whose wielder was panting heavily. For a few moments this hard breathing was the only sound; then he commanded: "Come on out!" No answer from within the cabin, and he shouted more fiercely: "Come out; or do you want me to drag you?"

From inside came the voice of Captain Fitz-Laing: "Put the ax down."

"Oh, I'm not going to hit you," replied Ezra. "I just wanted to see you. Come on out, you dirty skunk."

Fitzy came limping through the doorway, his handsome face very pale, his clothing in disarray. He passed the large and powerful soapman, watching him guardedly. The others made way for him, and he went down the corridor.

"You saw him, now take a look at her," said the man with the ax. He was speaking, not to his guests, but to the members of the crew; several others had come, and the owner of the yacht ordered them to the doorway, insisting: "You have seen her? I shall need you for witnesses." Thus directed, they peered into the cabin, from which came now the sounds of Edna Hackabury's weeping.

"You know her?" demanded Ezra, relentlessly. He set his ax against the wall, and took from his pocket a pencil and some paper.

"I want your names and addresses, some place where I can reach you," he said. From one man after another he got this information and wrote it down carefully, while the sobbing inside the cabin went on, and the guests stood, helpless with embarrassment, not saying a word.

"Now then," said Ezra, when he had what he needed, "I'm through." He turned to the group of guests. "I'll leave you this floating whore-house," he declared. "Take it any place you please. I'm going back to God's country, where people still have a sense of decency."

There came a scream from the cabin, and Edna rushed out, half undressed as she was, and flung herself at her husband. "No, Ezra, no!" She started to plead that she hadn't meant it—she had been too much tempted—she would never do it again—he must forgive her. But he said: "I don't know you," and pushed her away and went on down the corridor.

The first person he had to pass was Lanny, and he stopped and put his hand on the lad's head. "I'm sorry you had to see this, son," he remarked, kindly. "You're in a tough spot. I hope you get out of it some day." He walked by the others without looking at them, and went into the cabin he had been sharing with Lanny and started throwing his belongings into a couple of suitcases. His wife followed him, weeping hysterically. She groveled at his feet, she begged and besought him; but each time he shoved her out of the way. When he had what he needed in the suitcases, he took one in each hand and strode out of the cabin and up the companionway, crossed the gangway to the shore, stepped into one of the waiting hacks— and that was the last they saw of him.

VIII

Doubtless things like that have happened in the Isles of Greece on many occasions, both ancient and modern; but none of these people had ever seen it, and they found it more exciting than looking at ruins or buying picture post cards of the Parthenon. The ladies gathered in poor Edna's cabin, and did what they could to console her, telling her that she had got rid of a great burden, and ought to be thankful. Ceddie Fashynge and Eddie Patterson went out and found Captain Andrew Fontenoy Fitz-Laing bracing himself with a few drinks in a café, and brought him back to the *Bluebird*.

When they had time to think matters over, they realized that it wasn't so bad; they had got rid of a dreadful bore, who in a crisis had shown himself a ruffian as well. Edna and Fitzy would no longer have to hide and cower. The latter, being a gentleman, would of course offer to marry her; but unfortunately he had nothing but his army pay, and couldn't keep a wife on that. Perhaps the soapman would make a settlement; anyhow, if he stuck by his word and left her the yacht, it would make a tidy nest egg.

The question was, what should they do next? They had been having such a jolly time, and it would be a shame to end it. Fortunately there was a person on board who could afford to keep the cruise going, and that was Eversham-Watson—or rather, his wife. Prompted by her, he said he would see them back to Cowes, which they had chosen as the place for the ending of their cruise. "The honor of England is at stake," said his lordship; his bright and chirrupy little American wife had told him that, and he said it—solemnly and heavily, so that it sounded like a political speech instead of a joke.

Everybody wanted to get away from the Piraeus, before the madman from Indiana changed his mind and came back and turned them out. Edna gave the order to put to sea and she moved into Fitzy's cabin—it was necessary, really, since the door of her own was split to pieces and the carpenter had to make a new one. There were now three pairs of happy lovers on the yacht, to say nothing of one married couple who had learned to get along reasonably well. There was no longer anything to be concealed, and nobody to embarrass anybody else.

Lanny had a cabin to himself now, and if he missed his elderly friend, he did not tell anyone. He was left to speculate by himself about the strange scene he had witnessed; for nobody on board seemed to want to talk to him about it. Despite his having acquired a complete supply of the facts of life, his mother was greatly embarrassed, and considered that Mr. Hackabury had committed an outrage in allowing a child to witness such a scandal. All Beauty said was that the soap manufacturer had shown himself a crude and boorish person; "one of those men who think they can buy a woman's heart and hold it like a chattel."

All the party seemed to sympathize with Edna, except Marcel Detaze. From remarks he made to Beauty, Lanny gathered that he had his own ideas; but he didn't explain them to Lanny, and the boy was shrewd enough to realize that he must never under any circumstances come between Marcel and his mother, and had better not even know if there was any difference between them.

The *Bluebird* steamed south to Crete and then to the coast of Africa. The weather was hot, the sea blue and still, no one seasick, and no cloud in anyone's sky. They had hundreds of records for the phonograph, and played American ragtime and danced under the awnings which covered the after part of the deck. When they came to Tunis, and the ruins of what had been Carthage, they were in the midst of a long siege of poker; but the yacht stopped to get fresh fruits and vegetables, so Marcel and Lanny went ashore, and saw strange dark men wearing white hoods, and women going about completely veiled, with eyes black as sloes peering out seductively. They saw another sunset over broken shafts of marble, and Marcel told about Hannibal who had driven the elephants across the Alps, and Cato who had said every day all his life that Carthage must be destroyed. Lanny hadn't known that ancient history was so interesting, and went looking for a bookstore in Tunis, something hard to find.

Then Algiers, and they all went ashore and paid strange musicians and dancers to entertain them. They hired camels and rode into the interior, and saw date-palms growing, and poked into native houses, and Marcel sat for hours making sketches which he would use by and by. Lanny stuck to him, asking questions and learning about lines and shadows. The boy had now decided that he liked painting best of all the arts; for dancing was being ruined, nobody cared for anything but hugging each other and moving around in a slow kind of stupefied stagger.

But painting was something you could do by yourself. Lanny dreamed of some day achieving what Marcel had given up in despair —to convey, on canvas, that sense of melancholy which came over them, watching a sunset behind the ruins of old civilizations, and thinking about the men who had lived in those days and tried to make the world more beautiful. You wanted to call to those men to come back. You couldn't bear to know that they would never hear you; that they were gone, and all their dreams, their music and dancing, their temples and the gods who had dwelt in them! Some day you also would be gone, and other men would stand and call to you, and you, too, would not hear.

8

This Realm, This England

I

THE harbor of Cowes lies on the sheltered side of the Isle of Wight, and is the headquarters of the Royal Yacht Squadron and scene of the great regatta every summer. Here came the *Bluebird* at the beginning of May, in time for the pleasant weather and the opening of the London "season."

The gay company broke up. Edna Hackabury received a communication from a firm of solicitors representing her husband, and went up to the city to learn her fate. Beauty Budd was going to visit the Eversham-Watsons at their town house. Marcel Detaze was returning to his studio on the Cap d'Antibes, to put upon canvas his memories of Africa and Greece. The plan had been for Lanny to return with him; but here was a letter from Eric Vivian Pomeroy-Nielson, to whom Lanny had written from Athens. Rick begged: "Oh, please don't go away without seeing me! I'll come to town to meet you, and we'll go to the opera and the Russian ballet. Pretty soon school will be over, and you can come to the country with me. Kurt Meissner is coming, and we'll have a grand time."

Kurt wrote from his school. He had worked hard and won prizes, and his father had promised him a reward. He had an uncle who was an official in a rubber company and had business in London, and was willing to take him along, to see the Russian ballet, and to hear the symphony orchestra and the opera, and to learn all he could about English music. So of course Lanny began begging to stay, and Lady Eversham-Watson said: "Why not? The dear little fellow can enjoy himself at our country place as long as he pleases, and if he wants to come to town, there will be someone to bring him."

If you have ever drunk Kentucky Bourbon, you have probably contributed to the fortune of Margy Petries; if you have ever read a magazine in the English language, you have surely not escaped the self-praises of "Petries' Peerless." Lord Eversham-Watson had met the creator of this beverage at one of the racing meets, and had been invited to come to the bluegrass country and see how they raised horses. He had come, and seen, and conquered, or so he had thought; but that was because he didn't know Kentucky girls. Margy was one of those talkative little women who make you think they are shallow, but underneath have a sleepless determination to have their own way. His lordship—"Bumbles" to his friends—was heavy and slow, and liked to be comfortable; Margy was his second wife, and all he demanded was that she shouldn't go too far with other men. She had paid his debts, and he let her spend the rest of her father's money for whatever she fancied.

As a result, here was an old English country house that you could really live in. All the rooms had been rearranged and everybody had a bathtub. The old furniture, dingy, smelling of the Wars of the

Roses—so Margy said, though she had the vaguest idea what or when they were—had been sold as antiques, and everything was now bright chintz or satin, with color schemes that said, gather ye rosebuds while ye may. There were light wicker chairs and tables, and twin beds for fashionable young wives. Old tapestries in the billiard room had been replaced with a weird device called "batik," and there was a bar in the smoking room, patronized mainly by the ladies, and having decorations out of a children's nursery tale. The rugs were woven in futurist patterns, and on them lay two Russian wolfhounds with snow-white silky hair; when these noble creatures went out in wet weather they donned waterproof garments of a soft gray color edged with scarlet and fastened with two leather straps in front and another about the middle.

If you were a guest at Southcourt you could have anything there was in the Empire; all you had to do was to indicate your wish to one of the silent servants. This silence was to Lanny the most curious aspect of life in England; for in Provence the servants talked to you whenever they felt like it, and laughed and joked; but here they never spoke unless it was part of a ritual, such as to ask whether you wanted China or Ceylon tea, and white or Demerara sugar. If you spoke an unnecessary word to them, they would answer so briefly that you felt you were being rebuked for a breach of form. They wanted you to assume that they did not exist; and if one of them forgot something, or did it wrong, the usually placid "Bumbles" would storm at the unfortunate creature in a manner that shocked Lanny Budd far more than it did the creature.

You weren't supposed to notice this, and if you didn't, you would find Southcourt a delightful place to stay. There were plenty of horses, and generally somebody wanting to ride. There was a comfortable library, and Margy had not bothered to change the books. The pleasantest part of life at an English country house was the way you were let alone to do what you pleased. The rule of silence applied only to house servants; the gardener would talk to you about flowers, and the kennelman about dogs, and the stableman about horses. The place was in Sussex, and there were rolling hills, now fresh with spring grass; Lanny had thought of England as a small island, but there seemed to be great tracts of land that nobody wanted to use except for sheep. The shepherds, too, didn't mind talking—the only trouble was they used so many strange words.

I I

Somebody was motoring to town, and Lanny went along. Automobiles were becoming faster and more dependable every year, also more luxurious. It had suddenly occurred to many persons at once that they didn't need to ride in the open, with a gale blowing on them, and ladies' hats having to be tied on with many yards of chiffon. No, they were now enclosing cars like little rooms. The one Lanny rode in was called a "sporting saloon," and consisted of a square black box in the rear, with a long black cylinder in front for the engine; it was heavy and the tires were small, but Lanny had never seen anything so elegant, and it was marvelous to come rolling into London in your own private parlor. The chauffeur sat out in the wind, and wore goggles, and his cap was fastened to them, and a high tight collar made him sit up straight and stiff. He drove on the left side of the road, and Lanny couldn't get over the idea that somebody would forget about that and run into them.

Rick came to town to spend Saturday and Sunday, and they fell into each other's arms. He was English, but being a devotee of the arts, he didn't mind letting a friend know that he was glad to see him. Rick was such a handsome fellow, with dark eyes and hair very wavy; he had a slender figure, elegant manners, and fastidious tastes —Lanny was quite overwhelmed by him, and proud to introduce him to his friends.

And what a lot they had to talk about! Lanny had been to Silesia, and to Greece and Africa, while Rick had been coming in week-ends to theaters and operas. They were both at the growing age, and measured each other, and tried each other's muscles, and danced a bit, and played odds and ends of music, and chatted about the Russian ballet which was to open next week, and they would make a date for the Saturday matinees and get their tickets right away.

This was at the town house of the Eversham-Watsons, where Beauty was staying, and also Edna Hackabury. The latter had been to see her husband's solicitors, and had been informed that he had filed suit for divorce in Indiana. If Mrs. Hackabury contested the action, she would undoubtedly lose and get nothing; if she agreed not to contest, Mr. Hackabury would give her the choice of the following: the yacht, to be placed in escrow and to become her property on the day the decree was final; or an income of ten thousand dollars a year for life.

Edna had been making inquiries, and learned that yachts were a standard commodity, bringing good prices, so she was all for proposition number one. But her military gentleman announced that his rights as a future husband were not going to be put in escrow. He said if Edna got the price of the yacht she would spend it on clothes and parties in a year; whereas Bluebird Soap stood close to British consols in the estimation of "the City," and two thousand pounds a year was a sum on which a retired army officer and his spouse could live comfortably in some not too fashionable part of the Riviera. So it was settled; and Edna's friends agreed that she was fairly lucky. She had her clothes for the present season, and would be "top-notch" for that long. She must put on a bold front and not let anything get her down.

There was gossip, of course; you couldn't keep such a story from the journalists, who flutter like hummingbirds over the social flower beds, sticking their long noses into everything. There were paragraphs of the sort known as "spicy": a yacht that was in the social as well as the marine register, and an owner in the role of infuriated husband chopping down a cabin door with an ax intended for a different sort of fire. No names were given, but "everybody" knew who it was, and ladies whispered and put up their lorgnettes when the soapman's wife and her slightly lame captain came strolling across the greensward at Ranelagh. Edna wore a genuine Paquin creation —it was a "Paquin year," and the famed woman dressmaker had set off the American's soft white skin and raven-black hair with a strik-

ing ensemble of the same bold contrasts. Picture a dashing wide
black hat with three saucy corners, and with aigrettes sticking in
several directions like broom-tails; a black riding jacket and white
blouse with rolling collar and tie like a man's; a huge muff of black
fur with tails nearly to the ankles; a tall white cane like a shepherd's crook; and on a leash the world's wonder, one of those priceless Japanese Chin dogs famed for their resemblance to a chrysanthe-
mum—a black "butterfly" head with a white blaze over the skull,
and long white hair almost to the ground, and a tail curved exactly
like the petals of a great flower. That was "swank" of the season of
1914; it was *vif*, it was *chic*, it was *la grande tenue*.

III

The social whirl was now in full career. There were two or three
smart dances every night; also people had taken to dancing at teas
and at supper parties after the theater. The Argentine tango was the
rage, also the maxixe—"a slide, a swing, and a throw away." In short,
the town had gone dance-crazy, and some of the fetes were of mag-
nificence such as you read about in the days of Marie Antoinette.
The Duchess of Winterton turned the garden of her town house
into a dancing pavilion, with a board platform and the shrubs and
trees sticking through holes. With a rustic bandstand and colored
lanterns at night it was a scene from the Vienna woods—but no
waltzes, no, the music of a famous "nigger-band."

A half-grown boy wasn't invited to such affairs, but there were
plenty of other things he could do to keep "in the swim." He could
walk by Rotten Row, and see the great ladies and gentlemen of fashion in their riding costumes, and crowds of people lined up to stare,
separated from them only by a wooden railing. He could go to hear
the "bell-ringing" for the Queen's birthday. He could see the coach-
ing parade; the smart gentlemen, and even one smart lady, driving
fancy turnouts with four horses, an array of guests, and two grooms
sitting in back as stiff as statues. He could attend the military tourna-
ment at Olympia, and see a score of riders charging at a long hurdle

from opposite directions, all leaping over it at the same moment, passing each other in the air so close that the knees of the riders often touched.

Also Lanny was invited to ride on a coach with his mother's friends to the races on Derby Day. That was the time you really saw England. Three or four hundred thousand people came out to Epsom Downs, on trains, in carriages or motorcars, or in the huge motorbusses which were the new feature of the town. The roads were packed all day long, first going and then coming; Epsom was described as a vast garage, and people said that soon there would be no horses at the Derby except those in the races. The common people were out for a holiday, and ate and drank and laughed and shouted without regard to etiquette. The people of fashion were there to be looked at, and they put on the finest show that money could buy.

Everybody agreed that the styles for that summer of 1914 were the most extreme since the Restoration, the Grand Monarque, the Third Empire—whatever period of history sounded most impressive. Svelte contours were gone, and fluffiness was the rule; waists were becoming slimmer, side panniers were coming back, flounces were multiplied beyond reason; skirts were tight—a cause of embarrassment to ladies ascending the steps of motorcars and coaches, and the moralists commented sternly upon the unseemly exhibitions which resulted. They complained also that the distinction between evening and day frocks was almost lost; really, flesh-pink chiffon was too *intime* for open air! Fete and race gowns were cut low at the throat, and materials worn over the arms were so diaphanous that they were hardly to be seen at all.

Those who aimed to be really smart did not heed the moralists, but they had to heed the weather; so with these scanty costumes went capes. Everyone agreed that it was a renaissance of the cape; Venetian capes, Cavalier capes, *manteaux militaires,* all made of the most exquisite materials, of silk and satin brocade, sometimes embroidered with great flowers, painted ninons and delicate doublures; the linings were velvet, always of the brightest colors, and the capes

were weighted down with diamonds or other jewels, and held across
the figure by straps of plaid silk or chiffon, with jeweled buckles of
butterfly or flower design.

In short, the fancy of the dressmakers had been turned loose for
many months, and the product was set up conspicuously on the tops
of coaches or in open motorcars for the crowds to inspect. If they
liked it they said so, and if they didn't they said it even louder. Fashionable society tittered over the misadventure of the Dowager
Duchess of Gunpowder, a stout old lady who arrayed herself in
pink taffeta, with a wide hat of soft straw covered with pink chiffon
and roses, known as a "Watteau confection." In a traffic jam her
carriage was halted, and some navvies working by the road leaned
on their shovels and had a good long look at the show. "Wot ho,
Bill!" one of them shouted. "Wot price mutton dressed as lamb!"

Inside the racetrack the big busses were lined all the way down
the straight. The weather was fine, and everybody happy. The royal
family put in an early appearance, and the King and Queen stood in
the royal box and received a hearty ovation. "Bumbles" pointed out
to Lanny the precautions taken to keep the suffragettes from interfering with the race; for last year one of them had dashed out and
thrown herself under the horses' hoofs and got killed—"the daughter
of a very good family, too," said his lordship, with disgust. To keep
that from happening a second time the track had been lined with
three sets of railings, and police and soldiers were watching all the
way around. Every Derby receives a name, and this one was dubbed
"the silent Derby," because a French horse won and two outsiders
were placed; the favorites were nowhere, so that everybody lost
money except the bookies.

IV

At the next week-end came the art lover Rick, and they saw the
Russians in *Le Coq d'Or* by Rimsky-Korsakov. They saw the foolish King Dodon with a tall gold crown and a great black beard to
his waist, and a huge warrior in chain mail, with a curved sword half

as big as himself and shining like a bass tuba. This was the Tsar's own ballet troupe, trained for the dance since early childhood, and all London raved over them. Lanny's enthusiasm for dancing came back, and he and Rick exhausted themselves trying to reproduce those amazing Muscovite leaps.

Also, they went to hear Chaliapin, an enormous blond man with a voice that filled the firmament. They went to see Westminster Abbey, and found a fashionable wedding going on; they heard the clamor of high-toned bells, and got a glimpse of the bridal pair emerging, one in a cloud of tulle, the other with a pale, peaked face, dwarfed by a tall black cylinder on top. Rick didn't seem to think very highly of the old families which ruled his country; he said the groom was probably dim-witted, while the bride would be the daughter of a brewer or a South African diamond king.

Later on came the Trooping of the King's Colours on the Horse Guards' Parade, the occasion being the King's "official birthday": a gorgeous ceremony with a troop of horsemen wearing huge bearskin hats. The King rode at their head, a frail-looking gentleman with dark brown mustaches and beard closely trimmed. They had mounted one of those bearskins on top of him, also a uniform much too large for him, loaded with gold epaulets and a belt, a wide blue sash, and a variety of stars and orders. The young Prince of Wales looked still more uncomfortable, having a pathetic thin face and a sword which he would have had a hard time brandishing.

They made the Queen colonel-in-chief of a regiment; her uniform was blue, all over gold in front, and her hat was of fur with a blue bag hanging from it, and a tall white pompon standing up a foot in the air. Lanny had seen in an American magazine a picture of a drum major in such a costume. He said that to Rick, who replied that the influence of this royal family was a very bad thing for England. "They give themselves up entirely to the tailoring and dressmaking business," said the severe young art lover. "Their friends are the big money snobs. If an artist receives honors, it is some painter of fashionable portraits. Titles are entirely a question of finance; you pay so much cash into the party treasury, and become Sir Snuffley Snooks or the Marquess of Paleale." In short, Sir Alfred Pomeroy-Nielson having got no honors for his efforts to promote little theaters in England, his eldest son thought ill of the government. ·

"Go and see it in action," he advised. So Lanny went on a weekday to Westminster, and was admitted to the visitors' gallery of the House of Commons, now covered with heavy wire net on account of suffragettes' attempts to throw themselves over the railing. Lanny looked down upon the members of the House, mostly wearing top hats, except for the Labour non-conformists. The front-benchers sprawled with their feet upon the bench in front of them. Any of the members, when they didn't like what was said, shouted loudly. The Labour men hated the Tories, the Tories hated the Liberals, and the Irish hated everybody. A fierce controversy was under way over the question of self-government for Ireland; the Ulstermen were swearing they would never be ruled by Catholics, and Sir Edward Carson was organizing an army and threatening civil war. In short, the Mother of Parliaments was hardly setting the best of examples to her children all over the world.

V

There were two "Courts," at which fashionable American ladies dreamed of being presented; but not Beauty Budd, a divorced woman. The same applied to the "state ball," and to the levee at St. James's Palace. But there were plenty of private balls—it was becoming the fashion to give them at West End hotels, where there was room enough for everybody you knew. There would be dinner parties in advance. Margy, Lady Eversham-Watson, was having one at the Savoy; Lanny Budd, so proud of his beautiful blond mother, saw her in a state of exaltation, being got ready for this grand occasion, and her friends Margy and Sophie in the same state of mind and body.

Lanny knew a lot about women's costumes, being a little ladies' man, and hearing them talking all the time, and going with them to be fitted, or seeing it done at home. Just as lovers of painting hoped to find a genius whom they could buy up cheap, so women like Beauty Budd, forced to economize, dreamed of finding a seamstress of talent who would make them something as good as the great establishments could turn out. And when they got it, was it really good? They would torment themselves, and would ask even a boy who loved beautiful things, and knew the names of materials and ways of cutting them, and what colors went together.

Here was Beauty ready to be launched in a costume about which her son had been hearing talk for weeks: a ball dress of pink tulle, with simili diamonds put on the skirt in three-tier pleated flounces. The corsage was a little coat of heavy guipure lace embroidered with amethysts and gold. It was cut in that ultra style which had caused an old gentleman at a dinner party to say that he couldn't express an opinion of the ladies' costumes because he hadn't looked under the table. The plump and creamy-white bust of Beauty appeared on the point of emerging from the corsage, like Venus from the waves, all that prevented it being two little straps made of flat links of gold. The tiny dancing slippers were of tissue of gold incrusted with gems, and the high heels took you back to Empire days, having flower designs worked on them in jewels.

"Well, how do you like me?" asked the mother, and Lanny said he liked her well enough to dance with her all night if she needed him. She gave him eager little pats on the head, but he mustn't kiss her because of her powder.

Then he had to admire the costume of the Baroness de la Tourette, likewise completed after labors and consultations. Sophie's crown of henna hair topped a gown of brocade; roses and rose leaves in silver on a ground of rich blue, very supple, and draped graciously—so said its creator, a *couturier* who was on hand to approve the final effect, and who rubbed his hands together with delight. The gown had a narrow train from the waist, to be held up for dancing, and a deep belt of dark blue velvet, with pleatings of silver lace carried to make kimono sleeves. There was a Cavalier cape of fine old Brussels lace weighted with embroidery of diamonds and gold; and slippers of stamped velvet to match, also embroidered with diamonds. The only difference was that Sophie's were real, while Beauty's were not, and would people notice the difference? It was terrible to feel yourself just an imitation.

But Sophie, good soul, said: "Nonsense! None of the richest people wear their valuable gems any more. They keep them stored in vaults and wear replicas."

"Yes, of course," said Beauty. "But then everybody knows they have the real ones; and everybody knows I haven't!"

"Forget it!" commanded the hardware manufacturer's daughter. "You've got what not one in a hundred has, and most of them would give their eyeteeth for." Kind Sophie said things like that.

Beauty put one more dab of powder on her little white nose, and there was Harry Murchison waiting for her, tall, well set up, looking like a fashion plate. Lanny watched them get into the rich young American's motorcar, and went back into the house, reckoning the months before he, too, would have a full-dress suit and an opera hat, and be able to take his mother to balls at the Savoy Hotel!

VI

Lanny, left alone, went out for a walk. He liked to walk anywhere, but especially in the streets of London. At this time of year it didn't get dark until after nine o'clock, and meantime there were mists and haze and pastel colors in the sky. Lanny would walk by the Serpentine River in Hyde Park, and watch the beautiful black and white swans; he would walk along the Embankment, observing the clouds across the river, and the tugs and launches gliding over the dull gray surface. Sometimes he would climb to the top of one of those new motorbusses, from which for thruppence you could see everything there was in London—seven million people, and nobody had ever counted how many houses, or how many cabs, carriages, and automobiles.

The city had been laid out by ancient Saxon or Roman cows, and rarely had their paths been straight. One village had run into another, all higgledy-piggledy; and where was Bandbox Lane High

Court, or Old Pine Hill New Corners?—you might be within a quarter of a mile of the place, but you couldn't find a soul who had ever heard of it. Few streets had the same name for any distance; you would start walking on the Strand, and presently it was Fleet Street, and then it was Ludgate Hill, Cannon Street, Fenchurch, Aldgate—and like as not would evaporate and disappear entirely. The same peculiarity was shared by the old buildings; you would go down a corridor, and descend three steps, and turn to the left, pass three doors and climb a winding stairway, turn to the right, walk a dozen steps—and knock on a door which hadn't been opened for a hundred years.

Lanny felt in an adventurous mood that evening and started off in a new direction. For a while he was on a wide thoroughfare, with motorcars taking people to the theaters, and crowds looking into windows of gaily decorated shops. Then little by little the neighborhood changed; the shops became poorer, the men wore caps, and the women dingy shawls. The street began to ramble, and Lanny did the same; he was keeping in a general easterly direction, but that didn't mean anything special, for he had never heard of the East End of London. He had the general idea that the seven million population was composed mainly of ladies and gentlemen such as he had seen in Mayfair, with their servants and tradespeople, and a sprinkling of saucy flower girls, lively newsboys, and picturesque old beggars trying to sell you "a box o' lights."

But now Lanny had walked through a looking glass, or plunged down a shaft to the center of the earth, or to the bottom of the sea; he had taken a drug, or fallen into a trance—something or other that had transported him into a new world. He couldn't believe his eyes, and walked on, fascinated, staring; it just couldn't be real, there couldn't be such creatures on earth! English men and women were tall, and stood up straight, and took bold strides, and had long thin faces, sometimes a little too long, especially the women—Robbie impolitely called them horse-faces! Both men and women whom Lanny had met had rosy complexions, sometimes alarmingly so, suggestive of apoplexy. But suddenly here were creatures squat and stooped, that shambled instead of walking; their legs were short and their arms long—they looked like apes more than human beings! Features crooked, teeth missing, complexions sallow or pasty—no, this couldn't be England!

And the clothes they had on! Lanny had never seen such rags, never dreamed they existed on earth. Clothes that were not fitted to the human form, but dangled as on scarecrows, and when they threatened to fall to pieces were fastened with pins or bits of string, or even pieces of wood. They were filthy with every sort of grime and grease, and gave out the musty acrid smell of stale human sweat; the sum total of it filled the streets and polluted the winds that blew from the North Sea.

And the swarms of these creatures! Where did they come from, and where could they go? The sidewalks were crowded, so that you had to jostle your way. There were no longer any motorcars or carriages, and few horse-drawn vehicles, only pushcarts, called "barrows." Many had things to sell, things that must surely have been gathered out of dustbins: old rags of clothing, as bad as what the people had on; worn, badly patched shoes set in rows along the curb; the cheapest vegetables, wilted and bruised; stinking fish, scraps of meat turned purple or black, old rusty pans, chipped and damaged crockery, all the rubbish of the world. Shops had it spread out in front, and shopkeepers stood watching, while dingy women with bedraggled skirts pulled things about and smelled and chaffered and argued. Tired workingmen sat on the steps, puffing at pipes. Babies swarmed everywhere, ghostly death's-head children suckled on gin. There were innumerable garbage cans, and hardly one without some human creature digging in it for food.

Every other place, it seemed, was a pub. Murmurs and sometimes uproar came from within, and now and then a drunken man would push back the swinging doors and stagger forth—bringing with him a reek of alcohol, and more of that dreadful animal stench, and shouts and curses in a language bearing odd resemblances to the one that Lanny used. He would listen and try to puzzle out the words. A young woman with a ragged straw hat, pulling herself loose from a man: "Blymee, I 'ave ter git the dyner fer me bybee!" What was that? And two fellows coming out of a pub wiping big mustaches on coatsleeves and carrying on an argument, one shouting at the other: "Ow, gow an' be a Sowcialist!"

VII

The sun had gone down behind Lanny's back, and twilight was letting down its veils over this strange nightmare. One who thought of being a painter might have noted interesting effects of darkness and shadow; somber brick tenements, three or four stories high, blackened with the smoke of centuries; forests of chimney pots pouring out new blackness all the time; sodden human figures, shawl-clad and hunched, growing dimmer in the twilight, blending into the shadows of walls and doorways and dustbins full of trash. But Lanny wasn't thinking about art; he was overcome with more direct, more human emotions. That there should be a world like this, so near to the glittering hotel where his mother and her friends were dancing in their jeweled gowns and slippers! That there should be human beings of English blood, sunk to this state of squalor!

Lanny was beginning to be uneasy. This slum appeared to be endless, and he didn't know how to get out of it. He had been told that any time he lost his way, he should ask a "bobby," but there appeared to be none in this lost world, and Lanny didn't know if it was safe to speak to any of these lost people. The men seemed to be looking at him with hostile eyes, and the leering women frightened him no less. "Two bob to you, mytey!" a girl would say, holding out her hands with what she meant for a seductive gesture. Starved children followed him, beggars whined and showed their sores and crippled limbs; he hurried on, being afraid to take out his purse.

Darkness was falling fast. The shopping district of the slum came to an end, and Lanny, trying to find a better neighborhood, followed a street that widened out. There were sheds, and gravel under foot; dimly he could see benches, and people sitting on them—the same terrible ape figures in stinking rags, men and women and children:

a baby laid on its back, and no one even troubling to put a cover on it; whole families huddled near together; a bearded man with his head back, snoring, a woman curled up against him; a man and a woman lying in each other's arms.

A raw wind had sprung up, and Lanny felt chilly, even while he was walking; but these people sat or lay, never moving. Could it be that they had no place to go? The boy had observed human forms curled up alongside dustbins and sheds, and had supposed they must be drunk; but could it be that they slept out all night?

He pressed on, still more hurriedly; he was beginning to be really afraid now. He had broken his promise to his mother, never to go anywhere except where plenty of people were to be seen. He was in a dark street, and the figures that passed were slinking and furtive, and many seemed to be watching him. He saw two women fighting, shrieking at each other, pulling hair; children stood watching them, apathetic and silent.

It was a street of tenements, but now and then came a pub, with lights and sounds of roistering. A man came out, and as he swung the doors open, the light fell on Lanny. The stranger fell in beside him on the narrow sidewalk. " 'Ullo, little tyke!" said he.

Lanny thought he ought to be polite. "Hello," he replied; and the fellow doubtless noted something different about his accent. "Whur yer bound fer, mytey?" he demanded.

"I don't know," replied Lanny, hesitatingly. "I'm afraid maybe I'm lost."

"Ho! Little toff!" exclaimed the other. "Little toff come inter the slums lookin' fer mayflowers, eh, wot?" He was a burly fellow, and in the light of the pub the boy had seen that his face was grimy, as if he were a coal heaver; or perhaps it was several days' growth of beard. His breath reeked of alcohol. "Listen, mytey," he said, leaning over cajolingly, "gimme a bob, will yer? Me throat is so dry it burns up, it fair do."

This was a problem for the boy. If he took out his purse the fellow would probably grab it. "I'm sorry, I haven't any money with me," said he.

"Garn!" snarled the other, turning ugly at once. "A toff don't go withaht no brass."

They had come to a dark place in the street, and Lanny had just decided to make a dash for it, when to his terror the man grabbed him by the arm. "Cough up!" he commanded.

Lanny struggled; then, finding that the fellow's grip was too strong, he screamed: "Help! Help!"

"Shut yer bloomin' fyce," growled the man, "or I'll bryke every bone in yer body!" He fetched the boy a cuff on the side of the head. It was the first time that Lanny had ever been struck in his whole life, and it had a terrifying effect on him; he became frantic, he twisted and struggled, harder than ever, and shouted at the top of his lungs.

The ruffian began to drag him toward a dark opening leading into a court. Lanny's cries brought people to doors and windows, but not one moved a hand to help him; they just stood and looked. They were interested, but not concerned—as if it were a Punch and Judy show.

But suddenly a door in the court was flung open, and a light streamed upon the scene. A young woman emerged, wild-looking, with tousled black hair and a blouse open at the throat and hanging out at the waist, as if she had put it on in a hurry. When she saw the man and his victim, she darted toward them. "Wot yer doin', Slicer?"

The answer was, "Shut yer silly fyce!" But the girl began shouting louder: "'Ave yer gone barmy, ye bleedin' fool? Carnt yer see the kid's a toff? An' right in front of yer own drum!" When the man continued to drag Lanny into the court, she rushed at him like a wildcat. "Cut it, I sye! Yer'll 'ave the tecs 'ere, an' we'll all do a stretch!"

He called her a "bitch," and she told the world in return that he was a "muckworm." When he still wouldn't give up, she began clawing at his face in a fury. He had to take one hand to push her away, and that gave Lanny his chance; with a frantic effort he tore himself loose and dashed for the street.

The crowd gave way; it wasn't theirs to stop him. The man came pounding behind, cursing; but Lanny hadn't been climbing mountains and swimming in the Golfe Juan and practicing Muscovite leaps for nothing. He was built like a deer, whereas the man was heavy and clumsy, and presently he gave up. But the boy didn't stop until he had got to a thoroughfare thronged with long-bearded Jews and curly-headed babies, and having signs that said: "Whitechapel High Street."

Then a blue uniform, the one sight that could really bring an end to Lanny's terror. The London bobby didn't carry weapons, like the French gendarme, but he was a symbol of the Empire. Lanny waited until he got back his breath and could speak normally, then he approached and said: "Please, would you tell me how to get to the tube?"

The bobby had a large blue helmet, with a strap across his chin. He answered like an automaton: "First t'right, second t'left." He said it very fast, and when Lanny said: "I beg pardon?" he said it again, even faster than before.

The boy thought it over, and then dropped a delicate hint: "Please, might I walk with you if you're going that way?" It was obviously not the right accent for Whitechapel, and the "copper" looked him over more carefully, and then said: "Right you are, guv'nor."

They walked together in silent state. When they parted, Lanny wasn't sure if the symbol of the Empire would accept a tip, but he took a chance, and held out a shilling which he had denied to "Slicer." The symbol took it with one hand and with the other touched his helmet. "Kew!" said he. The visitor had already had it explained to him that this was the second half of "Thank you," doing duty for the whole.

VIII

Lanny decided to say nothing to his mother about his misadventure. It would only worry her, and do no good; he had learned his lesson, and wouldn't repeat the mistake. He brooded all by himself over the state of the people of East London. When he went to call for his mother at a tea party in Kensington Gardens, the sight of exquisite ladies on the greensward under the trees made him think of the families that were lying out on benches all night because they had no place to go. Instead of snow-white tulle and pink mousseline de soie, he saw filthy and loathsome rags; instead of the fragrant concentrations of the flower gardens of Provence, he smelled the stink of rotting bodies and the reek of gin.

They drove to Ascot on the second day of the races, the day of the gold vase. It was known as a "black and white" Ascot, because of the costumes decreed by the fashion dictators. He saw black and white striped taffeta dresses with black and white parasols to match. He listened to the chatter of his mother and her friends, commenting upon the fashion parade—froufrou hats, broché effects, corsage prolonged into polonaise, shot silk draped as tunic, butterfly wing confection, black liseré straw, poufs of tea-rose taffeta, bandeau hats and plume towers, cothurns of lizard-green suede—and all the while he would be seeing babies lying on benches with only rags to cover them. He watched the royal procession, the King and Queen riding across the turf amid thunderous cheers from the crowd, and he thought: "I wonder if they know about it!"

The person he took into his confidence was Rick; and Rick said that people knew if they chose to know, but mostly they didn't. He said those conditions were as old as England. The politicians talked about remedying them, but when they got elected they thought about getting elected again. He said it was a problem of educating those slum people; of raising the tone of the intellectual and art life of the country. He took Lanny to a matinee of a play by Bernard Shaw which was the rage that season, and dealt with a flower girl who talked just the sort of Cockney that Lanny had heard during his descent into hell. A professor of phonetics succeeded in correcting her accent, making her into a regular lady of Mayfair. It was most amusing—and it seemed to be in line with Rick's suggestion.

Kurt Meissner arrived, and he, too, was taken into the discussion.

Said Kurt: "We don't leave our poor to the mercies of the wage market. The Germans are efficient, and provide decent housing for the workers, and insurance against sickness, old age, and unemployment." Kurt was perhaps a little too well satisfied with conditions in his country, and too contemptuous of British slackness. Rick, who was willing to make any number of sarcastic remarks about his native land, wasn't so pleased to hear them from a foreigner. Rick and Kurt didn't get along so well in London as they had in Hellerau.

Lanny talked about the question of poverty with his mother also, and Beauty assured him that the kind English people were not overlooking the problem. He would soon see proof of it; the twenty-fourth of June was known as "Alexandra Day," and the fashionable ladies of England honored their Queen Mother by putting on their daintiest white frocks and hats with many flowers and going out on the streets of the cities to sell artificial pink roses for the benefit of the overcrowded hospitals. Lanny saw his mother, the loveliest sight in Piccadilly Circus, taking in silver coins hand over fist; he had to drive three times in one of Lord Eversham-Watson's cars to keep her supplied with stock in trade. He hoped that he might be able to provide accommodations for all those babies who were sleeping outdoors on benches.

9

Green and Pleasant Land

I

THE home of Sir Alfred Pomeroy-Nielson was called "The Reaches," and was close to the Thames River some way below

Oxford. It was a very old place, and not much had been done to modernize it, because, as Rick explained, his father was too poor; they had all they could do to keep the place, and not much left for their beloved arts. There was a little bit of everything in the architecture of the house: an old tower, a peaked roof with gables, mullioned windows, a crenelated wall, a venerable archway through which you drove to the porte-cochere. The structures were jammed one against another, and topping them all were chimney pots, sometimes three or four in a row. This meant that all the year except summer the maidservants were busy carrying coal scuttles; and since there was very little running water, when they had finished with scuttles they carried pails.

But, of course, in summertime everybody went to the river, crossing a beautiful sloping lawn under an archway of aged oaks. It was a new kind of swimming for Lanny, and he thought he could never get enough of it. The boys lived in bathing suits, and "punted" in a long flat-bottomed boat with a ten-foot pole. It was a nice friendly little river, neither wide nor deep. Boathouses lined it, and gaily decorated motorboats went by, and long thin shells, with oarsmen practicing for the coming races. It was a holiday thoroughfare, and there was laughter and singing; the three musketeers of the arts sang all the songs they knew.

Rick had a sister, two years older than himself, and therefore too old for either of the visitors; but she had friends with younger sisters, so there was a troop of English girls bright-cheeked and jolly, interested in everything the boys were doing, and sharing their sports. Lanny was just at the age where he was preparing to discover that girls were wonderful, and here they were.

Sir Alfred Pomeroy-Nielson was a middle-aged gentleman, tall and slender, with handsome dark mustaches turning gray, sharp features, a hawk's nose, and keen dark eyes. He had a Spanish mother, and maybe a trace of Jewish blood, as Rick had said. He was a lover of all the arts and friend of all the artists. He knew many rich people, and acted as a sort of go-between for the bohemian world; telling the "swells" what was what in art and helping the struggling

geniuses to find patrons. An impecunious playwright would bring
him a blank-verse tragedy, and Sir Alfred would decide that it was
a masterpiece, and would design a group of magnificent sets for it;
then he would set out to find a backer, and when he failed he would
declare that England was going to the dogs. He had very high standards, and would relieve his disappointments by composing sharp
epigrams.

It was a free and easy world which he had made for himself within
his castle. The most extreme opinions were freely voiced, and it was
everybody's pride not to be shocked. But at the same time it would
be better not to commit any lapse of table etiquette, and when you
took off your bathing suit you put on the right sort of clothes. This
made an odd mixture of convention and scorn for convention, and a
boy with American parents had now and then to ask his friend for
guidance. Rick would give it with an apology. "The older people
try to be mod'n, but they really aren't quite up to it."

Kurt Meissner found even greater difficulties, because he was stiff
and serious and couldn't get used to the idea of saying things that
you didn't entirely mean. "In a Pickwickian sense," was the English
phrase, and what was a youth from a province of Prussia to make of
it? Kurt was puzzled by their habit of running down their own
country; what they said about the state of England was what Kurt
himself believed, but he couldn't get used to the idea of Englishmen
saying it. They would even discuss the desirability of getting rid of
their royal family. "The Prince of Wales is going to turn out to be
another dancing boy," Sir Alfred would remark blandly; "a ladies'
man like his grandfather."

And then the suffragettes! The son of the comptroller-general of
Castle Stubendorf had read in the newspapers about maniacal creatures who were pouring acids into letter boxes and chaining themselves to the railings of the House of Commons in order to prove
their fitness to have the vote; but never in his wildest moment had
it occurred to him that he might be called upon to sit at dinner
table with one of these creatures, and to take her punting upon the
Thames! But here was Mildred Noggyns, nineteen years old, the

daughter of a former undersecretary in the government; pretty, but pale and rather grim, only three weeks out of Holloway gaol after having chopped a hole in the painted face of the Velásquez Venus, most highly prized treasure of the National Gallery. And talking quite calmly about it, discussing the "cat-and-mouse act," by which the authorities were combating hunger strikes; they let you out of jail when they thought you were near dying, and took you back again as soon as you had picked up a bit.

Rick's sister, Jocelyn, abetted her; and of course these saucy ladies soon found out what was in the haughty soul of the Junker from Silesia, and it became their delight to tease him beyond endurance. They wouldn't let him help them into a punt. "No, thank you, all that nonsense is over, chivalry, and bowing and scraping before women; we're quite able to get into punts by ourselves, and we'll do our share of handling the pole, if you please. And what do you mean when you say that man is gregarious, and that man is a spiritual being, and so on? Do you refer to lordly males like yourself, or do you deign to include the females? And if you include us, why don't you say so? Of course, we know it's just a way of speaking, but it's a benighted way devised by men, and we object to it."

"Yes, Miss Noggyns," Kurt would reply, "but unfortunately I have not learned any word in your language which expresses the concept 'man and woman.'" When the feminist lady proposed that they should create such a word, Kurt replied, gravely: "I have found it hard enough to learn the English language as it exists, without presuming to add anything to it."

II

The three boys discussed the matter among themselves. Kurt thought that the revolt of women meant the breakdown of English society; it was like the "war of the members" in one of the fables of Aesop. Lanny hoped that, if women got the vote, society might be kinder and there wouldn't be so much talk about war. Rick said: "It won't make much difference, one way or the other; the women'll

divide about as the men do, and there'll be more votes to count."
Generally when these three argued they had different opinions—and
when they finished, they still had them.

Of course they talked about girls, and what was called the "sex
problem." No one of the three had as yet had a sex experience. Kurt
said that he had had opportunities; the peasant girls were often willing enough, and looked upon it as an honor that a gentleman would
do them; but Kurt had the idea of saving himself for a great and
worthy love. Lanny remembered what the Social-Democratic editor
had said about Kurt's father, but of course he wouldn't breathe a
word of that.

Rick said, rather casually: "If a sex experience comes my way I'll
probably take it; I think people make more fuss about it than is
necessary—especially since methods of birth control are generally
known. It seems to me the women are waking up and will attend to
changing our ideas."

"I'd hate to put Miss Mildred Noggyns in charge of *my* ideas,"
replied Kurt; and they all laughed.

Lanny, desiring to contribute something to the conversation, told
about his unpleasant experience with Baron Livens-Mazursky. Rick,
young man of the world, said that homosexuality was spreading, it
was one of the consequences of the false morality of Puritanism.
"There's a plague of it in our public schools," he declared. "The
boys hide their share from the masters, and the masters hide their
share from the boys, or think they do."

This was one time that Kurt didn't try to prove that Germany
was superior to England. "It's bad in our army," he said. Lanny decided to tell how he had unwittingly got into conversation with a
Social-Democratic editor in a railway station, and the man had repeated evil rumors about high-up persons. "Such an editor would
believe the worst about our ruling classes," said Kurt.

They talked also about something that had happened the other
day in Sarajevo, capital of the province of Bosnia; the Austrian arch-
duke, heir to the throne of the Empire, had been on an official tour
with his wife, and the two of them had been murdered while riding

in their motorcar. Rick and Lanny had heard their elders discussing
it, but hadn't paid much attention; Kurt now explained that Bosnia
was a province of Austria inhabited mostly by Slavs, an inferior and
disorderly people. "They are always agitating against the Austrian
authorities," he said, "and the Serbians across the border encourage
them. The murder was committed by students, and naturally the
Austrians will have to take strong measures to punish the conspirators."

The other two were interested in the story, but as something far
off that didn't mean much to them. It was politics; and they were
all agreed that politics was an activity which artists were in duty
bound to look upon with contempt. All three were dedicated to the
service of the ideal. "*Im Ganzen, Guten, Wahren resolut zu leben*"
—so Goethe had taught, and Kurt repeated it to the other two. The
diplomats in the Balkans would continue to squabble, but men of
superior mind would pass over such headlines in the newspapers,
and give their attention to the reviews of Ravel's *Daphnis and Chloe*,
then being superbly danced by the Russian ballet.

III

Another event of the moment was the Royal Regatta at Henley-
on-Thames. Amateur oarsmen from many parts of the world assembled, and the river was put upon the map for three days. There were
two American crews among them, so Lanny had a chance to feel
patriotic. The finals were rowed on Saturday, and Lanny's mother
came with a motoring party from London, and met the family who
were hosts to her boy. Of course these free and "mod'n" people
didn't concern themselves about her divorce, and she was lovely in
her simple white frock, of what the French call *mousseline de com-
munion*, and a jardiniere hat with pink hedge roses held in place by
a white chiffon veil several yards in length. At her throat was a
diamond bow brooch that also looked simple—unless you knew that
it was set in platinum.

Harry Murchison drove the party, and had servants following in another car, to set up tables and spread an elaborate "breakfast" on the lawn of The Reaches. It was a festivity without a single flaw—unless you counted the fact that wasps persisted in getting stuck in the jam. Afterwards they motored to Henley, and the Pomeroy-Nielsons invited them to a private enclosure of one of the rowing clubs, from which they had a view of the finish. The course had been marked off with piles driven, and booms, and there were no launches and no high wind to trouble the oarsmen, as you had on the big rivers of America: just a nice friendly sort of tea-party place, so that oarsmen rowing down the course could hear the conversation of spectators on both banks. On one side was a towpath, on which the crowd ran or bicycled; on the other side, behind the booms, were punts and rowboats crowded together like sampans on a Chinese river.

It was a gay scene; the men wore blazers with the colors of their rowing clubs, while the ladies in their bright gowns lolled upon silken cushions. Of course you wouldn't expect an English crowd to roar and cheer like an American one. "Well rowed, Harvard!" would be the proper expression of enthusiasm. It happened that the final in the eight-oar event for the Grand Challenge Cup was rowed by two American crews, one composed of Harvard undergraduates, and the other of Harvard graduates; so there were many crimson flags and nasal New England accents. Oddly enough, the race was rowed on the Fourth of July, so the Americans had to be careful not to give offense to their well-mannered hosts.

Only one thing marred a perfect day for Lanny Budd: that was the attention which Harry Murchison was so obviously paying to his mother. It was Harry who helped her out of the motorcar, and Harry who helped her in again, and it happened to be Harry who caught her when one of her fancy high-heeled slippers caused her ankle to turn. He was a good-looking and agreeable fellow, and the Pomeroy-Nielsons could have no reason to criticize his interest in an unattached woman—but that would be because they didn't know about Marcel Detaze. But Lanny thought of Marcel down there at the Cap, painting diligently; he must be lonely, and wondering when his Beauty would get through with the social whirl and return to the life of art and love.

She was going back to France right after this race—but not going home yet. She had been invited to spend a fortnight with Mrs. Emily Chattersworth, an American friend who lived on the Riviera in winter and in a château near Paris in summer. From a bit of conversation Lanny now gathered that Harry Murchison was motoring her there, and would be in Paris and take her to a fête champêtre. Lanny couldn't get away from the disturbing thought: was this too-agreeable heir of a plate-glass factory in Pennsylvania trying to win the love of his mother? And if so, where did Marcel come in? Had Beauty begun to tire of her painter? A whole new set of problems for a youngster who was supposed to have learned all the facts of life!

IV

Among the girls who came to The Reaches was the daughter of an army officer by the name of Rosemary Codwilliger, which you pronounced Culliver. She had hazel eyes and smooth thick hair the color of straw, and very regular, rather grave features—she might have served as model for a girlish Minerva, goddess of wisdom. She was a year older than Lanny, and took a maternal attitude toward him, which he liked, being a mother's boy. Rosemary was fascinated by "Dalcroze," and would watch Lanny and Rick and imitate what they did, and was very good at it. She had been to the Riviera and knew the places Lanny knew, so they had plenty to talk about.

When the young couples strolled apart, it would be Rosemary and Lanny. They were sitting near the river, watching the last tints of the fading day; a single very bright star, and no sound on the river, but up at the house Kurt Meissner playing the slow movement of Mozart's D minor piano concerto. A lovely melody, tender and touching, floated down to them; it died to a whisper, rose again, and then again, in different forms, an infinite variety. It whispered of love and beauty, it captivated the soul and led it into a heaven of ecstasy, pure yet passionate.

It was one of those rare moments in which new possibilities of the
spirit seem to be unveiled; and when at last the music died away,
neither of them moved for a while. Lanny felt the girl's hand touching his; he returned the pressure gently, and again they were still.
A faint breeze stirred tiny ripples on the surface of the water, and
caused the evening star's reflection to shiver and tremble. In the soul
of Lanny something of the same kind began to happen, the strangest,
indescribable sense of delight pervading his being. He leaned closer
to the girl, who seemed to feel the same way.

The music had begun again. Kurt was playing something that
Lanny didn't know. It sounded like Beethoven; slow and mournful,
a lament for mankind and the suffering men inflict upon one another. But the magic of art turns sorrow into beauty, pain into ecstasy; the young people were flooded with an emotion which caused
their two hands to tighten and tremble, and tears to start down their
cheeks. When the music died again, Lanny whispered: "Oh, that
was so sweet!" Not a brilliant observation, but the tones of his voice
were eloquent.

Rosemary's reply startled him. "You may kiss me, Lanny."

He hadn't known that he wanted to kiss her; probably he wouldn't
have dared to think of it. But he realized at once that it would be
pleasant to kiss her—very gently, respectfully, of course. So he
planned; but when he touched his lips to hers, her arms folded about
him, and they clung together in a long embrace. Those strange thrills
became more intense, they suffused the boy's whole being. He seemed
to know what all the music of the world was about, what it was
trying to express. He wanted nothing but to stay there, perfectly
still, and have Kurt go on playing sweet, sad melodies.

Somebody came along, interrupting them, so they got up and
went into the house. Lanny's cheeks were flushed, but Rosemary
was as cool and serene as the girlish Minerva, goddess of wisdom.
Whenever she looked at Lanny she smiled, a gentle smile, at once a
reassurance and a pledge of happiness to come.

So after that, whenever circumstances permitted, those two wandered off by themselves. As soon as they were alone, their hands

would come together; and when they found a sheltered spot, or darkness to protect them, their arms would be about each other and their lips would meet. They never went any further; Lanny would have been shocked by the idea, and the girl did not invite it. They were at a stage where happiness came easily, and in satisfactory abundance.

It was long before Lanny admitted to himself that these thrills had anything to do with that puzzling thing called "sex" that people were always talking about. No, this was something rare and exalted, a secret bliss which they alone had discovered, and concerning which they would breathe no whisper to anyone else. At least that is what Lanny said, and Rosemary smiled her wise, motherly smile, and said: "You dear!"

They both kept the secret; and when the time came for Lanny to go back to town, the girl told him it would be just "*au revoir.*" "My mother is talking about the Riviera for next winter," she said. "We'll write to each other, and surely not forget how happy we've been."

Lanny answered: "I'll think of it every time I listen to music or play it. And that will be often!"

V

One other adventure before the boy left that green and pleasant land. Kurt had gone up to London to meet his uncle's friends. Rick had to do some studying; owing to his preoccupation with the arts, he had failed in his mathematics and had to stand an examination in the fall. Lanny read for a while, and then went for a walk.

It was delightful country, with a great variety of prospects; the land owners had a right to bar you from their property, but they generally didn't, and there were lanes and footpaths, with stiles over the fences, and little dells with streams running through them. Summer was at its height; the sun, not having long to stay, did its best by shining for long hours, and the green things made the most of their opportunity, crowding to the light. A very different world from Provence; greener trees, and landscapes more intimate and friendly, warmer to the heart if not to the thermometer.

Lanny rambled, turning wherever he saw anything that interested him, and not caring where he went; he knew the names of villages near The Reaches, and anybody could tell him the way. When it was time to go back, he trusted to luck. He found himself on the edge of a patch of woodland, with a fence as you entered, and a stile to enable you to step over it; he sat there to rest, and saw a figure moving on another path, which crossed his at the farther edge of the patch of woods. It was a girl, and Lanny couldn't see clearly, but it appeared that she was carrying something over her shoulder; then, as he watched, she suddenly disappeared and he didn't see her again. He was puzzled, because there seemed to be no drop in the ground. Could it be that the girl had fallen?

His curiosity was aroused, and he climbed over the stile and went toward the place. Sure enough, there was the girl lying flat on the ground, and a sack of turnips, some of them having spilled out when she fell. Lanny ran toward her, and saw that she was about of his own age, barefooted, wearing a torn and dirty old skirt and blouse; her hair hadn't been combed, and she was far from prepossessing. It looked as if she had fainted; anyhow, there she lay, and Lanny noticed that her skin was bloodless and that she was emaciated to a painful degree. He might have decided that she was drunk, but instead he guessed that she hadn't had enough to eat.

He had heard somewhere that when people fainted you dashed cold water in their faces and slapped their hands. He tried the latter, but perhaps didn't put enough energy into it. He looked and saw buildings some distance beyond the wood, and ran toward them and found a row of cottages close together, of the sort which look picturesque in old etchings. They might have been as old as Queen Anne, or as Elizabeth; they had low thatched roofs, small windows, and doorways not quite regular, and so low that even Lanny had to bend his head to enter. He saw a woman in front of them and ran to her, calling that there was a girl lying out there on the ground. The woman was tousle-headed and red-faced, and she said, dully:

"It'll be that Higgs gel, over thurr," and pointed to one of the cottages.

Lanny ran to the place and knocked on the door. It was opened after a while by a woman with straggly hair and only three teeth visible. The English poor, whenever they had a toothache, simply pulled the tooth out; no doubt many a woman who looked like this one had been hanged or burned for a witch. "Aye, it'll be Madge," she said, with no great excitement. She got him some water in a pail, and he went running with it.

By dint of throwing handfuls in the girl's face he got her eyes open by the time the woman arrived. They lifted her to her feet and the woman helped her to the cottage, while Lanny lugged the turnips. Stooping under the doorway, they laid the girl on the bed, which consisted of a mattress stuffed with straw on a board frame. The girl's skin was transparent and looked like wax; she closed her eyes, and Lanny couldn't be sure whether she had fainted again or not.

"Hadn't you better give her something to eat?" he asked; and the reply was: "There's nowt in the house." This bewildered him. "But what do you do?" he demanded, and the woman said, dully: "The man'll bring summat when he comes, belike."

That didn't satisfy this good Samaritan. He wanted to know if there wasn't some place where he could purchase food, and the woman told him where to find a shop. It proved to be a miserable place, with flyspecked peppermints and gumdrops in the window. He bought a loaf of bread, a tin of beans, and a rusty one of salmon, his guess at a balanced diet. When he got back to the cottage he found that there was no tin-opener, and he had to break into the tins with a knife and a block of wood. When he put the food before the girl, she wolfed it like a famished animal, leaving only part of the bread.

Lanny looked about him. He had read a poem called "The Cottar's Saturday Night." He hadn't been quite sure what a "cottar" was, but now he was in the home of one. It didn't bear much resemblance to the poem. A dark-colored clay had been stuffed into chinks of the walls, and the floor was of planks, very old and worn. The fireplace was black with the smoke of ages. There was another bed like the one the girl was lying on, and a table apparently knocked together by amateur hands, and three stools, each with three peg legs. There was also a row of shelves with a few pans and dishes, and some ancient clothing hanging on the walls, and a water bucket on the floor. That was about all.

One place on the floor was wet, and the woman saw Lanny's eyes resting upon it. "It's the roof," said she. "The blurry landlord won't have it fixed." Lanny asked who was the landlord, and the reply was: "Sir Alfred." It gave the boy a start. "Sir Alfred Pomeroy-Nielson?" The woman answered: "Aye, he's the stingy one, he'll do nowt for ye, not if the house was to blow down."

VI

So Lanny had something to think about on his short walk to The Reaches. He wasn't sure if he ought to mention the matter to his hosts, but he decided that they'd be apt to hear about it, and would think it unnatural that he had kept silence. Lanny went to Rick and told him; good old Rick, who never got embarrassed about anything. Rick said: "It's that good-for-nothing old laborer, Higgs. He's a sot that spends every penny he can get his hands on for drink. What can you do for such a family? The pater's been talking of getting rid of him for a long time, and he should have done it." Rick added that he'd tell his father; but he didn't invite Lanny to the conference. Lanny had an uncomfortable feeling, as if he had opened a closed door and a family skeleton had tumbled out.

The Pomeroy-Nielsons thanked him for his good deed, and Rick took the trouble to explain matters further. The land on which those cottages stood belonged to the family, but the tenants worked for other people. "Most of them are behind with their rent," said Rick, "because the pater's reluctant to press them as other landlords do. The old tenements are nothing but a nuisance, and he has often thought of razing them and plowing the land." The son of the family added, with one of his dry smiles, that of course that wouldn't go very far toward solving the housing question; but you couldn't expect a man to be an authority on both art and economics.

Lady Pomeroy-Nielson was a stoutish, motherly person who looked after the boys and made them change their shoes when they got wet. She was kind, and told Lanny that she would take the poor child a basket of food. "But I fear it won't do much good," she added, "unless I stay and see it eaten. That Higgs is a rough fellow, and he'll take anything he can get his hands on and sell it for a drink."

Rick discussed with his guest the problem of poverty in England's green and pleasant land. He declared that when human beings got below a certain level, it was very difficult to help them; drink and drugs took the place of food and they finished themselves off. Lanny said his father had explained that to him, but he had thought it applied only to city slums; it had never occurred to him that there might be slums in the country. Rick said there could be little difference between country and city; if there was an oversupply of labor in one it shifted immediately to the other. In the hop-picking season, hundreds of thousands of people from London's East End spread out over the country looking for work, and if they found conditions a bit better on the land, some of them would stay.

It was an insoluble problem—as Rick, and Rick's father, and Lanny's father agreed; but all the same Lanny couldn't forget the feel of the pitiful thin body that he had lifted, the waxen skin, and the frantic look in the girl's eyes when food was held out to her. Nor could he drive from his mind the impolite thought that, if he were an English landed gentleman, he would have his lovely green lawn a trifle less perfectly manicured, and spend the money on keeping the roofs of his cottages in repair.

VII

There had come a cablegram from Robbie; he was sailing from New York on the *Lusitania*, and would be at the Hotel Cecil on a certain day. Of course a summons from Robbie took precedence over all other affairs. Lanny went to town the night before, and telephoned the steamship office to find out at what hour the steamer was due. The boy was sitting in the lobby, reading a book, but looking up every few minutes, and when the familiar sturdy figure appeared in the doorway, he sprang up to welcome his father. It was a hot July morning, and perspiration glistened on Robbie's forehead, but he looked well and vigorous as always, and everything he wore was fresh and spotless.

It had been four or five months since his last trip, and they had a lot of news to swap. At lunch Lanny told about Greece and Africa, and the scene on board the *Bluebird*. Then he told about his adventures in the slums of London and of Berkshire. The father said: "That's the curse of England. The most depressing thing I ever saw in my life was the people of London's slums spread out on Hampstead Heath on a bank holiday; men and women lying together on the ground in broad daylight."

Robbie Budd had come on an interesting errand. The firm had completed a new gun on high-angle mountings, to be used for protection against airplanes; the season's best-seller in the armaments trade, he predicted. It would mean another battle with Zaharoff, because Vickers already had one, but it wasn't nearly so good and couldn't be fired so fast. "Are we going to wipe him out?" asked the boy eagerly; and Robbie said they would if there was such a thing as justice in the world. He said this with one of his boyish grins, and added his fear that there wouldn't be any in England for Budd's.

They made themselves comfortable in their suite. Robbie got a bottle of whisky out of his suitcase, and ordered soda and ice—the London hotels were quite "American" now, and ice was one of the signs. For Lanny there was ginger beer, the father having asked him to wait many years before he touched liquor, or smoked, or learned to play poker. He said he wished he had waited longer himself. Lanny was interested to note in how many ways parents expected their children to be wiser than themselves.

Robbie telephoned the manager of Budd's London office, and while waiting for him to arrive, they talked about the English and their Empire. Lanny knew the country now and took a personal interest in it, but he found that his father didn't share his enthusiasm. Robbie had been in business competition with the English, which was different from being a guest in their well-conducted homes. "They are sharp traders," he said, "and that's all right, but what gets your goat is the mask of righteousness they put on; nobody else sells armaments for the love of Jesus Christ." The Empire, he added, was run by a little group of insiders in "the City"—the financial district. "There are no harder-fisted traders anywhere; power for themselves is what they are out for, and they'll destroy the rest of the world to get and keep it."

Lanny had got the impression that they liked Americans; but Robbie said: "Not so. All that talk about 'Hands across the sea,' don't let it fool you for a moment. They're jealous of us, and the best thing they can think of about us is that we're three thousand miles away."

Lanny told about a talk with Sir Alfred, in which the baronet had deplored the great amount of graft in American political life, and had expressed satisfaction because they had nothing of the sort in Britain. "They have a lot more," said the munitions salesman, "only they call it by polite names. In our country when the political bosses want to fill their campaign chest, they put up some rich man for a high office—a 'fat cat' they call him—and he pays the bills and gets elected for a term of years. In England the man pays a much bigger sum into the party campaign chest, and he's made a marquess or a lord, and he and his descendants will govern the Empire forever after—but that isn't corruption, that's 'nobility'!"

You could see the effect of such a system in the armaments industry, Robbie went on to explain; and he didn't have to do any guessing, he was where he could watch the machinery working. "I've come to England with a better gun than Vickers is making; but will the British Empire get that gun? I'm going to do my best, but I'll make a private wager that it'll be the Germans who come across first. The reason is Zaharoff and his associates. They're the best blood, so called, in England. On the board of Vickers are four marquesses and dukes, twenty knights, and fifty viscounts and barons. The Empire will do exactly what they say—and there won't be any 'graft' involved."

VIII

Robbie went about his important affairs, while Lanny learned to know the pictures in the National Gallery. Also he met Kurt's uncle, a stout and florid gentleman who told him about rubber plantations in the Dutch East Indies, and took them to lunch at a place where they could have a *rijstafel*. Rick came to town over the week-end, and they went to the opera and concerts, and to a cricket match. They had lunch with Robbie, who was glad Lanny had picked two such intelligent fellows as friends; he said he would take them to a place that would give them a thrill—the War Planes Review now being held on Salisbury Plain. Robbie had been invited by an army captain who had to do with his negotiations.

The boys were delighted, of course. They had been hearing a lot about the picturesque idea of battles fought in the air. The four of them were up early in the morning, and took a train for Salisbury, some eighty miles west of London, where Captain Finchley had a car to meet them and bring them to the camp. They spent the whole day wandering about seeing the sights. The Royal Flying Corps had put up sheds for seventy planes, and most of them were in the air or lined up on the field, a spectacle the like of which had never before been seen. The officers, of course, were proud of the enterprise and might of Britain.

The largest and newest of the machines was a Farman, and the men dubbed it "the mechanical cow." It was a frail-looking structure, a biplane spreading nearly forty feet across, the wing frames of light spruce and the surface of canvas, well coated and waterproofed. The flier sat in the open, and of course a mighty gale blew around him when he was in the air, so he was muffled up and wore a big helmet. The principal service expected of him was to obtain information as to enemy troop movements and the position of artillery; some planes were provided with wireless sets, others with photographic apparatus. That lone fellow up there was going to be pretty busy, for he also had a carbine and a couple of revolvers with which to defend himself; or he might have an explosive bomb attached to a wire cable, the idea being to get above an enemy plane and run the cable over him.

Many planes were diving and swooping, acquiring the needed skill. Some were learning a new art called "flying in formation"; others were practicing dropping objects upon stationary targets. The visitors watched them until their eyes ached, and the backs of their necks. Every now and then a new plane would take off, and the moment when it left the ground always came to the beholder as a fresh miracle: man's dream of ages realized, the conquest of the last of the elements. The visitors were introduced to some of the pilots, well-padded fellows who of course made it a matter of pride to take it all in the day's work; going up was no miracle to them, and flying around was, to tell the truth, a good deal of a bore, once you got the hang of it. One place in the sky was exactly like another, and the ground beneath was no more exciting than your parlor rug. They were practicing night flying—and that, they admitted, was something that kept you awake. Also, they were very proud because they had succeeded in "looping the loop" in a biplane, for the first time in history.

Lanny was interested to see the effect of all this upon his English friend. Eric Vivian Pomeroy-Nielson, young man of the world whose "note" was sophistication and whose motto was *nil admirari*, was stirred to eloquence by the idea of military aviation. He remarked to Lanny's father that after all England wasn't as backward as the Americans might have thought. He began asking technical questions of Captain Finchley and the fliers; he wanted to know if it wouldn't be possible to mount a machine gun in a plane, and they told him that the French were trying it. "That would be a fight to put a man on his mettle!" exclaimed Rick; a surprising remark from a youth who had been heard to speak of army men as "troglodytes."

Captain Finchley was pleased by this enthusiasm. "I wish more English boys felt that way," he remarked; "the failure of the recent recruiting is a cause of deep concern to all friends of the Empire."

Robbie Budd took the occasion to speak about the effect which this new kind of warfare was bound to have upon the position of Englishmen. It deprived them of the advantage of their island solitude. Planes were now flying the Channel, and the Americans had even devised a sort of catapult that could launch a plane from a ship. It was certain that in the next war bombs would be dropped upon munitions centers and factories; and guns that could be fired at planes and airships would surely have to be mounted at vital points. Lanny understood that his father was giving a sales talk—Captain Finchley was on the board which had to decide about the Budd gun with high-angle mountings. Robbie had told his son the previous evening that they were trying to "stall" him; they wouldn't say they would buy the gun, yet they were obviously worried by the idea of his taking it anywhere else.

IX

On their way back to town in the evening the four talked about what they had seen, and the likelihood of these dangerous contrivances being actually put to the test. Kurt Meissner was worried by a letter he had received from home; the situation in the Balkans was more serious than anybody in England seemed to realize. Robbie said, yes, but it was always that way; the English were an easygoing people and left problems for others to solve as much as possible. This was just one more crisis.

"But," exclaimed Kurt, "do the English or anybody else expect the Austrians to let Serbian hooligans incite the murder of Austrian rulers on Austrian soil?"

"The diplomats will get together and stop it," Robbie told him soothingly. Nothing to worry about.

"But it is said that the Russians are backing the Serbs!"

"I know; they're always shoving one another about. The Russians say: 'You let my Serbian friends alone.' The Germans say: 'You let my Austrian friends alone.' The French say: 'You let my Russian friends alone'—so it goes. They've been making faces at one another for hundreds of years."

"I know it, Mr. Budd—but they've been going to war, too."

"The world has been changing so fast that it no longer pays to go to war, Kurt. The nations couldn't finance a war; it would bankrupt them all."

"But," argued Kurt, "when people get angry enough, they don't stop to calculate."

"The masses don't, but they don't have the say any more. It's the financiers who decide, and they're first-class calculators. What's happened is, we've made weapons so destructive that nobody dares use them. Just to have them is enough." Robbie paused for a moment, and smiled. "Did Lanny ever tell you about his meeting with Zaharoff? The old man was worried by the thought that his armaments might some day be put to use; I suggested to him that the ideal of civilization was to spend all our energies making things we never meant to use." Robbie chuckled, and they all chuckled with him, though a bit dubiously.

A few days later Lanny set out for France to join his mother, and Robbie was packing up his Budd gun, preparatory to taking it to Germany, in an effort to wake the British up—or so he confided to his son. On that day King George was reviewing the might of the British navy off Spithead. His flagship was the *Iron Duke*, a dreadnought that could shoot away fifty thousand dollars in a single minute. Included in its armament were two twelve-pounder guns with high-angle mountings against airplanes. On that day . . .

It was the twentieth of July 1914.

10

La Belle France

I

MRS. EMILY CHATTERSWORTH was the widow of a New York banker who had once held great power, controlling railroads and trust companies and what not; he had become involved in some Congressional investigation—it had been a long time ago, and nobody remembered just what it was, but the newspapers had exhibited bad manners, and the banker had decided that his native land was lacking in refinement. His widow had inherited his fortune and, being still good-looking, was described by Sophie, Baroness de la Tourette, as "an island entirely surrounded by French suitors." Perhaps the country's laws regarding the property rights of married women were unsatisfactory to Mrs. Emily; anyhow, she had remained for years the sole mistress of Les Forêts, as her country estate was called.

The château was in French Renaissance style, a four-story structure of gray stone, built at the head of a little artificial lake. There was an esplanade in front, resembling the docks of a port, complete with several small lighthouses; when the lights were turned on at night the effect was impressive. At the front of the house, beyond the entrance drive, was a garden, the central feature of which was a great fleur-de-lis made of gold and purple flowers. Surrounding the place were smooth lawns shaded by chestnut trees, and beyond them were dark forests of beeches, for which the place had been named. In them were deer and pheasants, and in the kennels were dogs used for hunting in the fall. Among other interesting things was an orchid house, in which you might examine the strange and costly products of the jungles of South America, for as long as you could stand the moist heat in which they throve.

The rooms of this château were splendid, and had tapestries and works of art which connoisseurs came to study. Mrs. Emily knew what she had, and spoke of them with authority. She lived and entertained in the French manner, conducting what was called a salon—an arduous undertaking, a career all in itself. It meant inviting a number of celebrated men at regular intervals and giving them a chance to air their wit and erudition before others. Each one of these personages was conscious of his own importance, and resentful of the pretended importance of his rivals; to know who could get along with whom, and to reconcile all the vanities and jealousies, took skill and energy enough for a diplomat guarding the fate of nations.

Beauty Budd had very few pretensions to wit, and still fewer to erudition, but she possessed a treasure appreciated in any drawing room—she was easy to look at. She also possessed a full supply of womanly tact, and was naturally kind, and didn't quarrel with other ladies or try to take away their men. The weaker sex was supposed to do little talking at a salon; as among the fowls, it was the males who displayed the gorgeous plumage and made the loud noises. The company did not break up into groups, as was the custom in English and American drawing rooms. There would be a super-celebrity who would set the theme and do most of the expounding; the other celebrities would say their say, and the function of the hostess was to supervise and shepherd the conversation. The other ladies listened, and did not interrupt unless they were quite sure they had something supremely witty that could be uttered in a sentence or two. Generally they thought of it too late, and for that misfortune the French had a phrase, *esprit de l'escalier*, that is to say, staircase wit.

Of course it was not possible for an American woman, however wealthy, to have a really first-class salon in France. The fashionables and the intellectuals of that land were clannish, and it took a full lifetime to learn the subtleties of their differentiations. There were royalist salons and republican salons, Catholic salons and free-thought salons, literary and art salons, each its own little world, with but slight interest in foreigners. However, an American could provide a way for her fellow-countrymen to meet such Frenchmen as were international-minded, and Mrs. Emily, a handsome and stately lady, was conscientious about performing this service.

She would give dinner parties, also in the French manner, the hostess sitting midway between the ends of the table, putting the most important guest directly across from her, and then shading off to persons of least importance, who sat at the ends. There was a French phrase for that too, *le bout de table*. At dinner parties you did not chat with the person on either hand, but listened to those whose importance had been indicated by their seating. One of these was privileged to hold forth for a few minutes on any subject, and then he was expected to let the hostess indicate another performer. A cultivated people had been centuries evolving this routine, and to them it was extremely important.

II

There wasn't much place for children in Les Forêts, and they were rarely invited. But Mrs. Emily had met Lanny on the Riviera, and knew that he could be counted upon to wipe his feet before treading the heavy red velvet carpets which covered the entrance hall and went up the central stairway. He would stand for a long time looking at a painting in silence, and if he asked a question it would be an intelligent one. He never interrupted the conversation of his elders, and had listened to so many conversations that he was almost an elder himself. Mrs. Emily had suggested to Beauty that he might come and stay until they both were ready to return to Juan-les-Pins.

So here was Lanny, playing tennis with the children of the steward who managed the estate, swimming in the lake, riding the fine, high-strung horses, playing not too loudly upon a sonorous piano, and reading in a library where a pale and black-clad scholar had spent a lifetime cataloguing and watching over treasures. Here was a person worth listening to, and glad to have an audience. A week with M. Priedieu meant as much to Lanny Budd as a term in college. The old gentleman helped to orientate him in the world of books, making known to him the writers from whom he could find out about other writers; it was like giving him a map of the forests, so that he could go out and explore for himself.

Another educational influence was Mrs. Emily's mother, who was history. She had been a "Baltimore belle," and told how beautiful she used to be and how the beaux had swarmed about her. Now she was in her mid-seventies, and had lovely golden curls which looked quite natural; Lanny was surprised when his mother told him how once the sprightly old lady had rocked with laughter and thrown her curls into her plate of soup. She was painted all pink and white over her many wrinkles, and was automatically driven to exercise charm upon anything that came along in trousers.

Lanny fell under her spell, and she told him how her daughter Emily had been born amid the sounds of battle; the Fifth New York regiment, marching through Baltimore on its way to defend Washington at the outbreak of the American Civil War, had fired upon the citizens. "That fixes her age at fifty-three, so she doesn't like to have it told on her, and you must keep it a secret; but Emily herself won't be able to keep it much longer unless she consents to dye her hair. Dear me, how I do rattle on!" said Mrs. Sally Lee Sibley; and she added: "What a hideous and ruinous thing that war was, and how lucky we are who don't have to see such things!"

Lanny was moved to tell how yesterday he had heard Prince Skobelkov remark that Russia ought to bring war on right now, because his country was ready and could never be more so. The old lady looked at the boy in horror and whispered: "Oh, no, no! Don't let anybody say such a thing! Oh, what wicked people!" Mrs. Sally Lee Sibley lived in Europe because it was her fate, but privately she hated it.

III

Of course a half-grown boy was not invited to a salon or to formal dinner parties; but there were house guests, and callers in great numbers, and Lanny met them, and listened to conversations about the state of Europe, in which persons who were on the inside of affairs talked freely, being among those who had a right to know. There was a Russian military mission in Paris, and the famous general, Prince Skobelkov, was a member of it; he found time to motor out and have tea, even in the midst of a world-shaking crisis. Also the French Senator Bidou-Lascelles, who said, in American poker language: "Germany is trying to use Austria to bluff Russia, and this will go on indefinitely unless we call the bluff." The Prince assented, and added: "Our official information is that Austria is unprepared, and will prove a weak ally."

Lanny listened, and thought that he didn't like these two old men. The Russian was large, red-faced, and tightly laced up, and spoke French explosively. The senator was baldheaded and paunchy, with a white imperial that waggled somewhat absurdly; he was an ardent Catholic, and fought for his Church party in the Senate, but to Lanny he didn't seem religious, but rather a little gnome plotting dreadful things. Lanny recollected the beautiful Austrian country through which he had passed, the mountain cottages with steep roofs to shed the snow, and the inns with fancy gilded signs. He thought of Kurt Meissner, and his brothers who were in the German army. Kurt was to come to Paris in a few days, to meet his "rubber" uncle and return home with him. Lanny had thought of having him invited to Les Forêts, but decided that it wouldn't do, with people voicing opinions like these.

Mrs. Emily had thrown her estate open for a charity bazaar, and booths had been set up, decorated with bunting and huge quantities of flowers. Everybody donated things to be sold, and the crowds came and bought them. It appeared that there were vast numbers of persons who had money enough to wear fashionable clothes, but couldn't get into the right society. Here they would have a chance, not merely to look at the *gratin,* as the inner circle was called, but even to speak to them.

It was a scheme devised to turn the weaknesses of human nature to a useful purpose. There were "cabbage patches" in Paris, too, and the poor who lived in them sometimes fell ill, and had to be cared for in hospitals, and this was the established way to raise the money. The most aloof of the great ladies of society offered themselves as bait, duchesses and countesses of the old nobility putting themselves on exhibition, and you might have the honor of addressing them. But you weren't to expect to have it cheaply, for the prices were graded according to those laws of precedence which ruled at dinner parties. A cousin of the Russian Tsar was in charge of the booth where Mrs. Emily's orchids were sold, and for the commonest of them you would have to part with a hundred-franc note, or twenty American dollars. Along with it you would get a charming smile from a regal person, and if you paid double the price asked, she might even hold out a hand to be kissed.

This was like a debut party for Lanny; he was to act as a sort of page, and run errands for the ladies, and he had on long trousers for the first time—a neat white linen suit made especially for the occasion. He felt extremely self-conscious, but knew he mustn't show it; he strolled about the soft green lawns and was introduced to many persons, and made himself helpful in every way he could think of. The grounds presented a gay picture; so many ladies with striped parasols and hats full of flowers and feathers and even whole birds.

Beauty was selling little bouquets, as she had done in London; she was notable in pale yellow taffeta embroidered with large green berries; the corsage prolonged into a polonaise, and the skirt of soft white muslin, cut narrow. With a throat low and sleeves short, Beauty made the most of her numerous charms and was in a state of exaltation, as always when there were many people about and she knew they were admiring her; she had a smile for everybody, and a happy greeting, especially for gentlemen whom she discovered without a boutonnière. She would extend one seductively, saying:

"*Pour les pauvres.*" When they asked the price she would say: "All you have," and when they handed her a ten-franc note, she would thank them soulfully, and they would have to forget about the change, because she didn't have any.

Harry Murchison was there, following her everywhere with his eyes. He was a fair mark for the ladies, for he was known as a rich American, and handsome; they lured him to the booths, and he would buy whatever they offered, and then take it to another booth to be sold again by ladies equally charming. They made a game out of the whole thing—it could be nothing but that, of course, because there were persons here who could have built hospitals for all the poor of Paris if they had wanted to. But what they wanted was to dress up and display themselves. They sat at little tables and had Mrs. Emily's uniformed servants bring them tea and little cakes; they sipped and nibbled while they chatted, and paid double prices for what they got, and if there were any tips, these also went *pour les pauvres.*

I V

A day or two later there was a more exclusive tea party; Mrs. Emily's friends were invited to meet a famous writer. He was no stranger to Lanny Budd, because he had a villa at Antibes, and came there often, and went around wearing little round skullcaps of silk or velvet, always of a bright color and always different—he must have had a hundred of them. He was an old gentleman, tall and thin, with a large head and a long face, like a horse's. His name was Thibault, but he went by his pen name of Anatole France. Everybody talked about his books, but Lanny had got the impression that they were not for the young.

Now he came in a blue velvet coat and a large brown felt hat. He descended slowly from a motorcar, and was escorted to the shade of a great chestnut tree; once he was seated in a lawn chair, all the ladies and gentlemen brought their chairs where they could sit and look and listen. As soon as he got started, everyone else was silent;

they had come to hear him, and he knew it, and they knew it, and he knew that they knew it, and so on. Had he rehearsed in his mind what he was going to say? Very probably; but nobody minded that. He poured out for them a stream of ironic remarks, in an even tone, with a serious mien except for a twinkle in the bright old eyes. Now and then he would put his fingers together in front of him, and move them as if he were telling off the points in his mind.

Most of his talk was too subtle for a youngster. M. France had read everything that was old, and his mind was a storehouse of anecdotes and allusions to history, religion, and art; it was as if you were wandering through a museum so crowded that you hardly had room to move or time to see anything properly. Possibly there was only one person in the company who could understand everything the great man was saying, and that was M. Priedieu, the pale, ascetic librarian, who stood humbly on the outskirts and was not introduced. Lanny thought there was pain in his face, he being a reverent scholar, whereas M. France made mockery of everything he touched.

Somebody started to ask him a question beginning: "What do you think—?" and he answered quickly: "I am trying to cure myself of the habit of thinking, which is a great infirmity. May God preserve you from it, as He has preserved His greatest saints, and those whom He loves and destines to eternal felicity!"

Sooner or later the conversation of French ladies and gentlemen was apt to turn to the subject of love. On this also it appeared that the elderly author was skeptical. A saucy young lady asked him something about love in South America, and he made a laughing reply, and the company was vastly amused. Lanny didn't understand it, but afterward he gathered that M. France had once taken a lecture trip to the Argentine, and on the steamer had met a young actress; he had traveled with her, introducing her as his wife. Later, when he returned to France, he did not want her as a wife, but the young lady was disposed to insist, and there resulted a considerable scandal.

Also Lanny heard about a wealthy lady of Paris to whom this story had caused great distress. Madame de Caillavet was her name, and she was credited with having made the fame and fortune of Anatole France, setting up a salon for the display of his talents and driving this most indolent person to the task of writing books. She and her husband had maintained with France the relationship known as *la vie à trois*—life in threes, instead of pairs. No one had objected to that, but the Argentine actress had made four, and everyone considered her *de trop*.

Madame de Caillavet was dead now, so Anatole France no longer had a salon. Perhaps that was why it was possible for an American hostess to lure him to a tea party. After he had taken his departure, they all gossiped about him, saying as many malicious things as he himself had said about Cicero, Cleopatra, St. Cyprian, Joan of Arc, King Louis XV, the Empress Catherine of Russia, and many other personages of history whom he had quoted. However, all agreed that he was an extremely diverting person; they had been so well entertained that for two hours they had forgotten the disturbing news that the Austrian government had delivered to the Serbian government an ultimatum which practically required the abdication of the latter and the taking over of its police functions by Austrian officials.

V

Beauty went motoring with Harry Murchison. She was gone all day, and came back looking flushed and happy, and Lanny went to her room to chat. They would have little snatches like that—she would tell him where she had been, and the nice things that Prince This and Ambassador That had said to her.

But this time she wanted to talk about Harry. He was such an obliging and generous fellow, and his family in Pennsylvania was a very old one; he had an ancestor who had been a member of the First Continental Congress. Harry liked Lanny very much, calling him the best-mannered boy he had ever met; but he thought it was too bad for him not to have a chance to know his own country. "That's what Mr. Hackabury said, too," remarked the boy.

But Beauty didn't want to talk about soap just then; she was interested in plate glass. "Tell me," she persisted, "do you really like him?"

"Why, yes, I think he's all right." Lanny was a bit reserved.

But then came a knockout. "How would you feel if I was to marry him?"

The boy would have had to be a highly trained diplomat to hide the dismay which smote him. The blood mounted to his cheeks, and he stared at his mother until she dropped her eyes. "Oh, Beauty!" he exclaimed. "What about Marcel?"

"Come sit here by me, dear," she said. "It's not easy to explain such things to one so young. Marcel has never expected to marry me. He has no money and he knows that I have none."

"But I don't understand. Would Robbie stop giving you money if you married?"

"No, dear, I don't mean that. But I can't always live on what Robbie gives me."

"But why not, Beauty? Aren't we getting along all right?"

"You don't know about my affairs. I have an awful lot of debts; they drive me to distraction."

"But why can't we go and live quietly at Bienvenu and not spend so much money?"

"I can't shut myself up like that, Lanny—I'm just not made for it. I'd have to give up all my friends, I couldn't travel anywhere, I couldn't entertain. And you wouldn't have any education—you wouldn't see the world as you've been doing——"

"Oh, please don't do it on my account!" the boy broke in. "I'd be perfectly happy to stay home and read books and play the piano."

"You think you would, dear; but that's because you don't know enough about life. People like us have to have money and opportunities—so many things you will find that you want."

"If I do, I can go to work and get them for myself, can't I?"

Beauty didn't answer; for of course that wasn't the real point; she was thinking about what she herself wanted right now. After a while Lanny ventured, in a low voice: "Marcel will be so unhappy!"

"Marcel has his art, dear. He's perfectly content to live in a hut and paint pictures all day."

"Maybe he is, so long as you are there. But doesn't he miss you right now?"

"Are you so fond of him, Lanny?"

"I thought that was what you wanted!" the boy burst out. "I thought that was the way to be fair to you!"

"It was, dear; and it was sweet. I appreciate it more than I've ever told you. But there are circumstances that I cannot control."

There was a pause, and the mother began to talk about Harry Murchison again. He had been in love with her for quite a while, and had been begging her to marry him; his love was a true and unselfish one. He was an unusually fine man, and could offer her things that others couldn't—not merely his money, but protection, and help in managing her affairs, in dealing with other people, who so often took advantage of her trustfulness and her lack of business knowledge.

"Harry has a lovely home in Pennsylvania, and we can go there to live, or we can travel—whatever we please. He's prepared to do everything he can for you; you can go to school if you like, or have a tutor—you can take Mr. Elphinstone to America with you, if you wish."

But Lanny didn't care anything about Mr. Elphinstone; he didn't care anything about America. He loved their home at Juan, the friends he had there and the things he did there. "Tell me, Beauty," he persisted, "don't you love Marcel any more?"

"In a way," she answered; "but"—then she stopped, embarrassed.

"Has he done something that isn't fair to you?"

The boy saw the beginning of tears in his mother's eyes. "Lanny, I don't think it's right for you to take up notions like that, and cross-question me and try to pin me down——"

"But I'm only trying to understand, Beauty!"

"You can't understand, because you aren't old enough, and these things are complicated and difficult. It's hard for a woman to know her own heart, to say nothing of trying to explain it to her son."

"Well, I wish very much that you'd do what you can," said Lanny, gravely. Something told him that this was a crisis in their lives; and how he wished he could grow up suddenly! "Can you love two men at the same time, Beauty?"

"That is what I've been asking myself for a long while. Apparently I can." Beauty hadn't intended to make any such confession, but she was in a state of inner turmoil, and it was her nature to blurt things out. "My love for Marcel has always been that of a mother; I've thought of him as a helpless child that needed me."

"Well, doesn't he still need you? And if he does, what is going to become of him?"

Tears were making their way onto Beauty's tender cheeks. She didn't answer, and Lanny wondered if it was because she had no answer. He was afraid of hurting his mother; but also he was afraid of seeing her hurt Marcel. He had watched them both on the yacht, and impressions of their love had been indelibly graven upon his mind. Marcel adored her; and what would he do without her?

"Tell me this, Beauty, have you told Harry you will marry him?"

"No, I haven't exactly said that; but he wants me so much——"

"Well, I don't think you ought to make up your mind to such a step in a hurry. If it's debts, you ought to talk to Robbie about them."

"Oh, no, Lanny! I promised him I wouldn't have any debts."

"Well, don't you think you ought to wait and talk to Marcel at least?" Lanny was growing up rapidly in the face of this crisis.

"Oh, I couldn't do that!"

"But what do you expect to do? Just walk off and leave him? Would that be fair, Beauty? It seems to me it would be dreadfully unkind!"

His mother was staring at him, greatly disconcerted. "Lanny, you oughtn't to talk to me like that. I'm your mother!"

"You're the best mother in the world," declared the boy, with ardor. "But I don't want to see you do something that'll make us all unhappy. Please, Beauty, don't promise Harry till we've had time to think about it. Some day you may see me making some mistake, and then you'll be begging me to wait."

Beauty began sobbing. "Oh, Lanny, I'm in such an awful mess! Harry will be so upset—I've kept him waiting too long!"

"Let him wait, all the same," he insisted. He found himself suddenly taking the position of head of the family. "We just can't decide such a thing all at once." Then, after a pause: "Tell me—does Harry know about Marcel?"

"Yes, he knows, of course."

"But does he know how—how serious it is?"

"He doesn't care, Lanny! He's in love with me."

"Well, he oughtn't to be—at least, I mean, he oughtn't try to take you away from us!"

VI

Lanny Budd, in the middle of his fifteenth year, had to sit down and figure out this complicated man and woman business. He had been collecting data from various persons, over a large section of Europe. They hadn't left him to find out about it in his own way, they had forced it upon him: Baron Livens-Mazursky, Dr. Bauer-Siemans, the Social-Democratic editor, Beauty, Marcel and Harry, Edna and Ezra Hackabury, Miss Noggyns and Rosemary, Sophie and her lover—Lanny had seen them embracing one evening on the deck of the *Bluebird*—Mrs. Emily, who had a leading French art critic as her *ami*, old M. France and his Madame de Caillavet and his Argentine actress—to say nothing of his jokes about the leading ladies and gentlemen of history, rather horrid persons, some of them. King Louis XV had said to one of his courtiers that one woman was the same as another, only first she must be bathed and then have her teeth attended to.

In this world into which Lanny Budd had been born, love was a game which people played for their amusement; a pastime on about the same level as bridge or baccarat, horse racing or polo. It was, incidentally, a duel between men and women, in which each tried to achieve prestige in the eyes of the other; that was what the salons were for, the dinner parties, the fashionable clothes, the fine houses, the works of art. Lanny couldn't have formulated that, but he observed the facts, and in a time of stress understanding came to him.

Concealment was an important aspect of nearly all love, as Lanny had observed it; and this seemed to indicate that many people disapproved of the practice—the church people, for example. He had never been to church, except for a fashionable wedding, or to look at stained-glass windows and architecture. But he knew that many society people professed to be religious, and now and then they repented of their love affairs and became actively pious. This was one of the most familiar aspects of life in France, and in French fiction. Sophie's mother-in-law, an elderly lady of the old nobility with a worthless and dissipated son, lived alone, wore black, kept herself surrounded by priests and nuns, and prayed day and night for the soul of the prodigal.

Of course, there were married persons who managed to stay together and raise families. Robbie was apparently that sort; he never went after women, so far as Lanny had heard; but he seldom referred to his family in Connecticut, so it hardly existed for the boy. Apparently the Pomeroy-Nielsons also got along with each other; but Lanny had heard so much of extramarital adventures, he somehow took it for granted that if you came to know a person well enough, you'd find some hidden *affaire*.

The fashionable people had a code under which they did what they pleased, and he had never heard any of them question this right. But evidently the outside world did question it, and that seemed to put the fashionable ones in a trying position. They had always to guard against a thing called "a scandal." Lanny had commented upon this to Rick, who explained that "a scandal" was having your *affaire* get into newspapers. Because of the libel laws, this could happen only if it was dragged into court. In English country houses, everybody would know that Lord Black and Lady White were lovers, and all hostesses would put them in adjoining

rooms; but never a word would be said about it, except among the
"right" people, and it was an unforgivable offense to betray another
person's love affair or do anything that would bring publicity
upon it.

Lanny had been officially taught the "facts of life," and so was
beginning to know his way about in society. He had come to know
who was whose, so to speak, and at the same time he knew that he
wasn't supposed to know—unless the persons themselves allowed
him to. There were things he mustn't say to them, and others he
must never say to anyone. The persons he met might be doing
something very evil, but if there hadn't been "a scandal," they would
be received in society, and it wasn't his privilege to set up a code
and try to enforce it.

It had never before occurred to Lanny to find any serious fault
with his darling Beauty. But now his quick mind could not fail to
put two and two together. For years he had been hearing her tell
her friends that she refused to "pay the price"; and now, how could
he keep from believing that she was changing her mind? It was
painful to have to face the idea that his adored mother might be
selling herself to a handsome young millionaire in order to be able
to have her gowns made by Paquin or Poiret, and to wear long
ropes of genuine pearls as her friend Emily Chattersworth did! He
told himself that there must be some reason why she was no longer
happy with Marcel. The only thing he could think of was the
painter's efforts to keep her from gambling, and from running into
debt and losing her sleep. But Lanny had decided that Marcel was
right about that.

VII

"I must go and see Isadora," said Mrs. Emily. "Maybe Lanny
would like to go along."

Lanny cried: "Oh, thank you! I'd love it—more than anything."
For years he had been hearing about Isadora, and once he had seen
her at a lawn party at Cannes, but he had never had an opportunity

to meet her or even to see her dance. People raved about her in such terms that to the boy she was a fabulous being.

Harry Murchison telephoned, and when Beauty told him about the proposed trip, he begged to be allowed to drive them. Mrs. Emily gave her consent; it appeared that she was promoting the affair between Harry and Beauty, giving the latter what she considered sensible advice.

They set out, Lanny riding in the front seat beside the young scion of plate glass, who laid himself out to be agreeable. But Lanny was hard to please; he was polite, but reserved; he knew quite well that he wasn't being wooed for his own beautiful eyes. Harry Murchison was well dressed and dignified, and had been to college and all that, but his best friend couldn't have claimed that he was a brilliant talker. When it came to questions of art and the imagination, he would listen for a while, trying to find something to say that was safe.

For example, Harry had seen Isadora Duncan dance; and what could he say about it? He said that she danced on an empty stage, and with bare feet, and that people in Pittsburgh had considered that decidedly *risqué.* He said that she had an orchestra, and danced "classical" music—as if anybody had imagined her dancing a cake-walk! If you made him search his memory he might add that she had blue velvet curtains at the back of the stage, and wore draperies of different colors according to the music, and that people clapped and shouted and made her come on again and again.

But imagine Marcel Detaze talking about Isadora! In the first place, he would know what was unique in her art, and how it was related to other dancing. He would know the difference between free gestures and any sort of conventionalized form. He would know the names of the compositions she danced, and what they expressed —poignant grief, joy of nature, revolt against fate, springtime awakening—and as Marcel told you about them he would grieve, rejoice, revolt, or awaken. He would use many gestures, he would make you realize the feat that was being performed—one small woman's figure, alone and without the aid of scenery, embodying the deepest experiences of the human soul; struck down with grief, lifted up in ecstasy, sweeping across the stage in such a tumult that you felt you were watching a great procession.

In short, Lanny was all for French temperament, as against American common sense. Of course, plate glass was useful, perhaps even necessary to civilization; but what did Harry Murchison have to do with it, except that he happened to be the grandson of a man who had known about it? Harry got big dividend checks, and would get bigger ones when his father and mother died; but that was all. He had sense enough to find Pittsburgh smoky and boring, and had come to Paris in search of culture and beauty. And that was all right—only let him find some other beauty than that upon which Lanny and Marcel had staked their claims!

Mrs. Emily in the back seat was telling about the *affaires* of Isadora, and Lanny turned his head to listen. The dancer was another person who had been experimenting with the sex life. She was a "free lover"—a new term to Lanny. He gathered its meaning to be that she refused to conceal what she did. Defying the dreadful thing called "scandal," she had had two children, one by a son of Ellen Terry, the actress, and the other by an American millionaire whom she called "Lohengrin." The smart world could not overlook such an opportunity for entertaining itself, and delighted in a story that Isadora had once offered to have a child by Bernard Shaw, saying that such a child would have her beauty and his brains; to which the skeptical playwright had replied: "Suppose it should have my beauty and your brains?"

The jealous fates would not permit a woman to believe too much in happiness, or to practice what she preached. Early in the previous year a dreadful tragedy had befallen those two lovely children. They had been left in an automobile, and apparently the chauffeur had failed to set the brakes properly. The car had rolled down hill, crashed into a bridge, and plunged into deep water; the children had been taken out dead. The distracted mother had wandered over Europe, hardly knowing what she did; but now her friend "Lohengrin" had taken charge of her, and had purchased a great hotel in the environs of Paris, and Isadora was trying to restore herself to life by teaching other people's children to dance—and incidentally, so Mrs. Emily revealed, by having another child of her own.

VIII

The hotel at Bellevue was a large place with several hundred rooms; a commonplace building, but with lovely gardens sloping to the river, and from the terrace in front of it a view over the whole of Paris. The dining room had been turned into the dancing room, and there were Isadora's blue velvet curtains. Tiers of seats had been built on each side, where the pupils sat while the lessons were given on the floor. The teachers were the older pupils; the school had been going for only a few months, but already they had been able to give a festival at the Trocadéro and rouse an audience to transports of delight.

Isadora Duncan was a not very large woman, with abundant dark brown hair, regular features, a gentle, sad expression, and a figure of loveliness and grace. She had come from California, unknown and without resources, except her genius, and had created an art which held vast audiences spellbound in all the capitals of Europe and America. Even now, expecting a baby in a few days, she would step forward to show her troop of children some gesture; she would make a few simple movements against the background of her blue curtains, and something magical would happen, a spirit would be revealed, an intimation of glory. Even reclining on a couch, making motions with arms and hands, Isadora was noble and inspiring.

The music of a piano sounded and a group of children swung into action, eager, alert, radiating joy. Lanny Budd's whole being leaped with them. It took him back to Hellerau, but it was different, more spontaneous, lacking the basis of drill. In "Dalcroze" there was science; but these children caught a spirit—and Lanny, too, had that spirit; he knew instantly what they were doing. He could hardly keep his seat; for dancing is not something to be watched, it is something to be done.

Afterward they had lunch in the garden, the visitors, the teachers, and the children. "Lohengrin" was pouring out this prodigality, and to Lanny the place seemed a sort of artists' heaven. The children, boys and girls of all ages, wore tunics of bright colors; they lived on vegetarian foods, but it didn't keep them from having bright cheeks and eyes, and hearts full of love for Isadora, and for the beauty they were helping to create. Lanny exclaimed: "Oh, I'd like to come here, Beauty! Do you suppose Isadora would take me?"

"Perhaps she would," said Beauty; and Mrs. Emily said she would ask her, if they meant it. Mrs. Emily had helped Isadora to become known, and the lovely white feet had danced more than once on the lawn under the chestnut trees at Les Forêts.

But suddenly Lanny thought, was he free just then to think about dancing? Didn't he have to stay with Beauty, and watch over her, and try to save poor Marcel from having his happiness ruined? Oh, this accursed sex problem!

Artists came to Bellevue, and sat upon a platform in the center of the hall and made sketches of the dancing children. At Meudon, not far away, was the studio of a famous sculptor, Auguste Rodin; a sturdy son of the people with a great spade beard, broad features, and ponderous form. He was an old man now, becoming feeble, but he could still make wonderful sketches. He sat near Lanny and, when the dancing was over, talked about the loveliness of it, and wished he could have had such models for all his work—models who lived, and moved, and brought harmony before the eyes in a thousand shifting forms. Lanny thought that this old man himself had been able to make marble and bronze live and move; he tried to say it, and the sculptor put his big hand on the boy's head, and told him to come to the studio some day and see the works which had not yet been given to the world.

Driving into Paris, the ladies talked about Rodin, who also was providing evidence about the love life! He was getting into his dotage, and had fallen prey to an American woman, married to a

Frenchman who bore one of the oldest and proudest names in history. "But that doesn't keep them from being bad characters," said Mrs. Emily. She told how this pair had preyed upon the old artist and got him to sign away much of his precious work.

"Oh, dear, oh, dear!" exclaimed Beauty Budd. "What pitiful creatures men are!" She meant it for Harry, of course; but Lanny heard it and agreed. People wished to take love as a source of pleasure, but it seemed to bring them torment. The primrose path had thorns in it, and as time passed these thorns became dry and hard and sharper than a serpent's tooth.

They came into Paris at the hour when the shops and factories were closing, and the streets swarming with people. The crowds did not seem to be hurrying as usual; they would form groups and stand talking together. The newsboys were shouting everywhere, and the headlines on the papers were big enough so that motorists could read without stopping. LA GUERRE! was the gist of them all. Austria had that day declared war upon Serbia! And what was Russia going to do? What would Germany do? And France? And England? People stared at one another, unable to grasp the awful thing that was crashing upon the world.

11

C'est la Guerre

I

BEAUTIFUL flowers bloomed in the garden that was Europe. They spread wide petals to the sunshine, trusting the security of the warm and sheltered place. Over them fluttered butterflies, also of splendid hues and delicate structure, loving the sunlight, floating upon peace and stillness. But suddenly came a tempest, harsh and blind, tearing the fragile wings of the butterflies, hurling them against the branches of trees or into the sodden ground; ripping the petals off the flowers, stripping the foliage, leaving bare wrecked limbs to mock the lovers of beauty. So it was with Lanny Budd during the next dreadful week, and so with all the persons he knew, and with countless millions of others, from Land's End to Vladivostok, from Archangel to the Cape of Good Hope. It was the worst week in the history of Europe—and there were many more to follow.

Lanny had been expecting his friend Kurt Meissner in Paris; but several days before had come a letter from Kurt, written on a Channel steamer, saying that his father had telegraphed him to return home at once, taking the first boat by way of the Hook of Holland. Kurt had been worried, thinking there must be illness in his family; but now Lanny understood what had happened—Herr Meissner had known what was coming. In London and Paris one heard many stories about Germans who had received such warnings, and had taken measures for their personal safety or their financial advantage. Here and there one had even passed on a discreet "tip" to an American friend.

Lanny and his mother came to Paris, and Robbie showed up there on the morning after Austria declared war. He wouldn't lack advance information, be sure! He said that a salesman of armaments wouldn't have to do any more traveling now; the governments would find him wherever he was. The thing had come which Robbie had said couldn't possibly come; but it didn't take him long to adjust himself to it. "All right, it's what Europe wants, let them have it." Budd's would continue to turn out products, and anybody could buy them who came with the cash. Somebody had been telling Robbie about Shaw's *Major Barbara*, so now he talked impressively about "the Creed of the Armorer."

It was good to have Robbie at hand in a time like this; self-possessed as ever, a firm rock of counsel, also a checkbook open to friends in trouble. He and Beauty and Lanny settled down to a conference; and presently Harry Murchison came into it—forcing himself in, by taking his problem to Robbie. They had met once before and were on friendly terms, Harry being the sort of fellow that Robbie approved.

"Mr. Budd," said he, "I don't know why you and Beauty parted, and I'm not interested; but I know you're still her friend, and she listens to you, and I wish you'd give her sensible advice. I want to marry her—right now—today—and take her out of this hell that's starting here. She can have a new life in America; I'll do most anything she asks, give her anything she can think of. As for Lanny, I'll take care of him, or you can—I like the boy, and we'll be the best of friends if he'll let me. Surely that's a fair offer!"

Robbie thought it was; and so the whole situation was forced into the open. Lanny talked to his father, not merely about Marcel, but about Baron Livens-Mazursky, and Dr. Bauer-Siemans, and the Hackaburys, and Isadora, and Anatole France, and all the rest; he had to make Robbie understand how he came to know so much about love, and why he was taking it upon himself to keep a French painter from losing his beautiful blond mistress. Robbie didn't have much use for either Frenchmen or painters, but he was very much for Lanny, and couldn't help being tickled by this odd situation, a sensitive, idealistic kid undertaking to make a hero out of his mother's lover—and seeming very likely to get away with it. It was clear that Beauty was still half in love with her painter; the other half in love with the idea of becoming a respectable American lady, wife of a man who could give her security and position. Which would she choose?

II

It was a time for showdowns. In the crash of kingdoms and empires, human blunders and failures shrank to smaller proportions. Beauty took her son into a room apart, and told him a story which so far she had kept from nearly everyone she knew. She couldn't look him in the eyes, and blushed intensely—her throat, her cheeks, her forehead. "Your father and I have never been married, Lanny. The story that we are divorced is one that I made up to protect you and me. I didn't want people to know that you are illegitimate, and make it a handicap to your life."

She rushed on to pour out the details, defending both herself and Robbie. They had met in Paris when they were very young, and they had loved each other truly, and had planned to marry. But Beauty had been an artist's model, and had been painted in the nude. Lanny would understand that, he knew what art was; one of the pictures had been exhibited in a salon, and was much admired. But some malicious person had sent a photograph of it to Robbie's father, the head of an old and proud family of Puritan New England. It had meant only one thing to him, that Beauty was an indecent woman; he was a harsh and domineering man, and was he going to have his son marrying a painter's model, and having her picture in the newspapers naked instead of in the usual bridal costume? That was what he said, and he laid down the law: if Robbie married such a woman his father would disown and disinherit him.

Robbie wanted to do it, even so, but Beauty wouldn't let him; she loved him and wouldn't wreck his life. They had lived together without marriage; the father had consented to ignore his son's mistress, something not so unusual, even for Puritans in New England. It was hard on Lanny, but they hadn't meant for him to happen—Lanny had been an accident, said his mother at the climax of her confusion and blushes.

She had thought she would never have the courage to tell this story to her son; she took it for granted that he would receive it with shame, and perhaps with anger toward her. But Lanny had by now seen so much of lawless love, and heard about so much more, that the distinctions were blurred in his mind. He said it didn't worry him to be illegitimate; it hadn't hurt his health, and it wouldn't hurt his feelings if somebody called him a bastard—he had read about them in Shakespeare and had got the impression that they were a lively lot. What did give him shivers was the idea of having been an "accident." "Where would I have been, and what would I have been, if you and Robbie hadn't had me?"

Tears came into the mother's bright blue eyes; she saw that he was trying to spare her; he was being a darling, as usual. She hastened to explain the situation which now confronted her, the reasons why her decision was so important. If she were to marry Harry Murchison, that would cover all her past and make her a "respectable" woman; it wouldn't make Lanny legitimate, but it would keep anybody from bothering about it—and anyhow Robbie intended to acknowledge him as his son.

Lanny could understand all that; but he said: "What good will it do you to be respectable if you aren't happy?"

"But, Lanny!" she exclaimed. "I mean to be happy with Harry."

"Maybe," said he; "but I don't believe you'll ever forget that you left Marcel without any cause. Suppose he goes and jumps off the Cap?"

"Oh, Lanny, he won't do that!"

"How can you be sure? And then, suppose that France mobilizes? Marcel will have to go to war, won't he?"

Beauty turned pale; that was the horror she couldn't bring herself to face. The boy, seeing that he had the advantage, pushed harder. "Could you bear to leave him if you knew he had gone to fight for his country?" All Beauty could do was to bury her face in her arms and weep. Lanny said: "You better wait and see what happens."

III

They wouldn't have to wait long. Surely nobody could complain of the slowness of events at the end of July 1914! First it was Russia mobilizing one and a quarter million men; then it was the German Kaiser serving an ultimatum to the effect that Russia had to cease mobilizing. Paris buzzed like a beehive at swarming time; for France was Russia's ally and was bound to go to war if Russia was attacked.

Robbie had said that the governments would find him, and they did. By one means or another, word spread that the representative of Budd's was staying at the Hotel Crillon, in a front suite with a pleasant view up the Champs-Élysées. Military gentlemen representing most of the governments of Europe came to enjoy that view, and partake of the array of drinks which Robbie had upon the sideboard in his reception room—all going onto the expense account of a munitions salesman. The immaculately uniformed gentlemen came to find out what stocks Budd's had on hand at present—of guns and ammunition, of course, not of whiskies, brandies, and liqueurs.

Robbie would smile suavely, and say that he regretted that Budd's was such a very small plant, and had practically no stocks on hand. "You know how it is, I begged your General So-and-So to place an order last year. I warned you all what was coming."

"Yes, we know," the military gentlemen would reply, sorrowfully. "If the decision' had rested with us, we should have been prepared. But the politicians, the parliaments"—they would shrug their shoulders. "What could we do?"

Robbie knew all about politicians and parliaments; in his country they were called Congress and had steadily refused to vote what the safety of the country required. Now, of course, there would be a quick change, the purse strings would be loosened. The policy of Budd's was fixed; it was "first come, first served" to all the world. The terms in this present crisis would be fifty percent of the purchase price to be placed in escrow with the First National Bank of Newcastle, Connecticut, before the order was accepted; the balance to be placed in escrow a week before the completion of the order, to be paid against bills of lading when shipment was made. Munitions makers had grown suddenly exacting, it appeared. Robbie added confidentially—to everyone—that he had cabled his firm recommending an immediate increase of fifty percent in its entire schedule of prices: this to meet inevitable rises in the cost of materials and labor.

The visitors would depart; and while the next lot cooled their heels in the lobby, the salesman would take off the heavy alligator-skin belt which he always wore, slip a catch, and draw out several

long strips of parchment with fine writing on them. He would sit
at his portable typewriter, the newest contraption created by Yankee
ingenuity, and would study the parchment strips and proceed to
type out a cablegram in code.

That secret code had been one of the thrills of Lanny's life for
several years. It was changed every time Robbie made a trip, and
there were only two copies of it in existence; the other was in the
possession of Robbie's father. The one other person who knew
about it was the confidential clerk who devised it, and who did the
decoding for the president of the company. The belt in which
Robbie kept his own copy was never off his person except when he
was in the bathtub or in swimming; usually he swam from a boat,
and before he sank down among the fishes he would make sure
there were no agents of foreign governments near by.

Robbie had talked quite a lot about ciphers and codes. Any cipher
could be "broken" by an expert; but a code was safe, because it
gave purely arbitrary meanings to words. The smartest expert could
hardly find out that "Agamemnon" meant Turkey, or that "hippo-
griff" meant the premier of Rumania. Robbie would use the cable
company's code-book for the ordinary phrases of his message: "I
have promised immediate delivery," or "I advise acceptance," and
so on; but crucial words, such as names of countries, of individuals
he was dealing with and the goods they were ordering, were in the
private code. These precautions had been adopted after a deal had
been lost because Zaharoff had a man in the office of Budd Gunmakers and was getting copies of Robbie's messages.

Seeing how overwhelmed his father was, Lanny asked if he could
help; and the father said: "It's too bad you don't know how to type."

"I can find the letters on the keyboard," replied the boy, "and
you don't hit 'em so fast yourself."

"You'll find it's pretty poor fun."

"If I'm really helping you, I'll think it's the best fun there is."

So Robbie wrote his cablegram in English, and showed the boy
how to look up phrases in the regular code-book, and underlined
those words which would be in his own list. While Robbie inter-

viewed a friend of Captain Bragescu, just arrived from Rumania,
Lanny worked patiently by the "hunt and peck" method, producing
a long string of ten-letter words: "California Independed Hilarioust
Scorpionly Necessands," and so on. Lanny's grandfather, who had
tried hard not to let him be born, and who so far had refused to
recognize the failure of that effort, would learn from this pains-
taking service that the government of Holland was anxious over the
possibility of invasion, and would pay thirty percent premium for
delivery of twenty thousand carbines during the month of August.

By the time Robbie's interview was concluded, the message was
ready, and he went over it and found only two or three errors, and
said it was a great help; which of course made the boy as proud as
Punch. Robbie burned the original message, and let the ashes drop
into the toilet bowl. Then Lanny asked: "Do you ever add anything
out of code?"

"Sometimes," replied the father. "Why?"

"Just say: 'Lanny coded this.' "

Robbie chuckled, but he said: "Wait till he sells the guns and
gets the money!"

IV

The cablegram dispatched, the pair went for a stroll, to get some
fresh air into their lungs before lunch. The other delegations could
wait, said Robbie; no sense in killing yourself—anyhow, Budd's was
loaded up with orders; in the past couple of weeks they had accumulated a "backlog" for six months. For years Robbie had been urging
the family to expand the plant; Robbie's eldest brother, Lawford,
who was in charge of production, had opposed it, but finally their
father had adopted Robbie's program. Now he wouldn't have to
worry any more.

"What's he worrying about?" asked Lanny, and Robbie answered:
"Bankers! Once you let Wall Street get its claws into you, you
cease to be a family institution."

It was Friday, the last day of July. Newsboys were shouting

la guerre again. Germany had declared martial law. She was going to war with somebody, and it could only be with France's ally. People appeared to have lost interest in the ordinary tasks; they stopped on street corners, or in front of bistros, kiosks, and tobacco shops, to talk about the meaning of events. People spoke to you who wouldn't ordinarily have done so. "They're scared," said Robbie. "That brings human beings together."

There came the sound of drums; a regiment marching—toward the east, of course. The soldiers sweated under a load of equipment; rifle and bayonet, knapsack, a big blanket roll, a canteen, even a little spade. Their blue coats were long and heavy, their red trousers big and baggy. The crowds came running, but they didn't cheer. Neither the soldiers nor the people looked happy. "Is France mobilizing?" asked Lanny, and his father replied: "Troops would be moving toward the frontier in any case."

They returned to the Crillon, and while they were at lunch a cablegram was brought to Robbie. "From Newcastle," he said. It was in code, of course, and Lanny exclaimed eagerly: "Oh, let me try it!" The father said: "O.K."

When they went upstairs Robbie took off the magic belt, and Lanny shut himself in his bedroom with cablegram and code-book, leaving the father free for more interviews. The cablegram conveyed the information that Turkey was twenty-four hours overdue upon the first payment for ground-type air-cooled machine guns ordered. Might it not be wise to cancel the deal and dispose of the guns to the British army? Robbie was to advise immediately what increased price he thought the British would pay.

It sounded so important that Lanny took the decoded message to his father, and Robbie cut short his interview and got busy on the telephone to locate a member of the British military mission then holding consultations with the French Ministry of War. Lanny went back to put into code the words: "Advise cancellation Turkey am making inquiries Britain."

A man like Robbie Budd would normally have a secretary with him; but Robbie was active, and had always preferred to handle his own affairs and write his own letters to his father. Now he was caught in a sudden hurricane, and less willing than ever to trust anybody. So there was a chance for a fourteen-year-old boy to step into a secretary's job—for which he was not without some preparation.

Robbie checked the message and found it all right. He put on his magic belt and went down to take a taxi for an appointment with the British officer. Lanny filed the cablegram, and then went to the street and bought the latest newspaper. When he came back he found there was a letter for his mother—in the familiar handwriting of Marcel Detaze, and postmarked Juan-les-Pins. It was an unusually thick letter, and Lanny didn't have to guess that Marcel would be pouring out his soul. He took it up to his mother's suite. He would rest for a while from being a code expert, and resume his role as consultant upon affairs of the heart.

V

Beauty had been to lunch with her friend Emily Chattersworth, and was loaded up with "sensible" advice on the problem which was exercising her. But when she saw that letter, all the labors of her friend were undone. She paled and caught her breath, and her hands trembled while she read. When she had finished the long letter, she sat staring in front of her, biting her lip as if enduring pain.

Lanny had an impulse to say: "May I read it?" But he feared that wouldn't be polite, and merely asked: "Is he in trouble, Beauty?"

"He is uncertain about everything," she answered, and then started to read him the letter, which was in French, and began "*Chérie.*" Before she got very far, her voice broke, and she handed him the sheets, saying: "You have to know about it."

Lanny read: "I have been hoping every day to hear from you and to see you, but now I fear it will be too late. It looks as if there will be mobilization, and I cannot come to Paris because it would look like running away. I cannot be sure, but I expect my class will be called among the first. If I go, I will write you. I do not know where I shall be, but you can write me in care of my regiment.

"I keep reminding myself that you are an American, and I cannot be sure how you will feel about what is happening. But you know that I am a Frenchman and can have no doubt who is right in this unwanted conflict. It is cruel that our happiness has to be broken, and that millions of other women will be stricken with grief. It is perhaps a minor tragedy that men of talent have to be dragged from their task of making beauty, and instead must destroy it upon the battlefield. But it is our fate, and if the summons comes, I shall not permit myself to be weakened by repining. In this I hope for your help.

"One sad idea has been haunting my mind. It may be that Lanny's father will wish to take him out of this hell which Europe is about to become. It may be that you will wish to go with your son. I have thought about it day and night, and what it is my duty to say to you. I have written half a dozen letters and torn them up. I have pleaded with you for the right of our love; and then I have decided that I was being selfish, thinking about my own welfare while making myself believe I was thinking about yours. I have written a letter of renunciation, in the name of true, unselfish love, and then decided that I would seem cold, when in reality I was so trembling with grief and longing that my hand could hardly control the pen.

"If I could have one hour's talk with you, I could make it all clear. I expected that as my right, and you gave me to think that I was to have it. But you kept postponing your coming—and I felt that you must have known about this crisis, and the prospect of my being called to the defense of my country. This is not said in complaint, but merely to make plain my situation.

"In what you are about to read, I beg you to remember our hours of ecstasy. Remember our tears that mingled, and all the pulses of our hearts. Everything that I have ever been to you, I am today, and will be forever, if fate spares me. I love you; my being trembles when I think of you, my courage dissolves, I curse war, mankind, fate, and God Himself, that gives us such bliss and then tears it away. I feel all that, and I am all that. But also I am a citizen of France, with a duty there is no escaping. Also I am a rational man, knowing what the world is, and what can happen to a woman in it. I say: 'What have you to offer to this woman, or to any woman born to the pleasant things of life?'

"There are times when I feel that I know about the value of my own work. I say: 'It is good, and some day the world will know that it is good.' But then I remember how van Gogh succeeded in selling only one painting in his lifetime, and that to his brother. So I ask myself: 'Have I anything more than he had?' I tell myself there are hundreds, perhaps thousands of painters, each as sure of his own merits as I am of mine; and very few of them can be right. Who can say there is any sure guarantee that genuine merit will be recognized in the world? Why may it not be suffocated by indifference, just as life may be annihilated in the blast of war?

"I tell myself that if you go to America, you will almost certainly marry there, and I shall never see you again. Grief overwhelms me; but then reason speaks, reminding me that my life may be snuffed out in a few days—or worse, that I may be mutilated, and made into something you had better not see or know about. I say: 'If she takes her dear son to America, that will be the happiest path for her and for him. Her wise American friends must be telling her that. What right have I to add to the ache of her heart?'

"It may be, Chérie, that all this is fantasy. If so, call it a lover's nightmare, and laugh at it. But it is better to write something foolish than not to let you know my heart. If I am called, what I write thereafter will be under the eyes of an army censor. I beg you to learn not to worry about me, it is the destiny of the men of our time. France must be saved from the insolence of an autocrat, and whatever comes to each individual is his to endure. My love, my blessings go with you, and my prayers for your happiness."

Tears had come into Lanny's eyes as he read, and were trickling down his cheeks. When he was through he, too, sat staring before him, not seeing anything, not knowing anything to say. He didn't think that Marcel believed in prayers, or in blessings. Was it just a manner of speaking, or was it a cry wrung from him when his own forces were not enough to meet his need? Maybe he would be glad to go to war, and to get killed, as a way of escape from his grief.

"It's her own affair," Robbie had said to his son. "It's a mistake to urge people to any course, because then they hold you responsible for the consequences. Let her make her own decision." So the boy didn't say a word, just let the tears trickle.

"Oh, Lanny, what shall I do?" whispered Beauty, at last. When he didn't answer, she began to sob. "It's monstrous that a man like Marcel should be dragged away to war!"

"He doesn't have to be dragged," said the boy. "Don't you see that he would go anyway? We can't help that part of it. Most of the women of France will have that to endure." Robbie had said this, and the boy knew it was right.

But Beauty was a different kind of woman, belonging to the class which wasn't supposed to suffer. So far she had refused to do so. That was why it seemed such a perfect solution of the problem to flee to America, in the care of a capable man who had no part in Europe's hates and slaughters. That was undoubtedly the sensible way—as Robbie and Emily and all her friends kept assuring her. How provoking and unreasonable that a woman who had given her heart couldn't get it back without finding it all bleeding and torn!

"Tell me, what shall I do?" she repeated.

"Robbie doesn't want me to say any more about it," the boy answered. "You know what I think."

"Harry is coming to take me to dinner," persisted the mother. "What am I to say to him?"

The boy remembered what his father had told him during the *affaire* Zaharoff. "Tell him the facts, Beauty."

VI

Lanny returned to his other job. Robbie wrote out a long message to his father, advising him that Turkish officials were deeply involved in intrigues with Germany and the outcome might be a blockade of all Turkish ports. The British military mission advised that Britain would certainly want all the ground-type air-cooled machine guns it could get. Robbie advised against charging a higher price, except as part of a general boost in the price schedule. He recommended this latter more urgently than ever. Future quotations should be subject to increase depending upon raw-material prices certain to jump enormously.

A long message which would take a good part of the afternoon; Robbie hated to put it off on the youngster, but Lanny said he had never done anything he enjoyed more. He would stick right there and make himself an expert, and when Robbie was willing to send a message without checking it, he would be as proud as if he'd got the tiny red ribbon of the Legion of Honor.

So they went to work, Lanny at his table, and the father talking to harassed and exhausted military men. This went on until after seven o'clock, when Robbie said they'd eat, no matter what happened to Europe. "Let's go to a place where real Parisians eat," he suggested. "Fellow I know will be there."

They got into a taxi, and he gave an address on the Rue Montmartre. "We're to meet a journalist; a man who has worthwhile connections, and often brings me tips. I give him a couple of hundred-franc notes. It's the custom of the country."

It was a place Lanny had never heard of before. There were many tables on the sidewalk, but Robbie passed these by and strolled inside; he looked about, and went toward a table where sat a little man with heavy dark mustache and beard, pince-nez on a black silk cord, and a black tie. The man jumped up when he saw him. "Ah, M. Bood!" he exclaimed, trying to say it American fashion, but not succeeding.

"*Bon jour, M. Pastier*," replied Robbie, and introduced Lanny: "*Mon secrétaire*." The man looked puzzled; for not many businessmen have secretaries fourteen years old. Robbie laughed, and added: "*Aussi mon fils*."

"*Ah, votre fils!*" exclaimed the Frenchman, exuberantly, and shook hands with the lad. "*C'est le* crown prince, *hein?*"

"*Je l'espeer,*" replied Robbie; his French was no better than M. Pastier's American.

The other invited them to sit down. They ordered, and Robbie included a large bottle of wine, knowing that his acquaintance would assist them. The Frenchman was a voluble talker, and impressed Lanny greatly. The boy was too young to realize that persons in this profession sometimes pretend to know more than they can know. To listen to him you would have thought he was the intimate friend of all the prominent members of the cabinet, and had talked with several of them that afternoon.

He reported that Germany had been making desperate efforts to detach France from her Russian engagements. "The German ambassador pleaded with friends of mine at the Quai d'Orsay. 'There is and should be no need for two highly civilized nations to engage in strife. Russia is a barbarous state, a Tatar empire, essentially Asiatic.' So they argue. They would prefer to devour us at a second meal," added the Frenchman, his black eyes shining.

"*Naturellement,*" said Robbie.

"But we have an alliance; the word of France has been given! Imagine, if you can, the insolence of these Teutons—they demand of us the fortresses of Toul and Verdun, as guarantees of our abandonment of the Russian alliance. Is it probable that we built them for that?"

"*Pas probable,*" assented the American.

"When the French people hear that, they will rise as one man!" exclaimed the journalist, and illustrated with a vigorous rising of both arms.

"What will your workers do, your Socialists?" asked Robbie. It was a question which troubled everybody.

The other said: "Look," and indicated with his eyes. "Over there at that table by the window. The question is being settled tonight."

The American saw eight or ten men sitting at dinner, talking among themselves. They might have been journalists like M. Pastier, or perhaps doctors or lawyers. At the head of the table was a large stoutish man with a heavy gray beard, a broad face, and grandfatherly appearance. "Jaurès," whispered the Frenchman.

Lanny had heard the name; he knew it was one of the Socialist leaders, and that he made eloquent speeches in the Chamber of Deputies. What Lanny saw was a heavy-set old gentleman with baggy clothes, talking excitedly, with many gestures. "They are Socialist editors and deputies," explained M. Pastier. "They have just returned from the conference at Brussels."

The three watched for a while, and others in the restaurant did the same. The Socialists were men of the people, deciding the affairs of the people, and there was no need for them to hide themselves. Lanny decided that their leader must be a kind old gentleman, but he look exhausted and harassed.

"It is a grave problem for them," explained the journalist; "for they are internationalists, and against war. But Jaurès spoke plainly to the Germans at Brussels—if they obey their Kaiser and march, there will be nothing for the French workers to do but defend their *patrie*. Have you seen *L'Humanité* this morning?"

"I don't patronize it," said Robbie.

"Jaurès speaks of 'Man's irremediable need to save his family and his country even through armed nationalism.'"

"Too bad he didn't discover that before he began advocating the general strike in case of war!"

"Jaurès is an honest man; I say it, even though I have opposed him. I have known him for many years. Would you be interested to meet him?"

"No, thanks," said Robbie, coldly. "He's a bit out of my line." He led the conversation to the chances of British intervention in the expected war. He had his reasons for wanting to know about that; it would be worth many hundred-franc notes to Budd Gunmakers.

After dinner father and son strolled along the boulevards and looked at the crowds. When they got to the Crillon, there was another cablegram. Lanny began insisting that he wasn't at all tired;

surely he could work till bedtime, and so on—when the telephone
rang, and Robbie answered. "What?" he cried, and then: "*Mon
Dieu!*" and: "What will that mean?" He listened for a while, then
hung up the receiver and said: "Jaurès has been shot!"

It was the boy's turn to exclaim and question. "Right where we
left him," said the father. "Fellow on the street pushed the window
curtains aside and put a couple of bullets into the back of his head."

"He's dead?"

"So Pastier reports."

"Who did it, Robbie?"

"Some patriot, they suppose; somebody who thought he was going to oppose the war."

"What will happen now?"

Robbie shrugged his shoulders, almost as if he had been a Frenchman. "It's just one life. If war starts, there'll be a million others.
C'est la guerre, as the French say. Pastier says that Germany's expected to declare war on Russia tomorrow; and if so, France is in."

VII

It was hard upon a young fellow who had just assumed an important and responsible position to have to be distracted by the sex
problem. Lanny learned how it interferes with business, and all the
other serious things of life; he said a plague upon it—for the first
time in his life, but not for the last. Here he was, the next morning,
comfortably fixed by the window in his bedroom, with the code
material and a long message from Connecticut, badly delayed by
congestion of the cables. But instead of looking up the word "marketless," he was sitting lost in thought, and presently interrupting
his father's reading of the mail. "Robbie, don't you think one of us
ought to see Beauty for a few minutes?"

"Anything special?" asked the other, absentmindedly.

"Harry told her last night that she'd have to make up her mind,
or he's going back to the States without her. She says it's an ultimatum."

"Well, there's a lot of ultimatums being served right now. One more hardly counts."

"Don't joke, Robbie. She's terribly upset."

"What's she doing?"

"Just sitting staring in front of her."

"Has she got a looking glass?"

Lanny saw that his father was determined to keep out of it; so he looked up the word "marketless." But before he started on the word "lightening," he interrupted again. "Robbie, does it often happen that a woman thinks she is in love with two men and can't decide which?"

"Yes," said the father, "it happens to both men and women." He put down the letter he was reading and added: "It happened to me, when I had to decide whether I was going to get married or not." It was the first time Robbie had ever spoken of that event to his son, and the boy waited to see if he'd say more. "I had to make up my mind, and I did. And now Beauty has to do it. It won't hurt her to sit staring in front of her. She's owed it to herself for a long while to do some serious thinking."

So Lanny looked up "lightening," and three or four words more. But he couldn't help trying once again. "Robbie, you don't want me to give Beauty advice; but I've already given her some, and I know it's counting with her. You don't think it was good advice?"

"It wasn't what I'd give her; but it may be right for her. She's a sentimental person, and it seems she's very much in love with that painter fellow."

"Oh, really she is, Robbie. I watched them all the time on the yacht. Anybody could see it."

"But he's a lot younger than she is; and that's going to make a tragedy some day."

"You mean, Marcel will stop loving her?"

"Not entirely, perhaps; he'll be torn in half, just the way she is now."

"You mean he'll get interested in some younger woman?"

"I mean he'll have to be a saint if he doesn't; and I haven't met any saints among French painters."

"You ought to know Marcel better, Robbie. He is one of the very best men I ever have met."

"I'm taking your word for him. But there's a lot you still must learn, son. Beauty would be poor—that is, by the standards of everyone she knows or wants to know. And that's awful hard on the affections. It gets worse and worse as you get older, too."

"You think it's right for people to marry for money, then?"

"I think there's an awful lot of bunk talked on the subject. People fool themselves, and try to fool other people. I've watched marriages, scores of them, and I know that money was the important element in most. It was dressed up in fine words, of course; it was called 'family,' and 'social position,' and 'culture,' and 'refinement.'"

"But aren't those things real?"

"Sure they are. Each is like a fine house; it's built on a foundation—and the foundation is money. If you build a house without any foundation, it doesn't last long."

"I see," said the boy. It impressed him greatly, like everything his father said.

"Don't let anybody fool you about money, son. The people who talk that nonsense don't believe it themselves. They tell you that money won't buy this, that, and the other thing. I tell you that money will buy an awful lot, especially if you're a good shopper. You get my point?"

"Oh, sure, Robbie."

"Take Edna Hackabury. Money bought her a yacht, and the yacht got her a lot of friends. Now she's lost her yacht, and she and her captain will have to live on two thousand pounds a year; and how many of her old friends will come to see her? She'll be embarrassed if they do, because she can't keep up with them. She'll find that she's forced to get some cheaper friends."

"I know, Robbie, there are people like that; but others are interested in art, and music, and books, and so on."

"That's quite true; and I'm glad to see that you prefer such friends. But when those friends grow old, and their blood flows slower, they'll want a warm fire, and money will buy the fire. Money won't buy them appreciation of books, but it will buy them books, and what's the use of appreciation if you haven't anything to use it on? No, son, the only way to be happy without money is to go and live in a tub, like Diogenes, or be a Hindu with a rag around your loins and a bowl to beg for rice. Even then you can't live unless other people have cared enough for money to grow rice, and to market and transport it."

"Then you don't think there's anything we can do for Beauty?"

"What I think, son, is that one or the other of us has got to work at that code; because this is a time of crisis, and a whole lot of women have worse troubles than trying to make up their minds which man they want."

VIII

That was the first of August; and early in the day came the news that Germany had declared war on Russia. Soon afterward it was reported that both Germany and France had ordered general mobilization.

The temper of Paris changed in an hour. Previously everything had been hushed; people anxious, frightened, horrified. But now the die was cast. It was war! That hateful Kaiser with his waxed mustaches, those military men who surrounded him, strutting and blustering—they had thrown Europe into the furnace. At least, that was the way the Paris crowds saw it; and business came to an end for the day, everybody rushed into the streets. Bugles sounding everywhere, drums rolling, crowds marching and cheering. They were singing the "Marseillaise" on every street corner; and "Malbrouck s'en va-t-en guerre"—to which Americans sing "For He's a Jolly Good Fellow"; also the "Carmagnole," which Americans do not know—all the old revolutionary songs of France, now become patriotic and respectable.

Lanny finished his secretarial labors and went out to see the sights, the most stirring any boy could have imagined. Pink mobilization orders posted on kiosks and walls; young men assembling and marching to the trains; women and girls running beside them, singing, weeping hysterically, or laughing, borne up by the excitement of the throngs; people throwing flowers at them, putting roses in the soldiers' red caps, in the hair of the girls. And the regiments marching to the railroad stations, or being loaded into trucks—it wouldn't be long before you could no longer find a taxicab or even a horse in Paris.

And then back to the Hotel Crillon. The Champs-Élysées, that wide avenue, and the great open spaces, the Place de la Concorde, the Place du Carrousel, now like military encampments; regiments marching, horses galloping, artillery rumbling, people singing, shouting: "*La guerre! La guerre!*"

Inside the hotel another kind of tumult, for it appeared that there were thousands of Americans in Paris, and they all wanted to get out quickly. Many were caught without funds; they wanted food and shelter, railroad tickets, steamer accommodations, everything all at once. They had been reading about a new kind of warfare, and had visions of squadrons of German airplanes dropping bombs upon Paris that afternoon. It seemed that every person who had ever met Robbie Budd was now asking him for advice, for the loan of money, for his influence in getting something from the embassy, from the consulate, from railroad and steamship and travel bureaus.

When they couldn't get hold of Robbie, they would go to his former wife, who had always been able to get anything from him. Beauty, who wanted to sit and stare in front of her and think, who wanted to weep without anybody seeing her ruined complexion, had to put on a few dabs of paint and powder, and her lovely blue Chinese morning robe with large golden pheasants on it, and receive her friends, and the friends of her friend Emily and her friend Sophie and her friend Margy, and tell them what Robbie said, that there wasn't any immediate danger, that the embassy would advance money as soon as they had time to hear from Washington, that Robbie himself couldn't possibly do anything, he was besieged by military men trying to buy things which he didn't have and couldn't make for months yet.

They even fell upon Robbie's newly appointed secretary, to ask what he knew and what he thought. Lanny had never had such an exciting time; it was like going to war himself. He would run to his father with something he thought especially urgent, and there would be that solid rock of a man, hearty, serene, smiling. He'd say: "Remember, son, there've been lots of wars in this old Europe, and this will pass like the others." He'd say: "Remember, some of these are real friends, and some are spongers who won't ever repay the money they're trying to borrow." He'd see Lanny standing at the window, watching the troops march by and the flags flying, listening to the drums beating and the crowds shouting; he'd see the color mounting in the boy's cheeks and the light shining in his eyes, and he'd say: "Remember, kiddo, this isn't your war. Don't make any mistake and take it into your heart. You're an American!"

IX

That was the line the father was going to take. Budd's didn't engage in any wars; Budd's made munitions, and played no favorites. The father found time, in the midst of excitements and confusions, to hammer that fact in and rivet it. "I'll have to go back to Newcastle, to try to straighten out my father and brothers; and I don't want my son to step into anybody's bear trap. Remember, there never was a war in which the right was all on one side. And remember that in every war both sides lie like hell. That's half the battle—keeping up the spirits of your own crowd, and getting allies to help you. Truth is whatever you can get believed. Remember it every time you pick up a newspaper."

The father went on to prove his case. He told how Bismarck had forged a telegram in order to get the Franco-Prussian war started when he was ready for it. He told about the intrigues of the Tsar's government, the most despotic and corrupt in Europe. He explained how the great financial interests, the steel cartels, the oil and electrical trusts, and the banks which financed them, controlled both France and Germany. They owned properties in both countries, and would see that those properties were protected; they would make billions of profits, and buy new properties, and be more than ever masters, however the war might end.

"And that's all right," continued the father; "that's their business; only remember it isn't yours. Remember that among their properties are all the big newspapers. Find out who owns the one you read." Robbie took up several that were lying on the table. "This is the de Wendels'," he said; "the Comité des Forges—the steel trust that runs French politics. This one is Schneider-Creusot. And here's your old friend Zaharoff!"

The father opened one paper, and asked: "Did you get this little story?" He pointed to an account of a state ceremony which had taken place on the previous day—Zaharoff had been promoted to commander of the Legion of Honor. A strange bit of irony, that it should have happened the day that Jaurès was shot! "I don't hold any brief for Socialist tub-thumpers," said Robbie; "but he was perhaps honest, as you heard Pastier say. They shoot him, and they give one of their highest honors to an old Levantine trader who would sell the whole country tomorrow for a hundred million francs."

Practically all the Americans in Paris sympathized with France, because they believed that France had wanted peace, and because it was a republic. But Robbie wouldn't leave it at that. What counted nowadays was business, and the oil, steel, and munitions men of France wanted what all the others wanted. "Is it peace when you lend billions of francs to Russia, and force them to spend the money for arms to fight Germany?"

"I suppose you're right," the boy had to admit.

"Put yourself in the place of the German people—your friend Kurt, and his family, and millions like them. They look to their eastern border——"

"A dark cloud of barbarism, the Graf Stubendorf called it," Lanny remembered suddenly.

"Russian diplomacy has one purpose—to get Constantinople, and that means to keep Germany from getting it. Russia is called a steam roller, and it's built to roll westward; the French paid for it, and taught the Russians how to run it. Of course the Germans will fight like hell to stop it."

"Who do you think's going to win, Robbie?" Purely as a sporting proposition, it got a boy keyed up.

"Nobody on earth can say. The French are setting out for Berlin, and the Germans for Paris; they'll meet, and there'll be a smash, and one side or the other will crumple. The only thing you can be sure of is that it won't be a long war."

"How long?"

"Three or four months. Both sides would go bankrupt if it lasted longer."

"And what will England do?"

"I could make a pile of money if I knew. The men who have to make the decision are running around like a lot of ants when you turn over a stone. If England had said she'd defend France, there wouldn't have been any war. But that's the trouble with countries that have parliaments, they can't make up their minds to anything—not until it's too late."

X

Harry Murchison had put down his money and engaged a stateroom for two on a steamer sailing the next day; also a berth for Lanny in another stateroom. He had done this before the rush began, and now it was a part of his "ultimatum." He and Beauty could be married that night; or they could be married by the captain of the steamer. Harry came two or three times during the day to plead his cause and argue against the folly of hesitation. He would lock the door so that nobody could interrupt them, and he wouldn't let her answer the telephone; he was a young man who had been used to having his own way most of his life. He hadn't much consideration for Beauty's feelings; he said that she was somewhat hysterical right now, and didn't really know her own mind. Once the die was cast, the marriage words spoken, she'd settle down and be glad somebody had acted for her.

It was the technique known in America as "high-pressure salesmanship." Beauty would beg for time, but Harry would insist: "I've got to sail on that steamer. There's going to be an awful lot of plate glass smashed in the next few months, and I've got to be in Pittsburgh to see about replacing it."

"Don't leave me, Harry," the tormented woman pleaded. "Surely you can put it off one more week."

"If you don't go now you mayn't be able to go until the war's over. Call up the steamship company and see what they tell you. Everything is booked for months ahead, and there's talk of our government having to send steamers to get Americans out of Europe."

Robbie decided suddenly that he had better go too. Cablegrams were being delayed and censorship might stop them entirely. He told Harry that if Beauty rejected the chance, he'd take her half of the stateroom. "But don't let her know it!" he hastened to add. "If she goes, I'll manage to get on board somehow." Robbie was a friend of all the steamship people, and knew discreet ways to arrange matters. "They can put a cot in the captain's cabin," he remarked, smiling.

It was a trying position for Lanny, not knowing whether his future was to be on the French Riviera or in a smoky valley of steel and coal three thousand miles to the west. He made no complaint for himself, but he did think that the cards were being stacked against Marcel. It was an elementary principle of justice that both sides should be represented in any court. Lanny had a strong impulse to represent the painter, but Robbie had asked him to keep his hands off, and Robbie's wish was a command.

In between codings and decodings, Lanny would go to see his mother, and tell her that he loved her—that was about all he could say. Toward evening he found Mrs. Emily with her; and these two fashionable ladies had tears running down their cheeks. It wasn't because of Beauty's problems, nor was it the million Frenchwomen left at home to face the thought of bereavement. It was a terrible story which Mrs. Emily had brought. While troops were marching and crowds shouting and singing in all the streets, fate had chosen to strike another blow at Isadora Duncan. She had lain in agony for many hours, trying to bear her baby; and at last when it was placed in her arms, she had felt it suddenly beginning to turn cold. She screamed, and the attendants came running and tried to save it, but in vain; in a few minutes the spark of life had expired, and that unhappy woman was desolate again.

"Oh, my God, what has happened to the world?" whispered Lanny's mother. It certainly seemed as if some devil had got hold of affairs, at least temporarily. Everybody had been so happy, the playground of Europe had seemed such a delightful place—and here it was being turned into a charnel house, a sepulcher not even whited.

"I see those pitiful men marching away," said Mrs. Emily, "and I think how the hospitals and the graves will be filled with them, and it just seems more than a woman can bear."

"I know," said Beauty; "it's one of the reasons why I'm so tempted to flee from France."

"If the Germans break through," said the other woman, "my home lies directly in their path."

"Surely the Germans wouldn't harm that beautiful place!" exclaimed Lanny's mother. But then right away she remembered having heard how the Turks used the Parthenon to store powder in!

XI

Robbie and his son went to dinner. Beauty declined their invitation; she couldn't eat anything, she said. They guessed that Harry was coming again. The time was getting short; if she was going she had a lot of packing to do. Apparently she was, for Mrs. Emily had given her another talking to. Also Robbie had been with her—and Robbie was not following the course he had advised for his son.

Father and son came back to the hotel, and there were more delayed cables. But Beauty phoned; she wanted very much to talk to Lanny—just a few minutes, she promised—and Robbie said all right, he'd go on with the decoding himself.

Beauty was pale, seeming more distraught than ever; she was walking up and down the room, twisting her hands together. "Marcel has gone to war," she announced.

There was a telegram lying on the table, and Lanny read it. "I have been called to the colors. God bless you. Love." No high-pressure salesmanship here!

"Lanny I've got to make up my mind now!" exclaimed the mother. "I've got to decide our whole future."

"Yes, Beauty," said the boy, quietly.

"I want to think about your happiness, as well as my own."

"Don't bother about me, Beauty. I'm going to make the best of whatever you decide. If you're Harry's wife, I'll make myself agreeable and never give you any worry."

"It'll mean that you go to live in America. Will you like that?"

"I don't know, because I don't know what I'll find; but I'll get along."

"Tell me what you really prefer."

Lanny hesitated. "Robbie doesn't want me to interfere, Beauty."

"I know; but I'm asking. I have to think about both of us. If you had your choice—if you had nothing to consider but your own wishes—where would you go?"

Lanny thought for a while. His father could hardly object to his answering a straight question like that. Finally he said: "I'd go back to Juan."

"You like it there so well?"

"I've always been happy there. That's my home."

"But now there's going to be war. It mayn't be safe any more."

"Those French warships will stay in the Golfe, I imagine; and it isn't likely anybody's going to lick the British and French fleets."

"But Italy has some sort of a treaty with Germany and Austria. Doesn't she have to help them fight?"

"Italy has just announced that she will take a 'defensive attitude.' Robbie says that means they'll wait, and see which side offers them the most. That's bound to be England, because she has money."

"Our friends all talk about going back to America. It'll be lonely at Juan."

"Maybe for you," said the boy. "But you know how it is—I never did see enough of my mother. We could read, and play music, and swim, and wait for Marcel to come back." Lanny stopped, not being sure if it was fair for him to mention that aspect of the matter.

The mother's voice trembled as she said: "He may never come back, Lanny."

"There's a chance, of course. But Robbie says the war won't last long. And Marcel may never see any fighting—Robbie thinks the Provençal regiments will be kept on the Italian border, at least till they're sure what Italy's going to do. And then again, Marcel might come back wounded, and we'd both want to take care of him. It wouldn't be nice to know that he was hurt, and in need of help, and we couldn't give it."

"I know, Lanny, I know." The tears were starting again in the beautiful blue eyes. "That's what has been tearing my heart in half." She sat with her hands clasped tightly together, and the boy watched her lips trembling. "That's really what you want to do, isn't it, Lanny?"

"You asked me to tell you."

"I know. I couldn't decide it all by myself. If I do what you say, I may be a forlorn and desolate old woman. You won't get tired of me?"

"You can bet I won't."

"And you'll stand by Marcel? You'll help us, whatever hard things may come?"

"Indeed I will."

"You'll be a French boy, Lanny—not an American."

"I'll be a bit of everything, as I am now. That hasn't hurt me." He tried to conceal his joy, but didn't succeed altogether. "You really mean it, Beauty?"

"I mean it. Or, rather, I'll let you mean it for me. I'm a weak and foolish woman, Lanny. I oughtn't to have got into this jam at all. You'll have to take charge of me and make me behave myself."

"Well, I've wanted to sometimes," admitted the youngster. He wasn't sure whether he ought to laugh or cry. "Oh, Beauty, I really think it's the right thing to do!"

"All right, I'll believe you. I'll have to write a note to Harry. I just haven't the courage to see him again."

"That's all right—he ought to stop worrying you. He really hasn't any claim to you."

"He has, Lanny—more than you can guess. But I'll tell him it's all over—and we'll never see Pittsburgh."

"I can get along without so much smoke," declared the boy.

"I think I'd better tell Robbie first," said the mother. "Maybe he can help to break the shock to Harry. He'll tell him I'm not really as good as I look!"

"Harry won't suffer so much," said the young man of the world. "There'll be plenty of girls on the steamer willing to marry him."

"He's a dear, kind fellow, Lanny—you're not in a position to appreciate him. I'll write him, and he can sail tomorrow, and you and I will go to Juan right away. I'll save and pay my debts, and give up trying to shine in society—do you think there'll ever be any more society in Europe, Lanny?"

So it was settled at last; and so it was done. Robbie and Harry sailed the next day—with nobody to see them off. Beauty was packing up her many belongings, with the help of the maid whom she had engaged for her Paris sojourn, but whom she was not taking to the Riviera. Lanny was helping all he could, and writing a letter to Rick, and also one to Marcel, which he hoped would some day be delivered by the postal service of the French army. The army was rather preoccupied on that particular day—since it happened to be the one which the Kaiser's troops had chosen for the invading of Luxembourg and France.

BOOK THREE

Bella Gerant Alii

12

Loved I Not Honour More

I

THE August sun on the Riviera is a blinding white glare and a baking heat. In it the grapes ripen to deepest purple and olives fill themselves to bursting with golden oil. Men and women born and raised in the Midi have skins filled with dark pigments to protect them, and they can work in the fields without damage to their complexions. But to a blond daughter of chill and foggy New England the excess of light and heat assumed an aspect hostile and menacing; an enemy seeking to dry the juices out of her nerves, cover her fair skin with scaly brown spots, and deprive her of those charms by which and for which she had been living.

So Beauty Budd had to hide in the protection of a shuttered house, and have an electric fan to blow away the heat from her body. She rarely went out until after sundown, and since there was no one to look at her during the day, she yielded gradually to the temptation of not taking too much trouble. She would wear her old dressing gowns to save the new ones, and let her son see her with hair straggling. She got little exercise, there being nothing for her to do in a house with servants.

The result was that terror which haunts the lives of society ladies, the monster known as *embonpoint*, a most insidious enemy, who keeps watch at the gates of one's being like a cat at a gopher hole. It never sleeps, and never forgets, but stays on the job, ready to take advantage of every moment of weakness or carelessness. It creeps upon you one milligram at a time—for the advances of this enemy are not measured in space but in avoirdupois. With it, everything is gain and nothing loss; what it wins it keeps. The battle with this unfairest of fiends became the chief concern of Beauty's life, and the principal topic of her conversation in the bosom of her family.

No use looking to the government for help. During the course of the war the inhabitants of the great cities would be rationed, and those of whole countries such as Germany and Britain; but over the warm valleys of the Riviera roamed cattle, turning grass into rich cream, and there were vast cellars and caves filled with barrels of olive oil, and new supplies forming in billions of tiny black globes on the gnarled and ancient trees. Figs were ripening, bees were busy making honey—in short, war or no war, a lady who received a thousand dollars' worth of credit every month in the invulnerable currency of the United States of America could have delivered at her door unlimited quantities of oleaginous and saccharine materials.

Nor could the trapped soul expect help from the servants who waited upon her. Leese, the cook, was fat and hearty, and Rosine, the maid, would become so in due course, and both of them were set in the conviction that this was the proper way for women to be. "*C'est la nature,*" was the formula of all the people of the South of France for all the weaknesses of the flesh. They looked with dismay upon the fashion of Anglo-Saxon ladies to keep themselves in a semi-starved condition under the impression that this was the way to be beautiful; they would loudly insist that the practice was responsible for whatever headache, *crise de nerfs*, or other malaise such ladies might experience. Leese fried her fish and her rice in olive oil, and her desserts were mixed with cream; she would set a little island of butter afloat in the center of each plate of potage, and crown every sort of sweet with a rosette or curlicue of fat emulsified and made into snow-white bubbles of air. If she was asked not to do these things, she would exercise an old family servant's right to forget.

So in desperation Beauty turned to her son. "Lanny, don't let me have so much cream!" she would cry. She adopted the European practice of hot milk with coffee; and Lanny would watch while she poured a little cream over her fresh figs, and would then keep the pitcher on his side of the table. "No more now," he would say when he caught her casting a glance at the tiny Sèvres pitcher. But

the boy's efforts were thwarted by the mother's practice of keeping
a box of chocolates in her room. She would nibble them between
meals; and very soon it became evident that the cunning monster of
embonpoint could utilize the bean of a sterculiaceous tree exactly as
well as the mammary secretion of *Bos domestica*. Beauty would be
in a state of bewilderment about it. "Why, I hardly eat anything at
all!" she would exclaim.

II

The explanation of all this was obvious. Beauty Budd was a social
being, who could not live without the stimulus of rivalry. When
she was going out among people, she would be all keyed up, and
when food was put before her, she would be so absorbed in conversation that she would take only absentminded nibbles. But when
she was shut up in the house alone, or with people upon whom she
did not need to "make an impression," then, alas, she had time to
realize that she was hungry. Not even the thought of a world at
war, and the sufferings of millions of men, could save her from that
moral decline.

There were friends she might have seen; but in the tumult of
fear which had seized the world she preferred to keep to herself.
All the Americans in France were hating the Germans; but Beauty
hated war with such intensity that she didn't care who won, if only
the fighting would end. As for Lanny, he was doing what his father
advised, keeping himself neutral. This being the case, they couldn't
even speak to their own servants about the terror that was sweeping
down upon Paris.

Lanny had to be "society" to his adored mother. He would invite
her to a *thé dansant*; putting a record on the phonograph, and letting her show him the fine points of the fashionable dances. He in
turn would teach her "Dalcroze," and make her do "plastic counterpoint"; she would be required to "feel" the music, and they would
experiment and argue, and have a very good time. Then he would
invite her to a concert, in which they would be both performers and

audience; they would play duets, and he would make her work at it. No fun just playing the same things over; if you were going to get anywhere you had to be able to read. He would put a score before her and exhort and scold like a music master.

When Beauty was exhausted from that, he wouldn't let her lie down by the box of chocolates; no, it was time for their swim. When she got into her suit, he would walk behind her to the beach and survey the shapely white calves, and worry her by saying: "They are undoubtedly getting thicker!" The water was warm, and Beauty would want to float and relax, and let him swim around her; but no again, he would challenge her to a race along the shore. He would splash and make her chase him. But he never did succeed in persuading her to put on Robbie's goggles and sink down among the fishes.

They would read aloud, taking turns. Beauty couldn't concentrate upon a book very long, she was too restless—or else too sleepy. But when she had someone to read to her, that was a form of social life. She would interrupt and talk about the story, and have the stimulus of another person's reactions. In course of the years many books had accumulated in the house; friends had given them, or Beauty had bought them on people's recommendation, but had seldom found time to look at them. But now they would enjoy the company of M. France, whom they had met so recently. Lanny found *Le Lys Rouge* on the shelves, a fashionable love story treated with touches of the worldling's playful mockery. It had been his popular success, and proved a success with Beauty. It took her back to the happy days, the élite of the world enjoying the impulses of what they politely termed their hearts—the glands having not as yet been publicly discovered. Without difficulty Beauty saw herself in the role of a heroine who had become involved with three men, and couldn't figure out what to do. Having visited in Florence, she recalled the lovely landscapes, and they discussed the art treasures and art ideas in the book.

Lanny remembered that M. Priedieu, the librarian, had spoken about Stendhal. A copy of *La Chartreuse de Parme* had got onto the shelves, they had no idea how. Once more Beauty saw herself as a heroine, a woman for whom love excused all things. She was enraptured by detailed and precise analysis of the great passion. "Oh, that is exactly right!" she would exclaim, and the reading would stop while she told Lanny about men and women, and how they behaved when they were happy in love, or when they were sad; of different types of lovers, and what they said, and whether they meant it or not; how it felt to be disappointed, and to be jealous, and to be thwarted; how love and hatred became mixed and intertangled; the part that vanity played, and love of domination, and love of self, and love of the world and its applause. Beauty Budd had had a great deal of experience, and the subject was one of unending fascination.

Perhaps not all moralists would have approved this kind of conversation between a mother and a son. But she had told Lanny in Paris that if they came back to Juan, he would be a French boy. So he would have to know the arts of love, if only to protect himself. There were dangerous kinds of women, who could wreck the happiness of a man, old or young, and care not a flip of the fan about it. One should know how to tell the good ones from the bad—and generally, alas, it was not possible until it was too late.

There was another purpose, too; Beauty was defending herself, and Marcel, and Harry, or rather what she had done to Harry. Perhaps her conscience troubled her, for she talked often about the plate-glass man, and what might be happening to him in Pittsburgh. Love was bewildering, and many times you wouldn't be happy if you did and wouldn't be if you didn't. You might make a resolve to go off by yourself and have nothing more to do with love; but men had refused to let Beauty do it, and some day soon women would be refusing to let Lanny do it.

After which they would go back to Henri Beyle, soldier, diplomat, and man of the world, who had written under the pen name of Stendhal, and who would tell them how love had fared in the midst of the last World War—just a hundred years earlier, not so long ago in Europe's long story.

III

There came post cards from Marcel Detaze; he was well, busy, and happy to know they were safe at home. He was not permitted to say where he was, but gave the number of his regiment and battalion. The censoring of mail was strict, but no censor in France would object to a painter's declaring that he loved his beautiful blond mistress or to her replying that the sentiments were reciprocated. Beauty fed her soul upon these messages—plus Robbie's assurance that the war couldn't last more than three or four months. Maybe Marcel wasn't going to see any fighting; he would come home with a story of interesting adventure, and life would begin again where it had left off.

Everybody they had met in Paris, and everybody they met now, was confident that the French armies were going to hold the Germans while the Russian steam roller hurtled over Prussia and captured Berlin. The French military authorities had been so confident that they had planned a giant movement of their forces through Alsace and Lorraine; they would break the German lines at the south, then, sweeping north, cut the communications of the enemy advancing through Belgium and northern France. The papers told about the beginning of this counterattack and what it was intended to do; then suddenly they fell silent, and the next reports of fighting in this district came from places in France. Those who understood military affairs knew what this meant—that the armies of *la patrie* had sustained a grave defeat.

As to what was happening farther north, not all the censorship in the land could hide the facts from the public. One had only to take a map and mark on it the places where fighting was reported, and he would see that it was the German steam roller which was hurtling —and at the rate of ten or twenty miles a day. The little Belgian army was fighting desperately, but was being swept aside; its forts were being pulverized by heavy artillery, and towns and villages in the path of the invasion were being wrecked and burned. The still smaller British army which had been landed at the Channel ports

was apparently meeting the same fate. The Kaiser was on his way
to Paris!

IV

There came a letter from Sophie, Baroness de la Tourette. That
very lively lady had been having an adventure, and wrote about it
in detail—being shut up in a room in a fourth-class hotel in Paris,
much bored with nothing to do. She had gone to spend the month
of August with friends at a country place on the river Maas, which
flows through the heart of Belgium. Sophie was a nonpolitical person, entirely devoted to having a good time; she rarely looked at
newspapers, and when she heard people talking about war threats,
she paid no attention, being unable to take seriously the idea that
anybody would disturb the comfort of a person of her social position.

The ladies she was visiting shared her attitude. News traveled
slowly in the country; and when at last they heard that the Germans
had crossed the frontier, they did not worry; the army would be
going to France, and it might be interesting to watch it pass. Only
when they heard the sound of heavy guns did they realize that they
might be in danger, and then it was too late; a troop of Uhlans with
long lances came galloping up the driveway, and the automobiles
and horses on the place were seized. Soon afterward arrived several
limousines, and elegant officers descended, and with bowing and
heel-clicking informed the ladies of the regrettable need to take the
château for a temporary staff headquarters. They all had wasp
waists, and wore monocles, long gray coats, gold bracelets, and
shiny belts and boots; their manners were impeccable, and they
spoke excellent English, and seemed to be well pleased with a lady
who was introduced as Miss Sophie Timmons from the far-off state
of Ohio.

Her friends had suddenly realized that under the law, being married to a Frenchman, she was French and might be interned for the
period of the war. That night she sent her maid to the village and

succeeded in hiring a cart and an elderly bony white horse; taking only a suitcase, she and the maid and a peasant driver had set out toward Brussels. There was fighting everywhere to the south and east of them, and the roads were crowded with refugees driving dogcarts, trundling handcarts, or carrying their belongings on their backs. More than once they had had to sit for long periods by the roadside to let the German armies pass, and the woman's letter was full of amazed horror at the perfection of the Kaiser's war machine. For a solid hour she watched motorized artillery rolling by: heavy siege guns, light field-pieces, wicked-looking rapid-firers; caissons, trucks loaded with shells, and baggage trains, pontoon trains, field kitchens. "My dear, they have been getting ready for this all our lifetime!" wrote the Baroness de la Tourette.

She watched the marching men in their dull field-gray uniforms, so much more sensible than the conspicuous blue and red of the French. The Germans tramped in close, almost solid ranks, forever and ever and ever—in one village they told Sophie of an unbroken procession for more than thirty hours. "And so many with cigars in their mouths!" she wrote. "I wondered, had they been pillaging the shops."

The fugitives slept in their cart for fear it might be stolen; and after two days and nights they reached Brussels, which the Germans had not yet taken. From there they got to Ostend, where the British were landing troops, and then by boat to Boulogne, and to Paris by train. "You should see this city!" wrote Sophie. "Everybody has gone that can get away. The government has taken all the horses and trucks. Maybe the taxicabs have been hired by refugees—I'm hoping that a few will come back. All the big hotels are closed—the men employees are in the army. The Place de la Concorde is full of soldiers sleeping upon straw. The strangest thing is that gold and silver coins have disappeared entirely; they say people are hoarding them, and you can't get any change because there's only paper money. I am waiting for a chance to come south without having to walk. I hope the Germans do not get here first. It would be embarrassing to meet those officers again!"

V

When Marcel departed to join the army, he had brought the keys of his cottage to the servants at Bienvenu and left them for Madame Budd. The servants being French, the occasion had not been casual; they had wept and called upon God to protect him, which in turn had brought tears to the eyes of Monsieur. He had said that it was *pour la patrie*, and that they should take care of the precious Madame, if and when she returned; after those wicked Germans had been driven from the soil of France, they would all live happy forever after, as in the fairy tales.

Leese and Rosine of course knew all about the love affair. To them it was romance, delight, the wine and perfume of life; they lived upon it as women in the United States were learning to live upon the romances, real and imaginary, of the movie stars of Hollywood. Beauty's servants talked about it, not merely among themselves, but with all the other servants of the neighborhood; everybody watched, everybody shared the tenderness, the delight; everybody said, what a shame the young painter was so poor!

Now Beauty received a card from Marcel, saying that, if anything should happen to him, he wanted her to have his paintings. "I don't know if they will ever be worth anything," he wrote; "but you have been kind to them, while to my relatives they mean nothing. Perhaps it might be well to move them to your house, where they would be safer. Do what you please about this."

Beauty, watching for every hint in his messages, clasped her hand to her heart. "Lanny, do you suppose that means he's going to some post of danger?"

"I don't know why it should," said the boy. "We have our own paintings insured, and certainly we ought to take care of his."

Beauty had been going to the little house and sitting there, remembering the times when she had been so happy, and reproaching herself because she had not appreciated her blessings. Now she went with Lanny to carry out Marcel's commission. There were more than a hundred canvases, each tacked upon a wooden frame, and stacked in a sort of shed-room at the rear of the house. One by one Lanny brought them out and studied them—all those aspects of Mediterranean sea and shore which he knew better than anything else. He exclaimed over the loveliness of them; he was ready to set himself up as an art critic against all the world. Beauty wiped the tears from her eyes and exclaimed over the wickedness of a war that had taken such a lover, and stopped such work, and even made it impossible for Sophie to come to the Riviera unless she walked!

There was a group of paintings from the trip to Norway. Lanny had never seen these or heard of them, for it had been before he was told about Marcel. The boy had heard so much about this cold and shining country, and here it was by the magic of art. Here was more than fiords and mountains and *saeters* and ancient farmhouses with openings in the roofs instead of chimneys; here was the soul of these things, old, yet forever new, so long as men loved beauty and marveled at its self-renewal. Here, also, was Greece with its memories, and Africa with its grim desert men, muffled and silent. The *Bluebird* was being made over into a hospital ship right now; but its two cruises with the soap king would live—"well, as long as I do," said Lanny.

V I

The whereabouts of Marcel was supposed to be a secret, upon the preserving of which the safety of *la patrie* depended. But when you take thousands of young men from a neighborhood and put them into encampments not more than a hundred miles away, it soon becomes what the French call *un secret de Polichinelle*, something which everybody knows. The truck drivers talked when they came to the towns for supplies, and pretty soon Leese and Rosine were able to inform the family that the painter's regiment was on guard duty in the Alpes Maritimes.

Italy had declared for neutrality in this war; but it could not be forgotten that she had been a member of the so-called Triple Alliance with Germany and Austria. There was a powerful Italian party known as the Triplicists, who wanted to carry out the pledges, and

in these days of quick political overturns France dared not leave her
Provençal border unguarded. So Marcel had for a while what the
British called a "cushy" job. But the trouble was that as the menace
of the German steam roller increased, more and more men were
being grabbed up and rushed to the north. Right away Beauty decided that she must visit that camp. She didn't wait to write, not
knowing if the censor would let such a letter pass; she would just go
to the place and lay siege to whatever authorities might be in command. Beauty had arts which she trusted, but which could not be
exercised by mail.

The difficulty lay with transportation. They had their car, but
Pierre Bazoche was in the army—oddly enough he was a sergeant,
and gave orders to the beloved of his former employer. This seemed
to the employer among the atrocities of war, but it amused Lanny,
and he was sure it wouldn't worry Marcel. Pierre was a capable fellow, and his orders were doubtless proper.

Leese could always find among her innumerable relatives a man or
woman to do anything that was needed, and she now produced an
elderly truck driver of the flower farms of the Cap d'Antibes, who
could be spared for this journey of romantic interest. He was washed
and made presentable in Pierre's uniform, and managed to solve the
problem of getting the *essence*, which had suddenly grown scarce
and high in price, being needed in huge quantities to move the
troops and guns for the saving of Paris.

Lanny sat in the front seat and made friends with old Claude
Santoze, who was dark and hook-nosed, and doubtless descended
from the Saracen invaders. His black hair was grizzling, and he had
half a dozen children at home, but he wanted nothing so much as a
chance to fight, and wanted to talk about the war and what Lanny
knew about it. The youngster put on the mantle of authority, having a purpose of his own, which was to persuade Claude to say that
a boy so intelligent and sensible was old enough to learn to drive a
car, and that he, Claude, was willing for a suitable fee to take the
time off to teach him.

Having accomplished this much, Lanny moved into the back seat and began a campaign with his mother. He could sail a boat, and run a motorboat, and why was a car any different? Like all boys of his time, Lanny was fascinated by machinery, and listened to the talk of motor owners and drivers and asked all the questions he dared. Now even the women of France were learning to drive, and surely the son of Robbie Budd, maker of machines, ought to be allowed to try. So in the end Beauty said yes; it was one of her characteristics that she found it so hard to say anything else.

VII

They were traveling up the valley of the river Var, amid scenery which took their minds off their troubles. Before many hours they were winding along the sides of mountains, and could only hope that the descendant of the Saracens was as alert as he looked. The chill of autumn was in the air, and the wind blew delightful odors from the pine forests. They were in what seemed a wilderness, when they came suddenly upon the encampment; Beauty was surprised, for she had taken it for granted that soldiers in wartime slept like rabbits in holes in the ground. She had not realized that they would have a town, with excellent one-story wooden buildings and regular streets laid out.

The exercising of feminine charm was going to be difficult. There was a barrier across the road, and the men on duty could not be cajoled into raising it for a car whose occupants had no credentials. The lady would have to submit her request in writing; so they drove back to a tiny village which had what called itself an *auberge*, and Beauty hired the only two bedrooms it contained. There she penned a note—could you guess to whom? Respectfully and with due formality she addressed herself to Sergeant Pierre Bazoche—the bright idea having occurred to her that a person of rank might be able to pull more wires than a humble private, even though a man of genius. Beauty informed the sergeant that she was the fiancée of Private Detaze, and requested the sergeant's kind offices to obtain a leave of absence for the private.

Lanny handed this in at the barrier, and after that there was nothing to do but wait. It was dark before the answer came, in the shape of the sergeant himself, looking distinguished in his long blue coat and baggy red pants, but not presuming on his new status. He lifted his képi and bowed, and said that he was delighted to see them both. Like everybody else, his first wish was to know about the terrible events in the north; could it be that Paris was in danger? Could it be that the capital had been moved to Bordeaux? Only afterwards did he mention the matter which was so close to Beauty's heart. Nothing could be done that night, but he was taking steps to arrange matters in the morning so that Madame's wishes might be granted.

How were Beauty and her son going to spend an evening in that wretched village, with only a few huts of woodsmen and charcoal burners, and only candles in their rooms? Lanny had an original suggestion, fitting his own disposition: why not sit in the public room and talk with whoever might come in? The possibility of such a proceeding would never have crossed the mind of Beauty Budd; but the boy argued they would be nothing but peasant fellows, with whom he had chatted off and on all his days. If there was a lady in the room, they would surely mind their conversation. They would sip their wine, play their dominoes, sing their songs. If they were soldiers, they would want to be told about the war, like Pierre. They were Marcel's comrades, and one of them might some day save his life.

That settled it. Beauty decided that she wanted to know them all! So the two had their supper at one of the rough wooden tables in the little drinking place; fried rabbit and onions and dried olives and bread and cheese and sour wine. When they were through they did not leave, but called for a set of dominoes; and when the soldiers came straggling in—what a sensation! Lanny talked with them, and the whisper passed around: *"Des Américains!"* Ah, yes, that accounted for it; in that wonderful land of millionaires and cinema stars it must be the custom for rich and divinely beautiful blond ladies to sit in public rooms and chat with common soldiers. Before long Lanny revealed why they were there, and the sensation was magnified. *Sapristi! C'est la fiancée de Marcel Detaze! Il est peintre! Il est bon enfant! C'est un diable heureux!*

It happened just as Lanny said it would; they all wanted to know about the war. Here were rich people, who had traveled, had been in Paris when the war broke out—what had they seen? And a friend who had been in Belgium—what had *she* seen? Was it true, Madame, that the Germans were cutting off the hands of Belgian children? That they were spearing babies upon their bayonets and carrying them on the march? Beauty reported that her friend had not mentioned any such sights. She did not express opinions of her own. They were not there to make pro-German propaganda, nor to excite disaffection among the troops!

VIII

In the course of the next morning came Marcel; young, erect, and happy, walking upon air. He caught Beauty in his arms and kissed her, right there in front of an audience, including Lanny, and mine host with long gray mustaches, and several mule teams with drivers, all grinning. Romance had come to the Alpes Maritimes! The men could not have been more interested if it had been a company of movie stars to put them into a picture.

The military life agreed with Marcel; why shouldn't it? asked he— in that bracing mountain air, at the most delightful season of the year, living outdoors, marching and drilling, eating wholesome food, and not a care in the world, except the absence of his beloved. "*Regardez!*" he cried, and pointed to the mountains. "I will have something new to paint!" He showed Lanny the far snowy peaks, and the valleys filled with mist. "There's a new kind of atmosphere," he said, and wanted to start on it right away. He had just come from sentry duty; on that mountain to the east he paced back and forth many hours at a stretch; it was good, because it gave him time to think and to work out his philosophy of life—and of love, he added. When Beauty spoke of danger, he laughed; he and the Italian sentries exchanged cigarettes and witticisms—"Jokes and smokes," said Marcel, who was brushing up his English.

They had lunch in the *auberge*, and Marcel was like all the other soldiers, he wanted to talk about nothing but the war. "Did you bring me any papers?" Yes, Lanny had had that kind thought, and Marcel wanted to see them at once. The boy could see that his mother's feelings were hurt; the painter could actually look at an old newspaper when he had Beauty Budd in front of him! But that's what has to be expected, thought she. "Man's love is of man's life a thing apart; 'Tis woman's whole existence."

Worse than that: before the lunch was over, Marcel revealed that he wasn't content with this idyllic existence in the mountains; he was pining to get up to the north, into the hell of death and destruction. He undertook to defend this attitude, even though he saw that it brought tears to the eyes of his beautiful blond mistress. *"La patrie est en danger!"* It was the war cry of the French Revolution, and now, more than a hundred years later, it was shaking the soul of Marcel Detaze. How could any Frenchman know that the goosestep was trampling the banks of the river Marne, only a few miles from Paris, and not desire to rush there, and interpose his body between the most beautiful city in the world and the most hateful of enemies?

Lanny knew that they wanted to be alone; their every glance revealed it, and he said that he would take a walk and see all he could of those grand mountains. Marcel pointed to the west and said: "All France is that way." Then he pointed to the east and added: "All that is forbidden."

So Lanny walked to the west, and when he was tired he sat and talked to a shepherd on a hillside; he drank the clear icy water of a mountain stream, and saw the trout darting here and there, and a great bird, perhaps an eagle, sailing overhead, and large grouse called capercaillie whirring through the pine forests. When he came back, toward dark, he saw by the faces of the lovers that they were happy, and by the quivering gray mustaches of the *aubergiste* and the smiles of his stout wife that all the world loved a lover. Madame had prepared a sort of wedding cake for the occasion, and it was washed down with wine by mule drivers and soldiers who sang love songs, for all the world like a grand opera chorus. *"Nous partons, courage; courage aux soldats."*

IX

When they got home again they found that the Baroness de la Tourette had returned to Cannes; she and her maid had managed to crowd into a train, sitting up the whole night—but that was a small matter after the hardships they had been through. Sophie had tales to tell about Paris under what had so nearly been a siege. The German army of invasion had come swinging down on the city, turning like the spokes of a wheel with far-off Verdun as the hub. But when they got close to Paris they veered to the east, apparently planning to enclose the French armies at Verdun and the other fortifications. The minds of their commanders were obsessed by the memory of Sedan; if they could make such a wholesale capture, they could end this war as they had ended the last.

There is around Paris a convergence of waters known as "the seven rivers"; gentle streams, meandering through wooded lands with towns and villages along the banks, and many bridges. The Marne flows into the Seine just before it enters the city at the east. It was along the former river that the German von Kluck contemptuously exposed the right wing of his army; and General Gallieni assembled all the taxicabs and trucks in a great metropolis, rushed his reserves to the front, and hurled them against the enemy forces.

You saw hardly any young men in Paris during those fateful days of the battle of the Marne. The older men and women and children listened to the thunder of the guns that did not cease day or night; they sat upon the parapets of the river, and saw the wreckage of trees and buildings, of everything that would float, including the bodies of dead animals—the human bodies were being fished out before they got into the city. Overhead came now and then a sight of irresistible fascination, an aeroplane soaring, spying out the troop movements, or possibly bringing bombs. The enemy plane was known as a *Taube*—an odd fantasy, to turn the dove of peace into a cruel instrument of slaughter. Already they had dropped explosives upon Antwerp and killed many women and children. Nevertheless, curiosity was too great, and everywhere in the open places you saw crowds gazing into the sky.

The sound of the guns receded, and by this the people knew that one of the great battles of history had been fought and won. But they did not shout or celebrate; Paris knew what a victory cost, and waited for the taxicabs to bring back their loads of wounded and their news about the dead. The Germans were thrown back upon the Aisne, thirty miles farther north; so the flight of refugees from Paris stopped—and at last it became possible for a lady of title to get to the Riviera without having to walk.

With Sophie came Eddie Patterson, her amiable friend whose distinction in life was that he had chosen the right grandfather. The old gentleman had once engineered through the legislature of his state a franchise to build a railroad bridge; now he drew a royalty from the railroad of one cent for every passenger who crossed the river. Eddie was an amateur billiard player with various medals and cups, and was also fond of motorboating. He talked of giving his fastest boat to the French government to be used in hunting submarines; he would soon see it cruising the Golfe Juan day and night with a four-pounder gun bolted onto the bow.

Eddie Patterson was a slender and rather stoop-shouldered fellow who talked hardheadedly, and had never given any indication of having a flighty mind; but now he had somehow worked himself into a furious rage against the Germans and was talking about volunteering for some kind of service. Sophie was in a panic about it, and of course appealed for the help of her friend Beauty Budd, who agreed with her that men were crazy, and that none of them ever really appreciated a woman's love.

At any hour of the day or night Sophie and Eddie would get into an argument. "All that talk about German atrocities is just propaganda," the baroness would announce. "Haven't I been there and

seen? Of course the Germans shoot civilians who fire at them from
the windows of houses. And maybe they are holding the mayors of
Belgian towns as hostages; but isn't that always done in wartime?
Isn't it according to international law?" Sophie talked as if she were
a leading authority on the subject, and Eddie would answer with an
impolite American word: "Bunk!" After listening to a few such discussions, Lanny made up his mind that neither of them really knew
very much about it, but were just repeating what they read in the
papers. Since there were hardly any but French and English papers
to be had, a person like himself who wanted to be neutral had a hard
time of it.

X

What women have to do is to keep their restless and frantic men
entertained. So Lanny would be pressed into service to take Eddie
Patterson fishing, or tempt him into roaming the hills to explore ancient Roman and Saracen ruins. But truly it was impossible to get
away from the war anywhere in France.

Once they stopped to watch the distilling of lavender, high up on
a wind-swept plateau. There were odd-looking contrivances on
wheels, with an iron belly full of fire, and a rounded dome on top
from which ran a long spout, making them look like fantastic birds.
A crew of women and older men were harvesting the plants, tend-
ing the fires, and collecting the essence in barrels. Pretty soon Lanny
was talking with them, and they became more concerned to ask him
questions than to earn their daily bread. Americans were rich and
were bound to know more than poor peasants of the Midi. "What
do you think, Messieurs? Will *les Allemands* be driven from our
soil? And how long will it take? And what do you think the Italians will do? Surely they could not attack us, their cousins, almost
their brothers!"

On Lanny's own Cap d'Antibes the principal industry was growing flowers for perfumes, and in winter this is done under glass. It
was estimated that there were more than a million glass frames upon
that promontory; and naturally those people who owned them were

troubled to hear about bombs being dropped from the sky, and about strange deadly craft rising from the sea and launching torpedoes. Such things sounded fabulous, but they must be real, because often you could see war vessels patrolling, and now and then a seaplane scouting, and there were notices in all public places for fishermen and others to report at once any unusual sight on the sea.

Now came the flower growers, wanting to talk about *les affaires.* What did these foreign gentry think about the chances of enemy bombing of the Cap? What would be the effect, supposing that a stray torpedo were to hit the rocks? Would it have force enough to shatter those million glass frames? And what did it mean that people who were supposed to be civilized, who had come to the Riviera by the tens of thousands, as the Germans had done—many great steamers loaded with them every winter—should now go away and repay their hosts in this dreadful manner?

There came a letter from Mrs. Emily Chattersworth, who had fled from Les Forêts when the Germans came near, and after the great battle had returned to see what had become of her home. "I suppose I can count myself fortunate," she wrote, "because only half a dozen shells struck the house, and they were not of the biggest. Apparently they didn't get their heavy guns this far, and the French retired without offering much resistance. The Uhlans came first, and they must have had an art specialist with them, because they packed up the best tapestries and most valuable pictures, and took them all. They dumped a lot of furniture out of the windows —I don't know whether that was pure vandalism or whether they were planning to build breastworks. They did use the billiard table for that purpose, setting it up on edge; it didn't work very well, for there are many bullet holes through it. They used the main rooms for surgical work, and just outside the window are piles of bloody boots and clothing cut from the wounded. They raided the cellars, of course, and the place is a litter of broken bottles. In the center of my beautiful fleur-de-lis in the front garden is a shell hole and a wrecked gun caisson with pieces of human flesh still sticking to it.

"But what breaks my heart is the fate of my glorious forests.

There was a whole German division concealed in them, and the French set fire to the woods in many places; the enemy came out fighting and were slaughtered wholesale. The woods are still burning and will never be the same in our lifetime. The stench from thousands of bodies which have not yet been found loads the air at night and is the most awful thing one could imagine. I do not know if I can ever endure to live in the place again. I can only pray that the barbarians will not have a second chance at it. The opinion of our friends here is that they are through and will be entirely out of France in another month or two."

So there was more ammunition for Eddie Patterson! One by one the militarists among the Americans were joining up; some in the Foreign Legion, others in the ambulance service, many women for hospital work. The French aviation service was popular among the adventurous-minded young men—but to Sophie this was the most horrible idea of all, for those man-birds were hunting one another in the skies, and the casualties among them were appalling. In the first days all France had been electrified by the deed of one flier, who had driven his plane straight through the gasbag of a Zeppelin, and out at the other side. The mass of hydrogen had exploded and the huge airship had crashed, an inferno of flame; the aviator, of course, had shared its fate.

Beauty Budd would fling her arms about her boy and cry: "Oh, Lanny, don't ever let them get you into a war!" And then one day she received a letter which made her heart stand still:

"Chérie: Your visit shines as the most precious jewel of my memory. The news which I have to tell will make you sad, I fear—but be courageous for my sake. Your coming was the occasion of my having the opportunity to make the acquaintance of my commandant, and being able to volunteer for special service. I am being sent elsewhere to receive training, concerning which it is not permissible for me to write. For the present you may address me in care of l'École Supérieure d'Aéronautique at Vincennes.

"Your love is the sunshine of my life, and knows neither clouds nor night. I adore you. Marcel."

13

Women Must Weep

I

IT WAS going to be some time before Lanny Budd would see his father again. The warring nations would have their "missions" in New York for the purpose of buying military supplies; Robbie's headquarters would be there, and he would make a great deal of money. The various governments would float bonds in the United States, and persons who believed in their financial stability would buy the bonds, and the money would be spent for everything that was needed by armies. Robbie explained these matters in his letters, and said that England and France had placed enough orders with Budd's to justify great enlargements of the plant.

Robbie wrote cautiously, being aware that mail would be read by the French censor. "Remember what I told you about your own attitude, and do not let anybody sway you from it. This is the most important thing for your life." That was enough for Lanny; he did his best to resist the tug of forces about him. Robbie sent magazines and papers with articles that would give him a balanced view; not marking the articles—that would have made it too easy for the censor—but writing him a few days later to read pages so-and-so.

"One thing I was wrong about," the father admitted. "This war is going to last longer than I thought." When Lanny read that, the giant armies were locked in an embrace of death on the river Aisne; the French trying to drive the Germans still farther back, the Germans trying to hold on. They fought all day, and at night food and ammunition were brought up in *camions* and carts, and the armies went on fighting. Battles lasted not days but weeks, and you could

247

hardly say when one ended and the next began. The troops charged and retreated and charged again, fighting over ground already laid waste. They dug themselves in, and when rain filled up the trenches they stayed in them, because it was better to be wet than dead.

It was the same on the eastern front also. The Russian steam roller had made some headway against the Austrians, but in East Prussia it had got stuck in the swampy lands about the Masurian Lakes. The Russians had been surrounded and slaughtered wholesale; but many had got away, and fresh armies had come up and they were pushing back and forth across the border, one great battle after another.

It was going to be that way for a long time—the fiercest fighting, inspired by the bitterest hatreds that Europe had known for centuries. Each nation was going to mobilize its resources from every part of the world; resources of man power, of money, of goods, and of intellectual and moral factors. Each side was doing everything in its power to make the other odious, and neither was going to have any patience with those who were lukewarm or doubting. A mother and son from America who wanted to keep themselves neutral would be buffeted about like birds in a thunderstorm.

II

Traveling by himself to a new post of duty, Marcel was free of censorship for a day or two. He wrote on the train and mailed in Paris an eloquent and passionate love letter, inspired by their recent day and night together. It filled Beauty with joy but also with anguish, for it told her that this treasure of her heart was going to one of the most terrible of all posts of danger. He was to receive several weeks of intensive training to enable him to act as observer in a stationary balloon.

He had suggested this post as one for which his career as a painter fitted him especially. His ability to distinguish shades of color would enable him to detect camouflage. He had studied landscapes from mountain tops, and could see things that the ordinary eye would miss. "You must learn to be happy in the thought that I shall be of real use to my country"—so he wrote, and perhaps really believed it, being a man. What Beauty did was to crumple the letter in her hands, and sink down with her face upon it and wet it with her tears.

After that there was little peace in Bienvenu. Beauty went about with death written on her face; Lanny would hear her sobbing in the night, and would go to her room and try to comfort her. "You chose a Frenchman, Beauty. You can't expect him to be anything else." The boy had been reading an anthology of English poetry, which Mr. Elphinstone had left behind when he went home to try to get into the army. Being young, Lanny sought to comfort his mother with noble sentiments expressed in immortal words. "I could not love thee, dear, so much, Loved I not honour more."

So he quoted; but it only seemed to make Beauty mad. "What do you mean, 'honour'? It's nothing but the desire of powerful men to rule over others. It's a trick to get millions of people to follow them and die for their glory."

Going about the house brooding, did Beauty Budd regret the choice she had made? If so, she didn't say it to Lanny. What she told him was that life was a thing too cruel to be endured. It could not be that there was a God—the idea was crazy. We were being mocked by some devil, or by a swarm of them—a separate devil in the heart of every man who sought to kill his fellows.

Beauty's good friend Sophie and her young man, Eddie Patterson, rallied to her support. They brought with them an elderly retired Swiss diplomat who bore the distinguished name of Rochambeau; having been behind the scenes of Europe most of his life, he was not to be deceived by any propaganda, and could not be offended by the antimilitarist utterances of a self-centered American lady. These four played bridge; they played with a kind of desperation, all day and most of the night, stopping only when Leese put a meal upon the table and tapped a little tune on the Chinese gongs that hung by the dining-room door. They played for very small stakes, but took their game with the utmost seriousness, having their different systems of play, and discussing each hand, what they had done and whether some other way might not have been better. They never mentioned, and they tried never to think, how men were being mangled with shot and shell while these fine points of bidding and leading and signaling were being settled.

A convenient arrangement for Lanny, because it set him free to read. Also he could play tennis with boys and girls of the near-by villas, and keep the household supplied with seafood. But he had to promise not to go sailing upon the bay, because of Beauty's fear that a German submarine might rise up without warning and torpedo the pleasure boats in the Golfe Juan.

III

Lanny kept up a correspondence with his friend Rick, and learned once more how difficult was going to be the role of neutral in this war. Rick said that the way the Germans were behaving in Belgium deprived them of all claim to be considered as civilized men. Rick hadn't been as much impressed by Kurt's long words as had Lanny, and he said that anyhow, what was the use of fancy-sounding philosophy if you didn't make it count in everyday affairs? Rick said furthermore that from now on America's safety depended on the British fleet, and the quicker the Americans realized it the better for them and for the world.

Lanny was at a disadvantage in these arguments, because he was afraid that if he repeated what his father had told him, the censor wouldn't allow the letter to pass. So he just mentioned what he was reading, and the sights he was seeing. The French had what was called an "aérohydro," a plane that could land upon water, and one of them, having sprung an oil leak, had come down by the quay at Juan; Lanny had watched it being repaired, and then had seen it depart. It carried a machine gun, a Hotchkiss—Lanny knew all the types of guns, as other boys knew automobiles. Rick in return told about the London busses being made over into "transports" for troops, and about crowds of clerks and businessmen drilling in

Hyde Park, still in their civilian clothes, and with only sticks for guns.

But Rick's principal interest was in the air. He wrote a lot about having met one of the fliers with whom they had talked at Salisbury Plain; this officer had fought a pistol duel in the sky, and had got his German. The British, too, were putting machine guns in their planes; but it was a problem, for most planes had the propeller in front, and that was where you wanted to shoot if you were following an enemy. The idea now was to shoot through the propeller, and the British had devised one with flanges which would turn aside whatever bullets struck its blades.

"That's the service I'm going into," said Rick. "But I've promised the pater to wait until next year. The age requirement is eighteen, but a lot of the fellows do a little fibbing. I could, because I'm tall. It is hard to do any studying in times like these. No doubt it's easier for an American."

Lanny corresponded also with Rosemary Codwilliger—pronounced Culliver. He always felt funny when he wrote that name; but he knew that many English names were queer, especially the fashionable ones; the owners carefully preserved this queerness as a form of distinction, as one way of showing that they didn't care a hang whether anybody agreed with them about the way to spell, or to pronounce, or to do anything else. It did not occur to Lanny that people like that might be difficult to get along with in other ways; all he remembered was that Rosemary was delightful to look at, and how sweet it had been to sit with his arms around her in the moonlight.

He didn't write anything about that. They exchanged placid and friendly letters that would make proper reading for both censors and parents. She said that her father was commanding a regiment somewhere in France, and that her mother's nephew, the Honorable Gerald Smithtotten, had been killed after holding the Condé Canal near Mons against seven enemy attacks. "This war is rather hard on our best families," explained the daughter of Captain Codwilliger, "because they have to show themselves on the parapets or whatever it is, to set an example for the men. I want to take up nursing, but mother keeps begging me to finish this year's school. Mothers always think that we are a lot younger than we are really. Are American mothers like that?"

IV

Lanny could not help thinking about Kurt all the time, and wondering what he was doing and thinking. Of course Kurt would be patriotic. Would he blame Lanny for not taking the side of Germany? What reason would he give? Lanny wished he could find out; but of course no letters were allowed to come or go between countries at war.

One day it happened that Lanny was poking into a bureau drawer where he kept handkerchiefs and a fishing reel and some cartridges and photographs and old letters and what not. He picked up a business card and read: "*Johannes Robin, Agent, Maatschappij voor Electrische Specialiteiten, Rotterdam.*" What a lot had happened in the world since Lanny had talked with that Jewish gentleman on the train last Christmas! "I wonder if I'll ever see him again," the boy reflected.

He remembered that he had intended to write to Mr. Robin; and this brought another idea, that possibly the salesman of gadgets might be willing to mail a letter to Kurt for him. Lanny had learned, from the conversation of his mother's friends, that one could communicate with Germans in this way; it was against the law, but much business was still being carried on by way of neutral countries. "It couldn't do Mr. Robin any harm," the boy decided, "because I won't say anything the censor can object to; I won't even need to say that I'm in France."

He sat himself down and composed a letter to his friend in Germany. To set the German censors straight he began:

"My father has told me that it's an American's duty to keep neutral, and I am doing it. I don't want to lose touch with you, so I write to say that I am at home, and that my mother and I are well.

My father is back in Connecticut. I am studying hard, reading the best books I can get, and not forgetting the ideals of the nobler life. I am also practicing sight reading, although my piano technique is still mixed up. I have no teachers at present, but my mother has met a young American college man who came over on a cattle boat for the adventure and now thinks he may stay for a while because he has become interested in a young lady who lives near us. He may want to earn some money, so may teach me what he learned at college, if he has not forgotten it. Please give my sincere regards to all the members of your family, and write your affectionate friend, Lanny."

Certainly that letter could do no injury to any nation at war; and Lanny wrote the salesman in Rotterdam, recalling their meeting on the train and hoping that this would find Mr. Robin well, and that his business had not been too greatly injured by the war. Lanny explained that here was a letter to the friend he had visited in Silesia. Mr. Robin was welcome to read the letter, and Lanny assured him that it contained no war secrets; Mr. Robin would be at liberty to test the paper with lemon juice or with heat—Lanny had been reading and hearing about spies and the way they operated. He hoped that this request would not embarrass Mr. Robin in any way; if it did, he was at liberty to destroy the letter; otherwise would he please mail it in a plain envelope addressed to Kurt Meissner at Schloss Stubendorf, Upper Silesia.

Lanny posted the two letters in the same envelope, and then waited. In due course came a reply from Mr. Robin, cordial as Lanny had expected. Mr. Robin was pleased to take his word about the letter, and would mail future letters if so desired. He recalled his fellow-traveler with pleasure and hoped to meet him again some day. No, the war had not injured his business; on the contrary, he had been able to expand it along new lines, not so different from those of Lanny's father. Mr. Robin told about his family; he had two little boys, one ten and the other eight, and he took the liberty of enclosing a snapshot, so that Lanny might feel that he knew them.

Lanny studied the picture, which had been taken in the summertime, and showed the family standing at the entrance to a pergola, with a Belgian shepherd dog lying on the ground in front of them. Mr. Robin had on an outing shirt with a soft collar such as Lanny himself wore; Mrs. Robin was stoutish and kind-looking, and the two little boys gazed soberly at Lanny, as if they had known that he was going to be seeing them, and wondered what sort of fellow he might be. They had dark wavy hair like their father, and large, gentle eyes; on the back their names were written, Hans and Freddi, and the information that the former played the violin and the latter the clarinet. Lanny thought once more that he liked the Jews, and asked his mother why they didn't know any. Beauty replied that she hadn't happened to meet them; Robbie didn't like them any too much.

A couple of weeks later came a letter postmarked Switzerland, without the name of any sender. It proved to be from Kurt—evidently he too had some friend whom he trusted. It was in the same cautious tone as Lanny's. "I am glad to hear about an American's attitude to present events. You will of course understand that my point of view is different. You are fortunate in being able to go on with your music studies. For me it has become necessary to make preparations for a more active career. Whatever happens, I will always think of you with warm friendship. My soul remains what it has always been, and I count upon yours. I will write you when I can and hope that you will do the same. The members of my family are well at present. All, as you can imagine, are very busy. Those who are at home join me in kindest regards. Kurt."

Lanny showed this to his mother, and she agreed that Kurt must be preparing for some sort of military service. He was only sixteen, but then the Germans were thorough and began young. His brothers, no doubt, were in the fighting now. Lanny tried to read between the lines; that sentence about his friend's soul meant to tell him, over the censor's shoulder, that even though Kurt went to war, he would still believe in the importance of the ideal, and in art as an instrument for uplifting mankind. The war was not going to make any difference in their friendship.

V

Since Kurt was counting upon Lanny's soul, Lanny must be worthy of it. He decided that he spent too much time reading love stories, and should begin at once upon something uplifting. He was wondering what to choose, when he happened to hear M. Rochambeau, the retired diplomat, remark that the priests and bishops who were blessing the instruments of slaughter in the various nations were not very well representing the spirit of Jesus. Lanny reflected that he had seen many pictures of Jesus, and of Jesus's mother, and of apostles and angels and saints and what not, yet he knew very little about the Christian religion. Both his mother and his father had had it forced upon them in their youth, and hated it. But as a matter of art education, shouldn't Lanny read up on it?

He asked the white-haired and courtly ex-diplomat where he could find out what Jesus had said, and was reminded that the words were set down in some old books called the Gospels. M. Rochambeau didn't happen to own a copy, and Beauty's friends, of whom the boy made inquiry, found the idea amusing. Finally Lanny found in a bookstore a copy of this ancient work.

Winter was coming now. In Flanders and through northern France a million men were lying out in the open, in trenches and shell holes half full of filthy water which froze at night. They were devoured by vermin and half paralyzed by cold, eating bread and canned meat, when it could be brought to them over roads which had been turned into quagmires. All day and night bullets whistled above them and shells came down out of the sky, blowing bodies to fragments and burying others under loads of mud. The wounded had to lie where they fell until death released them, or night made it possible for their fellows to drag them back into the trenches.

And with this going on a few hundred miles away, Lanny was

reading the story of Jesus, four times over, with variations. He was deeply touched by it each time, and wept over the way that poor man had been treated, and loved him for the kind and gentle things he had said. If somebody had happened along to speak for one of the religious sects—almost any of them—that person might have made a convert. As it was, Lanny had no one to consult but a worldly-wise ex-diplomat, who told him that if he wanted to follow Jesus he would have to do it in his own heart, because none of the churches were traveling in that path or near it.

So Lanny didn't go to church. Instead he studied arithmetic, algebra, and modern history with his new tutor, Jerry Pendleton, a happy-go-lucky fellow whom Beauty Budd had met in the way she met most persons, at a party for tea and dancing; she liked him because he had red hair, a gay disposition, and good manners. He had come to Europe with a chum, working their way, and had got caught, first by the war, and then by a mademoiselle whose mother conducted the *pension* at which he was staying. Instead of going back to finish his senior year in a fresh-water college, Jerry had lingered on, and a job as tutor presented itself as a happy solution of several problems.

The young man's account of education in the United States was not exactly favorable; he said that the main thing you learned was how to get along with other fellows, and with girls. He confessed, as Mr. Elphinstone had done, that he had forgotten all the subjects he was going to teach, but he and Lanny could read together, and there was that magnificent encyclopedia which could never go wrong. Jerry would at least keep the kid out of mischief—and at the same time Mrs. Budd could give him kindly advice about the most bewildering love affair he had ever run into. Mlle. Cerise, it appeared, was being brought up in French fashion, which meant that she couldn't see a young man without her mother being close by, and he couldn't even bring her to one of Mrs. Budd's tea parties without a chaperon. At home you took a girl motoring, or if you didn't have a car, you bicycled and had a picnic in the woods; but here they were all nuns until after they were married—and then, apparently, you could pick them up in the gambling rooms at the casino.

"Not quite all of them," said Beauty, beginning the education of her son's tutor.

VI

Once again, for a day, Marcel Detaze was free from the censor. He was on his way to his post of duty, and poured out his heart to his beloved. This time he didn't hide from her the dangers to which he was going. The hour had come when she had to steel her soul.

Marcel was gay, as always; that was the way you had to take life, if you didn't mean to let it get you down. Make a work of art of it; put your best into it; play your little part, and be ready to quit before the audience got tired of you. Marcel described a "sausage balloon" as a grotesque and amusing object, in rebellion against the men who had created it and obstinately trying to break out of their control. It was huge and fat, and assumed changing shapes, and danced and cavorted in the air. A net of cords imprisoned it, and a steel cable bound it to the earth. The cable was on a pulley, and two stout horses or oxen plodding across a field let the balloon up or pulled it down.

All this for the sake of an observer who sat in a bulletproof basket underneath the balloon, equipped with field glasses and measuring instruments, and a telephone set. It was his task to spy out enemy entrenchments, and the movements of troops and guns. He had to have a keen eyesight, and be trained to recognize the difference between branches growing on trees and the same when cut down and made into a screen for a heavy gun. He had to know Birnam Wood when it was removed to Dunsinane. Also, he had to be a man who had traveled to the fiords of Norway and the Isles of Greece without getting seasick; for the winds which blew off the North Sea would toss him around like a whole yachtful of soap kings—so wrote the painter, who had been sorry for poor Ezra Hackabury, but couldn't help finding him funny.

Of course such a balloon would be a target for the enemy. Airplanes would come darting out of the clouds at a hundred miles an hour, spitting fire as they came. "We have guns on the ground to stop them," wrote Marcel; "guns with high-angle mountings designed especially to shoot at planes, but I fear they are not very good yet, and Lanny should tell his father to invent better ones for my protection. The shells from these guns make white puffs of smoke when they explode, so that the gunner can correct his aim. The English call the guns 'Archies,' and I am told that this comes from some music-hall character who said: 'Archibald, certainly not!' It is wonderful, the humor with which the English fellows take this messy business. I have had one as an instructor and he has explained their jokes to me. The heavy shells which make an enormous cloud of black smoke they call 'Jack Johnsons,' because of a Negro prize fighter who is dangerous. Also they call them 'black Marias' and 'coal boxes.' Doubtless there will be new names by the time I get to the front."

Beauty broke down and couldn't read any more. It seemed to her horrible that men should make jokes about death and destruction. Of course they laughed so that they might not have to weep; but Beauty could weep, and she did. She was certain that her lover was gone forever, and her hopes died a new death every time she thought of him. Lanny, talking with M. Rochambeau, learned that his mother had cause for fear, because the job which Marcel had chosen represented just about the peak of peril in this war. A single correct observation followed by a well-placed shell might put a battery of guns out of action; so the enemy waged incessant warfare upon the stationary balloons. This far the French had managed to keep the mastery of the air, but the fighting was incessant and the death rate high. "Women must weep," a poet in Lanny's anthology had said.

VII

Mrs. Emily Chattersworth wrote the news. Learning of the dreadful sufferings of the wounded after the great battle of the Aisne, she had lent the Château Les Forêts to the government for a hospital. Then she had been moved to go and see what was being done, and had been so shocked by the sight of mangled bodies brought in by the hundreds, and the efforts of exhausted doctors and nurses to help them, that she had abandoned her career as *salonnière* and taken up that of hospital director. Now she was helping to organize a society in Paris for the aid of the wounded and was asking all her friends for help and contributions. Would Beauty Budd do something? Mrs. Emily said that Marcel might some day be brought to Les Forêts; and of course that fetched Beauty. Despite her vow to economize and pay her debts, she sent a check to her friend.

Then Lanny began to observe a curious phenomenon. Having given her lover, and then her money, Beauty could no longer refuse to give her heart. So far she had been hating war; but now little by little she took to hating Germans. Of course she didn't know about *Weltpolitik*, and didn't try to discuss it; Beauty was personal, and recalled the hordes of Teutons who had come flocking to the Riviera in recent winters. The hotelkeepers had welcomed them, because they spent money; but Beauty hadn't welcomed them, because she loved the quiet of her retreat and they invaded it. The women were enormous and had voices like Valkyries; the men had jowls, and rolls of fat on the backs of their necks, and huge bellies and buttocks which they displayed indecently to the winter sunshine. They drank and ate sausages in public, made ugly guttural noises—and now, as it turned out, they had all the time been spying and intriguing, preparing huge engines of destruction and death!

Yes, Beauty decided, she hated all Germans; and this made for disharmony in the little island of peace which she had created at Bienvenu. Sophie didn't want to hate the Germans because it might start her Eddie off to be a hero, like Marcel. M. Rochambeau didn't want it because he was old and tired, and liable to heart attacks if he let himself get excited. "Dear lady," he would plead, "we in this crowded continent have been hating each other for so many centuries—pray do not bring us any more fuel for our fires." The re-

tired diplomat's voice was gentle, and his manner that of some
elderly prelate.

Lanny agreed that things were going to be harder for him if his
mother became warlike. He would remind her of Kurt, and of great
Germans like Goethe and Schiller and Beethoven, who belonged to
all Europe. He would repeat to her the things which Robbie had told
him—and of which the father kept reminding him, in carefully veiled
language. When Beauty burst out that Robbie was thinking of the
money he was going to make out of this war, Lanny was a bit
shocked, and withdrew into himself. It wouldn't do to remind his
mother that it was Robbie's money on which they were both living,
and which she was giving to Mrs. Emily.

VIII

Jerry Pendleton was being a good companion. He liked to do the
things that Lanny liked, and they climbed the hills and played tennis and swam and fished, and Jerry cultivated the mother of Mlle.
Cerise by bringing in more seafood than the *pension* could consume.
They enjoyed torch-fishing especially, and made themselves expert
spearsmen, and got many a green moray, but never one as big as
Captain Bragescu's. One night a strange adventure befell them—
oddly enough the very thing that Beauty had been worried about,
and for which everybody had laughed at her. It was to be that
way all through the war; truth would outrun fiction, and if anybody said that a thing couldn't happen, then right away it did.

A still night, something not so common in the month of Decem-
ber, and two young fellows in fishing togs and sweaters, because it
was cold in spite of the lack of wind. They had a torch set in the
bow of the boat, blazing brightly, and were lying, one on each side,
with their heads over the gunwales, looking down into the crystal-
clear water. The sea growths waved gently to and fro, and it was
like some enchanted land; the *langoustes* poked their heads out from
the rocks, and fish idled here and there, many of them camouflaged,
just like the Germans. Lanny thought about Marcel, doing the same

kind of work, but high in the air instead of on top of the sea.

The Cannes lighthouse was flashing red and green. Not many lights on the shore, for the night life of the Golfe Juan was dimmed that winter. Not many sounds, just the murmur of distant traffic, and now and then the put-put of a motorboat. But suddenly a strange sort of splashing, the movement of a great bulk of water, and a series of waves rushing toward them, rocking their little boat so that they could no longer look into the depths. They stared toward the sound, shading their eyes from the torchlight, and gradually made out something, a dim shape. Impossible to believe it and equally impossible to doubt it—a round boxlike object arisen from the depths of the sea, and lying there, quite still!

"A submarine!" whispered Lanny; and his companion exclaimed: "Put out the torch!" Lanny was nearer, and grabbed it and plunged it into the water. A hissing sound, then silence and darkness, and the rowboat rocking in the swells.

The two listened, their hearts thumping. "They must have seen us," Jerry whispered. They waited and wondered what to do. They had both read stories about submarines sinking vessels, and not even bothering to save the crews. This might be an enemy one, or again it might be French or British.

Sounds travel clearly over smooth water. They heard footsteps, people moving; then came splashing and, unmistakably, the sound of muffled oars. "They're coming after us!" exclaimed Lanny; and his tutor grabbed their oars and began to row for dear life for the shore, less than a hundred feet away.

Would the people on the submarine turn on a searchlight and open fire on them? It was something they both thought of, and they had a good right to be scared. But nothing of the sort happened. They got to the shore and crept out of the boat; then, safe behind rocks, they listened again, and heard the muffled oars, undoubtedly coming nearer—but a little farther down the shore. Very plainly they heard the rowing stop, and after a minute or less it began again—the boat, or whatever it was, was going back to the submarine.

"They came to get somebody," whispered Jerry.

"Or else to put somebody ashore."

"It must be an enemy. No French boat would behave like that." A moment later the tutor added: "Somebody on shore may be looking for us." That called for no argument, and the pair got up and started to climb toward the road.

"Look here," whispered Jerry, suddenly; "this may be very serious, and we ought to tell the police or the military. If anybody was put ashore, he'd be armed, and he'd mean business."

"That's right," answered the younger boy, in a delightful state of excitement.

"Do you know where there'd be a telephone?"

"In almost any of the villas along the road."

"Well, let's go quietly; and if anyone tries to stop us we'll bolt— you go one way and I'll go another. They can hardly get us both in the dark."

They tiptoed down the road, and presently came to a house with lights, and asked permission to telephone the nearest police station. The police ordered them to wait right there, which they were glad to do, and meanwhile told their story to a family of English people who were greatly excited. A car with gendarmes arrived soon, and another with military men a little later. They took the Americans down to the shore and asked them a hundred questions. There was no sign of any submarine, only Lanny's boat, which the tide was about to float away. Launches came, and men searched the shore, finding no trace of anything—but would there have been, on those masses of rocks? The two young fellows managed to convince the authorities of their good faith, and one of the army men said that it must have been an Austrian submarine from the Adriatic.

That was all they said. A curtain of silence fell about the matter; nothing was published—but there was a lot of patrolling by torpedo boats and "aérohydros" in the neighborhood. M. Rochambeau, who knew about military matters, said that the enemy's purpose must have been to put ashore some important agent who was too well known to come in with a neutral passport. Doubtless he would have a place of refuge prepared. The secret service of the Allies would be trying to find out who he was and what he had come for.

Besides the open war of arms, there was this underground war of spying and sabotage always going on; both sides had their agents in all the services of the enemy, and were spending fortunes to corrupt and undermine. The French had gathered up the known enemy aliens in the Midi and interned them on the Île Ste.-Marguerite, which lay just offshore from Cannes, and had been the peaceful home of some fifty nuns, and a place where tourists came to sit under the big pine trees and have tea. But of course there must be many Germans at large in France, posing as Swiss, or Danes, or citizens of the United States, or what not; they would be watching troop movements, perhaps planning to blow up railroad bridges, or to put bombs upon merchant vessels, or even warships. If they were caught, you wouldn't hear anything about it; they would be taken to some military fortress, and stood against a wall blindfolded and shot through the heart.

IX

The dread news came for which Beauty had been waiting many weeks. It was written by a comrade of Marcel's, a "ground man" whom he had pledged to this duty. The comrade regretted to inform Madame Budd that her friend had been severely injured; his "kite balloon" had been attacked by two enemy planes, and had been hauled down, but not quickly enough; some fifteen meters above ground it had caught fire, and Marcel had leaped out, and had been badly smashed up, also burned. He had been taken to the base hospital at Beauvais, and the writer could not say as to his present condition.

After her first collapse, Beauty's one idea was to get to him; she couldn't stop sobbing, and was in the grip of a sort of convulsion of shuddering—but she must go, she must go—right now, come on! She wouldn't even wait to put clothes into a suitcase. She had visions of her lover mutilated, defaced—he would be in agony, he might be dying at that moment. "Oh, God, my God, help me, help my poor Marcel!"

It happened that Jerry and M. Rochambeau were in the house, as well as Lanny. They tried to comfort her, but what could they say? They tried to restrain her, but she wouldn't listen to reason. "You must find out if you can get on the train," argued the diplomat. But her answer was that she would motor. "Then you must arrange to get *essence*"—but she said: "I'll find a way—I'll pay what it costs— you can always get things if you pay."

"But, my dear lady, you may not be able to get near the town— it's in the war zone, and they never allow relatives or visitors."

"I'll find a way. I'll go to Paris and lay siege to the government."

"There are many persons laying siege to the government right now—including the Germans."

"I'm going to help Marcel. I'll find a way—I'll take a job as nurse with Emily Chattersworth. She'll get me there somehow. Who will come with me?"

Lanny had learned to drive a car, but hardly well enough for this trip. Jerry Pendleton was a first-class driver, and knew how to fix carburetors and those other miserable devices that were always getting out of order. Jerry would go; and the terrified maids would rush to pile some clothes into suitcases—warm things, for Madame was declaring hysterically that if they wouldn't let her into the town she would sleep in the car, or in the open like the soldiers. None of her pretty things—but then she changed her mind, if she had to call on government officials she would have to look her best—nothing showy, but that simplicity which is the apex of art, and which costs in accordance. A strange thing to see a woman, so choked with her own sobs that she could hardly make herself understood, at the same time trying to decide what sort of dress was proper to wear in approaching the war minister of a government in such dire peril of its existence that it had had to move to a remote port by the sea!

Lanny packed his suitcase, taking a warm sweater and the overcoat he had worn in Silesia; a good suit also, because he too might have to interview officials. Beauty sent a wire to Mrs. Emily, asking her to use her influence; M. Rochambeau sent a telegram to an official of his acquaintance who could arrange it if any man could. "Only woman can do the impossible," added the old gentleman, parodying Goethe.

They piled robes and blankets into the car, filling up the seat alongside Beauty, who sat now, a mask of horror, gazing into a lifelong nightmare. They drove to the *pension* where Jerry stayed, and he ran upstairs and threw some of his things into a bag. Downstairs were Mlle. Cerise and her mother and her aunt, all shocked by the news. The red-headed tutor grabbed the proper young French lady and kissed her first on one cheek and then on the other. "*Adieu! Au revoir!*" he cried, and fled.

"*Ah, ces Américains!*" exclaimed the mother.

"*Un peuple tout à fait fou!*" added the aunt.

It was practically an engagement.

14

The Furies of Pain

I

THE little town of Beauvais lies about fifty miles to the north of Paris. It is something over a thousand years old, and has an ancient cathedral, and battlements now made into boulevards. It was like Paris, in that the Germans had got there almost, but not quite. Its inhabitants had heard the thunder of guns, and were still hearing it, day and night, a distant storm where the sun came up. Thunder-

storms are capricious, and whether this one would return was a subject of hourly speculation. People studied the bulletins in front of
the ancient Hôtel de Ville and hoped that what they read was true.

To keep the storm away, everybody was working day and night.
The Chemin de Fer du Nord passed through the town, which had
become a base: soldiers detraining, guns and ammunition being un-
loaded, depots established to store food and fodder and pass them
up to the front, everything that would be needed if the line was to
hold and the enemy be driven back. No use to expect comfort in
such a place; count yourself lucky that you were alive.

Beauty Budd was here because she belonged to that class of people who are accustomed to have their own way. She had met cabinet
ministers at tea parties and salons, she had given a generous check
for the aid of the French wounded, she bore the name of a munitions
family now being importuned to expand their plant and help to
save *la patrie*. So when she appeared at the door of an official, the
secretary bowed and escorted her in; the official said: "Certainly,
Madame," and signed the document and had it stamped.

So the car with the red-headed college boy chauffeur had been
passed by sentries on the edge of Beauvais, and the harassed authorities of the town did their best to make things agreeable for a lady
whose grief added dignity to her numerous charms. "Yes, Madame,
we will do our best to find your friend; but it will not be easy, because we have no general records." There was another battle going
on; the grumbling guns were making hundreds of new cases every
hour, and they were dumped here because there was no time to take
them farther.

"We will go ourselves and search," said Madame; and when they
told her that all the buildings in the town which could be spared
had been turned into hospitals, she asked: "Can you give me a list?"
The boys drove her to one place after another, and she would stand
waiting while a clerk looked through a register of the living and
another of the dead; her hands would be clenched and her lips trembling, and the two escorts at her side would be ready to catch her if
she started to fall.

At last they found the name of Marcel Detaze; in a dingy old inn, so crowded with cots in the corridors that there was barely room to get through. It was Milton's "Stygian cave forlorn, 'Mongst horrid shapes, and shrieks, and sights unholy." Beauty Budd, accustomed to every luxury, was plunged into this inferno, ill-lighted, clamorous with cries and groans, stinking of blood and suppurating wounds and disinfectants. Ambulances and carts were unloading new cases on the sidewalk; sometimes they were dead before a place could be found for them, and then they were carted to open graves outside the city.

II

Marcel was alive. That was all Beauty had asked for. They could not tell her much about him. His legs had been broken and had been set. His back was injured, they didn't know how badly. He doubtless had internal injuries. His burns had been dressed; very painful, of course, but they did not think he would be blind. "We have no time, Madame," they said. "We do not sleep, we are exhausted."

Beauty could see that it was true; doctors and nurses and attendants, all were pale and had dark rings under their eyes, and some of them staggered. "*C'est la guerre, Madame.*" "I know, I know," said Beauty.

They took her to where he lay upon a cot, with a dozen other men in the same room. There would have been no way of recognizing him; his head was a mass of bandages, only an opening for his mouth and nose, and these appeared to be open sores. She had to kneel by him and whisper: "Is it you, Marcel?" He did not stir; just murmured: "Yes." She said: "Darling, I have come to help you." When she put her ear to his lips, she heard faintly: "Let me die." There was something wrong with his voice, but she made out the words: "Don't try to save me. I would be a monster."

Beauty had never been taught anything about psychology; only what she had picked up by watching people she knew. She had never heard of a "death-wish," and if anyone had spoken of auto-hypnosis she would have wondered if it was a gadget for a motorcar. But she had her share of common sense, and perceived right away that she had to take command of Marcel's mind. She had to make him want to live. She had to find what might be an ear under the mass of bandages, make sure that the sounds were going into it, and then say, firmly and slowly:

"Marcel, I love you. I love your soul, and I don't care what has happened to your body. I mean to stand by you and pull you through. You have got to live for my sake. No matter what it costs, you must stand it, and see it through. Do you hear me, Marcel?"

"I hear you."

"All right then. Don't say no to me. You must do it because I want you to. For the sake of our love. I want to take you away from here, and nurse you, and you will get over this. But first you have to make up your mind to it. You have to want to live. You have to love me enough. Do you understand me?"

"It is not fair to you——"

"That is for me to say. Don't argue with me. Don't waste your strength. You belong to me, and you have no right to leave me, to deprive me of your love. I don't care what you say, I don't want to hear it—I want you. Whatever there is of you that the doctors can save—that much is mine, and you must not take it from me. You can live only if you try to, and I ask you to do that. I want your promise. I want you to say it and mean it. I have to go out and make arrangements to take you to Paris; but I can't go till I know that you will fight, and not give up. You told me to have courage, Marcel. Now I have it, and you have to repay me. Do you understand?"

"I understand."

"I want your promise. I want to know that if I go out to get help, you will fight with everything that's in you to keep alive, to keep your hope and courage, for my sake, and for our love. There's no use talking about love if you're not willing to do that much for it. Answer me that you will."

She put her ear to the opening again, and heard a whisper: "All right." She touched him gently on the shoulder, not knowing what part of him might be a wound, and said: "Wait for me. I'll come back just as quickly as I can make arrangements. Anything else I can do?"

"Water," he said. She didn't know how to give it to him, for she was afraid to lift his head, and she had no tube, and no one to ask. She dipped her handkerchief into a glass and squeezed a little into his mouth, and kept that up until he said it was enough.

III

The doctors made no objection to having a patient taken off their hands. They said he couldn't be crowded into an automobile, that would surely kill him; and there was no ambulance available. It was a question of making changes in Beauty's own car, one of the new and fashionable kind called a "limousine," a square black box. It might be possible to take out two of the seats, the right-hand ones, and make a place to lay a narrow mattress on the floor. Then Jerry made a suggestion—why not put a board platform on top of the two seats, with a mattress on that?

They drove to a garage; there was nobody but the wife of the proprietor and an elderly mechanic, both greatly startled by the idea of cutting out a piece of the back of a luxury car, so that a wounded soldier could be slid into it. The windshield was large, and the mechanic thought he might be able to remove that. Beauty said: "Break it if necessary. We can have it replaced in Paris." Jerry took the proprietress aside and spoke magic words: *"C'est l'ami de cette belle dame."*

"Ah, c'est l'amour!" That explained everything, and they went to work with enthusiasm. Love will find out the way! They managed to get the windshield off without too great harm, and they put some boards together and made a platform, and the proprietress brought an old mattress, and Lanny worked at it with his pocket knife, cutting it down to the right size. *"Ah, ces Américains!"*

While all this was being done, Beauty was out looking for a telephone, to call a surgeon she knew in Paris, and arrange for Marcel to be received at a private hospital. When she got back, the platform was in place, and the mattress on top of it, a reasonably good place for a wounded man to lie for the time it would take to get him to the big city.

Two tired attendants carried the patient down and slid him onto the mattress without damage. Beauty distributed money to every-one who helped them, and Jerry gave them cigarettes, which they wanted even more at the moment. It was dark when they set out, but no matter—Marcel was alive, and Beauty sat in the rear seat, which brought her head about level with his ear, and for two hours she whispered: "Marcel, I love you, and you are going to live for my sake." She found a thousand variations of it, and Lanny listened, and learned things about love. He was in a cramped position—they had taken out some of the bags and tied them onto the rear of the car, and Lanny was squatting on the floor at his mother's knees, un-derneath Marcel's mattress. He couldn't see anything, but he could hear, and he learned that love is not all pleasure, but can be agony and heartache, martyrdom and sacrifice. He learned what the clergy-man was talking about in the marriage service: "For better for worse, for richer for poorer, in sickness and in health, to love and to cherish, till death us do part."

IV

The human body is a complicated engine with many miles of elastic pipes large and small. In order that the engine may develop the max-imum horsepower per pound of weight, the pipes are made of fragile materials, and the framework which encloses and supports them is porous and brittle. When you take such a contraption fifty feet up in the air and explode a mass of hydrogen gas above it, and let it crash onto hard ground, you produce in a second or two results which surgeons and nurses may need a long time to remedy.

There were no physicians in Paris who were not overworked, and no hospital which was not crowded; but the lady with the mag-ical name of Budd used her influence, and Robbie, getting the news by cable from his son, replied: "Spare no expense." So Marcel was

X-rayed and investigated, and his burns were treated according to the modern technique of cleaning away damaged tissues. After several days of watching, the doctors said that he would live, if he did not become discouraged by the ordeals he would have to undergo, and if his *amour propre* was not too greatly wounded by the certainty of looking like a scarecrow.

It was up to Beauty. She could have that scarecrow if she wanted it, and she did. There were no more thoughts about Pittsburgh now; she had made her bed and she would lie in it—right here in a private room in a *maison de santé*. She got herself some nurse's uniforms and made a job of it; the people of the place were only too glad, having plenty to do without this difficult case. She had a cot in one corner of the room, and for weeks hardly ever left it; she took no chance of Marcel's *amour propre* breaking loose and causing him to throw himself out of the window. She would be right there, to keep reminding him that he belonged to her, and that her property sense was strong.

Troops of little demons came and sat upon the metal bars which made the head and foot of Marcel's bed. His physical eyes were swathed in bandages, but he saw them plainly with his mind's eye. Some had round shaven heads with *Pickelhauben* on; some had sharp-pointed mustaches which they twisted and turned up at the ends; others were just regular devils with horns and red tails. They came in relays, and pinched the painter's wounded flesh and poked needles into it; they twisted his broken joints, they pulled and strained his damaged pipes—in short, they gave him no peace day or night. The sweat would stand out on him—wherever he had enough skin left for that to happen. He would writhe, and do his best not to groan, because of that poor woman who sat there in anguish of soul, talking to him when he couldn't listen, trying to help him when there wasn't any help. When you are in pain you are alone.

There were the burns that kept having to be dressed; there were bones that had been set wrong and had to be broken again; he was always being transported to the operating room for more probing and poking. The doctors could give him opiates, of course, but there was a limit, if they intended to keep him alive. He just had to stand it; he had to learn to live with pain and make a game of it. The doctors would help him by making jokes, and letting him make them. He took to calling them "plumbers," and threatening to get an American one, because the French ones didn't know their business. They answered that they would know it a lot better before this war was over. Beauty could hardly stand such jokes, but she toughened herself. "*C'est la guerre.*"

V

The youth and his youthful tutor had rooms in a hotel near by. The walls had white wainscoting and pink flowered silk above it, and the chairs were upholstered to match. The elevators looked as if they were made of gold, and were of open grillwork, so that you could watch people rising up or sinking down. An elderly official in a grand uniform set the front doors to revolving for them, and young women musicians in red coats and gold braid played Hungarian dances while they ate their meals. It was a life of unimaginable luxury for Jerry Pendleton, whose father owned a couple of drug stores in a town of Kansas.

They got some books and faithfully studied every morning. After lunch they walked, and looked at pictures and the other sights of Paris, and then went to relieve Lanny's mother so that she could have a nap. The pair were a comfort to Marcel; for men have to be together, it appears; they just can't stand women all the time. Men understand why you have to get out into the world, in spite of danger and death. When Marcel was able to listen, he enjoyed hearing about American college life, including football; and about a trip on a cattle boat, and then tramping over Europe, sleeping in haystacks. He wished that he had thought of something so original when he was a youth.

Also, of course, he had to know about the war. Beauty had hoped never to hear of it again, but she had to read the news to him, and learn to think about strategy instead of broken bodies. Those two armies had locked themselves together, like wild stags which have got their horns caught and are doomed to butt each other around the forest until both of them drop. All that bitter winter the armies would thrust here and yield there, until gradually they got settled down into the earth. The Germans constructed an elaborate set of entrenchments, line behind line; to the defense of these lines they would bring up everything they had, and Britain and France would do the same on the other side of "no man's land." Each army was frantically getting ready for the spring "push" that was to end the war—so the experts all said, only they differed as to'what the ending would be.

Winters in Paris are disagreeable, and people of means do not stay if they can help it. But Beauty hardly ever went out, and the boys didn't mind, because they were young and everything was new and delightful. They saw motion pictures, French and American; they went to plays, and Jerry improved his French. They had a piano in their suite—for Robbie wrote that he was making a pile of money, and Lanny might have anything he wanted, provided he did not smoke or drink or go with prostitutes.

Friends came to see Beauty and Marcel: Emily Chattersworth, very serious now, completely wrapped up in the affairs of her *blessés;* Sophie and her Eddie, she trying so hard to keep her man entertained and hoping that the sight of poor Marcel might teach him the cruelty and wickedness of fighting. But it didn't work that way; men seemed to be drawn to death like moths into the flame; they thought of vengeance rather than of safety. Lanny wrote to Rick, telling what had happened, and it surely did not act as a deterrent with the English boy; he longed all the more to get up there in the air and hunt a *Taube.*

The time came when the sufferer's burns were healed enough so that the bandages could be taken off. That was a time of fresh trials for Beauty—the doctors had to warn her, she must be prepared for the worst, and not let Marcel see any trace of horror in her face. He wouldn't have a mirror, but of course he would put his fingers to his face and feel what was there. His friends must help him get used to it, and make him believe that it made no difference to them.

Beauty, who had been named for her looks, and valued hers and others' very high among the gifts of life, had chosen a man who possessed fine blond hair and mustaches, grave, melancholy features, and an expression of romantic tenderness. Now he had no hair at all, just a red scalp, and his face was a flaming scar. His lips were gone on one side, so that he could only make a pretense at articulating the letters b and p. Out of the gaping wound his teeth grinned hideously, and the gum of the lower jaw was all exposed. Some day a facial surgeon might replace the lip, so the doctors assured him. Fortunately his eyesight was uninjured, but one of his upper eyelids was gone, and most of his ears.

Beauty had to go and look at that mask, and smile affectionately, and say that it didn't matter a bit. Marcel's right hand was well enough to be kissed, and that was where she kissed him. Since he liked so much to make jokes, she told him that she would take up needlework, like other old ladies, and learn to patch up his skin. Seriously she insisted that it was his soul she cared about, and that wasn't changed. After saying all this, she went off to the little room which she had to dress in, and there wept hysterically, cursing God and the Kaiser.

Lanny and Jerry, duly warned, went in armed with cheerfulness. "Well, do you think you can stand me?" asked the victim; and Lanny said: "Don't be silly, Marcel. You know we'd like you in sections if you came that way."

Jerry added: "I read an article about what the surgeons are doing, making new faces. Gosh, it takes your breath away!"

"They've taken away pretty nearly everything but my breath," replied the painter.

Lanny said: "They've left your eyes and your hands, and you'll go back to the Cap and paint better than ever." That was the way to talk!

VI

What was Beauty going to make of this blow which fate had dealt her? She believed in happiness and talked about it as a right. A minister's daughter, raised in a stuffy, uncultured home, she had learned to loathe incessant droning of hymns and preaching of tiresome duty; she had fled from it, and still avoided every mention of its symbols. But suddenly all those hated things had sprung as it were out of the earth, had seized her and bound her with chains which there could be no breaking.

Lanny was all tenderness and kindness, and when she wanted to weep he was there to console her. In his presence she wept for Marcel; he never knew that she went alone and wept for herself. Over and over she fought this bitter battle. No use trying to get away from it—her bridges were burned. She couldn't desert this wreck of a man, and whatever happiness she found would have to be by his side. She who was so dainty had had to accustom herself to blood and stenches; and now she would have to eat and sleep and walk and talk in the presence of what ordinary people see only in nightmares.

Even from her devoted son she must hide her rage at this fate. Even to herself she was ashamed to admit that she regretted her bargain and dreamed of a happiness she might have had in a far-off land of plenty and peace. She had to force herself to be loyal to her choice; but this moral compulsion was associated in her mind with a dull and stolid religion, full of phrases which seemed to have been designed to take the gaiety and charm out of existence. Mabel Blackless, seventeen years old and bursting with the joy of life, hadn't wanted to lay her burdens at the foot of the cross, or to have any redeeming blood spilled for her; she had wanted to see Paris, and had borrowed money and run away to join her brother.

And now it seemed that she was back where she had come from; teaching herself to carry the cross. Her best friends mustn't know about it, because if they did they would pity her, and to be pitied was unendurable. She must tie herself down once for all! In that mood she went out one day and told her story to the *maire* of the *arrondissement*, and arranged for him to come to the hospital. She went back and told Marcel what she had done, and refused to hear any of his objections, pretending to have her feelings hurt by them. With two of the nurses for witnesses, they were married under the French civil law.

Did Marcel guess what was in her heart? She had to fight him, and lie vigorously; how else would he be persuaded to go on living? She and her son and her son's tutor had to make real to themselves the game they played. It wasn't hard for Lanny, because art counted for so much with him; also, it was wartime, and everybody was full of fervors, and wounds were a medal or badge of glory. The marriage made Beauty a "respectable woman" for the first time; but oddly enough it meant a social comedown, the name of Budd being one of power. She would have to get busy and boost Marcel's paintings, and make herself "somebody" again!

VII

The first thing was to contrive something for him to wear over his face. Hero or no hero, he couldn't bear to let anybody look at that mask of horror. He would cover the top of his head with a skullcap, and across his forehead would hang a close-fitting silk veil, with small holes for eyes and nose. Beauty went out and got some pink silk lingerie material, but he wouldn't wear pink; he wanted gray, so that it wouldn't show the dust; they compromised on white when Beauty said that she would make a lot of them and wash them with her own hands. She made a pattern, and after that had something to keep her fingers busy while she sat by his bedside.

It was springtime before he was able to move about, and they took him back to Juan in the car, making a two-day journey of it, so as not to put any strain on him. He looked not so bad with his skullcap and veil; the world was getting used to the sight of *mutilés* —and not yet tired of them. Jerry supported him on one side and Lanny on the other, and they got him into Bienvenu without mishap.

Oh, the glory of that sunshine in the little court; the almost over-powering scent of orange blossoms and jasmine in the evening, and the song of the nightingales! Here were three women to adore him and wait upon him, and nobody to disturb him; here Beauty meant him to spend the rest of his days in peace, and paint whatever wonderful things he might have in him. She was going to give up all her frivolous life—save only such contacts as might help in a campaign to win recognition for genius.

There were just a few painter friends Marcel wanted to see, and these would come to him, and bring their work for him to look at—or if it was too big, Lanny would bring it in the car. The patient was soon able to sit up and read, and there were plenty of books and magazines. Often they read aloud; Jerry came and tutored Lanny, and Marcel would listen and improve his English. They had music; and when he grew stronger he walked about the place. The furies of pain would never let him entirely alone, but he learned to outwit them. He was a more silent man than he used to be; there were things going on inside him about which he did not tell and did not wish to be asked by anyone.

VIII

The military deadlock at the front continued. All winter long the Allies had spent their forces trying to take trenches defended by machine guns—a weapon of which the Germans had managed to get the biggest supply. It was something that Robbie Budd had helped to teach them—and which he had tried in vain to teach the French and British. He couldn't write freely about it now, but there were hints in his letters, and Lanny knew what they meant, having been so often entertained by his father's comic portrayals of the British War Office officials with whom he had been trying to do business. So haughty they were, so ineffable, almost godlike in their self-satisfaction—and so dumb! No vulgar American could tell them anything; and now dapper young officers strolled out in front of their troops, waving their swagger sticks, and the German sharp-shooters knocked them over like partridges off tree limbs. It was sublime, but it wasn't going to win this war of machines.

All the nations had come to realize that they were facing a long struggle. Old M. Rochambeau, who came often to see Beauty and her husband, used a terrible phrase, "a war of attrition." It was like the game of checkers in which you had one more man than your enemy, so every time you swapped with him, you increased your advantage. "Yes, dear lady," said the ex-diplomat, in answer to Beauty's exclamation of horror, "that is the basis on which military strategy is being calculated, and no one stops to ask what you or I think about it."

Man power plus manufacturing power was what would count. Britain had sacrificed her little professional army in order to save the Channel ports, and now she was rushing a new army into readiness, a volunteer army of a million men. There would be a second million, and as many more as needed; they would be shipped to some part of the fighting line, and swapped for Germans, man for man, or as near to it as possible.

The Turkish politicians had been bought into the war on the German side; which meant that the Black Sea was shut off, and nothing could be sent into Russia's southern ports. So a British expedition had been sent to take the Dardanelles. Rick informed Lanny that a cousin of his was going as a private in one of these regiments; Rosemary wrote that her father had been promoted to the rank of colonel, and was to command this same regiment. Rosemary had extracted a promise from her mother to be allowed to study nursing after one more year, and perhaps she would some day be on one of those ships. She promised that she would wave to Lanny as she went by!

It wasn't long before Italy was bought by the Allies, and that was important to people who lived in Provence. It lifted a fear from their souls, and freed the regiments guarding the southeastern border. "You see," said Marcel to his wife, "I saved a few months by volunteering!" It had been a sore point, that he had gone out of his

way to get himself smashed up. Now she could congratulate herself
that it had been done quickly!

IX

Marcel's paintings had been stored in the spare room of the villa,
and now he would set them up one by one and look at them. He
wanted to see what sort of painter he had really been, in those days
that now seemed a different lifetime. Lanny and Jerry and M.
Rochambeau would join him, and make comments, more or less expert. Lanny and his tutor thought they were marvelous, but the
painter took to shaking his head more and more. No, they weren't
much; it was too easy to do things like that; there was no soul in
them. Lanny protested; but the old diplomat said: "You've become a
different man."

It was something which happened now and then to painters,
poets, musicians. Sometimes it amounted to a transformation. Verdi
had changed his style entirely in his middle years; Tolstoy had decided that his greatest novels were useless, even corrupting. Van
Gogh had painted everything gloomy and grim in Holland, and
then had come to the Midi and exploded in a burst of color. "You
will start work all over," said the old gentleman; "find some new
way to say what you feel."

People who didn't understand art—people like Marcel's wife, for
example—were going to have an unhappy time while he was groping his way into that new stage of life. He became restless and dis-
contented; he found fault with everybody and everything; his life
had come to nothing. He took to going out at night, when people
couldn't stare at his mask, and wandering about the roads on the
Cap. Beauty was exasperated, but she dared not show it; she was
haunted by the idea that if she made him unhappy he might try to
get back into the army, or else in some fit of melancholia he might
seek to release her from her burden by jumping off the rocks. She
had never forgotten Lanny's suggestion of that possibility, at the
time when she was thinking about Pittsburgh, Pennsylvania.

She ordered built for her genius a little studio in an out of the way corner of the place; north light, and all modern conveniences, including a storeroom for his canvases; the whole place of stone, entirely fireproof. She got him a new easel, and a pneumatic cushion for his chair, to spare his sore bones. There was everything ready for him—everything but his own spirit. He would go to the place and sit and brood. He would spend much time stretching canvases on frames, and would sit and dab paint on them, and finally would take them out behind the studio and burn them, saying that he was no good any more. What he wanted to say couldn't be said in any medium known.

Blazing hot summer had come. It was before the Riviera had been discovered as a summer resort, but Lanny, now fifteen, went about all day in bathing trunks and loved it. Marcel sat in his studio in the same costume—with nobody to look at his scarred and battered body. He had taken to staying by himself; he painted or read all day, and ate his meals alone, and only came out after dark. Then he would take a long walk, or if there were visitors he cared about, he would sit on the veranda in the dark with them. Or he would sit alone and listen to Lanny playing the piano.

X

The war had lasted a year. Some thought it was a stalemate, and others thought that Germany was winning. She held her line in France, and let the Allies waste themselves pounding at it while she broke the Russian armies. She had launched gas warfare, a new device filling the world with dismay. She was answering the British blockade by submarine warfare; British waters were a "military area," and all vessels in them liable to be sunk without warning.

In May had come the attack upon the *Lusitania*, the incident which excited the greatest horror in the United States. This great passenger liner, with more than two thousand persons on board, was passing the Irish coast in a calm sea: two o'clock in the afternoon, and the passengers had come from lunch, and were walking the

decks, or playing cards, reading or chatting, when a submarine
rose from the depths and launched a torpedo, blowing a hole in the
huge vessel's side. The sea rushed in and sank her in a few minutes,
drowning some twelve hundred persons, including more than a hundred babies.

When Americans read about the sinking of merchant vessels,
British or neutral, and the drowning of the crews, they didn't know
any of the people, and their imagination didn't have much to take
hold of. But here were people "everybody" knew—society people,
rich people, some of them prominent and popular—writers like
Justus Miles Forman and Elbert Hubbard, theatrical people like
Charles Frohman and Charles Klein, millionaires like the Vander-
bilts. Their friends had gone to the pier in New York to see them
off, or to the pier to welcome them—and then they read this horror
story. When the boatloads of survivors were brought in, the papers
of the world were filled with accounts of families torn apart, of
fathers and mothers giving their lives to save their little ones, of
quiet heroism and serenity in the face of death.

Americans in France felt the shock even more intensely, for
nearly everyone had friends, American or English, on board. Two
of Mrs. Emily's oldest friends had given their lives to save children
not their own. The sister of Edna Hackabury, now Mrs. Fitz-Laing,
was among those of whom no word was heard. Beauty counted half
a dozen persons of her acquaintance on the passenger list, and found
only two on the list of survivors. Not much of the spirit of "neutrality" was left in the minds of ladies and gentlemen who discussed
such matters over their afternoon tea.

Thus America was dragged into the center of the world debate.
President Wilson protested, and the German government answered
that submarines could not give warning without risking destruction,
and manifestly could not take off passengers and crew. The *Lusitania* had carried cartridges—so Germany charged, and the British
denied it, and how was the truth to be known? The Germans agreed
to sink no more such vessels, but they did not keep the promise. All
passenger vessels carried cargo, and most merchant vessels carried

passengers, and how could a submarine under war conditions make certain? The Germans demanded that President Wilson should resist the British attempt to starve the German people and should insist that American ships be allowed to carry to Germany food which Germany had bought and paid for. When President Wilson wrote letters· denouncing German barbarity, the Allies were delighted; when he wrote letters denouncing British violations of American trade rights, all sympathizers with the Allies denounced him.

For a year Robbie had kept writing to his son, never failing to warn him against losing his head. Robbie was determined that no Budd should be drawn into Europe's quarrels; Budds were business-men, and did not let themselves be used to pull anybody's chestnuts out of the fire. Robbie had been on the inside, and knew that every one of these nations was thinking about its own aggrandizement. Twice it happened that an employee was coming to France, and Robbie took the trouble to write a long letter and have it mailed in Paris, so that it wouldn't be opened by a censor. "Study and think and improve your mind, and keep it clear of all this fog of hatred and propaganda." Lanny did his best to obey—but it is not pleasant to differ from everybody you meet.

XI

For several months Marcel worked at his painting and burned up everything he produced. Lanny got up the courage to protest, and got his mother to back him. One day when he was at the studio he began begging to be allowed to see what was on the easel, covered up with a cloth. He was so much interested in his stepfather's devel-opment that he could learn even from his failures. "Please, Marcel! Right now!"

The painter said it was nothing, just a joke; he had been avoiding an hour of boredom. But that made Lanny beg all the harder—he was bored too, he said. So finally Marcel let him take off the cloth. He looked, and laughed out loud, and was so delighted that he danced around.

Marcel had painted himself lying on that bed in the hospital, head swathed in bandages, two frightened eyes looking out; and all around him on the bed crowded the little furies of pain, as he had watched them for so many months. It happened that Mr. Robin had sent Lanny a copy of a German weekly magazine, containing pictures of some of the national heroes, and Marcel had turned them into a swarm of little demons with instruments of torture in their claws. There was the stiff Prussian officer with his lean face, sharp nose, and monocle; there was Hindenburg with his shaven head and bull's neck; there was the Kaiser with his bristling mustaches; there was the professor with bushy beard and stern dogmatic face. The whole of German *Kultur* was there, and it was amazing, the different kinds of malice that Marcel had managed to pack into those faces, and still keep them funny.

Lanny argued harder than ever. If it gave him so much pleasure, why shouldn't the family share it? So they took it up to the house, where Jerry did a war dance, and M. Rochambeau forgot his usual gravity, and even Beauty laughed. Lanny said it ought to be shown somewhere, but Marcel said, nonsense, it was just a caricature, he didn't wish to be known as a cartoonist. But the elderly diplomat came to Lanny's support; he said there was a lot of German propaganda all over the world, and why shouldn't the French use their genius for ridicule? The four of them wrung this concession from the stubborn man of art—they might have a photograph of it and send copies to their friends.

They got a real photographer and had a big one made, and wrote on the bottom of the negative: "Soldier in Pain." Lanny sent one to his father, and one to Rick—whose father was now in charge of precautions against spies and saboteurs in his part of England. Beauty sent one to several of her friends; and the first thing she knew came a telegram from Mrs. Emily, saying that one of the big weekly papers in Paris offered two hundred francs for the right to reproduce the painting. When this magazine appeared there came a cablegram from one of the big New York newspapers offering a hundred dollars for the American rights; and on top of that a concern which was making picture post cards asked Marcel's price to let them use it.

The New York paper came out with a story about the painter, saying that he had been in an air crash, and this was his own experience. Marcel was annoyed for a while; he hated that sort of publicity. But to Beauty it was marvelous; it set everybody to talking about her husband, and visitors came to the house again, and she · had an excuse to get out her pretty clothes. She had a vision of her husband becoming a famous and highly paid magazine illustrator; but Marcel said, to hell with it, and jammed his red silk skullcap down on his head and stalked off to the studio to brood there. So Beauty had to run to him, and fall on her knees and admit that she was a cheap and silly creature, and that Marcel was to paint whatever he wanted, and needn't see a single one of the curiosity seekers —they would disconnect the bell at the gate if he wished it.

However, Lanny managed to get his way about one thing; Marcel promised not to burn any more of his work. On this point the boy collected historical facts from painter friends and retailed them to his stepfather. "We have all Michelangelo's sketches, and Leonardo's, and Rembrandt's, and Rodin's—so we can follow their minds, and learn what they were thinking and trying. We learn from what they rejected as well as from what they kept." So it was agreed that everything Marcel did from that time on was to be put away on shelves in the storeroom; and, furthermore, Lanny might be allowed to see something now and then—but no more publicity.

15

Amor inter Arma

I

JUST before Christmas, Mrs. Emily Chattersworth returned to Cannes, and opened her winter home. She needed a rest, so she told her friends; but she didn't take it for long. There were too many wounded French soldiers all over the Midi; tens of thousands of them, and many as bad as Marcel. The casino at Juan—a small place at that time—had been turned into a hospital, as had all sorts of public buildings throughout France. But there was never room enough, never help enough. Frenchwomen, who as a rule confined their activities to their own homes, were now organizing hospitals and relief depots; and of course they were glad to have help from anyone who would give it.

So it wasn't long before Mrs. Emily was agitating and organizing, making her American friends on the Riviera ashamed of wasting their time playing bridge and dancing; she told them stories about men deprived of hands and feet and eyes and what not, and facing the problem of how to keep alive. In the end, impatient of delays, Mrs. Emily turned her own home into an institution for what was called "re-education": teaching new occupations to men so crippled they could no longer practice their former ones. A man who had lost his right hand would learn to do something with a hook, and men who had lost their legs would learn to make baskets or brooms. Mrs. Emily moved herself into what had been a maid's room, and filled up her whole mansion with her "pupils," and when that wasn't enough, put up tents on her lawns.

The wife of Marcel Detaze was especially exposed to this vigorous lady's attacks. "Don't you care about anybody's husband but your own?" Beauty was ashamed to give the wrong answer, and after she had made sure that Marcel was occupied with his painting, Lanny would drive her up to Sept Chênes, as the place was called, and give what help she could. She didn't know how to make brooms or baskets, and as a "re-educator" she wasn't very much, but she was the world's wonder when it came to uplifting the souls of men. Suffering had dealt kindly with her, and added a touch of mystery to her loveliness, and when she came into the room all the *mutilés* would stop looking at brooms and baskets, and if she said something to a poor devil he would remember it the rest of the day. After what she had been through with Marcel, she didn't mind seeing scars of war, and she learned to get the same thrill which in the old days she had got from entering a ballroom and having "important" people stare at her and ask who she was.

It was good for Lanny too, because the world he was going to live in was not to be composed exclusively of "important" persons, manifesting grace and charm at enormous expense. Going to Mrs. Emily's was a kind of "slumming" which not even Robbie could have objected to; and Lanny had an advantage over his mother in that he knew Provençal, and could chat with these peasants and fishermen as he had done all his life. Several of them were the same persons he had known, fathers or older brothers of the children he had played with.

And oddest circumstance of all—Lanny's gigolo! That happy and graceful dancing man whom he had picked up in Nice, and who had come to Bienvenu and spent an afternoon playing the piccolo flute and demonstrating the steps of the farandole! Here he was, drawing a harsh breath now and then, because he had got trapped in a dugout full of fumes from a shell; and surely he would never dance again, because his right leg was gone just below the hip. Instead he was learning to carve little dancing figures out of wood, and when he was through with that form of education, he would go back to his father's farm, where there was wood in plenty, and the organization which Mrs. Emily had formed would try to sell his toys for the Christmas trade. M. Pinjon was the same kindly and gentle dreamer that Lanny recalled, and the boy had the satisfaction of seeing his mother willing to talk to him now, and hearing her admit that he was a good creature, who doubtless had done no harm to anyone in his life.

II

One of Mrs. Emily's bright ideas was that men who had hands and eyes but no feet might learn to paint. Of course it was late in life for them to begin, but then look at Gauguin, look at van Gogh —you just could never tell where you might find a genius. Might it not be possible for Marcel to come now and then and give a lesson to these pitiful souls?

Marcel was coming to care less and less for people. Even the best of them made him aware of his own condition, and it was only when he was alone and buried in his work that life was bearable to him. But he heard Beauty talking for hours at a time about Emily Chattersworth, and of course this work came close to his heart. He too was a *mutilé*, and a comrade of all the others. He couldn't teach anything, because he couldn't talk; even Mrs. Emily had a hard time understanding him, unless Beauty sat by and said some of the words over again. But he offered to come and entertain them by making sketches on a blackboard—for example, those little German devils that seemed to amuse people. Somebody else might explain and comment on the work as he did it.

So they drove up to Sept Chênes one evening. Mrs. Emily had set up a blackboard, and had got one of her patients to do the talking, a journalist who had lost the fingers of his right hand and was learning to write with his left. He was an amusing talker, and Marcel with his skullcap and veil was a figure of mystery. He was clever and quick at sketching, and his Prussian devils made the audience roar. The deaf ones could see them, and the blind ones could hear about them. If the lecturer missed a point, Marcel would write a word or two on the board. It wasn't long before the men were shouting what they wanted next, and Marcel would draw that. He had been at the front long enough to know the little touches that made things real to his comrades.

He drew a heroic figure of the *poilu*. *Poil* means your hair, and is a symbol of your power. The *poilu* was a mighty fellow, and wore a red military *képi*, with a depression in the round top like a saucer. When Marcel drew a rough wooden cross in a field, and hung one of those battered caps on top of it, every man in the room knew what that meant, for he had seen thousands of them. The *poilu* wore a long coat, and when he was marching he buttoned back the front flaps to make room for his legs, so when you saw that, you knew he was on the march. If his face was set grimly, you knew he was going to say: "*Nous les aurons*," that is: "We'll have them, we'll get them."

What he was going to get was the *boche*. That was another word of the war. The British called him "Jerry," and the Yanks, when they came along, would call him "Heinie," and sometimes "Fritzie"; but to the *poilu* he was *le boche*, and when Marcel drew him, he made him not ugly or hateful, just stupid and discouraged, and that too seemed right to *anciens combattants*. When Marcel desired to draw something hateful, it wore a long coat to the ankles, tightly drawn in at the waist, and a monocle, and a gold bracelet, and an expression of monstrous insolence.

III

That visit was important to the painter because it gave him a place to go. With these poor devils he need never be ashamed, never humiliated. He would return now and then to entertain them; or he would go and just talk with them, or rather, let them talk to him. One of them had been with Marcel's own regiment in the Alpes Maritimes, and from him Marcel learned that his comrades had been moved to the front in the Vosges mountains, and what had happened to them there.

The men wouldn't talk to strangers about the war; it was too terrible, it would discourage people. But among themselves it was all right, and Marcel's mutilated face was a passport to all hearts. He heard about winter fighting in heavy snow, with the trenches only a few yards apart, so that you could hear the enemy talking, and shout abuse and defiance at him; if you lifted your cap an inch above the parapet, it would be riddled with bullets in a second or two. Shelling was incessant, day and night, and hand grenades were thrown; only a few sentries stayed to watch, while the rest hid in dugouts underground. Great tracts in the forest had been reduced to splinters, and in the *poste de secours*, a shelter dug half under the hillside, a dozen doctors had been killed in the course of a year. No going about at all in the daytime; yet you could hear the church bells ringing in a village behind the lines. One of the stories was about a man who picked up an old hand organ in one of the buildings wrecked by shells, and brought it up one rainy night to one of the *cagnas*, or dugouts, and stood outside in the rain playing it, and men began singing, hundreds of them all over the place, even with the shells falling around. "Sidi Brahim," they sang.

Among other things, Lanny learned what had happened to his mother's former chauffeur and handy man, Sergeant Pierre Bazoche. He had taken part in one of those innumerable attempts that came to nothing. Line after line of men had charged across an exposed place on a hillside, and just lay where they fell. There was no way to get to them; those who were not killed at once died slowly—but in any case they stayed all winter, and the smell of them made an invisible cloud that drifted slowly over the trenches, sometimes to the poilus and sometimes to the boches.

After talks like that Marcel would go back and paint. He made a painting that he called "Fear," and for a while he didn't want anybody to see it; perhaps it was a confession of something in himself. He was so proud, so serene, and full of ardor for his beloved France —could it be that he had ever been terrified? The truth is that this complicated arrangement of pipes and tissues that comprise a man is so fragile, so soft and easily damaged, that nature has provided an automatic impulse to protect it. There are parts of it that can hurt so abominably—and in truth you would have difficulty in naming any part that you would care to have struck by a little steel cylinder moving at the rate of half a mile per second. The boches had this same feeling, and many Catholics among them carried on their persons magic formulas containing detailed specifications. "May God preserve me against all manner of arms and weapons, shot and cannon, long or short swords, knives or daggers, or carbines, halberds, or any thing that cuts or pierces, against thrusts of rapiers, long and short rifles, or guns, and suchlike, which have been forged since the birth of Christ; against all kinds of metal, be it iron or steel, brass or lead, ore or wood." The poor devils lay dead upon the field with these prayers in their pockets.

Marcel painted a dim, mysterious form, the upper part of a human being, you couldn't be sure whether it was man or woman; it was shrouded in a sort of dark hood, and you saw only the face, and at first only the eyes, which had a faint glow, and were staring at you with a look that seized your own. The face was not distorted, the expression was subtler than that, it was a soul which had been acquainted with fear for a long time; and not just a physical fear, but a moral horror at a society in which men inflicted such things upon one another.

At least, that is what M. Rochambeau said after he had looked at the picture for a long time. He said it was quite extraordinary, and certainly none of the persons who saw it ever forgot it. But Marcel put it away. He said it wasn't a picture for wartime—not until the enemy could see it too!

IV

The British had failed in their efforts to take the Dardanelles, largely because they couldn't decide whether the taking was worth the cost. Now they were starting an advance from Salonika, a harbor in the north of Greece. That country had a pro-German king, and those beautiful islands which the *Bluebird* had visited had become lurking places of submarines seeking to destroy British commerce and the troopships which came heavily loaded from India and Australia. The entire Mediterranean was the scene of unresting naval war, and Lanny didn't need to look at war maps, because he had been to the places and had pictures of them in his eager mind.

When he and Jerry went fishing they watched every ship that passed—and there were great numbers—knowing that at any moment there might be an explosion and a pillar of black smoke. They never happened to see that, but they heard firing more than once, and ran to a high point of the Cap and with field glasses watched a sinking ship, and saw motorboats hurrying out to bring off survivors. Up and down the coast people told stories of hospital ships sunk with all on board, of loaded troopships torpedoed, of submarines rammed, or sunk by a well-aimed shot, or getting entangled in the chains and nets now set in front of harbors.

The fighting at Gallipoli had one important consequence for Lanny. The father of Rosemary Codwilliger was wounded, and in a hospital in Malta; this made the mother decide to spend the winter on the Riviera, where he could join her when he was able to be moved. "She says she's in need of a rest," wrote the girl, "but I think it's to get me out of the notion of nursing. She's afraid I'll get to know people outside our social circle."

The family wanted a quiet place, Rosemary added, and it happened that the Baroness Sophie had a little villa on the Cap, not the one she lived in. Lanny sent a snapshot of it to the girl, and as a result her family rented the place and set a date for their arrival; the mother, a widowed aunt, Rosemary herself, and her father whenever the doctors and the submarines would let him.

Lanny was sixteen now, and old enough to know that he was interested in girls. This grave and sweet English lass had captured his imagination, and he looked back upon the river Thames and its green and pleasant land as one of his happiest memories. He had met other girls on the Riviera, and had swum and boated and danced with them, but principally they interested him because they reminded him of Rosemary.

A year and a half had passed, and now she was coming, and Lanny hoped to be included in her social circle. His mother was a respectable married woman, and his stepfather had all but given his life in the war which was England's. Lanny had never met Rosemary's mother or aunt, but he hoped for success with them as in the case of the Frau Doktor Hofrat von und zu Nebenaltenberg— who now, by the way, was among the Germans interned on the Île Ste.-Marguerite, which Lanny could view from the veranda of his home.

The boy had told his mother about the English girl and how much he liked her; it would have been cruelty to withhold such news from Beauty, to whom it was the most interesting of subjects. She warned him not to expect too much from the English, because they were a peculiar people, rigidly bound by their own conventions. With Americans they were apt to go so far and no farther.

Just now Beauty had another love affair on her hands, that of Jerry Pendleton, who clamored for advice about French girls. He was finding in one of them such an odd mixture of fervor and reserve; and such a complication of mothers and aunts! Did Mrs. Detaze think that an American could be happy with a French wife? And would such a wife be happy in America? The situation was complicated by the fact that Jerry didn't know what he wanted to do with himself. He had come away fully determined to escape the drug store business; he dreamed of being a newspaperman, perhaps a foreign correspondent. But what would he do with a wife under those circumstances? Lanny's tutor, torn between his destinies, was much like Beauty having to choose between Pittsburgh and the Cap d'Antibes. Lanny's lessons suffered during the discussions—but he could always go and read the encyclopedia.

V

The three ladies and a maid arrived, and Lanny was at the train to meet them and take them to the villa. He had the keys, and knew the place and showed it to them. He had lived on the Cap all his life, and could tell them about the shops and services and other practical matters. Also he knew about servants—the innumerable relatives of

Leese were available and the ladies had only to choose. The most exclusive English family could hardly reject the assistance of such a polite and agreeable youth.

Mrs. Codwilliger was a tall, thin-faced lady from whom Lanny might have learned how Rosemary would look when she was forty; but he didn't. She and her sister, tall and still thinner, were the daughters of Lord Dewthorpe, and estimated themselves accordingly. But when Lanny's mother offered to call, they could not say no; and when they heard the romantic story of the painter who stayed in his studio alone, never appearing in public without a veil, their deep English instincts of self-sufficiency were touched. When Lanny offered to lend them several of his stepfather's seascapes to remedy the rather crude taste in art of the baroness, they had to admit that the habitability of their home had been increased.

Rosemary was a year older than Lanny, which meant that she was now a young lady. As it happened, she was a very grand one, belonging to a set which managed to impress other people—they "got away with it," to use the American slang. The youth was prepared to worship her at a distance. But they strolled off, and sat where they could see the moonlight flung across the water in showers of brilliant fire. There was a distant sound of music from the great hotel—all the lovely things which they remembered on the banks of the Thames.

So Lanny was moved, very timidly, to draw closer to this delightful being, and she did not seem to mind. When he gently touched her hand she did not draw it away, and presently they resumed, quite naturally and simply, the relation they had had in the old days. He put his arm about her, and after a while he kissed her, and they sat dissolved in the well-remembered bliss. But this time it did not stop at the same point.

Rosemary Codwilliger was a friend and admirer of that ardent suffragette, Miss Noggyns, who had so upset Kurt Meissner at The Reaches. With the coming of the war these redoubtable ladies had dropped their agitation, but they expected to have their demands granted before the war was over; and what were they going to do with their new freedom? That they would go into Parliament, attend the universities, and move into all the professions—such things went without saying. But what would they do about love and sex and marriage? What would they do about the so-called "double standard," which permitted men to have premarital sex relations without social disgrace, but denied that privilege to women?

Obviously, there were two alternatives. Women could adopt the double standard, or they could demand that men conform to the single standard. It soon appeared that the latter was very difficult, whereas the former was easy. The subject was made more complex by the possibility that not all women were alike; what might be pleasing to some might not be to all. In magazines, pamphlets, and books of the "feminist" movement these questions were vehemently debated, and the ideas were tried out by numbers of persons, with results not always according to schedule.

Rosemary's young mind was a ferment of these theories. First of all, she had been taught, you must be frank. You couldn't be so with the old people, of course; but young people in love, or thinking of being in love, had to be honest with each other and try to understand each other; love had to be a give and take, each respecting the other's personality, and so on. The problems of sex had apparently been changed by the discovery of birth control, which Mr. Bernard Shaw called "the most revolutionary discovery of the nineteenth century." Since you no longer needed to have babies, the question to be considered was whether love would bring happiness to the lovers.

Rosemary was blond, with features regular and a manner gentle and serene. In many ways she reminded Lanny of his mother, and perhaps that was why she had drawn him so strongly. He was a mother's boy, used to being told what to do, and Rosemary was prepared to deal with him on that basis—it was, apparently, what they all meant by "women's rights." Anyway, they sat in a remote and well-shadowed part of the garden, with arms around each other; and it seemed unavoidable that they should talk of intimate matters. Lanny told about love problems which puzzled him, and Rosemary

imparted ideas which she had gathered from a weekly journal called
the *Freewoman*.

When Lanny had listened to Kurt Meissner's expositions of German philosophy, he had attributed it all to Kurt's wonderful brain;
so now he thought that Rosemary had worked out the theory of
sexual equality for herself. Of course he was deeply impressed, and
at first rather frightened. But after these ideas had been discussed for
two or three evenings, they no longer seemed so strange; the boy
who had become a man within the last year began to wonder
whether all those words about freedom and happiness might possibly
apply to him and his lovely friend. This had an alarming effect; a
wave of excitement swept over him, and his teeth began to chatter
and his hands to shake uncontrollably.

"What's the matter, Lanny?" asked the girl.

He didn't dare to answer at first, but finally he told her: "I'm
afraid maybe I'm falling in love with you." It was all as if it had
never happened in the world before.

"Well, why not, Lanny?" she asked, gently.

"You mean—you really wouldn't mind?"

"You know I think you are a very dear boy."

So he kissed her on the lips—the first time he had ever done that.
They sat clasped together, and a clamor arose in him. He pressed
her to him, and when she submitted, he began to fondle her more
and more intimately. He knew then that the experience had come to
him about which he had heard everybody talking, and which had
been such a mystery in his thoughts.

The girl stayed his trembling hands. "You mustn't, Lanny. It
wouldn't be safe." Then she whispered: "I'll have to go to the house
first, and get something."

So they got up and walked. Lanny found his knees shaking,
which perplexed him greatly. It must be what the French novelists
call *la grande passion!* He waited some distance from the house
while Rosemary went in—as it happened, there was company and no
one paid any heed to her. Presently she came back, and they lost
themselves in a secluded part of the garden, and there she taught

him those things about which he had been so curious. At first his agitation was painful, but presently he was dissolved in a flood of bliss, which seemed to justify the theories of the "new women." If he was happy and she was happy, why should the vague and remote "world" of their elders concern itself with their affairs?

VI

It wasn't long before Lanny told his mother about this affair. Impossible not to, because she asked pointed questions, and it would have been hurting her feelings to evade. Beauty's reaction to the disclosure was a peculiar one. She had been what you might call a practicing feminist, but without any theories; she had had her own way about love, but always with the proper feeling that she was doing wrong. It was hard to explain, but that feeling seemed necessary; you knew it was wrong, and that made it right. But to assert that it was right was a shocking boldness. And when a girl was only seventeen! "Was she virgin?" asked Beauty, and added with distaste: "Certainly she didn't act like it." Lanny didn't know and couldn't make inquiries.

Beauty couldn't altogether dislike Rosemary, but she never got over the idea that there was something alarming about her—a portent of a new world that Beauty didn't understand. The mother's feeling was that her dear little boy had been seduced, and that he was much too young. She took the problem to her husband, but failed to get him excited. "Nature knows a lot more about that than you do," said the painter, and went on painting.

Springtime again on the Riviera, to Lanny the most delightful he had ever known. The flesh of woman was revealed to him, and the discovery transfused everything else in his life. The world and every common sight to him did seem appareled in celestial light, the glory and the freshness of a dream. Now for the first time he knew what music was about, and poetry, and dancing, not to mention the birds and the butterflies. The flowers had the colors of Rosemary, and she had their perfume. She was to him a being of magic, and when he was with her he never wanted to take his eyes from her, and when he wasn't with her he wished he was.

Of course he couldn't be with her all the time; because "what would people say?" The "world" did matter after all, it appeared. Cool and serene, Rosemary took charge. Lanny must go on with his studying, and not make her feel that she was a bad influence. When they boated and swam and played tennis, they must be with other young people, for appearance' sake; and the same in the evening— there must be some sort of pretext, a dance, a party, a sail—the young people all understood that, they all had the same desires, and would stroll away in couples, casually and innocently. They protected one another, a conspiracy of the new against the old.

Did Rosemary succeed in fooling her mother and her aunt? In those early days of the revolt of youth the old were in a peculiar state of emotional paralysis. They didn't dare to know; it was too awful to let themselves know—and yet of course they did. They would look at the young with fright in their eyes, and seldom dare to speak—for what could they say? Rosemary had given her answer in advance—she wanted to go out and earn her own living. Girls were nursing, they were, even getting jobs in munitions factories, wearing black overalls and filling shells with explosives. They were going out on the streets delivering tirades, calling on men to enlist, pinning white feathers on those who looked as if they ought to. And the things they were reading, and left around the house, careless of who might see them!

It had been prior to the outbreak of the war that Rosemary had fallen under the spell of one of those suffragettes—a teacher, it was. Still a child, with pigtails down her back, she had walked into the National Gallery with a hand ax concealed under her skirt, and at a prearranged signal had passed it to one of those notorious women who hadn't dared bring it in herself, because she was known and might be searched. And that not a crazy whim or a lark, but a means of reforming the world! Something they took up as a religion, for which they were willing to die! You might put them in jail, but they would only try to starve themselves to death; you wanted to say to the devil with them and let them do it, but you didn't dare.

VII

The German high command had made up its collective mind that in order to win the war they had to break through on the western front, and they had picked the fortress of Verdun as the place. This was the head of the original French defenses, the part which had not given way; a complex of fortifications covering various heights along both banks of the river Meuse. Now that the war had been going on for a year and a half, the technique of taking such fortifications had become well settled. You had to bring up enough heavy guns, and pile enough ammunition behind them, to reduce the enemy entrenchments to dust and rubble; then you put down what was called a "creeping barrage" of shells which exploded in small fragments, to destroy the men who had been hiding underground and who came up after your heavy bombardment. The "creeping barrage" moved forward, just ahead of your lines of infantry, which could thus advance in comparative safety, and take what was left of the trenches, an operation known as "mopping up." The enemy would have line after line of trenches, and you had to repeat this same procedure and hope to break through finally and turn a "war of position" into a "war of movement."

To stop such an attack, the French gunners had to be better than the Germans, and have more shells. The French airmen had to keep the mastery and bring in more information as to what was happening. But more than anything else, the plain everyday poilu had to crawl into his rabbit warrens, and those of him who were left alive had to pop up at the right moment, and hide in whatever shell holes might be left and shoot enough of the advancing Germans to discourage the rest. That was all there was to it, you just had to outstay the enemy. When you had fired all your cartridges, you got more from a dead comrade in the same shell hole. If the night passed and nobody brought you food, you starved. If it rained, you lay in the mud, and if the mud froze, you tried to keep your hands alive so that you could shoot.

The Verdun area covered a hundred square miles or so, and during the fighting it was turned into a chaos of shell craters and nothing else. Places like Fort Douaumont were taken and retaken a half-dozen times, and the living fought among the dead of both sides. The main battle began in February of 1916 and lasted until July without cessation, and after that off and on for a year. The Germans brought sixty-four divisions, which was more than a million men. The French fired more than ten million shells from field guns, and nearly two million from medium and heavy guns.

The German Crown Prince was in command, and that was one more reason for the French wanting to win. The whole world watched and waited while the armies staggered back and forth. A break-through might mean the German conquest of France, and nobody knew that better than the poilu; he invented for himself a chant, which became a sort of incantation, a spell to rouse the souls of men perishing of wounds and exhaustion, who yet would kill one more enemy before dying. *"Passeront pas, passeront pas!"* they sang or gasped. "They shall not pass."

VIII

Such were the events some three hundred miles to the north of Lanny Budd while he was playing with love in springtime. He couldn't keep the war from troubling his conscience, but there was nothing he could do about it—especially not so long as he was under pledge to keep neutral. He was the one person of that sort he knew. Eddie Patterson was now driving an ambulance behind the lines at Verdun, and so his Sophie no longer had any motive for not hating the Germans, and she was hating them. All Lanny could say was: "Excuse me, I promised my father not to talk about the war."

Budd's were now making small arms and ammunition in large quantities, and exclusively for the Allies. There was no way to make

any for the Germans; the British blockade was too tight, and anyhow the British and French were on hand to buy everything you
could produce, paying top prices on the nail. The big Wall Street
banks took British and French bonds and sold them to the American
public, and Budd's got the cash. Under Robbie's contract he was entitled to a commission on every deal. He would spend this money
freely and gaily, as always; but he was a stubborn fellow, and
nobody was going to get him to say that any nation of Europe—
and that included the British Empire—was ever right about anything.
Robbie had been on the inside, and knew they were all wrong.

Out of this came the first little rift between Lanny and his girl-
friend. Rosemary wasn't satisfied to have him hold his tongue; she
began to pin him down and ask what he really thought. When he
repeated his formula, she wanted to know: "What are you, a man
or a dummy? Do you have to think everything your father thinks?
If I thought what my parents think, would I be here with you?"
Lanny was troubled, because he had taken it for granted that this
delightful young woman was as gentle as she looked. But apparently
a sharp tongue was part of the equipment of every "feminist," and
first among "women's rights" was the right to tell her man what she
thought of him.

Both British and French were bitter against the Americans, because they were not taking part in the war, but just making money
out of it, and at the same time making objections to the blockade.
Nearly all the Americans in France felt the same way, and were
ashamed of their country. The conversation at Bienvenu was all
along that line; and while Marcel was careful not to say anything in
Lanny's presence, the boy knew that Marcel blamed Robbie because
he was making money out of the French and at the same time with-
holding his sympathy from them. The painter was eaten up with
anxiety all during the battle of Verdun; he would burst out with
some expression of loathing for the "Huns," and Lanny wouldn't
say anything, and it would appear that a chill had fallen in the home.
The relationship of stepfather and stepson is a complicated one at
best, and this wasn't the best.

The boy would go off and try to think out by himself the problems of the war. He would remember things that Robbie had told him about the trickery of Allied diplomacy. Right now it was being said in America that the Allies had made secret treaties dividing up the spoils of the war they hadn't won; worse yet, they had promised the same territory to different peoples. Robbie would send articles about such matters to his son, finding ways to get them by the censor—and the consequence of knowing about such things was that the boy no longer fitted anywhere in France.

IX

Marcel painted a picture of the poilu, the savior of *la patrie*. He tried to put into it all his love for the men with whom he had trained and fought. When he was done, he said it wasn't good enough, he hadn't got what he wanted; but his friends thought differently; the painting was shown at a salon in Paris, and made a hit, and was taken up and reproduced in posters. Beauty thought that her husband would get satisfaction out of that service to his country; but nothing could please him, it appeared. He didn't want to be a popular painter—and anyhow, art was futility in a time like this.

So came a crisis in the affairs of this married pair. How rarely does it happen that two human creatures, with all their differences, weaknesses, moods can get along without quarreling! Beauty was carrying her cross, in the best evangelical church fashion; she was pouring out her own redemptive blood in the secrecy of her heart. But she couldn't be happy in her tragic situation, and the bitterness which she repressed was bound to escape at some spots in her life. She couldn't restrain her annoyance at this contrary attitude of Marcel. Why should a man go to the trouble of making pictures, and then not want to have people see them, even quarrel with those who wanted a chance to admire them? Why was it necessary to say something contrary every time his work was praised? In vain did Lanny, budding young critic, try to make plain to his mother that a true artist is wrestling with a vision of something higher and better, and cannot endure to be admired for what he knows is less than his best.

Out of this clash of temperaments came a terrible thing: Lanny came home one evening from his love-making to find his mother lying on her bed sobbing. Her husband had broached to her the idea of going back into the army. He had the crazy notion that he ought to be helping to hold the line at Verdun; he was a trained man, and France needed every one. He was as good as ever, he in-insisted; he could march, and had tried long walks to make sure. He could handle a gun—the only thing wrong was that he was ugly, but out there in mud and powder smoke who would care?

Beauty had had a fit of hysterics and called him some bad names, an ingrate, a fool, and so on. If she meant no more to him than that, he would have to go—but he would never see her again. "I did it once, Marcel, but I won't do it a second time."

She really meant it, so she declared to her son. She had reached the limit of endurance. If Marcel went, *la patrie* could take care of him next time in some soldiers' home. She said it with hardness in her face that was a new thing to Lanny; one does not wrestle with duty for long periods without going back to the moods and even the facial expressions of one's Puritan forefathers. But five minutes later Beauty broke down; her lips were trembling, and she was ask-ing whether perhaps it was her impatience and lack of art sense which were making the painter dissatisfied with his lot.

So there was no peace in this woman's soul until midsummer, when the German attacks on the great fortress slowed up. By that time she had managed to get her man started upon another project —to paint a portrait of her. It is a use that every painter makes sooner or later of the woman he loves; if Marcel had it in him to do any portrait, she would be it. Beauty had changed, and what Marcel saw was the woman of anguish who had prayed to his soul, the woman of pity who talked to crippled soldiers and helped them to want to live.

She put on one of her nurse's uniforms and went over to the studio and sat for hours every day; an old story to her. Marcel painted her sitting in a chair with her hands folded, and all the grief of France in her face. "Sister of Mercy," he was going to call her; and Beauty didn't have to act, because of the terror in her heart. She couldn't tell what turn the next great battle might take. She could only urge Marcel to take his time and get it perfect; she wanted him to have something he really believed in—so that he would stay a painter instead of a poilu!

X

Lanny's young dream of love died early in the month of May, and it wasn't a merry month for him. At that time the thoughts of English people on the Riviera turned to their lovely green island with its chilly breezes. Furthermore it developed that Rosemary's father had to be examined by surgeons at home; he was brought to Marseille, and from there north, and Lanny never met him.

"Darling, we shall see each other again," said the girl. "You'll come to England, or I'll be coming here."

"I'll wait for you—always," said Lanny, fervently. "I want you to marry me, Rosemary."

She looked startled. "Oh, Lanny, I don't think we can marry. I wouldn't count on that if I were you."

The boy was startled in turn. "But why not?"

"We're much too young to think about it. I don't want to marry for a long time."

"I can wait, Rosemary."

"Darling, don't think about it, please. It wouldn't be fair to you." Seeing the bewilderment in his face, she added: "It would make my parents so terribly unhappy if I were to marry outside our own sort of people."

"But—but"—he had trouble in finding words. "Wouldn't it make them unhappy to know about our love?"

"They aren't going to know about that; and it's quite a different thing. Marriage is so serious; you have children, and property settlements, and all that bother; and there'd be the question whether

our children were to be Americans or English. You might want to
go to America to live——"

"I'm really not much of an American, Rosemary. I've never been
there, and may never go."

"You can't be sure; and my people wouldn't be sure. They'd make
an awful fuss, I know."

"Many English people marry Americans," argued the boy. "Lord
Eversham-Watson—I visited them, and they seemed quite happy."

"I know, darling, it's done; and don't have your blessed feelings
hurt—you know I love you, and we've been so happy, and will be
some more. But if we tie ourselves down, and get our families to
arguing and all that—it would be a frightful bore."

Lanny was imperfectly educated in modern ideas, and couldn't
get the thing clear in his mind. He wanted his adored one all the
time, and couldn't imagine that she might not want him. Why was
she so concerned about her family in this one matter, and so indif-
ferent, even defiant, in others? He asked her to explain it, and she
tried, groping to put into words things that were instinctive and
unformulated. It appeared that young ladies of the English govern-
ing classes who joined the movement for equal rights wanted certain
definite things, like being able to write M.P. after their names, and
to have divorce on equal terms with men; but they didn't mean to
interfere with the system whereby their families governed the realm.
They accepted the idea that when the time came for marriage
each should adopt some honored name with a peculiar spelling, and
become the mistress of some beautiful old country house and the
mother of future viscounts and barons, or at the least admirals and
cabinet ministers.

"It mayn't be so easy to find an upper-class Englishman," remarked the boy; "the way they're getting killed off in this war."

"There'll be some left," answered the girl, easily. She had only to
look in the mirror to know that she had special advantages.

Lanny pondered some more, and then inquired: "Is it because I
don't take sides in the war?"

"That's just a bit of it, Lanny. It helps me to realize that we shouldn't be happy; our ideas are so different, and our interests. Whatever happens to England, I have to be for her, and so will my children when I have them."

"They are apt to go just so far and no farther," Beauty had told her son. When he parted from Rosemary Codwilliger, pronounced Culliver, it was with tears and sighs on both sides, and a perfectly clear understanding that he might have a sweet and lovely mistress for an indefinite time, provided that he would come where she was, and do what she asked him to do. When Lanny told his mother about it, and she told Marcel, the painter remarked that the boy had been used as a guinea pig in a scientific experiment. When he learned that the boy was unhappy, he added that scientific experiments were not conducted for the benefit of the guinea pigs.

16

Business as Usual

I

WHEN the German army came to Les Forêts, old M. Priedieu, the librarian, had stayed to guard his employer's treasures. He had stood by, pale with horror, while drunken hussars cut the valuable pictures from the walls, rolled up the tapestries, dumped the venerable leather-covered chairs out of the windows, and swept the priceless books from the shelves in pure wantonness. They didn't do any physical harm to the white-haired old man, but they so wounded his sensibilities that he took to his bed, and a few days later died quietly in his sleep.

But his spirit lived on in Lanny Budd. All the boy's life he would remember what the grave old scholar had told him about the love of books. This was something that no misfortune or sorrow could take from a man, and its possessor had a refuge from all the evils of the world. Montesquieu had said that to love reading was to exchange hours of boredom for hours of delight; Laharpe had said that a book is a friend that never deceives. The librarian of Les Forêts had advised Lanny to seek the friendship of the French classic authors and let them teach him dignity, grace, and perfection of form.

Now misfortune and sorrow had come; love had dallied with Lanny Budd for a while and then tossed him away. The crisis found him without companionship, because Jerry Pendleton had come to an arrangement with his *belle amie* to wait for him, and had gone back to Kansas to complete his education. In this plight Lanny sought the friendship of one Jean Racine, who had died more than two hundred years previously but lived on by the magic of the printed page. He took disordered emotions and converted them into well-made dramas, in which exalted beings stalked the scene and poured out their sufferings in verses so eloquent that a youth of sixteen was moved to seek lonely places by the sea or in the forest and declaim them to tritons or hamadryads.

Also Lanny won the friendship of a severe and stern spirit by the name of Pierre Corneille, who had made over the French theater, and had had no easy time of it in his life. The aristocratic personages who had sprung from his brain, full panoplied in pride and owing fealty to duty alone, reminded a sensitive youth that the life of man had never been easy, and that fate appeared to have other purposes than to feed pleasure to avid lips. Since one had to die sooner or later, let it be magnificently, to the accompaniment of verses that had the sweep of an orchestra:

> *Je suis jeune, il est vrai; mais aux âmes bien nées*
> *La valeur n'attend point le nombre des années.*

After Lanny had read *Le Cid* and *Horace* and *Cinna*, he remembered the great hours he had spent among the Isles of Greece, and that these people also could be had in friendship by the magic of the printed word. M. Priedieu had told him about Sophocles, and Lanny got a French translation of the seven plays and read them aloud to his stepfather. Together they indulged in more speculation about the Greek view of life, which had begun with the worship of sensuous beauty and ended with a confrontation of dreadful and inexplicable doom. For what had this gay and eager people been brought into being on those bright and sunny shores, to leave behind them only broken marble columns, and a few thousand melodious verses embodying proud resignation and despair?

As a result of these influences, encountered at the most impressionable age, Lanny Budd became conservative in his taste in the arts. He liked a writer to have something to say, and to say it with clarity and precision; he liked a musician to reveal his ideas in music, and not in program notes; he liked a painter to produce works that bore some resemblance to something. He disliked loud noises and confusion, and obscurity cultivated as a form of exclusiveness. All of which meant that Lanny was out-of-date before he had got fairly started in life.

II

Inspired by sublime examples, the painter gave his stepson useful advice concerning love. It was good to do with it, but also good to be able to do without it. In this, as in other affairs, one must be master of one's self. There were a thousand reasons why love might fail, and one must have resources within and be able to meet the shocks of fate. Lanny knew that Marcel spoke with authority—this lover who had had to leave his love and go to war; this worshiper of beauty who now had to speak through a veil in order that his friends might not see his ugliness. When Marcel said that Lanny too might some day hear a call that would take him away from music and art and love—the youth trembled in the depths of his soul.

Lanny talked about these problems of love and happiness with his mother also. Strict moralists might have been shocked that

Beauty was willing to know about her son's too early entanglement, and to sanction it; but her course had this compensation, that when the youth was in trouble, now or later, he came to her and had the benefit of her experience.

She tried now to explain to him things that she didn't understand very well herself. No, she didn't think that Rosemary was heartless; it was evident that the girl had taken up the ideas of older women, who perhaps had suffered too much in a man's world, and had revolted from it and gone to extremes in the effort to protect themselves. Beauty told her son that kind and good people frequently had to suffer for those who were not so. Just so Kurt Meissner and other kind and good Germans might suffer for those cruel and arrogant ones who had dragged the nation into an awful calamity.

That was another problem with which Lanny wrestled frequently. Was Europe really going to be another Greece, and destroy itself by internecine wars? Would travelers some day come to Juan and to Cannes, and see the remains of lovely villas like Bienvenu and splendid palaces like Sept Chênes, and dig in the ruins and speculate concerning the lives of those who had built them, and the hostile fate which had driven them upon a course of self-destruction?

Lanny had written several times to Kurt, through the kind agency of the Jewish salesman of electrical gadgets, now engaged in buying from the United States such devices as magnetos for automobiles and airplanes, and reshipping them to Germany. Lanny wrote Kurt about the tenderness of Racine and the stern pride of Corneille and the moral sublimity of Sophocles; and Kurt replied that his friend was fortunate in being able to devote himself to these lofty themes. He, Kurt Meissner, was now taking up practical duties, and soon would be engaged in what he considered the most important work in the world. Lanny had no difficulty in understanding that his German friend was going into the war, and didn't wish, or perhaps wouldn't be allowed, to say where or when or how.

Lanny had to think of Kurt as fighting, and he had to do the same for Rick, who had finished his final year of school and was soon to have his heart's desire. "Sophocles is fine," wrote the English youth on a post card, "but I am reading Blériot"—that being the type of airplane the British were using. Rick didn't say where he was, but Rosemary had brought news about him, and Lanny knew that his friend was in touch with that Captain Finchley whom they had met at the review on Salisbury Plain, and was expecting to go to the camp which this officer now commanded. Lanny knew that the training was intensive and quick, for the need of the Allies for young fliers was desperate. A cousin of Rosemary's had been sent out after only some twenty hours of practice flying, and on his very first flight in France had been shot down by a German outfit. Kurt and Rick were going to fight each other; and suppose they were to meet up in the air!

Lanny took upon himself the duty of serving, at least in his own thoughts, as mediator between these two. It was obvious that when such high-minded youths disagreed so bitterly, there must be truth on both sides and a middle ground where sooner or later they would have to meet. This cruel war must come to an end, and when it did, there would be needed a friend who could speak to both of them and bring them together again.

III

No easy matter to keep that attitude, surrounded as Lanny was with persons whose hatred of Germans kept heating itself up like a furnace fire. Lanny would try to make a compromise by saying that the German rulers were wicked men, while the poor German people were deceived; but his mother said, no, they were a blood-thirsty race, they rejoiced in the infliction of suffering; you could never have got English sailors to send ships to the bottom and leave women and children to drown. Lanny saw that it was useless to argue; he went on playing the music of Mozart and Beethoven, who spoke directly to his soul. He knew they were not bloodthirsty, and neither were the people who had loved and cherished them and made them part of a national tradition.

No, there was something wrong with the world's thinking, and the young fellow's expanding mind kept trying to find out what it was. He wished very much that he might have the help of his father, whom he had not seen for two years. He was often tempted to write and ask Robbie to come to him; but he remembered the deadly submarines lurking all around France and Britain, and he would write: "I'm getting along O.K., and we'll have a lot to talk about when this is over."

Everybody was saying that it was bound to be over in a few months more. Never had wishes been father to so many thoughts. Each new offensive was going to be the final break-through; the Germans would be driven out of France, and the morale of the deceived people would crack. The German authorities kept saying the same thing, except that it was the French line that would crack, and Paris that would be taken. Both sides went on calling their young men, training them as fast as possible, and rushing them into the line; manufacturing enormous quantities of shells and using them in earth-shaking bombardments to prepare for infantry attacks. The battle of Ypres was opened by the British firing a hundred and ten million dollars' worth of ammunition.

The Germans had offered poison gas as their contribution to the progress of military science; and now it was the British turn to have a new idea. Early in the war an English officer had realized the impossibility of making infantry advances against machine guns, and had thought of some kind of steel fortress, heavy enough to be bulletproof, and moving on a caterpillar tread, so that it could go over shell holes and trenches. With a fleet of those to clean out machine-gun nests, it might at last be possible to restore the "war of movement."

It was nearly a year before the British officer could get anything done about his idea; and when after another year it was tried, it wasn't tried thoroughly; there weren't enough tanks and they weren't used as he had planned. All that fitted in exactly with the picture of the British War Office which Robbie had sketched for his son long before the conflict started.

Since Lanny couldn't talk about these matters with his father, he took M. Rochambeau as a substitute. This fine and sensitive old gentleman represented a nation which had maintained its freedom for four hundred years in the heart of warring Europe. It was because of the mountains, he said; and also because they were so fortunate as not to have any gold or oil. M. Rochambeau had surveyed Europe from a high watchtower; he pointed out that most of the Swiss were German-speaking, and French and Germans there had learned to live together in peace, and some day Europe must profit by their example. There would have to be a federation of states like the Swiss cantons, with a central government having power to enforce law and order. This was a vital idea, and Lanny stowed it away among others which he would need.

IV

Three years had passed since Robert Budd had forbidden Lanny to talk with his Uncle Jesse Blackless, and during that period the painter had come perhaps half a dozen times to call upon his sister. When Lanny happened to encounter him, the boy said a polite "How do you do, Uncle Jesse?" and then betook himself elsewhere. He had no reason to be particularly interested in this rather odd-looking relative, and never thought about him except when he showed up. There were so many worthwhile things in the world that Lanny did no more than wonder vaguely what might be so shocking and dangerous about his uncle's ideas.

Jesse and Marcel knew each other. Marcel didn't think much of Jesse as a painter, but they had friends in common, and both were interested in what was going on in the art world. So now when the older man came he went down to Marcel's studio and sat for a while, and Lanny went fishing or swimming.

Did Robbie's prohibition against his son's talking with Uncle Jesse include also talking about him? It was a subtle point of law, which Lanny would have asked Robbie about if it had been possible. On one occasion, after Jesse had called, the stepfather remarked: "Your uncle and your father ought to meet each other now. They could get along much better."

Lanny had to say something, so he asked: "How come?"

"They feel the same way about the war. Jesse can't see any difference at all between French and Germans."

"I don't think that's exactly true of Robbie," said the boy, hesitatingly—for he didn't like to talk about his father in this connection. He added: "I've never understood my uncle's ideas, but I know how Robbie despises them."

"It's a case of extremes meeting, I suppose," remarked the other. "Jesse is an out-and-out revolutionist. He blames all the trouble on big financiers trying to grab colonies and trade. He says they use the governments for their own purposes; they start wars when they want something, and stop them when they've got it."

"Well, it looks like this one might have run away with them," commented the boy.

"Jesse says not so," replied the other. "He thinks the British oil men want Mesopotamia, and they've promised Constantinople to Russia, and Syria to France. Also they want to sink the German fleet. After that their oil will be safe, and they'll make peace."

"Do you believe anything like that, Marcel?"

The voice that came from behind the white silk veil had a touch of grimness. "I'd hate having to think that I'd had my face burned off to help Royal Dutch Shell increase the value of its shares!"

V

Lanny wrote to his father: "I am finding it hard to think as you want me to." And of course Robbie understood that. He had met Americans returned from France, and seen how bitter they were against the Germans; he knew how many of the young fellows had joined the French Foreign Legion, or the Lafayette Escadrille, a group of American fliers fighting for France. One day Lanny received a long typewritten letter from his father, postmarked Paris.

He understood that it had been brought across by some friend or employee.

"If I were with you," wrote the father, "I could answer all the things that people are telling you. As it is, I have to ask you to believe that I have the answers. You know that I have sources of information and do not say that I know something unless I do. I am making this emphatic because your happiness and indeed your whole future may be at stake, and I could never forgive myself if you were to get caught in the sticky flypaper which is now being set for the feet of Americans. If I thought there was any chance of this happening to you I would come at once and take you away."

After that solemn preamble, the head of the European sales department of Budd Gunmakers went on to remind his son that this was a war of profits. "I am making them myself," he said. "Budd's couldn't help making them unless we gave the plant away. People come and stuff them into our pockets. But I don't sell them the right to do my thinking for me.

"Germany is trying to break her way to the east, mainly to get oil, the first necessity of modern machine industry. There is oil in Rumania and the Caucasus, and more in Mesopotamia and Persia. Look up these places on the map, so as to know what I'm telling you. England, Russia, and France all have a share, while Germany has none. That's what all the shooting is about; and I am begging you to paste this up on your looking glass, or some place where you will see it every day. It's an oil man's war, and they are all patriotic, because if they lose the war they'll lose the oil. But the steel men and the coal men have worked out international cartels, so they don't have to be patriotic. They have ways of communicating across no man's land, and they do. I'm a steel man, and they talk to me, and so I get news that will never be printed."

What the steel men were doing, Robbie explained, was selling to both sides, and getting the whole world into their debt. Robbie's own income for this year of 1916 would be five times what it had been before the war, and the profits of the biggest American powder

and chemical concern would be multiplied by ten. "The gentleman whom you met with me in Monte Carlo is keeping very quiet
nowadays; he doesn't want to attract attention to what he is doing,
which is stuffing money into all the hiding places he can find. I
would wager that his profits before this slaughter is over will be a
quarter of a billion dollars. He has put himself in the same position
as ourselves—he couldn't help making money if he wanted to."

But that wasn't all. These international industrialists had taken
entire charge of the war so far as their own properties were concerned. The military men were allowed to destroy whatever else
they pleased, but nothing belonging to Krupp and Thyssen and
Stinnes, the German munitions kings who had French connections
and investments, or anything belonging to Schneider and the de
Wendels, masters of the Comité des Forges, who had German connections and investments. Any army man who attempted to win the
war by that forbidden method would be sent to some part of the
fighting zone that was less dangerous for the steel kings and more
dangerous for him.

Said the father: "I could tell you a hundred different facts which
I know, and which all fit into one pattern. The great source of steel
for both France and Germany is in Lorraine, called the Briey basin;
get your map and look it up, and you will see that the battle line
runs right through it. On one side the Germans are getting twenty
or thirty million tons of ore every year and smelting it into steel,
and on the other side the French are doing the same. On the French
side the profits are going to François de Wendel, President of the
Comité des Forges and member of the Chamber of Deputies; on the
other side they are going to his brother Charles Wendel, naturalized
German subject and member of the Reichstag. Those huge blast
furnaces and smelters are in plain sight; but no aviators even tried to
bomb them until recently. Then one single attempt was made, and
the lieutenant who had charge of it was an employee of the Comité
des Forges. Surprisingly, the attempt was a failure."

Robbie went on to explain that the same thing was happening to
the four or five million tons of iron ore which Germany was get-

ting from Sweden; the Danish line which brought this ore to Germany had never lost a vessel, in that service or any other, and the Swedish railroads which carried the ore burned British coal. "If it hadn't been for this," wrote the father, "Germany would have been out of the war a year ago. It's not too much to say that every man who died at Verdun, and everyone who has died since then, has been a sacrifice to those businessmen who own the newspapers and the politicians of France. That is why I tell you, if you are going to be patriotic, let it be for the American steel kings, of whom you may some day be one. Don't be patriotic for Schneider and the de Wendels, nor for Deterding, nor for Zaharoff!"

VI

Lanny kept that letter and studied it, and thought about it as hard as he knew how. He did not fail to note the curious thing that Marcel had commented upon, the similarity of his father's views with those of the outlawed uncle. The uncle and the father agreed upon the same set of facts, and they even drew the same conclusion —that nobody ought to be patriotic. The point where they split was that Robbie said you had to stuff your pockets, because you couldn't help it; whereas Uncle Jesse—Lanny wasn't sure what he wanted, but apparently it was to empty Robbie's pockets!

Lanny took this letter to his mother, and it threw her into a panic. Politics and high finance didn't mean much to her, but she thought about the effect of such news upon her husband, and made Lanny promise not to mention it to him. Just now he was putting the finishing touches on his "Sister of Mercy," and was much absorbed in it. If the French weren't winning the war, at least they weren't losing it, so Marcel could be what his wife called "rational." As it happened, it was in that Briey district that he had been sitting in a kite balloon, surveying those blast furnaces and smelters which were the source of the enemy's fighting power. He had been praying for the day when France might have enough planes to destroy them. If now the terrible idea was suggested to him that *la patrie* had the power, but was kept from using it by traitors, who could guess what frenzy might seize him?

So Lanny took the letter to his adviser in international affairs, M. Rochambeau. This old gentleman represented a small nation which was forced to buy its oil at market prices, and had never engaged in attempts to despoil its neighbors; therefore he could contemplate problems of high finance from the point of view of the eighth and tenth commandments. When Lanny expressed his bewilderment at the seeming agreement between his conservative father and his revolutionary uncle, the retired diplomat answered with his quiet smile that every businessman was something of a revolutionist, whether he knew it or not. Each demanded his profits, and sought the removal of any factor that menaced his trade or privileges.

Lanny, whose mind was questioning everything and wondering about his own relation to it, was thinking a great deal about whether he wanted to follow in his father's footsteps and become the munitions king of America, or whether he wanted to play around with the arts. And now he heard this old gentleman, who knew the world and met it with suavity, point out the difference between business and art. One might look at a Rembrandt picture, or hear a Beethoven symphony, without depriving others of the privilege; but one couldn't become an oil king without taking oil away from others.

Said Lanny: "My father argues that the businessman creates wealth without limit."

Replied the other: "The only thing that I have observed to be without limit is the businessman's desire for profits. He has to have raw materials, and he has to have patents, and if he has too many competitors, his profits vanish."

"But Robbie argues that if he invents a machine gun"—the boy stopped suddenly, as if doubting his own argument.

"Every invention has an intellectual element," conceded the other. "But the machine gun is obviously intended to limit the privileges and possessions of other men. Just now it is being used by the oil kings to make it impossible to get any oil except on their terms. And isn't that a sort of revolution?"

Having thus disposed of Robert Budd as a "Red," the elderly ex-diplomat went on to deal with him as a pacifist; remarking, with the same gentle smile, that it had been long since kings were men of brawn, riding at the head of their retainers and splitting skulls with a battle-ax. The invention of machinery had produced a new kind of men, who sat in offices and dictated orders which put other men at work. If they felt that their interests required war they would have it; but they themselves would remain safe.

"Do you know any Latin?" asked M. Rochambeau; and when the answer was no, he quoted a verse of the poet Ovid, beginning: "Let others make war." The old gentleman suggested that these words might serve one of the great munitions families on its coat of arms. "*Bella gerant alii!*" He was too polite to name the Budd family, but Lanny got the point, and reflected that if his father had heard this conversation, he might have put M. Rochambeau on the prohibited list along with Uncle Jesse!

VII

Rosemary was back in England, and wrote now and then, letters cool and casual as herself. "I enjoyed our meeting so much," she said—just like that! You could hear Miss Noggyns or some other of those feminist ladies telling her: "Don't take it too seriously. That's the way women are made to suffer. Let the men do the suffering!"

So Lanny learned his own lessons. Don't wear your heart on your sleeve; don't make yourself too cheap. Among the fashionable young people at Juan was an American girl who gave evidence of being willing to console him; she was pretty, and svelte, as they all kept themselves, and her silks and satins and lawns and what not were cut to the latest pattern; she cast seductive glances at a handsome playmate, just emerged into manhood and conscious of it, blushing easily, and with strange messages flashing along his nerves. The world was at war, and nothing was certain, and young and old were learning to take their pleasures as they found them.

But Lanny had dreams of shining and wonderful things in love.

He thought it over, and told his mother about this too willing miss, and Beauty asked: "Is she interested in what you are thinking? Does she say anything that appeals to you especially?" When the boy admitted that she hadn't so far, Beauty said: "Then what will you talk about? How will you keep from being bored?"

So he would go off and lose himself in his piano practice. He could find highly exciting things in music and poetry. His anthology contained a poem by Bobby Burns, who spoke with authority concerning sexual prodigality: "But, och! it hardens a' within, An' petrifies the feelin'." Lanny resolved to wait awhile, and maybe Rosemary would find that she missed him more than she had expected.

She wrote about Rick, who had finished his training and left for France. He had had two days' leave and had come home, looking splendid in his khaki uniform. He had been so happy at getting what he wanted. Not a word about sadness in going away, and Lanny understood that there hadn't been many words—that was the English way. "Cheerio! Business as usual!"

A few days later a card came from Rick himself. No address on it, except the number of his unit in the Royal Flying Corps. "Fine setup here. Wish I could write you all about it. Jolly lot of fellows. Hope I can keep up with them. Write me the news. How's old Sophocles? And when are the Americans coming in? Rick."

Lanny could picture these jolly fellows in their camp a few miles behind the lines. It would be about the same as the one he had visited on the rolling Salisbury Plain. Eager young chaps with cheeks of bright red; smooth-shaven, except for now and then a dapper little mustache; no "side," provided you belonged in the right class; taking whatever came with a laugh; willing to die a hundred deaths but not to shed one tear. The English magazines were full of pictures of them, some smiling, some grave, all handsome; each with a string of old English names: "Lieutenant Granville Fortescue Somers, R.F.C. Killed in action, Vimy. Oct. 17, 1916." So it went.

VIII

There was mourning all around Lanny Budd; women in black everywhere on the streets. Women in terror, trembling every time they heard a knock at the door; afraid to look at a newspaper with its stories of wholesale slaughter. Poor Sophie de la Tourette was visiting Sept Chênes to help re-educate the victims; not really caring much about them, but feeling that she had to do something, because Eddie was doing something, everybody was doing it, you had to or you'd go crazy.

Letters came from the ambulance driver; his baroness brought them to Beauty, and Lanny had a chance to read them. The exciting occupation was having an unexpected effect upon a rather dull young American whose only previous achievements had been in billiard matches and motorboat races. He wanted Sophie to share his adventures, and wrote quite vivid prose.

He was sleeping in a half-demolished barn, and the French peasants' manure pile had become a leading feature of his life, the least unpleasant of the smells of war. He was living on bully beef, and a can of chicken from Chicago made a holiday. In front of him were the French trenches, and behind him the French artillery, and he tried to count the number of shots per minute, but it couldn't be done because they overlapped. You were on duty for a twenty-four-hour stretch, and the ambulance would be ordered out at any moment of the day or night. You drove without lights, in mud anywhere from three inches to three feet deep, and you heard all the familiar jokes about seeing a cap lying in the road and stooping to pick it up, and finding that there was a man under it, walking to town, or perhaps riding horseback. Keeping an ambulance right side up on such a road was really a lot of fun, and trying to see the shell holes at night made you wish you had a pet cat along. Sometimes the shell holes were made especially for your ambulance, and that was something you made bets about with your *brancardier*. You wore a helmet, "just in case."

"Have you seen Old Bill?" inquired Eddie, and enclosed one of Captain Bairnsfather's cartoons, with which the English at the front were teaching themselves to laugh at calamity. "Old Bill" was a Cockney with a large mustache and a serious expression; he was shown crouching in a shell hole with bombs going off all around him, and saying to his companion, angrily: "Well, if you knows of a better 'ole, go to it." And there was the elderly colonel who had come home for a brief leave and found that he couldn't get along outside the trenches. He had had one dug in his garden, and was sitting out in it on a rainy night, half covered with water, and with an umbrella over his head.

That was the sporting way to take war. The Americans living in France became ashamed of themselves and of their country. You just couldn't stay amid all that grief and desperate agony, and go on playing cards and dancing, going to the dressmaker and the hairdresser as you had done in the old days. It grew harder and harder for Lanny, and now and then he would find himself thinking: "I'll have to ask Robbie to turn me loose."

He helped himself a little by reading German books and playing German music, and remembering Kurt and the other warmhearted people he had met at Schloss Stubendorf. He hadn't heard from Kurt for quite a while, and could only wonder, did it mean that he had gone to the front and been killed, or had he too become disgusted with Americans—because they didn't do anything to stop the Allied blockade which was starving the women and children of the Fatherland? Lanny wrote another letter, in care of Mr. Robin, and received a reply from the oldest of the two little Robins:

"Dear Mister Lanny Budd: My papa has maled the letter that you sended. I am lerning to right the English but not so good. I have the picture that you sended my papa and feel that I know you and hope that I meat you when no more it is war. Yours respectful Hansi Robin. P.S. I am twelve and I practice now Beethoven's D-major romance for violin."

IX

The end of the year 1916 was a time of bitter discouragement for the Allied cause. Rumania had come into the war and been conquered. Russia was practically out, and Italy had accomplished little. The French armies were discouraged by having been too many times marched into barbed-wire entanglements and mowed down by machine guns. And on top of all that came the resumption of unrestricted submarine warfare. The German high command had made up their minds that even if America came in, the destruction of Allied commerce would be so great that Britain would be brought to her knees before America could do anything effective. At the end of January notice was given that all shipping in British and French waters, and in the Mediterranean, was subject to attack without warning. In January the total destruction of shipping was 285,000 tons; in the following April it rose to 852,000.

It was plain to everybody that Britain could not stand that rate of loss, and the American people had to face the question whether they were willing to see the British Empire replaced by a German one. At least everybody whom Lanny knew said that was the question, and no use fooling yourself. The youth found it a hard problem to think about, and wished more than ever to have his father at hand. He read bits of the speeches which President Wilson made, and the notes which he wrote to the German government, and it seemed to him that the only way he could comply with his father's orders was to start a new and determined campaign of sight reading at the piano.

The U-boats began sinking American ships; and then came the publication of an intercepted letter from the German government, inviting the Mexicans to enter the war on the German side, and promising them a handsome reward, including Texas, Arizona, and New Mexico. That helped Americans to understand what the war was about, and there was a general movement of the country to get ready.

An exciting time for Americans in France, and for none more

than Lanny. Would his father expect him to be neutral now? Or was he going to be free to feel the way everybody else did, and the way he wanted to—or at least thought he wanted to? Kurt Meissner seemed farther away, and the voices of Mozart and Beethoven grew fainter; France was all around, and its questioning was incessant: "Why don't you Americans help us?" Lanny heard it so often that he didn't go out any more, but became a sort of youthful hermit, swimming and fishing by himself, and reading books about other times and places. He wrote his father concerning these troubles, and added: "Tell me if America is coming in, and if so what I am to do."

Then one day late in March came a cablegram—one of the old-style ones such as Lanny had not received for more than two years and a half. "Sailing for Paris tomorrow wish you to join me there will wire upon arrival Robert Budd."

17

A Man's World

I

LANNY spent a whole week thinking about submarines. It was the time when the German campaign reached its high point; they were sinking thirty thousand tons a day, and one of every four vessels which left the British Isles never returned. Lanny didn't have to imagine a submarine rising from the sea—he had seen it. From eyewitnesses he had heard how torpedoes exploded, and people rushed into lifeboats, and men gave their lives to save women and children. Robbie was the sort of man who would do that, and Lanny felt as if he were tossing a coin every hour for his father's life.

At last a telegram from Le Havre. Thank God, he was on land! He was writing; and next day Lanny received the most important letter of his young life. Robbie was proposing to take him to Connecticut!

"I think the time has come when you ought to know your own country," wrote the father. "It appears certain that we are going into the war, and whatever part you take ought to be in America. My wife invites you to stay with us this summer; I will get you a tutor and you will study hard, and be able to enter prep school this fall and get ready for college." That meant Yale, which was Robbie's own college, and that of his forefathers for a hundred years or more.

There was a letter for Beauty also. Robbie hoped she would agree with him that a lad ought to have a chance to know his own people. Beauty had now had him to herself for thirty-two months —Robbie had an arithmetical mind. He said that if the war lasted, it would be better for Lanny to be in Connecticut, where Robbie could arrange for him to render service in the production of munitions. "You may put your mind at ease on one subject," he wrote. "Lanny will not go into the trenches. He is too valuable to me, and I will be valuable to the government." *Bella gerant alii!*

"What do you want to do?" asked the mother, after they had shared these letters.

"Well, of course, I'd like to see America," said the youth; and the mother's heart sank. Such a lovely safe nest she had made here, but of course he wouldn't stay in it; the last thing in the world that men wanted appeared to be safety.

"I suppose I'll have to give you up," she said. "The cards are all stacked against a woman."

"Don't worry, Beauty, I'll take good care of myself, and come back when the war's over. I don't think I'll want to live anywhere but here."

"You'll meet some girl over there, and she'll tell you what to do."

"I'm going to get tough," replied the boy; but he didn't look it.

"I knew this had to come, Lanny. But I hoped Robbie would wait till the sea was safe."

"Plenty of people are getting through; and he and I are pretty good swimmers." Lanny thought for a moment, then added: "I wonder what he's going to do about telling his friends the bad news about me."

"He told his wife about us both before they were married. I imagine he'll tell other people that you're his son, and let it go at that. Don't let it worry you."

"If anybody doesn't want me around," said the boy, "I can always go somewhere else. Shall you miss me too terribly, Beauty?"

"It'll be all right if I know you're happy. I ought to tell you a bit of news that I've just learned—I'm going to have a baby."

"Oh, gosh!" A wide smile spread over Lanny's face. "That's grand, Beauty! It will tickle Marcel, won't it?"

"Frenchmen are like that," she answered.

"All men are, aren't they?" After a while he inquired: "Was it another accident, or did you decide to do it?"

"Marcel and I decided."

"It's a grand place to bring up a child, Beauty—I can tell you that." He kissed her on both cheeks until she cried with happiness and sorrow mingled.

II

It seemed cruel that a youth should be so excited at the idea of leaving his mother; but he couldn't help it, and she understood. To be with Robbie in Paris, and travel on a great steamer, and see that city of New York which he knew from motion pictures, and the marvelous plant of Budd's, the economic foundation of his life. It was a center of his imaginings, a forge of Vulcan a million times magnified, a Fafnir and Fasolt cave where monstrous forces were generated. And to meet that mysterious family, so many of them that you couldn't keep their names straight, and all different and queer. Robbie didn't often talk about them, but behaved as if they were a dark secret. Or perhaps it was Lanny who was the dark secret!

He packed the few things he would take with him; that required only a couple of hours, and he was ready to go on the evening train. Beauty broke down and wept—it was such short notice. He was a mother's darling; and who else would love him as she had? The world was cruel, so many wicked people in it, women especially—she understood their hearts, the cold and selfish ones, the gold diggers, the harpies! So many things she ought to have taught him, and now it was too late, he couldn't remember them; he was crazy with eagerness to get out into that world which seemed to her so full of pain. She gave him many warnings, extracted many promises—and all the time aware that she was boring him a little.

Lanny had a good-by talk with Marcel, and this was more to the point. Marcel had left his family, respectable bourgeois in a provincial town; they had wanted him to be a lawyer, perhaps a judge, and instead he had come to Paris to dab paint on canvas. They gave him a small allowance, but didn't pretend to like his work. "You are lucky," Marcel said; "your parents are sympathetic, they'll stand by you even if you don't succeed. But don't be surprised if you don't like your relatives. Don't bare your heart to the hawks."

"What makes you say that?" asked the boy, puzzled.

"Rich people are pretty much the same all over the world. They believe in money, and if you don't make money they think there's something wrong with you. If you don't see life as they do, they take it as a criticism, and right away you're an outsider. If I were taking you to meet my family, that's how I'd have to warn you."

"Well, I'll write and let you know what I find, Marcel."

"If you like it, all right. I'm just putting you on guard. You've had a happy life so far, everything has been easy—but it can hardly be like that all the way through."

"Anyhow," remarked the boy, "Robbie says that America's going to help France."

"Tell them to hurry," replied the painter. "My poor country is bleeding at every vein."

III

Lanny was seventeen, and had grown nearly a foot in those thirty-two months since he had seen his father. For many youths it is an awkward age, but he was strongly knit, brown with sunshine and red with well-nourished blood. He came running from the train to welcome Robbie, and there was something in the sight of him which made the man's heart turn over. Flesh of my flesh—but better than I am, without my scars and my painful secrets! So Robbie thought, as the lad seized him and kissed him on both cheeks. There was a trace of down on Lanny's lips, light brown and soft; his eyes were clear and his look eager.

He wanted to know everything about his father in the first moment. That grand rock of a man, that everybody could depend on; he would solve all the problems, relieve all the anxieties—all in the first moment! Robbie looked just the same as ever; he was in his early forties, and his vigor was still unimpaired; whatever clouds might be in his moral sky showed no trace. He looked handsome in brown tweeds, with tie and shoes to match; Lanny, whose suit was gray, decided at once that he would look better in brown.

"Well, what do you think about the war?" The first question every man asked then.

The father looked grave immediately. "We're going in; not a doubt of it."

"And are you going to support it?"

"What can I do? What can anybody do?"

It was nearing the end of March. Relations with Germany had been severed for many weeks, and President Wilson had declared a state of what he called "armed neutrality." America was going to arm its merchant vessels, and in the meantime Germany was going on sinking them, day after day. Shipping was delayed, the vessels in American harbors were afraid to venture out.

"What can we do?" repeated Robbie. "The only alternative is to declare an embargo, and abandon our European trade entirely."

"What would that do?"

"It would bring a panic in a week. Budd's would have to shut down, and throw twenty thousand men out of work."

Driving to their hotel in a horse-drawn cab, Robbie explained this situation. A large-scale manufacturing enterprise was geared to a certain schedule. A quantity of finished goods came off the conveyors every day, and was boxed and put into freight cars or trucks—or, in the case of Budd's, which had its own river frontage, onto ships. Vessels were loaded and moved away, making room for others. If for any reason that schedule was interrupted, the plant would be blockaded, because its warehouses could hold only a few days' output. The same thing would happen at the other end, because raw materials came on a fixed schedule—they had been ordered and had to be taken and paid for, but there was place to store only a limited supply; they were supposed to go through the plant and be moved on.

That, said Robbie, was the situation not merely with steel mills and munitions plants, but with meat packing and flour milling, making boots and saddles, automobiles and trucks, anything you could think of. Rightly or wrongly, wisely or unwisely, American business had geared itself to the task of supplying the need of the nations of Europe. American finance had geared itself to taking and marketing their bonds. If all this were suddenly stopped, there would be such a breakdown as had never been known in the world before—"ten or twenty million men out of work," declared the representative of Budd Gunmakers Corporation.

Lanny had heard many persons express disapproval of those who were making money out of this war; Kurt, and Rick, and Beauty, Sophie, Marcel, and M. Rochambeau. But when he listened to his father, all that vanished like mist before the morning sun. He saw

right away that things had to be like this; if you were going to
have machinery, and produce goods on a big scale, you had to
do it in a fixed way. The artists and dreamers and moralists were
just talking about things they didn't understand.

At least that was the way it seemed until Lanny got off by himself. Then he began to have troubles in his thinking. Robbie was
all for Budd's, and defended the right of Budd's to get all the
business it could, and to keep its workers employed. But Robbie
didn't like Zaharoff, and had a tendency to resent the business that
Vickers got. Robbie blamed Schneider-Creusot because it sold
goods to neutral countries which resold them to Germany; he
objected to the French de Wendels' protecting their properties in
Germany. But suppose that Budd's had owned plants in Germany—
wouldn't Robbie be trying to take care of them, and pointing out
the harm it would do if they were bombed?

In short, wasn't there as much to be said for one set of businessmen as for another? As much for Germans as for British or French
or Americans? Lanny felt in duty bound to be fair to his friend
Kurt, and to Kurt's family who had been so kind to him. He could
not forget having heard Herr Meissner using these very same
arguments about the need of German manufacturers to get raw
materials and to win foreign markets, in order to keep their workers
employed and their plants running on schedule. It was extremely
puzzling; but Lanny didn't say much about it, because for two
years and a half he had been learning to keep his ideas to himself.
In wartime it appeared that nobody wanted to see both sides of
any question.

I V

Of course the father and son didn't spend all their time discussing
world politics. Lanny had to tell about Beauty and Marcel; about
the painter's wounds, and his way of life, and his work; about the
new baby they were going to have, on purpose—a somewhat rare
event nowadays, so Robbie remarked. And about Sophie and her
Eddie Patterson and his ambulance driving; about Mrs. Emily and

Les Forêts, and old M. Priedieu and how he had died; about Sept
Chênes, and the war victims who were being re-educated, including
Lanny's gigolo, who would never jig again. And about Mr. Robin,
and the letters to Kurt, and the little Robins, and the Jews, and
didn't Robbie like them, and why not? And about Rosemary—a
large subject in herself; and Rick and his flying—as soon as Lanny
learned that he was to have a few days in Paris he got off a card
to Rick, on the chance that he might be able to get a day's leave
and visit his friend.

Robbie would ask questions, and Lanny would think of details
he had left out. There was Marcel's painting; he was getting better
and better, everybody agreed; he was doing an old peasant woman
who grew roses on the Cap, and had lost three sons, one after
another, and it showed in her face, and still more in the portrait
that Marcel was making of her. The one he had done of Beauty,
called "Sister of Mercy," was to be shown at a salon in the Petit
Palais, and one of the things Lanny wanted to do was to find out
about it. If Robbie went to view it he would find a new woman,
one much more serious, and really sad. "Of course she's not that
way all the time," added the boy; "but that's how Marcel sees
things. He can't forgive fate for what it's done to his face—nor
for what it's doing to France."

Robbie also had things to tell. For the most part they had to do
with business; for he was not one of those persons who have states
of soul which require explanation. He had been making money
hand over fist, and it kept him in good humor; he found it pleasant,
not only for himself, but for many other people. He was troubled
because Lanny's wants were so modest in that regard; he seemed
to think they ought to celebrate their reunion by buying something handsome. The only thing Lanny could think of was one of
Marcel's paintings to take to America. But Robbie didn't think
that would be such a good idea—no use to say anything about a
stepfather right at the outset!

Lanny told how seriously Beauty was taking the re-education
of the *mutilés*, and so Robbie sent her a check for a couple of

thousand dollars, telling her she might use it for that purpose if she pleased. He added a friendly message for Mrs. Emily, knowing that Beauty would take it to her; in this way the money would win credit for Beauty with that socially powerful lady. Robbie explained this procedure, so that his son might learn how to make his way in the world. No use to have money unless you knew how to use it, and how to handle people. There were some to whom you gave it with a careless gesture, and others to whom you doled it out carefully.

Robbie remarked with a smile that there had been personal reasons for his opposition to America's entering the war; Budd's would now begin manufacturing for the United States government, and Robbie would get no commissions on that. "It will be a great satisfaction to my brother Lawford," he added. "It has pained · him to see me making more money than himself."

Lanny was going to meet this brother, so the time had come for Robbie to tell about him. "He will be polite to you, but don't expect him to be anything more, because nature hasn't made him that way. He's all right if you let him alone; but unfortunately I haven't—not since the day I was born, and attracted too much attention in the nursery. I was better-looking than he, and mother made too much fuss over me."

Robbie spoke playfully, but made it plain that there was something of a feud between his older brother and himself. When Robbie had come of age, he had offered to learn the selling end of the business, and the father had given him a chance, working on commission, plus an expense account. This latter had made much trouble, because Lawford objected to one item or another; when Robbie lost money to Captain Bragescu, his brother called it paying his gambling debts at the company's expense!

"And then came this war," said Robbie. "That was my good fortune, but surely not my fault. It resulted in my having an income two or three times his own—and he works hard running the plant, while I don't have to do another lick of work in my life unless I feel like it."

V

Just before Lanny left the Riviera a world-shaking event took place—the Russian revolution and the overthrow of the Tsar. Everybody was speculating as to what it meant, and what would be its effect upon the war. Most people in France believed it would help the Allies; the Russians would fight harder, now that they were free. But Robbie said that Russia was out, because of graft, incompetence, and the breakdown of her railroads. He said that freight had been landed from hundreds of steamers at Archangel in the far north, and at Vladivostok on the Pacific, and there was no way to get it to the war zones. Tens of millions of dollars' worth of goods was piled along the railroad tracks for miles, without more than a single tarpaulin to cover the boxes. Included in the stacks were Budd machine guns, and of course they were rusting and would soon be useless; meanwhile the Russian peasant-soldiers were expected to defend themselves with clubs and march to the attack with five men to one rifle.

"What is going to happen," said Robbie, "is breakdown and chaos; the country may be pillaged, or the Germans may take it. The German troops will be moved to the west, and may well be in Paris before the Americans can raise an army or get it across the ocean. That is what the German General Staff is reckoning on."

The father revealed the purpose which had brought him to Europe. The War Department of the United States government had sent an emissary to the president of Budd's, asking him to consider proposals for the licensing of Budd patents to various firms such as Vickers and Schneider, which were working day and night making munitions for the Allied governments. Under such licenses they would be permitted to make Budd machine guns, Budd anti-aircraft guns, and so on, paying a royalty to be agreed upon. If America should enter the war, Budd's itself would no longer be in position to manufacture for European nations, and it was desirable that our Allies should have the benefit of Yankee ingenuity and skill.

This question of patent licensing had been a subject of controversy inside the Budd organization for years. Foreign governments were always proposing it, offering handsome royalties.
Robbie had opposed the policy, while Lawford had favored it,
and each had labored to persuade the father to his point of view.
The older brother insisted that it was dangerous to expand the
plant any further; they would have to borrow money—and then
some day the pacifists would impose a scheme of disarmament,
Budd's wouldn't be able to meet its obligations, and some Wall
Street banking syndicate would gobble it up. Robbie, on the other
hand, argued that European manufacturers would make the most
generous offers and sign on as many dotted lines as you prepared
for them; but who was going to watch them, and know how many
shell fuses they really made?

Lanny got from this a clearer realization of the situation between
his father and his oldest uncle. The uncle was morose and jealous,
and a dispute which had begun in the nursery had been trans-
ferred to the office of the company. Lawford opposed everything
that Robbie advocated, and attributed selfish motives to him; as
for Robbie, he seemed convinced that the chief motive of the
brother's life was not to let Robbie have his way in anything. Now
the War Department had stepped in and given Lawford a victory.
Licenses would be issued to several European munitions firms, and
in order to salve Robbie's feelings, his father had sent him to do
the negotiating.

VI

Robbie telephoned to the home of Basil Zaharoff, which was on
the Avenue Hoche. Lanny was in the room and heard one-half
the conversation; the munitions king said something which caused
Robbie to smile, and reply: "Yes, but he's not so little now."
Robbie turned his eyes on Lanny as he listened. "Very well," he
said. "He'll be happy to come, I'm sure."

The father hung up the receiver and remarked: "The old devil asked if I had that very intelligent little boy with me. He says to bring you along. Want to go?"

"Do I!" exclaimed the intelligent little boy. "But what does he want with me?"

"Don't let your vanity be flattered. We've got something he wants, and he'd like to make it a social matter, not one of business. Watch him and see how an old Levantine trader works."

"Doesn't he have an office?" inquired the boy.

"His office is where he happens to be. People find it worth while to come to him."

Lanny dressed for this special occasion, and late in the afternoon of a day which promised spring they drove to 53, Avenue Hoche, just off the Parc Monceau. It was one of a row of stately houses, with nothing to make it conspicuous; a home for a gentleman who didn't want to attract attention to himself, but wanted to stay hidden and work out plans to appeal to other men's fears and greeds. A discreet and velvet-footed man in black opened the door, and escorted them into the reception room, which had furniture and paintings in excellent taste—no doubt the duquesa's. Presently they were invited to a drawing room on the second floor, where the first thing they saw was an elaborate silver tea service ready for action. The windows were open, and a soft breeze stirred the curtains, and birds sang in trees just outside. Presently the munitions king entered, looking grayer and more worn—one does not make a quarter of a billion dollars without some cares.

He had hardly finished greeting them when a lady entered behind him. Had she heard the story of the boy who had had such an odd idea about helping his father's business? Or was it the special importance of the contracts which Robert Budd was bringing? Anyhow, here she came, and Zaharoff said: "The Duquesa de Villafranca," with a tone of quiet pride. The duquesa bowed but did not give her hand; she said, very kindly: "How do you do, Messieurs?" and seated herself at the tea table.

She had been only seventeen when she had met this munitions salesman, and they had been waiting twenty-seven years for her lunatic husband to die. She was a rather small and inconspicuous person, gracious, but even more reserved than her companion. His blue eyes were watching the visitors, and her dark eyes for the most part watched him. She had the olive complexion of a Spaniard, and wore a teagown of purple, with a double rope of pearls nearly to her waist. "You have had a dangerous journey, M. Budd," she remarked.

"Many men are facing danger these days, Madame," replied Robbie.

"Do you think that your country will help us to end this dreadful war?"

"I think so; and if we come in, we shall do our best."

"It will have to be done quickly," put in the munitions king; to which Robbie answered that large bodies took time to get in motion, but when they moved, it was with force.

They talked about the military situation. Zaharoff set forth the extreme importance to civilization of overcoming the German menace. He told about what he had done to set up Venizelos in Greece and bring that country in on the side of the Allies; he didn't say how much money he had spent, but that he had moved heaven and earth.

"Greece is my native land," he said. "Love of Greece has been the first passion of my life, and hatred of Turkish cruelty and fanaticism has been the second." As he talked about these matters his voice trembled a little, and Lanny thought, was all that play-acting? If so, it was a remarkable performance. But Robbie told him afterward that it was genuine; the munitions king did really hate the Turks, and had spent millions buying newspapers and politicians, pulling wires against King Constantine and his German wife. Zaharoff had gone in for oil, and wanted Mesopotamia for his British companies. He used his money for things which the Allied governments wanted done, but which were too discreditable for them to do directly.

VII

Presently they were talking about President Wilson, who had said that Americans were "too proud to fight," and had been re-elected with the slogan, "He kept us out of war." Robbie explained the Presbyterian temperament, which would find some high moral basis for whatever it decided to do, and would then do it under divine direction. Now this President was talking about "war for democracy," and Zaharoff asked if that was supposed to be a moral slogan.

Robbie replied: "The founders of our nation didn't believe in democracy, M. Zaharoff, but it is supposed to be good politics now."

"Well, I should want to write the definition somewhat carefully." The old man smiled one of those strange smiles, in which his watchful eyes never took part.

"It is playing with fire," said the other, unsmiling. "We have seen in Russia what it may lead to, and not even Wilson wishes the war to end that way."

"God forbid!" exclaimed the munitions king; and no one could doubt the sincerity of that.

When you are having a lady of ancient lineage to pour tea for you, it is necessary to pay some attention to her. So presently Robbie remarked: "That is a lovely tea service you have, Duquesa."

"It is an heirloom of my family," replied María del Pilar Antonia Angela Patrocino Simón de Muguiro y Berute, Duquesa de Marqueni y Villafranca de los Caballeros.

"I had a gold one," put in the host. "But I have given it to the government, to help save the franc."

Was there just the trace of a frown on the gentle visage of the Spanish king's cousin? She had been laboring for a quarter of a century to make a gentleman out of a Levantine trader; and perhaps it cannot be done in one lifetime; perhaps in the midst of wars and revolutions one must excuse lapses from a much-burdened mind.

After they had had their tea, the old man remarked: "And now about that matter of business, Mr. Budd."

The hostess rose. "I am sure you gentlemen don't want an audience for your conference," she said; and added sweetly to Lanny: "Wouldn't you like to come and see my beautiful tulips?"

Of course Lanny went, and so lost his chance to observe the old trader in action. He was taken into a fine garden, and introduced to a pair of snow-white poodles, beautifully groomed and shaved to resemble lions. He learned about the tulips, which were just unfolding their beauties: the *bizarres*, which are yellow marked with purple and red; the *bybloemen*, which are white marked with violet or purple; also a new kind from Turkestan. The Dutch people had cultivated them for centuries, and once they had been the basis of a great financial boom.

"Do you really love flowers?" asked the duquesa; and Lanny told about Bienvenu, and the court full of daffodils and bougain-villaea where he did his reading. He was used to ladies with titles, and not awed by them. He suspected that one who had the munitions king for a companion didn't feel entirely safe or happy, so he was moved to be kind. He mentioned Mrs. Emily, and found that the duquesa knew her, and had aided her war work; so Lanny told what she was doing at Sept Chênes, and added the story of M. Pinjon, the gigolo, which the duquesa found *sympathique*. She remarked that she would like to send a present to that poor man; since he played the flute, perhaps he might like to have a good one.

Time passed, and the two men of business did not appear. Lanny didn't want to be a nuisance to his hostess, who must have other things to do than to entertain a casually met youth. He told her he was used to getting along by himself, and she offered to take him to the library. He had seen many large rooms in fine homes, having walls lined with volumes de luxe which were rarely touched save to be dusted. The munitions king's were all behind glass, but on the table were magazines, and he said he would be happy with those. So the gentle lady excused herself. Lanny understood that she was far too rich to ask him to call again; and besides, maybe this was all just a matter of business, as Robbie had said!

VIII

At last the two emerged from their conference; both suave as ever—but you couldn't tell anything from that. The father and son strolled down the street, and Lanny said: "Well, what happened?"

Robbie answered, with one of his grins: "I thought he was going to cry, but he didn't quite."

"Why should he cry?" The boy knew that he was supposed to be naïve, so that his father would have the fun of telling it.

"I hurt his feelings by suggesting that we should require observers in the Vickers plants, to check their production under our licenses."

"Is he going to let you?"

"He said it was a very serious matter to admit strangers to a munitions factory in wartime. I answered that they wouldn't be strangers very long; he would know how to become acquainted with them." Robbie began to laugh; he enjoyed nothing more than such a battle over property rights—especially when he held the good cards close to his chest. "They really need our patents," he said; "and, believe me, they won't get them without paying. Why should they?"

Lanny didn't know any reason, and said so.

"Well, the old devil thought he knew a number of them. He was horrified at the schedule of royalties I put before him; he said he had been given to understand that America wanted to help the Allies, not to bleed them to death, or drive them to bankruptcy. I said I hadn't heard of any bankruptcies among the hundred and eighty Vickers companies in England, or the two hundred and sixty of them abroad. He said they had cut their prices to the bone as a patriotic duty to the British and French governments. I told him it was generally understood that his companies were getting the full twenty percent profit allowed them by British law.

You can see it wasn't a conversation for a duquesa to hear. Was she nice to you?"

"Very," said Lanny. "I liked her."

"Oh, sure," said the father. "But you can't like the consort of a wolf beyond a certain point."

Lanny saw that his father was not going to like Basil Zaharoff under any circumstances. He said so, and Robbie replied that a wolf didn't want to be liked; what he wanted was to eat, and when it was a question of dividing up food with him, you had to have a sharp-pointed goad in hand. "We have paid out good American money, financing inventions and perfecting complicated machines. We're not going to give those secrets to Zaharoff, not even in return for a tea party and a smile from a duquesa. We're going to have our share of the profits, paid right on the barrel-head, and I'm sent here to tell him so, and to put before him a contract which our lawyers have constructed like a wolf trap. I said that very politely, but in plain language."

"And what did you decide?"

"Oh, I left him the contracts, and he'll weep over them tonight, and tomorrow morning I'm to see his French factotum, Pietri, and he'll plead and argue, and demand this change and that, and I'll tell him to take it as it's written, or the Allies can get along with a poorer grade of machine guns."

"Will they, Robbie?"

"Just stick by me the next few days, son, and learn how we businessmen pull wires. If they turn down my contracts, I know half a dozen journalists in Paris and London who will make a story out of it for a reasonable fee. I can find a way to have the merits of the Budd products brought to the attention of a dignified and upright member of Parliament, who wouldn't take a bribe for anything, but will endeavor to protect his country against the greed of munitions magnates and the bungling of War Office bureaucrats."

IX

Robbie's next conference was with Bub Smith, the ex-cowboy with the broken nose who had come down to Juan three or four years previously and demonstrated the Budd automatic for Captain Bragescu. Bub had given up his job in Paris to work for Robbie, and had made a couple of trips to America in spite of the submarines. It was he who had brought letters for Lanny into France.

Now Robbie told his son that Bub had proved himself an "ace" at confidential work, and was going to have the job of keeping track of the lessees of Budd patents. "Of course Zaharoff himself is a man of honor," said Robbie, with a smile. "But there's always the possibility that some of the men who run his companies might be tempted to try tricks. Bub is to watch the French plants for me."

"Can one man keep track of them all?" asked the youth.

"I mean that he'll be the one to watch the watchers."

Robbie went on to explain that it wasn't possible to carry on an industry without workers; and there were always some of these glad to give information in exchange for a *pourboire*. Bub would build an organization for knowing what was going on in munitions factories.

"Isn't it a rather dangerous job?" asked Lanny. "I mean, mayn't they take him for a spy?"

"He'll have a letter from me, and the embassy will identify him."

"And won't the munitions people find out about him?"

"Oh, sure. They know we're bound to watch them."

"That won't hurt their feelings?"

Robbie was amused. "In our business you don't have feelings—you have cash."

18

Away from All That

I

A TELEPHONE call for Lanny at the Crillon. He answered, and let out a whoop. "Where are you? Oh, glory! Come right up." He hung up the receiver. "It's Rick! He got leave!" Lanny rushed out to the lift, to wait for his friend; grabbed him and hugged him, then held him off at arm's length and examined him. "Gee, Rick, you look grand!"

The young flying officer had grown to man's stature. His khaki uniform was cut double in front, making a sort of breastplate of cloth; on the left breast was a white badge, indicating that he had a flying certificate, and high up on both sleeves were eagle wings. His skin was bronzed and his cheeks rosy; flying hadn't hurt him. With his wavy black hair cut close and a brown service cap on top he was a handsome fellow; and so happy over this visit—they were going to see Paris together, and Paris was the world!

"Gee, Rick, how did you manage it?"

"I had done some extra duty, so I had it coming."

"How long have you got?"

"Till tomorrow night."

"And how is it, Rick?"

"Oh, not so bad."

"You've been fighting?"

"I've got two boches that I'm sure of."

"You havent been hurt?"

"I had one spill—turned over in mud; but fortunately it was soft."

Lanny led him to the room, and Robbie was glad to see him, of

340

course; he set up the drinks, and Rick took one—they all drank in the air force, too much, he said, it was the only way they could keep going. Lanny drank soda, but said nothing about it. He sat, devouring that gallant figure with his eyes; so proud of his friend, thinking that he, Lanny, would never do anything as exciting and wonderful as that; his father wouldn't let him, his father wanted him to stay at home and make munitions for other men to use. But at least he could hear about it, and live it vicariously. He asked a stream of questions, and Rick answered casually, not much about himself, but about the squadron and what they were doing.

Of course Rick knew what was in his younger friend's mind, the adoration, the hero-worship; and of course it pleased him. But he wouldn't give a sign of it, he'd take it just as he took the job; nothing special, all in the day's work.

Rick could tell now what the censor wouldn't let him put on paper. He was stationed with General Allenby's Third Army, which lay in front of Vimy Ridge. He belonged to what was called the "corps wing," the group of fliers who served a particular body of troops. Observation planes equipped with two-way radios, or with photographic apparatus, went out to observe enemy positions, and fighting planes went along to protect them. Rick flew a machine known as a "Sopwith one-and-a-half strutter." It was a single-seater, such planes being lighter and faster, and the competition of the German Fokkers had forced it. Both sides now had what were called "interrupter gears"; that is, the action of the machine gun was synchronized with the propeller, so that the stream of bullets went through the whirling blades without hitting. So you didn't have to aim your gun, but just your plane; your job was to get on the other fellow's tail, and see him straight through your sights, and then cut loose. You would see two fighting planes maneuvering for position, darting this way and that, diving, rolling over, executing every sort of twist and turn. That sight was seen over Paris pretty nearly every day, and Lanny hadn't missed it.

His friend told many things about this strange new job of fighting in the air. In the sector where he flew, it was hard to distinguish the trenches, for the entire ground was a chaos of shell-craters. He flew at a speed of ninety miles an hour, and at a height of twelve hundred and fifty feet. When you came down suddenly from that height, you had headache, earache, even toothache, but it all passed away in three or four hours. The most curious thing was that you could hear the whine of the bullet before it reached you, and if you ducked quickly you might dodge it. Somehow that gave Lanny the biggest thrill of anything he had heard about the war; a mile and a half a minute, a quarter of a mile above the earth, and playing tag with bullets!

II

England and France were getting ready for the big spring "push"; everybody knew where it was to be, but it was a matter of good form not to name places. "Be silent," read the signs all over Paris; "enemy ears are listening." Rick said the air push was on all the time; the two sides were struggling incessantly for mastery. The English had held it pretty much through 1916; now it was a local matter, varying from place to place and from week to week. The Fokkers were fast, and their men fought like demons. The problem of the English was to train fliers quickly enough; they were used up faster than they could be sent across.

Rick stopped after he had said that; for it wasn't good form to reveal anything discouraging. But now and then he would mention a name. "Aubrey Valliance—you remember that fellow with the straw-colored hair you raced with, swimming? He was downed last week, poor chap. We don't know what happened—he just didn't come back." Lanny got the picture of those bright-cheeked English schoolboys, eighteen or nineteen, some younger, having told a fib about their ages. They would volunteer, and have a few tests of eyesight and sense of balance, and then be rushed to a training camp, listen to a few lectures, go up a few times with an instructor to be taught the rudiments, then go up alone and practice this and that, maybe a week, maybe less, thirty hours of flying, or even as few as twenty—and then off to France.

"Replacements," they were called; half a dozen would arrive in a truck at night and be introduced to their fellows; you hardly had time to remember their names. They would look on the bulletin board and see themselves scheduled to fly at dawn. They would have a drink, and a handshake, or maybe a salute. They would say: "Very good, sir," and step into their seats; the propellers would begin to roar, and away they would go, one after another. Maybe eight would go out, and only six would come back; you would wait, and listen, trying not to show your concern; after a certain period there was no use thinking about them any more, for the plane had only so much petrol, and no way to get any more. If the chap was down in enemy territory, you wouldn't know whether he was alive or dead; unless he had put up an extra-good fight, in which case an enemy flier might bring a bundle containing his boots and cap and pocketbook, and drop them onto the camp.

"Don't you ever get afraid, Rick?" asked Lanny. That was after Robbie had gone out to keep his engagements, and the two were alone.

Rick hesitated. "I guess I do; but it's no good thinking about. You've a job to do, and that's that."

Lanny recalled Mrs. Emily Chattersworth's mother, that very old lady who had told about the American Civil War. One of her stories had to do with a young Confederate officer whose knees were shaking before a battle, and someone accused him of being scared. "Of course I'm scared," he said; "if you were half as scared as I am you'd have run away long ago."

Rick said that was about it. He said that now and then there was some youngster whose nerves came near to breaking, and you had to figure out how to buck him up and get him started. The hardest job was that of the ground officer who had to send chaps out, knowing they weren't fit; but there was no choice, they had to keep up with the Germans. Apparently things weren't any better with them, because the score was about even. You'd soon know if they had the edge.

III

The pair went for a walk on the boulevards. Paris in wartime; every sort of uniform you could imagine, and Rick pointing them out to his friend: English Tommies out for a lark; Australians and New Zealanders, tall fellows with looped-up hats; Highlanders in kilts—the Germans called them "ladies from hell"; Italians in green; French zouaves with baggy knee-pants; African colonials, who fought fiercely, but looked bewildered in a great city. The poilus had a new uniform of gray-blue; the picturesque *képi rouge* and the baggy red pants had offered too good a target.

The two had lunch together; war bread, and very small portions of sugar, but anything else you could pay for. It was a special occasion, and Lanny wanted to spend all he had. He liked to be seen with this handsome young officer; his pacifist impulses weakened when put to such a test. He talked about Kurt, wishing he might be with them, instead of being on the other side of no man's land— or perhaps up in the air, fighting Rick! "I know he's in the army, but I've no idea where," said Lanny.

"We wouldn't get along so well," said the Englishman. "I always had the idea that German culture was a lot of wind and bluff." Rick went on like that at some length, saying that the reputation of Goethe was due to the fact of the Germans' wanting so badly to have a world poet; Goethe wasn't really so much. Lanny listened, thinking his own thoughts. If Kurt were here, would he say that Shakespeare was a barbarian, or something like that? It was going to take a long time to wipe the bitterness of this war out of the hearts of men. If America came in, what would happen to Lanny's own heart?

There is a saying: "Speak of angels and they flap their wings." The two friends came back from their stroll, and there was a letter for Lanny with a Swiss stamp on it, forwarded from Juan. "Kurt!" he exclaimed, and opened it quickly. His eyes ran over it. "He's been wounded!" Then he read aloud:

"Dear Lanny: It has been a long time since I have written. I have been very busy, and circumstances do not permit me to unbosom myself. Please believe that our friendship is not going to be ended, even by the news which I now read from abroad. I am now in hospital. It is not serious and I hope soon to be well again. It may not be possible for me to write for some time, so this is just to say Hello, and hope that you will not let anything interrupt your musical studies and the reading of the world's great poets. Ever your friend, Kurt."

The envelope showed that it had been opened by the censor. It was always a gamble whether any particular sentence might cause a letter to be destroyed. You had to read between the lines. The "news from abroad" of course meant America's coming into the war—which seemed certain, President Wilson having summoned a special session of Congress to meet in a few days. Kurt was telling Lanny that he hoped he wouldn't take part in fighting Germany.

"We mustn't let ourselves hate him, Rick," said the American.

The other answered: "The fighting men don't hate one another—not very often. What we hate is the damnable *Kultur* which has produced all these atrocities; also the rulers who impose it upon a credulous people."

Lanny could accept that; but would Kurt accept it? That was going to be a problem!

IV

Robbie was in the midst of conferences with the representatives of a half a dozen armaments concerns; but he found an hour to go with the pair to the exposition at the Petit Palais. It was a matter of *amour propre* with the French that not even a world war should stop the development of genius in their country; art lovers would come to see what was new in taste and culture even though bombs might be raining upon them from the sky. The younger painters of France were most of them putting camouflage on guns and ships;

but they had found time for sketches of war scenes. The older ones had gone on with their work, like Archimedes making scientific discoveries during the siege of Syracuse.

Battle pictures, of course, had always been found in every salon. Painters loved to portray thrilling conflicts: horses trampling men, sabers flashing, carbines spitting flame. Now there was a new kind of war, hard to know how to deal with. So much of it was fought at long distances, and with great machines—and how were you to make them dramatic? How were you to keep a picture of an airplane or a machine gun from looking like a photograph in *L'Illustration?* A general on horseback was an established figure of *la gloire;* but what could you do with a man in a tank or a submarine?

The answer of Marcel Detaze had been to go off in solitude and paint the figure of a woman in sorrow. Whether men were mutilated by sabers or by shrapnel made little difference to the wives and sweethearts of France; so said this young painter, and apparently the art lovers agreed with him. "Sister of Mercy" had been hung in an excellent position, and there were always people standing in front of it, and their faces showed that Marcel had conveyed something to their souls. Lanny listened to their comments, and little thrills crept up and down his spine. Even Robbie was moved; yes, the fellow had talent, you didn't have to be a "highbrow" to be sure of it.

Too bad that Beauty couldn't be on hand to share the sensation. She would have taken her friends, and stood and listened to what the crowds were saying; presently somebody would have glanced at her, and then at the picture, and then back at her again, in excitement and a little awe, and the blood would have started climbing to Beauty's cheeks, and even to her forehead; it would have been one of life's great moments. Call it vanity, but she was like that; "professional beauties" were amateur actresses, performing upon a larger stage with the help of newspapers and illustrated magazines. "I'll send her a ticket and tell her to come," said Robbie, who found her foibles diverting.

A further idea occurred to him, and he said to his son: "Do you remember what Beauty once told you about a painting that made my father angry?" Yes, that was one of the things Lanny wasn't going to forget—not in this incarnation! He said so, and Robbie inquired: "Would you be interested to see it?"

The youth was staggered. Somehow the idea seemed rather horrible. And with Rick along too! But he told himself that this was an old-fashioned attitude, unworthy of a connoisseur of art. Surely Rick would feel that way about it. So Lanny replied: "I would, of course."

"I've been told where it was. If it's been sold, maybe you can find out where it's gone." Robbie gave the name of one of the fashionable dealers on the Rue de la Paix, and told him to ask for the "Lady with a Blue Veil," by Oscar Deroulé. "You don't have to say that you know anything about it," added the father.

The two fellows set out. Lanny had to make some explanation, for of course Rick would recognize the portrait. Lanny couldn't say that he was an illegitimate son, and that this painting was to blame for it—no, that would be too much for even the coldest-blooded connoisseur! He said: "My mother posed for several painters when she was young, and I guess my father thinks I'm old enough to know about it now."

"Well, you surely can't blame the painters," was Rick's consoling reply.

V

The decorous and black-clad picture dealer found nothing out of the way in the fact that two young gentlemen wanted to see the "Lady with a Blue Veil" by Oscar Deroulé. It was his business to show pictures; a clerk went down some stairs and brought it up, and set it on a stand for them to look at, and then went to attend to another customer. So they had it to themselves, and no need to repress their feelings. "Oh, my God!" exclaimed Rick; and Lanny's heart hit him several blows underneath his throat.

There was Mabel Blackless, as she was in those days, just ripened into womanhood, a creature of such loveliness as made men catch their breath. The painter who had done her was a lover of the flesh, and had set himself to exploiting its lusciousness; the creams and whites and pinks, the velvety texture, the soft curves, the delicately changing shadows. Beauty was seated upon a silk-covered couch, half supported by one arm. There was a light blue veil across her hips, and the shower of her hair fell over one shoulder, half hiding a breast; she was in bright sunlight, and the fine strands gleamed like gold—not such an easy thing for a painter to get.

These were the modern days—they always are—and when a woman went swimming at Juan, she put on a fairly light bathing suit, and when it was wet it clung tightly, so really there wasn't so much in the picture that Lanny didn't know already. One thing he had never seen was her breasts, with nipples of delicate pink; he couldn't help thinking: "So that is where I was nourished!" He thought: "God, what a strange thing life is!" He confronted once more that most bewildering of ideas: "I was her accident! If it hadn't happened, where would I have been?"

He looked at the date in the corner of the painting; it was 1899, and he knew it was just before Robbie had come along and started him upon his strange journey into the present. Now, by the magic of art, the son could stand and look at the past; but no magic would enable him to look into the future, and know what he was going to do with his own power to create life. Were there baby souls waiting in the unknown, for him to decide whether or not they were to be?

His friend saw how deeply stirred he was; the blood had a way of mounting into Lanny's cheeks, just as you saw recorded in the portrait of his mother. Rick tried to ease him down by discussing the work from the technical point of view. Finally he allowed himself to remark: "If I owned that painting I don't think I'd ever marry. I'd expect too much!"

Lanny's reply was: "I think I'm the one who ought to own it." He recalled his father's wish to buy him something; and now he knew what it was going to be. When the dealer rejoined them he inquired: "What is the price of this painting?"

The man looked at him, and then pretended to look on the back of the painting. The artist was not a well-known one, and the price was thirty-two hundred francs, or six hundred and forty dollars. "I will take it," Lanny said. "I will pay you two hundred francs down, and if you send the painting to the Hotel Crillon this evening, I will have the rest." The dealer knew then that he should have asked a higher price, but it was too late.

When Lanny told his father what he had done, the latter was much amused. "Do you want to take it to America?"

Lanny laughed in turn. "I thought Beauty and I ought to have it. I'll send it to her, and she can stick it away with Marcel's work."

"It's a queer sort of a present," said Robbie, "but if it's what you want, O.K. There are half a dozen paintings of Beauty somewhere in the world, and you might hunt them up." Then the shrewd businessman added: "Buy options for two years, and you'll get some bargains that'll surprise you. The franc has been pegged, but it won't hold after the war!"

VI

The tongues of the two young men were loosened and they talked about love. Lanny told of his happiness with Rosemary, now almost a year past. He didn't have a right to say how far they had gone—but he found that Rosemary had told Rick's sister, and she in turn had told Rick. These young people had few secrets; their "emancipation" took the form of voluminous talk, and it was a mark of enlightenment to employ the plainest words.

When Lanny said he hadn't been able to be interested in any other girl, Rick told him it was hard luck that he had aimed too high. "I mean," he added, hastily, "from the English point of view. Her family puts on a lot of side. Of course, it's all bally rot; perhaps we'll sack the lot of them before this war is over."

Lanny told what his father had said to Zaharoff, that it might end as it had in Russia; to which Rick replied in his free and easy way that he'd take his chances with a new deal. He informed his friend

that the Codwilliger family was planning for Rosemary to marry
the oldest grandson of the very old Earl of Sandhaven; the grandson was the future heir, since his father had been killed in the same
siege of Gallipoli where Rosemary's father had been wounded.
Lanny could see how useless it was for him to hope—that is, of
course, from the English point of view. He gathered the impression
that he had been greatly honored by having had the future mother
of an earl for a temporary sweetheart.

It was Rick's turn to open his heart. "I've been meaning to tell
you, Lanny—I'm married."

"*What?*" cried the other, amazed.

"The night before I left for France. It's quite a long story. If
you want to hear it——"

"Oh, do I, Rick!"

The baronet's son had come to London to enlist in the Royal
Flying Corps, and at the home of one of his school friends had met
a girl just his age, a student at a college not far from his training
camp. They had hit it off together, and used to meet whenever
Rick had free time. "We talked about love," he said, "and I told
her I'd never had a girl. Of course all the chaps want to have one
before they go to the front—and all the girls want to have them, it
seems. She said she'd try it with me, and we were both quite happy
—only of course there wasn't very much time."

Rick paused. "And then?" said Lanny.

"Well, I knew I was going across in a week or so; and Nina—her
name is Nina Putney—told me she wanted to have a baby. I mightn't
come back—lots of the fellows have been downed on their first
flight."

"I know," said Lanny.

"I said: 'What will you do, alone?' And she said: 'I know what
I want. I can take care of it somehow.' She has a sister who's an
interior decorator, and would take her in. You know people don't
pay so much attention to illegitimacy in wartime; they make ex-
cuses. And Nina broke down—she said she had to have something
to remember me by. I couldn't very well say no."

"Is she going to have it?"

"So she writes me."

"You married her before that?"

"I thought I ought to tell the pater; if he was going to have a grandchild, he'd want to be sure about it. He looked up the family and found out they were all right—I mean, what he calls all right—so then he said we ought to get married. So we got a special license and went over to the church, the night before I reported for duty."

"Oh, Rick, what a story! Do you think she's a girl you'll be happy with?"

"I suppose we've as good a chance as most couples. Nina's game, and says she'll never hold me to it. She swears she wasn't trying to rope me in, and if I ever say it, she'll drop me flat." The young flying officer smiled a rather wry smile.

"You're supposed to be something of a catch, aren't you, Rick—I mean from the English point of view?"

Rick could talk about the social position of the Codwilliger family, but not of the Pomeroy-Nielsons. "The pater says we'll lose The Reaches if they keep piling war taxes on him. And what price a baronet if you have to live in lodgings?"

VII

Lanny was excited, of course. He wanted to know about Nina, and what she looked like—Rick had a little picture, which showed a slender, birdlike person with an eager, intense expression. Lanny admired her, and Rick was pleased. Lanny asked what she was studying, and about her family—her father was a barrister, but not a successful one; she would be one of these new women who had careers of their own, kept their own names, and so on. None of this clinging sort.

Lanny said that his father was taking him to London soon. Could he meet her? Rick said: "Of course."

"Could I give her a present, do you suppose? Would she like some picture that we could pick up for her?"

"You'd better wait," laughed the other, "and see what happens to me. If I'm put out, you'd better give her a baby basket."

"I'll give her both!" Lanny had recently become aware of the fact that his father had a pile of money.

"No Caliph of Bagdad business!" countered his friend. "You pick out a book that may keep her from being lonely, and write something in it, so she can remember you when you marry an oil princess in Connecticut."

"There isn't any oil in Connecticut, Rick."

"Well, nutmegs then. Your father says it's called the Nutmeg State. You'll make a whole crop of new princesses out of this war. They'll be bored, and they'll be crazy about you because you speak French, and dance, and have culture—you'll rank with a marquis or a Russian grand duke in exile."

Lanny was amused by this picture of himself in New England. He wanted to say: "They'll find out that I'm a bastard." But his lips were sealed.

Half a day, a night, and another day; never had thirty hours moved with such speed! They went to the Comédie Française, and sat in a box; they had a meal at midnight, and Robbie ordered an extra bottle of wine. They strolled on the boulevards in the morning, luxuriating in the sunshine, watching the crowds and gazing at the fine things for sale. Lanny bought a stock of chocolates, the one thing Rick admitted the chaps in the air force would appreciate. They picked up an old-fashioned open carriage with a bony but lively horse, and were driven about the Bois and the main boulevards, looking at historic buildings and remembering what they could of events. Rick knew a little about everything; he had all his old assurance, his worldly manner which impressed his younger friend so greatly.

Robbie came back to the hotel, feeling good, because Zaharoff's factotum had given way, and the other companies were giving way, and Robbie was collecting signatures on dotted lines. Lanny had to ask him not to be too exultant until Rick was gone. "You know how it is, he's giving his life, maybe, while we're making money."

"All right," said the salesman, with one of his chuckles. "I'll be good; but you tell Rick that if his old man wants to sell The Reaches, you'll buy it!" No use asking Robbie to shed any tears over the English aristocracy. They had had their day, and now the American businessmen were to have theirs. Gangway!

However, Robbie was very decent when the time for parting came. He had a big package delivered to Rick's room, and told him not to open it until he got back to camp. He told Lanny it contained cigarettes; the baronet's son would be the darling of the corps wing for a time. Robbie shook hands with him, and said "Cheerio," in the approved English fashion.

Lanny went to the train, and had tears in his eyes, he just couldn't help it. It would have been very bad form for Rick to have them; he said: "Thanks, old chap, you've been perfectly bully to me." And then: "Take care of yourself, and don't let the subs get you."

"Write me a post card every now and then," pleaded Lanny. "You know how it is, if I don't hear from you, I'll worry."

"Don't do that," said Rick. "Whatever comes, that's what comes." It was the nearest a modern man could approach to having a philosophy.

"Well, look out for the Fokkers—get them first!"

"Right-o!" The whistle blew, and Rick bolted, just in time for the train and for the honor of the Royal Flying Corps. Lanny stood, with tears flowing freely. "Good-by, Rick! Good-by!" His voice died into a sort of sob as the train moved on, and the face of Eric Vivian Pomeroy-Nielson disappeared, perhaps forever. That was the dreadful thing about wartime, you couldn't part from anybody without the thought: "I'll probably not see him again!"

VIII

The youth kept talking about this depressing idea until it worried his father. "You know, kid," he remarked, "you just can't be too soft in this world. It's painful to think of people getting killed, and I don't know the answer, except that maybe we put too much value on human life; we try to make more out of it than nature allows. This is certain, if you're too sensitive, and suffer too much, you wreck your own happiness, and maybe your health, and then what are you worth to yourself or anybody else?"

That was something to think about, and the youngster put his mind on it. What was the use of practicing the arts, of understanding and loving them, if you didn't dare let yourself feel? Manifestly, the purpose of art was to awaken feelings; but Robbie said you had to put them to sleep, or at any rate retire into a cave with them. Build yourself like a tortoise, with a hard shell around you, so that the world couldn't get hold of you to make you suffer!

Lanny voiced that, and the reply was: "Maybe it's a bad time for art right now. As I read history I see these periods come pretty frequently and last a long time, so you have to arm yourself somehow; unless, of course, you want to be a martyr, and die on a cross, or something like that. It makes good melodrama, or maybe great tragedy, but it's doggone uncomfortable while it's happening."

They were in their room, packing to leave for England; and Robbie said: "Sit down and let me tell you something I heard today." He lowered his voice, as if he thought that someone might be hiding in their room. Enemy ears are listening!

"Your friend is going off to fight the German Fokkers, and you're unhappy because they may get him. He's told you the Fokkers are fast and light, and that helps them, and may doom him. Do you know why they are so fast and light?'

"He says they're putting aluminum into them."

"Exactly. And where do they get it? What's it made from?"

"It's made out of bauxite, I know."

"And has Germany got any?"

"I don't know, Robbie."

"Few people know things like that; they don't teach them in the schools. Germany has very little, and she wants it badly, and pays high prices for it. Do you know who has it?"

"Well, I know that France has a lot, because Eddie Patterson drove me to the place where it's being mined." Lanny remembered this trip to a town called Brignolles, back from the coast; the reddish mineral was blasted from tunnels in a mountain, and brought down to the valley in great steel buckets rolling on a continuous wire cable. Lanny and his friend had been admitted to the place and had watched the stuff being dumped into lines of freight cars. It had been Lanny's first actual sight of big industry—unless you included the perfume factories in Grasse, where peasant women sat half buried in millions of rose leaves, amid an odor so powerful that a little of it sent you out with a headache.

Robbie went on with his story. "To make bauxite into aluminum takes electric power. Those lines of freight cars that you saw were taken to Switzerland, which has cheap power from its mountain streams. There the aluminum is made; and then it goes—can you guess?"

"To Germany?"

"It goes to whatever country bids the highest price for it; and Germany is in the market. So if your friend is brought down by a faster airplane, you'll know the reason. Also you'll know why your father keeps urging you not to tear your heart out over this war."

"But, Robbie!" The son's voice rose with excitement. "Something ought to be done about a thing like that!"

"Who's going to do it?"

"But it's treason!"

"It's business."

"Who are the people that are doing it?"

"A big concern, with a lot of stockholders; its shares are on the market, anybody can buy them who has the money. If you look up the board of directors, you'll find familiar names—that is, if you follow such things. You find Lord Booby, and you say: 'Zaharoff!' You see the Duc de Pumpkin, and you say: 'Schneider,' or perhaps 'de Wendel.' You see Isaac Steinberg, or some such name, and you say: 'Rothschild.' They have their directors in hundreds of different companies, all tied together in a big net—steel, oil, coal, chemicals, shipping, and, above all, banks. When you see those names, you might as well butt your brains out against a stone wall as try to stop them, or even to expose them—because they own the newspapers."

"But, Robbie," protested the youth, "doesn't it make any difference to those men whether the Germans take France?"

"They're building big industry, and they'll own it and run it. Whatever government comes in will have to have money, and will make terms with them, and business will go on as it's always done. It's a steam roller; and what I'm telling my son is, be on it and not under it!"

IX

The English and the French had made for themselves a sort of chicken run across the English Channel; a wide lane, fenced with heavy steel netting hung from two lines of buoys, and protected by mines. Back and forth through that lane went the troopships, the hospital ships, the freighters, the packet boats with passengers. Up and down the lines patrolled torpedo boats and destroyers, mine sweepers and trawlers; lookouts swept the sea with glasses, and gunners stood by their quick-firers, ready at a moment's notice to swing them into action. Overhead were airplanes humming, and silver blimps slowly gliding. The submarine campaign was at its peak, and the Allies were going back to the ancient system of convoys for merchant ships. They were doing it here, with fleets of slow-moving vessels laden with coal for France, escorted by armed trawlers.

At night the destroyers raced up and down, their searchlights flashing, making the scene bright almost as day. But the packet boats showed no lights, and passengers were not allowed on deck; you went on board after dark, and were escorted to your stateroom, and advised to sleep with your clothes on, and be sure to practice adjusting the life preserver which was overhead in your berth. Your porthole was sealed tightly with a dark cover, and to open it or show a light was a prison offense. You heard the sounds of departure, and felt the vibration of the screw and the tossing of the vessel. You slept, if your nerves were sound, and when you woke up you were in England, if your luck was reasonably good.

London in wartime was full of bustle, serious but not afraid. "Never say die," was the motto. England would follow her usual rule of losing every battle but the last. The theaters and the cinemas were crowded. Everybody was at work, both men and women; hours were long and wages high; the people of the slums had enough to eat for the first time in their lives. Lanny wondered: was that the solution to the problem of poverty and unemployment—to put everybody at work trying to blow some other people up?

Robbie had important men waiting to see him. There was no way for Lanny to help him; no more codes or ciphers now—whatever cablegrams you sent had to be in plain words, and signed by your full name; better not use any words the censor didn't know, and not too many figures. Robbie told a story about a man who tried to cable that he had purchased 12,462,873 sables; the military intelligence department got busy to find out how he had managed to get more sables than there were in the world.

Lanny had two young ladies to call on. Rosemary first, of course. She had got her heart's desire, and was working as a nurse. They called her a "student," but there wasn't much difference in these days, you went right to work, and learned by doing. She was in a big hospital which until recently had been a school. Her hours were long, and leave was hard to get; but when you are the granddaughter of an earl, you can manage things in England, even in wartime.

Toward sundown he went to meet her, expecting to see her in a nurse's costume of white; but she had changed to a blue chiffon dress and a little straw hat with blue cornflowers in it. The sight of her started something to tingling inside him. How lovely life could be, even with death ruling the world!

They walked in a near-by park, and she tried her best to be cool and matter of fact. But there was something between her and this young American that wasn't easy to control. They sat on a bench, and Lanny looked at her, and saw that she was afraid to meet his eyes, and that her lips were trembling.

"Have you missed me a little, Rosemary?"

"More than a little."

"I haven't been able to think about anybody else."

"Let's not talk about it, Lanny."

So he chatted for a while, telling her about Rick's brief holiday in Paris. He talked about his coming trip to America, and the reasons for it. "My father says we're surely coming into the war." Congress was then in session, and a fierce debate was going on; there might be a vote at any hour.

"Better late than never," replied Rosemary. The English in those days had become extremely impatient with the letter-writing of President Wilson.

"You mustn't blame me for it," said he. "But if we do come in, things will change quickly." He waited a reasonable time, then asked, with a smile: "If we do, Rosemary, will that make any difference in the way your parents feel about us colonials?"

"All that's so complicated, Lanny. Let's talk about nice agreeable things."

"The nicest agreeable thing I know is sitting on a park bench with the twilight falling about her and an evening star right in front of her eyes, and I haven't the least desire to talk about anything else. Tell me, darling: has there been any other man in your heart in the past eleven months?"

"There are hundreds of them, Lanny. I'm trying to help our poor boys back to life—or ease them out of it not too horribly."

"I know, dear," he said. "I've lived in the house with a war casualty for more than two years. But one can't work all the time, surely; one has to have a little fun."

Lanny didn't know England very well. He knew that the "lower orders" lay around in the parks in broad daylight; but just how dark did it have to be for a member of the nobility to permit a young man to take her hand, or put his arm around her on a park bench? He tried gently, and she did not repel him. Presently they were sitting close together, and the old mysterious spell renewed itself. Perhaps an hour passed; then he said: "Can't we go somewhere, Rosemary?"

Robbie had said: "Take her to one of the cheaper hotels; they don't ask questions." Robbie was practical on the subject of sex, as upon all others. He said there were three things a young fellow had to look out for: he mustn't get any girl into trouble; he mustn't get mixed up with any married woman unless he was sure the husband didn't care; and he mustn't get any disease. When Lanny had reassured him on these points, he said: "If you don't show up tonight, I won't worry."

X

So Lanny and Rosemary went strolling; and when they came to a place where they weren't apt to meet any of their fashionable friends, they went in, and he registered as Mr. and Mrs. Brown, and paid in advance, and no questions were asked. When they lay in the embrace which was so full of rapture for them both, they forgot the sordid surroundings, they forgot everything except that their time was short. Lanny was going out to face the submarines on the open ocean, and Rosemary was going to France, where the screaming shells paid no heed to a red cross on a woman's arm.

"Gather ye rosebuds while ye may, Old time is still a flying." Thus the English poet. The German has said: "*Pflücket die Rose, Eh' sie verblüht.*" So there was one thing about which the two nations could agree. In countless cheap hotels in Berlin, as in London, the advice was being followed; and the wartime custom was no different in Paris—if you could accept the testimony of Napoleon Bonaparte, who had stood on the field of Eylau, observing the heaps of the slaughtered and remarking: "One night in Paris will remedy all that."

Their happiness was long-enduring, and nothing in the outside world was permitted to disturb it. Not even loud banging noises, all over the city—one of them very close by. Lanny made a joke of it: "I hope that's not some morals police force after us." The girl explained that those were anti-aircraft warnings, made by "maroons," a kind of harmless bomb made of heavy paper wrapped with twine.

They lay still in the dark and listened. Presently came louder explosions, and some of them were near, too. "Anti-aircraft guns," said Rosemary; she knew all the sounds. There came dull, heavy crashes, and she told him those were the bombs. "You don't have to worry unless it's a direct hit."

"You surely can't worry if it is," said Lanny. It was his first time under fire, and he wanted to take it in the English manner.

"About as much risk as in a thunderstorm," said Rosemary. "The silly fools think they can frighten us by wrecking a house here and there and killing half a dozen harmless people in their beds."

"I suppose those'll be planes?" asked the youth.

"From occupied Belgium. The Zepps have stopped coming entirely."

The uproar grew louder, and presently there was a sharp cracking sound, and some of the glass in the window of their room fell onto the floor. That was getting sort of close! "A piece of shrapnel," said Rosemary. "They don't have much force, because the air resistance stops them."

"You know all about it!" smiled Lanny.

"Naturally; I help to fix people up. I'll have some new cases in the morning."

"None tonight, I hope, dear."

"Kiss me, Lanny. If we're going to die, let it be that way."

The uproar died away even more suddenly than it had come; they slept awhile, and early in the morning, when they got up, Lanny found a fragment of a shell near the broken window. It wasn't much more than an inch square, but had unpleasantly jagged edges. He said: "I'll keep it for a souvenir, unless you want it."

"We get plenty of them," replied the student nurse.

"Maybe it's a Budd." He knew, of course, that the British were using Budd shrapnel. "I'll see if my father can tell."

"They gather up the pieces and use them again," explained Rosemary.

That was her casual way. She told him to phone her or wire her as to when he would be sailing. She didn't know if she could get another leave, but she would try.

They went outside, and heard newsboys shouting, and saw posters in large letters: "U.S.A. IN WAR!" "AMERICA JOINS!" While the scion of Budd Gunmakers had been gathering rosebuds with the granddaughter of Lord Dewthorpe, the Senate of the United States had voted a declaration to the effect that a condition of war already existed between that country and Germany.

XI

It was a pleasant time to be in London. There were celebrations in the streets, and the usually self-contained islanders were hunting for some American, so that they could shake him by the hand and say: "Thanks, old chap, this is grand, we're all brothers now, and when will you be coming over?" Lanny asked his father if this would help him in getting contracts; Robbie said they'd expect him to give the patents now—but no such instructions had come from Newcastle, Connecticut!

Lanny went to call on Nina Putney, still a student in college in spite of being married. He took her to lunch, and they had a long talk. She was a brunette, slender and delicate, with sensitive, finely cut features. She seemed more like a French girl than an English one; she was like Lanny, eager and somewhat impetuous; she said what she felt, and then perhaps wished she hadn't. The two could get along easily, because they shared the same adoration, and wanted to talk about it.

Nina told about her meeting with the most wonderful of would-be fliers, whose dream had since come true. He might be in the air now—oh, God, at this moment he might be in a death duel with one of the German Fokkers, so light and fast because they were made of aluminum manufactured in Switzerland from French bauxite! Lanny didn't tell the young bride about that; but a shadow hung over their meeting, and what could he say? He couldn't deny

6 *WORLD'S END*

the mortal danger, or that it would last, day after day. No comfort that an airman came back alive, because he would be going out again so soon.

Business as usual! Lanny and Nina promised to write to each other, for Rick's sake, and she would tell him whatever news she got. America would hurry up, and this dreadful war would be won, and they would all live happy ever after. So, good-by, Nina, and take good care of that baby, and you're to have a basket, and remember, Budd's will stand back of you!

Robbie said he'd have all his affairs wound up in a couple of days, and no use to linger and be a target even for Budd shrapnel. He had engaged a stateroom, and Lanny, the lady-killer, might gather as many rosebuds as possible in that brief interim. He phoned to Rosemary, and she said, yes, she'd get away once more, even if they fined her for it. They went to the same hotel and got the same room—the pane of glass patched with brown paper. Once more they were happy, after the fashion that war permits—*amor inter arma;* concentrating on one moment, refusing to let the mind roam or the eye peer into the future.

In the morning, clinging to him, the girl said: "Lanny, you've been a darling, and I'll never forget you. Write me, and let me know how things go, and I'll do the same."

No more than that. She wouldn't talk about marriage; she would go on patching broken English bodies, and he would visit the home of his fathers, and come back as a soldier, or perhaps to sell armaments—who could say? "Good-by, dear; and do help us to win!"

So Lanny was through; and it was a good time to be leaving. The British were beginning their spring offensive, which would be drowned in mud and hung on barbed wire and mowed down by machine guns in the usual depressing way. The French had a new commander, Nivelle, and he would lead them into a slaughter that would bring the troops to the verge of mutiny. Away from all that!

They took a boat train at night, and went on board a steamship in darkness and silence. They knew they were being towed out into a harbor, and that tugs were pulling steel nets with buoys out of the way. But they couldn't see a thing, because the deck was covered with a shroud of burlap. They sat outside for a long while, listening to the sounds of the sea and conversing in whispers; not much chance to sleep, and nothing you could do. Everyone tried hard to seem unconcerned. Some men shut themselves up in their cabins and drank themselves insensitive; others played cards in the saloon and pretended not to care about death.

"Westward the star of empire takes its way," said Robbie. He was telling his son that they were off to God's country, the place to stay in, to believe in. He was telling him not to miss the granddaughter of an earl too much; there were plenty of delightful democratic maidens at home. He was saying that Europe was worn out; it would owe all its money to America, and collecting it would be fun. Yes, they were sitting pretty—unless by chance there should come a pale streak of foam out there on the starlit ocean, and a shattering explosion beneath them!